OUTSTANDING
NOVELS O

LIAR, LIAR

"Bestselling Jackson jam-packs the plot of her latest nail-biting novel with plenty of unexpected twists and turns, making *Liar, Liar* a terrific choice for readers who enjoy their literary adrenaline fixes on the darker side of the suspense spectrum."—*Booklist*

"Twisty . . . suspenseful. The many threads of this action-packed mystery are tied together by the mesmerizing, larger-than-life character of Didi Storm, who haunts the book to its final pages."—*Publishers Weekly* (starred review)

YOU WILL PAY

"This suspenseful thriller is packed with jaw-dropping twists." —*In Touch Weekly*

NEVER DIE ALONE

"Jackson definitely knows how to keep readers riveted." —*Mystery Scene*

CLOSE TO HOME

"Jackson definitely knows how to jangle readers' nerves . . . *Close to Home* is perfect for readers of Joy Fielding or fans of Mary Higgins Clark."—*Booklist*

TELL ME

"Absolutely tension filled . . . Jackson is on top of her game." —*Suspense Magazine*

CH

Books by Lisa Jackson

Stand-Alones
SEE HOW SHE DIES
FINAL SCREAM
RUNNING SCARED
WHISPERS
TWICE KISSED
UNSPOKEN
DEEP FREEZE
FATAL BURN
MOST LIKELY TO DIE
WICKED GAME
WICKED LIES
SOMETHING WICKED
WICKED WAYS
SINISTER
WITHOUT MERCY
YOU DON'T WANT
  TO KNOW
CLOSE TO HOME
AFTER SHE'S GONE
REVENGE
YOU WILL PAY
OMINOUS
RUTHLESS
ONE LAST BREATH
LIAR, LIAR
BACKLASH

Anthony Paterno/
  Cahill Family Novels
IF SHE ONLY KNEW
ALMOST DEAD

Rick Bentz/Reuben Montoya
  Novels
HOT BLOODED
COLD BLOODED
SHIVER
ABSOLUTE FEAR
LOST SOULS
MALICE
DEVIOUS
NEVER DIE ALONE

Pierce Reed/
  Nikki Gillette Novels
THE NIGHT BEFORE
THE MORNING AFTER
TELL ME

Selena Alvarez/
  Regan Pescoli Novels
LEFT TO DIE
CHOSEN TO DIE
BORN TO DIE
AFRAID TO DIE
READY TO DIE
DESERVES TO DIE
EXPECTING TO DIE

Published by Kensington Publishing Corporation

BACKLASH

LISA
JACKSON

ZEBRA BOOKS
KENSINGTON PUBLISHING CORP.
http://www.kensingtonbooks.com

ZEBRA BOOKS are published by

Kensington Publishing Corp.
119 West 40th Street
New York, NY 10018

All Kensington titles, imprints, and distributed lines are available at special quantity discounts for bulk purchases for sales promotion, premiums, fund-raising, educational, or institutional use.

Special book excerpts or customized printings can also be created to fit specific needs. For details, write or phone the office of the Kensington Sales Manager: Attn.: Sales Department. Kensington Publishing Corp., 119 West 40th Street, New York, NY 10018. Phone: 1-800-221-2647.

Zebra and the Z logo Reg. U.S. Pat. & TM Off.

First Zebra Books Mass-Market Paperback Printing: March 2019
ISBN-13: 978-1-4201-4821-3
ISBN-10: 1-4201-4821-4

ISBN-13: 978-1-4201-4822-0 (eBook)
ISBN-10: 1-4201-4822-2 (eBook)

10 9 8 7 6 5 4 3 2 1

Printed in the United States of America

Contents

Aftermath

Prologue

McLean Ranch, Montana

"I love you," Tessa Kramer whispered. Lying on the summer-dry grass, staring into eyes as blue as the sea, she smiled, blushing a little at the boldness of her words. At nineteen she was certain she was in love. And no one, not her overprotective father, nor her suspicious brother, nor even Denver McLean himself, could convince her otherwise.

Denver's thumbs traced the arch of her cheeks. Passion smoldered in his eyes. "You're sure?"

"Absolutely." Her lips quivered anxiously. "So don't try to tell me that I'm too young or too naive or too . . . whatever, to know what I'm talking about."

"Am I arguing?" He kissed her softly again, his lips warm and filled with promise as they brushed tenderly over hers. Strong fingers tangled in her long, strawberry-blond hair.

Winding her arms around his neck, she felt the weight of his chest crush her breasts, could see blue sky through the shifting pine needles of the branches overhead. The summer sun hung low over lazy mountains, and insects hummed in the whisper-soft breeze that ruffled Denver's coal black hair.

Nearby, the horses, a buckskin gelding and a sorrel mare, were tethered together. The animals stood nose to rump, nickering softly and switching their tails at the ever present flies.

The afternoon was perfect.

"I love you, too, Tessa," Denver vowed, moving gently above her.

Through her jeans Tessa could feel the heat of his body, the solid warmth of his legs entwined with hers.

Pressing eager lips against her neck, he groaned—a deep, primal sound that caused her heart to trip. Her breath caught somewhere between her throat and lungs as he said, "I want to make you mine."

She believed him. With all of her heart, she knew he wanted to marry her, intended to spend the rest of his life with her. Her heart began to clamor, her pulse jumping wildly as he circled the hollow of her throat with his tongue. His breath was as warm as the summer wind, the honesty in his eyes clear as a mountain lake.

"I trust you," she whispered.

She felt the buttons slide through the buttonholes in her blouse. The gauzy fabric parted, and sunlight warmed her bare skin. She smiled to herself, throwing caution to the wind. Today she would prove just how much she loved Denver, just how wrong her father was about him.

Shifting, he traced the sculpted lace of her bra with his tongue. Eager shivers darted down her spine. With ease he unlatched the fastening and tossed the scrap of white cotton into a clump of sagebrush.

She sucked in her breath. His hands moved protectively over her breasts, kneading each dark-crested mound until she burned inside with that same unsatisfied ache she felt when-ever they kissed. He touched one nipple with the tip of his tongue and she moaned, wanting more and responding by in-stinct, holding his head against her, whispering his name as her blood, like wildfire, ran hot and fast in her veins.

She couldn't think and didn't want to. Her fingers moved to the waistband of his faded jeans and she released the button, pushing worn denim over his legs, feeling for the first time the downy hair on his thighs as he, too, stripped her bare.

Sunlight danced through the trees, dappling their naked bodies as they gazed upon each other in silent rapture. She wasn't embarrassed and met his hungry gaze with her own. He swallowed.

She licked her lips. "I'll love you for the rest of my life," she said softly. Touching his bare chest, watching the muscles of his shoulders ripple and strain, she smiled up at him.

Her fingers traced a feather-light line against his ribs, and he groaned. "Tessa, don't tease me—"

"Never," she vowed, devouring him with her eyes.

At twenty-three, Denver had matured into a handsome man. Long and lean, with tanned skin, flashing blue eyes and hair as dark as the night, he was rugged and charming. His features were no longer boyish, but chiseled into manhood. He was everything she had ever wanted, and unless she convinced him otherwise, he was leaving.

"Oh, Tessa," he whispered hoarsely, smoothing her hair from her face, his palms caressing her cheeks. "I want to make you happy."

"Do I look so miserable?" she asked, chuckling deep in her throat.

He grinned crookedly. "You're gorgeous."

"So, Mr. McLean, are you."

"I never want to hurt you," he said, growing serious again.

"You won't."

Slanting his mouth over hers, he moved until he was lying over her, his knees between hers, his thighs rubbing sensually as he entered her quickly. A swift flame of pain burned for a second within her, only to be extinguished by the gentleness of his strokes.

Tessa gasped, her arms circling his neck, her lips pressed

to his as he began to move within her, enticing her to do the same. He kissed her eyes, her cheeks, her lips. The wild flames running through her blood leaped out of control and she was moving with him, riding on a storm as furious as a prairie fire, a tempest that swallowed them both.

"Love me," she whispered.

"I do—oh!" he cried, his voice raw as he stiffened above her, then fell spent into her waiting arms. "Oh, love."

The wind shifted silently, moving across the rugged ridge on which they lay, bending the dry grass and catching in Tessa's hair.

"Don't ever leave me," she begged, her mind still spinning in a kaleidoscope of colors as she clung to him and tried to still her racing heartbeat. She felt the dew of sweat on his arms, smelled the scent of lovemaking on his skin, saw smoky clouds swirl in a sky tinged with pink.

"I have to go to L.A."

His words were a cold dose of reality. "You don't have to," Tessa protested.

"Yes, I do, Tessa. I've got a job there in two weeks." Evidently seeing the disappointment in her eyes, he kissed the tip of her nose. "But you could come with me."

She swallowed back the urge to cry and looked away from him to the hazy heavens. "My dad—"

"Doesn't need you. I do. Come with me."

"What would I do in Los Angeles?" she asked, shifting her gaze back to his. "I train horses. I don't belong in the city. And neither do you." Blinking rapidly, she told herself not to cry, not this afternoon, not after loving him so completely. Clouds drifted overhead and the smell of smoke wafted through the trees.

"I'm an engineer, Tessa. I want to build bridges and skyscrapers and—" His nostrils flared and every muscle in his body flexed.

"And what?"

"Smoke!" he whispered, his gaze darting through the surrounding hills, to the valley floor far below. "Oh, God—"

"What?" she asked, reading the terror in his eyes. "Denver?" Her throat suddenly dry, she, too, smelled the biting odor of burning wood. *Fire!*

Scrambling into his jeans, Denver stared down the hillside, his face a mask of horror. "Oh, God, no!"

Tessa followed his gaze, only to see steel-gray smoke billowing from the stables of the McLean Ranch. She felt the blood rush from her face as she scrabbled on the dry ground for her jeans and blouse and struggled into her clothes.

Denver ran barefoot to his horse and grabbed the reins. While the poor beast sidestepped and tossed his head, he swung onto the gelding's back and kicked hard. Leaving behind a cloud of dust, the buckskin tore down the rutted trail, his hooves clanging sharply on the rocks.

"Wait!" Tessa cried, cursing the buttons of her blouse as she yanked on her boots, then ran to her sorrel mare and climbed into the saddle. "Come on," she urged, shoving her knees into the mare's ribs. The little quarter horse leaped forward, half-stumbling down the rocky trail. Tessa slapped her with the reins, and the mare scrambled down the hill.

Wind tore at Tessa's face and hair, and tears blurred her eyes as she clung burrlike to her horse's neck. Denver was yards in front of her, cutting away from the trail and through the trees. "Wait!" she called again.

He didn't even glance back. Tucked low over the buckskin's shoulders, he streaked ahead.

"Giddyap!" Tessa screamed, praying that the smoke pouring from the stables was from a fire already under control—trying to stop the horrid dread knotting in her stomach. Her game little mare sprinted into the pines, and Tessa had to duck to escape being scraped off by low-hanging branches. "Come on, come on," she whispered as they broke from the trees and raced across a long pasture leading to the stables.

The ranch was a madhouse. Stable boys, ranch hands and the kitchen help were running through the yard, yelling at one another, turning hoses onto the burning building. Thick, pungent smoke clogged the air, changing day to night. Flames crackled and leaped through the roof. Horses shrieked in terror, their horrific cries punctuating the ring of steel-shod hooves pounding against splintering wood.

"Dear God," Tessa prayed. "Dear God, save them!"

Denver yanked his horse to a stop, and as the buckskin reared, Denver jumped to the ground, then vaulted the fence.

"Stop! Denver, no!" Tessa cried, stricken as her sweaty mare slid to a halt near the gate. She leaped onto, then over, the top rail of the fence. Her eyes were glued to Denver as he raced, shouldering his way through useless ranch hands toward the stables. "Somebody stop him! Denver!"

Smoke burned her lungs and her eyes stung as she followed, stumbling forward. Somewhere in the distance she heard the wail of sirens. "Denver!"

"You can't go in there," her brother, Mitchell, commanded. He seemed to come from nowhere through the smoke.

"Like hell."

"Precisely." His gaunt face was streaked with soot, his hair grimy, his eyes red as he stared at the inferno. Hot, crackling flames knifed through charred shingles in the sagging roof. "Just like hell."

"Denver's in there!" she cried, still heading across the yard. But Mitchell had no trouble keeping up with her, taking one swift stride to her two.

"Listen to me, Tessa," he yelled over the roar of the fire, the shouts of men and the screams of terrified animals. "You can't—"

"I have to!" She was running now, only a few yards from the stables. Mitchell tackled her, his momentum pushing her to the ground. Her chin bounced on gravel, but she didn't care. She had to get to Denver.

"Damn it, Tessa," Mitchell's voice hissed urgently in her ear, "most of the McLean family's already trapped in there!"

"No!"

"When the fire broke out, Katharine and Robert tried to help save the animals and the ranch records stored in the office."

Struggling to a sitting position, Tessa clamped a trembling hand over her mouth and shook her head, staring at the burning building. Originally two stories, the stable had an upper floor used for storage and an office. The horses, the pride of the McLean Ranch, had been boxed in stalls on the ground level. Tessa thought she would retch.

"The fire department will be here soon," Mitchell said, his voice rough from the smoke, his strong arms holding her back. "There's nothing anyone can do until they get here."

"We can't just sit here and watch them burn!" she choked out, feeling helpless.

Sirens screamed nearby and heavy tires crunched on the gravel. Red and white lights flashed through the smoke. A paramedic van ground to a stop, followed by a red car from the fire department. Three huge, rumbling trucks roared behind.

The fire chief threw open the door of his car and shoved a bullhorn to his mouth. "Everybody get back!" he ordered, his eyes searching the grounds as he waved to the driver of the pumper truck. "There's a lake around behind!" The truck tore around the main house to the large pond now reflecting scarlet. Firemen jumped from the trucks, dragging heavy canvas hoses toward the stables. "I want that barn contained and the surrounding buildings covered. We can't trust the wind today."

Water began jetting from the hoses, arcing high in the air before spraying over the burning building, sizzling as the first jets hit scorched timbers.

Tessa broke away from her brother and ran to the chief, Mitchell on her heels. "You've got to save them!" Tessa cried over the deafening cacophony of pumps, screams, the roar of the fire and her own, hammering heart.

"The horses, or—?"

"The McLeans are in there," Mitchell clarified, yanking a thumb toward the stables. "They might be upstairs in the office or on the ground floor. They were trying to save the stock—"

"Christ!" the chief swore. "How many?"

"Five—no, four. Denver and his parents, Robert and Katharine. And . . . and Dad, Curtis Kramer, the ranch foreman."

"Dad, too?" Tessa whispered hoarsely.

"That's it?" the chief demanded, his tired eyes narrowing on Mitchell. "What about John McLean and the other McLean son—what's his name?"

"Colton," Tessa murmured, thinking of Denver's younger, daredevil brother and praying that he was safe.

Mitchell shook his head. "John and Colton are in town, and I think the rest of the hands are accounted for."

"Make sure," the chief insisted. Snapping the bullhorn over his mouth again, he barked, "Okay, we've got four people trapped inside, possibly more. Upstairs and down. Get 'em out!" He glanced back at Tessa and must have read the dread on her face. "Get her out of here," he said to Mitchell. "There's nothing she can do."

"I'm not leaving," she insisted.

"Come on, Tess—"

"Not when Denver and Dad are in there. No way!" She started forward and tripped over a hose.

"You're in the way, lady," the fire chief said.

"Hey, Chief! We got one!" One of the firemen was dragging a coughing, soot-streaked man from the fire. Tessa tried to run forward, but Mitchell's arms tightened around her waist.

"Maybe you don't want to see this," he said.

"Let me go!"

"It might be Denver—"

"Then I have to be with him!" Her heart pounding with dread, she shook him off and started running.

The paramedics reached the rescued man first. They were already working over him, forcing oxygen into his lungs when Tessa recognized her father, his face black, his white hair singed.

"Thank God," she whispered, falling to the ground near him.

"Hey, lady, give us a break! We need a little room," one paramedic snapped, and she backed away on her knees, her eyes glued to her father's face. Gray beneath the streaks of soot, his skin looked slack and old. His thick white hair had been singed yellow and he was coughing so hard he nearly threw up.

But he was alive. Closing her eyes, she prayed silently.

Her father blinked rapidly, still coughing, his eyes unfocused.

"Get him into an ambulance," the fire chief ordered. He glared grimly at her father. "You see anyone else in there?"

"I—I don't know," he mumbled, still coughing.

The paramedic glanced at the fire chief. "He wouldn't know. He's three sheets to the wind."

Tessa swallowed back a hot retort as she leaned over her father and smelled the familiar scent of whiskey on his breath.

A pickup roared down the drive and slammed to a stop. The driver, Denver's younger brother, Colton, jumped out of the cab and started forward, his boots crunching on gravel as he ran faster and faster toward the fire chief. "What the hell's going on here?" he asked, his face white as he stared at the stables. Orange flames shot out of the roof and heat rippled in sickening waves from the inferno.

Curtis coughed loudly and stirred, his red-rimmed eyes focusing on his daughter. "Tessa, gal?" he murmured, cracking a weary smile.

"Thank God, you're all right!" She wrapped her arms

around his grimy work shirt, buried her head in his chest. "Did you see Denver?"

"You were with him," Curtis said. He shook his head. "No one—"

"But Denver's in there! So are his parents," she protested, her head snapping up.

"Oh, God!" Colton cried. Without thinking he started for the stables.

"It's too late!" Mitchell yelled. "Colt—stop! Damn him!"

"Stay back!" the chief commanded through the horn. "Christ! Somebody stop him—"

A blast ripped through the stables, and the building exploded in a fiery burst. Glass shattered, spraying out. Timbers groaned and crashed to the ground. Flames crackled and reached to the sky in hellish yellow fingers. The earth shuddered.

Tessa fell to the ground sobbing, knowing in her heart that Denver would never survive.

"Come on, Tess," Mitchell whispered, picking her up and carrying her to his old, battered truck as the firemen and hands recovered and scurried toward the stables.

As if in a dream, Tessa saw her father being loaded into the ambulance, felt the scratchy denim of Mitchell's jacket against her cheek. "There's nothing more we can do here," Mitchell said softly. "I don't think there's anything anyone can."

"But Denver . . ."

"I know, Tess. I know."

Chapter One

Helena, Montana
Seven Years Later

"I don't want it!" Denver McLean declared as he dropped into a tufted leather chair close to Ross Anderson's desk.

"We're talking about the entire ranch," the young attorney reminded him. Ross was serious, his watery blue eyes steady behind thick lenses, his narrow features pulling together. He smoked a twisted black cigar.

The old-fashioned Western cheroot smelled foul and seemed completely out of place in this modern chrome-and-glass office building, Denver thought. He rubbed the scar on the back of his left hand. "I guess you didn't hear me. I don't want it. Sell the whole damned thing!"

"We can't do that without your brother's consent," Ross said in that soothing lawyer tone that irritated the hell out of Denver.

"No one knows where Colton is. I haven't heard from him in years."

"Nonetheless, half the ranch is his—half yours. Split fifty-fifty. That's the way your father wanted it, and your uncle saw fit to carry out his wishes."

"I wish John had talked to me first," Denver said flatly. If his uncle weren't already dead, he gladly would have wrung the old meddler's neck.

"Too late now," Ross said succinctly.

Denver's lips twisted at the irony. Though he'd been away from the McLean Ranch for seven years and had ignored his uncle's repeated pleas to visit, the old man had gotten him in the end. "Okay," he decided, flopping back in his chair. "Just sell my half."

"Can't do it. Back taxes."

"Son of a—"

The door opened and Ross's secretary, a willowy woman with pale blond hair, eyes heavy with mascara and a glossy smile, carried in a tray of coffee, cream and sugar.

"Just set it on the desk, Nancy," Ross instructed as he puffed on his cigar, gradually filling the room with bluish smoke.

Nancy did as she was bid, casting Denver an interested glance that made him shift uncomfortably in his chair. Even after three successful operations, he felt as if his burns were as red and harsh as when he was dragged barely alive from the fire.

The fire—always the fire. He had never escaped it. Not really. And he never would.

His guts churned at the memory, and he tried to concentrate on the plastic cup of black coffee Ross handed him.

"So, you think your uncle was getting back at you by leaving you the ranch?"

"Wasn't he?"

"It's over a thousand acres of Montana ranch land," Ross said dryly. "Doesn't seem like such a curse."

"No?" Denver sipped the coffee. It was scalding and bitter. He didn't really much care. "Why weren't the back taxes paid?"

"The ranch has been in the red for the past few years."

"I thought there were supposed to be huge silver deposits on the land," Denver said, thinking back to those years of speculation, before the fire, when both his parents and his uncle had been excited at the prospect of mining silver from the ridge overlooking the ranch—the ridge where he'd lain with Tessa while a smoldering cigarette butt ignited dry straw in the stables far below.

"I guess the silver didn't exist," Ross said.

"Too bad," Denver muttered. "What about the stock?"

"It's holding its own, I think. Your uncle seemed to think that he was on the brink of turning things around."

Denver doubted it. Ross was just giving him the sales pitch that good old Uncle John had peddled him time and time again over the past few years. Denver hadn't bought it then and he wasn't buying it now. "The stables were never rebuilt after the fire, right?"

"The insurance company paid reluctantly—claimed the fire was arson. The fire chief concurred. Unfortunately the building was grossly underinsured. The money only covered cleaning up the mess and adding a few stalls to the barn." Ross squinted through his glasses. "John was hell-bent on suing the insurance company—claimed he'd been misrepresented, that he'd paid higher premiums than he should have for the amount of coverage. But he finally gave it up."

"On your advice?"

Ross nodded and drew on his cigar. "What's your point?"

"The point is that the McLean Ranch is little more than a few decrepit buildings, some rangy cattle, a few horses and acres of sagebrush."

"Some people would see it differently."

Denver leaned back in his chair. "Maybe. I call 'em as *I* see 'em. The place isn't worth much. Let's get what we can out of it and call it good."

Ross sighed. "This is a mistake."

"Not my first." Tugging at his collar with two fingers,

Denver wished this whole mess were over and done with. He didn't need any reminders of the past.

Shoving a copy of the will across the desk, Ross said flatly, "There's nothing you can do until the taxes are paid."

"I'll pay them."

"Okay, that's the first hurdle. Now, what about Colton?"

"Find him."

"That won't be easy."

"There has to be a way," Denver said wearily. "Last I heard he was still a United States citizen. Start with the State Department, a private investigator, the IRS and the CIA."

"It'll take time."

Denver narrowed his eyes. "Maybe you'll get lucky."

"I tried writing him through that magazine he free-lanced for a couple of years back," Ross explained. "Never received a reply."

"Keep trying." Denver glared angrily at the will. "I can wait." He felt his jaw clench at his next thought. "Is old man Kramer still running the place?"

Shrugging slim shoulders beneath his jacket, Ross said, "Far as I know. But I heard John say once that Kramer's daughter is really in charge. I can't remember her name." He crushed out his cigar.

"Tessa," Denver bit out, her name stinging his tongue. After seven years, he still felt needlelike jabs of regret that had turned bitter with age. If he tried, he could still recall the taste of her skin that hot day. But he wouldn't. No need to dredge up a past based on lies.

"Yeah, that's it. John confided in me that she covers for her old man." Ross leaned back in his chair and regarded Denver carefully. "Apparently Curtis Kramer has a drinking problem."

"Some things haven't changed," Denver observed.

"You can do what you want, of course. But since you're in

Montana already, you may as well drive over and check out
the place, make sure you really want to sell."

"I do."

"So you've said. I just thought you might want to find out
why a ranch that was owned free and clear was losing money
hand over fist—at least until recently."

Denver considered. He knew why: poor management.
Curtis Kramer knew horses but couldn't handle a ranch.
Denver's father had seen it and had been ready to let Curtis
go just before the fire . . . the damned fire. Unfortunately
Uncle John had kept Tessa's old man on. No one could prove
Curtis had started the blaze, and John had been convinced of
the man's innocence. Denver wasn't so sure. He drummed his
fingers on the arm of his chair. "Isn't finding out how much
the ranch is worth and how much it earns a job for the bank
that's probating the estate?"

Ross smiled crookedly. "Are you willing to trust someone
from Second Western Bank to understand the ins and outs of
ranching?"

Denver snorted.

"Right." Ross tugged on his tie. "Of course it's up to you.
It's yours now."

"Great. Just great." Denver shoved his chair back and
strode angrily out the door, past the blond receptionist and
through the labyrinthine corridors of the law firm—the
largest in Helena, Montana. Although small compared to
most in Los Angeles, where Denver had lived for the past
seven years, the firm of O'Brien, Simmons and Taft was
top-notch even by California's high standards, and Ross
Anderson, a junior partner, knew his stuff.

Shouldering open the glass door, Denver stalked onto
the street. The pace in Helena was much slower than that in
Los Angeles and Denver was restless. Ross's advice followed
him into the parking lot where his rented car was baking in
the late-afternoon sun. Clouds gathered above, but there

wasn't a breath of wind, and the humidity was unusually high, the air sticky.

Denver climbed in and switched on the ignition, unwillingly remembering the inferno.

It had all happened so fast. One minute he'd been lying on Tessa, her dew-covered skin fusing with his own, her lips soft and sensuous, her hazel eyes glazed in passion—the next he'd witnessed the horror of the blaze, horses screaming in death throes, hooves crashing in the billowing, lung-burning smoke. He'd felt the explosion, been thrown to the floor.

When he finally awakened, his skin burning, his face and hands unrecognizable, it had been three days later. He'd learned the devastating news: both his parents had been killed.

Colton, eyes red and shadowed, coffee-colored hair falling over his eyes, had been waiting for Denver to wake up.

"It's old man Kramer's fault," Colton insisted as he huddled near Denver's bed, avoiding his eyes and watching the steady drip of an IV tube that ran directly into the back of Denver's right hand.

"How—how could it be?" God, he hurt all over.

"He's been stealing from the ranch. He was up in the office altering the books when the fire started. If you ask me, he did it to destroy the evidence."

"You can't prove it."

"Can't I?" Colton thundered, his gray eyes sizzling like lightning. "Weren't you supposed to go over the books that day? Didn't Tessa insist that you go riding with her instead?" He stood then, the back of his neck dark in anger, his boots muffled on the carpeting.

Denver's dry throat worked in defense.

"What did she do? Seduce you?" Colton must have seen

some betraying spark in Denver's eyes. "Of course she did," he muttered in disgust.

"No—"

"Don't you see? It was all part of the plan—Curtis's plan to rip off the ranch! Dad was on to him, and he had to cover his tracks."

"No way!" Denver rasped.

"Whose idea was it to go riding?"

Denver didn't answer.

"Right. And I'll bet Tessa was more than willing."

"Get out of here."

Colton didn't move. "You're a blind man, brother! She and that drunk of an old man of hers have been bleeding us dry. I'd even bet Mitch is in on it with them."

Denver tried to sit up, pushing aside the pain that scorched the length of his body. "I won't believe—"

"Then don't. But think about this. Mom and Dad are dead, Denver. Dead! Dad thought Curtis was embezzling, and he was out to prove it. Doesn't it seem a little too convenient that all the records were destroyed on the day Dad asked you to go over the books?"

"He didn't say a word about Curtis."

"He couldn't, could he?" Colton pointed out. "He wanted an impartial opinion!" Colton's furious gaze skated across the wrinkled sheets and gauze bandages to land on Denver's scarred face. "I know that you and I have never seen eye to eye, but I thought you'd agree with me on this one." His jaw worked for a minute. "They're gone, Denver. And you—look at you." Colton's eyes clouded with pity. "Look at what they did, for Christ's sake."

"Get out!" Denver didn't want to think about the damage to himself. He'd always been proud, and the look on Colton's face twisted his guts. He couldn't think about the pity in Tessa's eyes should she ever see him again.

Colton's gray eyes flashed furiously. "Any way you cut it,

Denver, Curtis Kramer is to blame." He strode out of the room then, leaving Denver alone with his scars and his memories.

Now, shaking his head to clear it of the unpleasant past, Denver rammed the car into gear and backed out of the law firm's parking lot. The car rolled easily onto the street and Denver turned north, toward the airport. Not once since the fire had he returned to the ranch. He'd never seen Tessa again.

At first pride had kept him from her, and eventually Colton had convinced him that she had, intentionally or not, conspired against him. He'd told himself he was doing her one big favor by leaving, and he'd been right. He had been badly scarred, physically and emotionally. Plastic surgery had fixed the exterior, he thought cynically as he glanced in the rearview mirror and saw the same blue eyes he'd been born with. One lid was a mere fraction lower than the other, but his skin was smooth, the result of more skin grafts than he wanted to count. But no surgeon or psychiatrist had been able to remove the bitterness he felt whenever he thought about that day.

"So don't think about it," he muttered aloud, scowling at himself. It was many miles north to the ranch, and the airport was only across town. He could drive to the airport and return to Los Angeles as he'd planned, or he could phone his partner and take time off—the vacation he hadn't allowed himself in years. Jim would understand, and business was unseasonably slow. But if he stayed in Montana, he'd have to face Tessa again.

His lips curved into a crooked, almost wicked smile. Maybe it was time. He saw the flashing neon sign of a local tavern and pulled into the pothole-pocked parking lot. One beer, he decided, then he'd make up his mind.

* * *

With one quick stroke of her jackknife, Tessa cut the twine. The bale split open easily. Snapping the knife closed, she shoved it into her pocket, then forked loose hay into the manger. Dust swirled in the air, and the interior of the old barn smelled musty and dry.

Though it was evening, no breeze whispered through the open doors and only faint rays from a cloud-covered sun filtered past the grime and cobwebs of the few circular windows cut high in the hayloft.

The air was still, heavy with the threat of rain. She hoped the summer shower would break quickly and give relief to the parched ranch land. The ground was cracked and hard. And it was only the middle of August.

She was already feeding the horses and cattle hay she'd cut barely a month before.

Frowning, she heard the familiar sound of thudding hooves. Tails up and unfurling like silky flags, several of the younger horses raced into the barn. Behind the colts, the brood mares plodded at a slower pace.

"Hungry?" Tessa asked as several dark heads poked through the far side of the manger. A gray colt bared his teeth and nipped at a rival as the horses shoved for position. "Hey, slow down, there's enough for everybody." She chuckled as she forked more hay, shaking it along the long trough that served all the McLean horses.

Once the McLean horses were fed, she tossed hay into a manger on the other side of the barn and grinned widely as three more horses plunged their heads into the manger. Their warm breath stirred the hay as they nuzzled deep, searching for oats. "In a minute," Tessa said, admiring the stallion and two mares. These were her horses, and her heart swelled with pride at the sight of them. She owned several—six in all—but these three were her pride and joy, the mainstay of her small herd. "Hasn't anyone told you patience is a virtue?" She petted the velvet-soft nose of Brigadier, the stallion.

A deep chestnut with a crooked white blaze and liquid eyes, he was spirited and feisty—and one of the best quarter horses in the state. At least in Tessa's opinion.

The two mares were gentler and shorter, one a blood bay, the other black. Both were with foal, and their bellies had started to protrude roundly. These three horses were the center of Tessa's dreams. She'd worked long hours, saved her money and even delayed finishing college to pay for them, one at a time. But the herd was growing, she thought fondly, eyeing Ebony's rounded sides, and finally Tessa was through school. She reached across the manger and patted Brigadier's sleek neck.

His red ears pricked forward then back, and he tossed his head, his mane flying and his dark eyes glinting.

"Okay, okay, I get the message." Grinning, Tessa poured oats for her horses and heard contented nickers and heavy grinding of back teeth.

Rain began to pepper the tin roof, echoing through the barn in a quickening tempo. "At last," Tessa murmured. She jabbed a pitchfork into a nearby bale, tugged off her gloves and tossed them onto the lid of the oat barrel. Stretching, she turned for the house. But she stopped dead in her tracks.

In the doorway, the shoulders of his denim jacket soaked, his wet dark hair plastered to his head, stood a man she barely recognized as Denver McLean. She hadn't seen him for so long—not since that awful day. Though his face was familiar, it had changed, the harsh angles and planes of his features more rugged than ever. His hair was the same coal black, shorter than she remembered, but still thick and wavy as he pushed a wet lock off his forehead.

"Denver?" she whispered, almost disbelieving. Her heart began to slam against her ribs. Her father and Milly, the cook, had both speculated that Denver might return to the ranch after his uncle's death, but Tessa hadn't dared think he would show up.

He crossed his arms and leaned one shoulder in the doorway. Behind him rain spilled from the gutters and showered the ground in sheets. The smell of fresh water meeting dusty earth filled the air. "It's been a long time, Tessa," he finally said.

Swallowing against a hard lump in her throat, she walked forward several steps. The horses snorted behind her and shifted restlessly, as if they, too, could feel the sudden electricity charging the air. "Yes, it has been a long time," she agreed, her voice as dry as the earth had been only a half hour before.

As she met his blue, blue eyes, painful memories crowded her mind. As vivid as the storm clouds hovering over the surrounding mountains, as fresh as the rain pelting the roof, the pain of his rejection flashed through her thoughts.

So many times she'd hoped she might meet him and not even mention the past—pretend total indifference to the wretched nights she'd lain awake, wounded to her very soul. But now that he was here, standing in front of her, she couldn't find one thread of that mantle of pride she'd sworn she'd wear. "I—I never thought I'd see you again."

"No?" His expression was wry, his tone disbelieving. "Haven't you heard? I own the place."

"Yes, I know, but—" Words failed her. Silence stretched heavily between them. "I—I knew it was possible, but it's just been so long." *So damned long.*

"I came back to straighten out a few things," he stated flatly, indifference masking his features. "I'll be here a couple of weeks. I thought I'd better tell someone I was here. I can't find your father or the cook, what's her name?"

"Milly Samms."

"Right. Anyway, you're the first person I've run into."

A little hurt tugged at her heart. Deep inside, she'd hoped he had been searching for her. She forced an even smile, though she couldn't help staring at his face, a face she'd loved so fiercely. Whatever scars had once discolored his skin were gone—faded to invisibility. Though he seemed changed, it was his callousness and age that caused the difference more than any surgery. But he was still handsome and earthy, she had to admit—and sensual in a way she hadn't remembered. "Most of the hands have gone into town," she said, struggling to keep her voice steady. "It's Friday night."

He raised one of his thick eyebrows skeptically. "So who's holding down the fort?"

"You're looking at her."

"You?" He held her gaze for a second before glancing at his watch and frowning. "I figured you might have a date later."

Damn him. "I do," she replied, a little goaded.

If the thought of her going out bothered him at all, he managed to hide it. *What did you expect after seven years?* she asked herself.

"A date with a hot bath and a good book." She found her work jacket on a hook near the door and slid her arms through the sleeves.

"That's not what I meant."

"I know," she admitted, trying to compose herself. Why after all these years did her heart race at the sight of him?

She dusted her hands and thought about the reason he'd come back: his uncle's estate. "I'm sorry about John."

"Me, too."

"He didn't want a funeral—"

Waving off her explanation, he shrugged. "Doesn't matter. I just came back to tie up a few loose ends, that's all. Where's your father? I thought he was running things."

"He is. He, uh, had business in town."

"But he's coming back?"

"Of course."

"When he gets back, tell him I want to see him. I'll be up at the house." He glanced through the rain toward the weathered two-story farmhouse across the yard.

Tessa's gaze followed his.

With its high-pitched roof, dormers and broad front porch, the old house had stood in the same spot for nearly a hundred years. It had been updated since the turn of the century—two bathrooms, central heat and electricity had been added— but it still appeared as it had when it was built by Denver's great-great-grandfather.

Denver cleared his throat then looked at her again, his eyes studying her face. She felt his gaze sliding from her straight red-blond hair past hazel eyes and a freckle-dusted nose to the sharp point of her chin. She wondered how he saw her—if she looked as he'd remembered. If he even cared.

"You know," she whispered, clinging to her rapidly escaping courage and feeling her fists curling into tight balls as she thought about the past, "I've waited all this time to ask you this one question."

His head jerked up. "Shoot."

"Why?" She stood dry-eyed in front of him, her chin tilted upward, her eyes searching his face—a face she'd loved with all her youthful heart. "Why wouldn't you talk to me?"

A muscle jumped angrily in his jaw. "Didn't seem the thing to do."

"But you could have called or something—" She lifted her hands helplessly and hated the gesture. Despite the fact that seeing him again opened old wounds, she couldn't let him see that she was still vulnerable to him in any way.

Shoving his hands into his jacket pockets, he crossed the weathered barn floor, eyeing the munching horses, the hay-loft now full of new-mown hay, and the bins and barrels of oats, wheat and corn. "By the time I thought about it, there was no point," he said. Then his gaze softened a little and he studied the rusted bit of an old bridle hanging on the wall. He ran his fingers slowly along the time-hardened leather reins. "I thought by now you'd be married with about five kids."

"So did I."

"What happened?" He regarded her with genuine perplexity, and she felt some of her old anger simmer again.

"The man I wanted to marry left town without saying a word."

He didn't move. The rain beat steadily on the roof, breaking the silence that stretched yawningly between them.

Tessa forced the issue. Though quaking inside, she sensed this might be her only chance to find out what had happened. "You wouldn't see me in the hospital," she accused, her voice surprisingly calm, "wouldn't take my calls and returned all my letters unopened."

His jaw hardened. He dropped the reins but didn't say a word. One horse nickered and Tessa glanced toward the manger.

The way she saw it, Denver's silence was as damning as if he'd said he hadn't cared. She drew on all her courage. "Before I knew what was happening, my dad told me you'd taken off for Los Angeles."

He almost smiled, his eyes narrowing. "I couldn't keep the plastic surgeon waiting."

"Without saying goodbye?" she asked, bewildered and wounded all over again. "After everything we'd planned?"

"We didn't plan anything, Tessa."

The wind shifted. Rain poured through the open door. "But you'd asked me to marry you, move to L.A.——"

"I *never* said a word about marriage," he cut in, his voice harsh. "Think about it. You were the one who wanted to tie me down."

Tessa nearly gasped. "I didn't——"

"Sure you did. You kept trying to convince me that I should stay here, with you, on this damned ranch." Standing at his full height, using its advantage to stare down at her and drill her with his frosty blue gaze, he added, "I had no intention of staying."

"I loved you," she said boldly, the words ringing in the barn. "I might have been naive, but I did love you, Denver."

Denver's muscles tensed, the skin over his features stretching taut. "We were two kids experimenting, Tessa—finding out about our bodies and sex. Love had nothing to do with it."

"You don't believe that!" she cried, feeling as if he'd slapped her. "You couldn't!"

"Time has a way of making the past crystal clear, don't you think?"

Tessa's chin wobbled, but she forced her head up proudly. He wiped the rain from his hair, and she saw his hand, the burns still visible. Suddenly she understood. "You were afraid to see me," she whispered, her eyes widening with realization as they clashed with his again.

His face was unreadable and stony. "Think what you want."

She walked toward him, her steps quickening as she closed the distance. "That's it, isn't it? You were afraid that because of your scars—"

"Has it ever occurred to you that maybe what happened between us just wasn't that important?"

"No!"

"Oh, God, Tessa. You always were a dreamer."

His words hit hard and stung, like the cut of a whip. As if to protect herself, she stumbled backward, wrapped her arms around her waist and leaned against one cobweb draped wall. "What happened to you, Denver?" she murmured, staring at the bitter man whom she had once treasured. "Just what the hell happened to you?"

"I got burned." Hiking his collar up, he turned and strode through the slanting rain. Ducking his head, he marched across the gravel yard, his boots echoing loudly as he disappeared into the house.

Tessa stared after him, her heart thudding painfully. Dropping onto the hay-strewn floor, she buried her face in her hands. For years she'd imagined running into him again, hoping deep in her heart that there might be some little spark in his eyes—a hint that he still cared. And even if he didn't love her again, she'd told herself, she could be content knowing that he, too, felt a special warmth at the thought that she had been his first love.

She'd been practical, not harboring any fanciful dreams that one day they could fall in love again. But she'd hoped that after an initial strained meeting, she and Denver would eventually become close—not as lovers, but as friends.

It had been a stupid, childish dream. She knew that now. Denver had changed so much.

Surprised that her hands were wet, that she'd actually shed tears for a man who had turned into such a soulless bastard, she sniffed loudly, wiped her eyes and tossed her hair over her shoulder. Never again, she told herself bitterly. These were the last tears she would ever shed for Denver McLean!

Chapter Two

Determined to be as cool and indifferent as Denver, Tessa marched through the rain to the house. The nerve of the man! she thought. He'd waltzed back into her life only to tell her that everything they had shared had been lies. He had twisted the truth to serve his own purposes. Well, he could twist it all he liked!

She wasn't afraid of Denver or his lies. He couldn't possibly hurt her more than he already had.

Seething, she kicked off her boots on the back porch and stalked into the kitchen in her stocking feet. The mingled smells of warm coffee, stale cigarettes and newsprint filled the air. Illuminated by the one remaining low-watt bulb, the room was muted, some of its defects hidden.

Tessa half expected to find Denver at the table, but the kitchen was empty. She knew he had to be in the house—or on the grounds nearby. His rental car was parked near the garage, under the overhanging branches of an ancient oak, and she'd watched him storm into the house just minutes before.

"So who cares?" she asked herself angrily. He'd made himself perfectly clear. She meant nothing to him and so much the better. At least now they could get down to business. She poured herself a cup of coffee from a glass pot still warming on the stove, took a sip and grimaced before tossing the remaining dregs down the drain. She refilled the cup with hot water for instant coffee and placed it in the microwave.

She listened, but didn't hear a sound other than the hum of the refrigerator, the gentle whir of the tiny oven and the drip of the rain outside. Maybe Denver had left through the front door.

Usually after chores, if Tessa found a few minutes to herself, she enjoyed the time, but now, as she stirred decaf crystals into her cup and pretended to read the headlines of the newspaper spread all over the kitchen table, she was tense.

The overhead bulb flickered, strobing the chipped Formica, the yellowed layers of wax on the old linoleum and the nicked cabinets. The entire ranch was falling apart, and the disrepair was glaringly evident. Denver would soon discover just how bad things were. Maybe she should tell him—get everything out in the open.

Still wrestling with that decision, she walked through the corridor leading to the stairs but stopped when she noticed a crack of light glowing under the study door. So Denver had holed up in the office. No doubt he was already poring over the books—searching for flaws. Her fingers curled tightly over the handle of her cup. If it took every ounce of grit within her, she had to find a way to work with him and get through the next few days without antagonizing him. Her father needed this job. Since the fire no one else in Three Falls would hire Curtis Kramer.

She twisted the knob, shoving on the door.

Denver was right where she expected him to be—seated behind John McLean's old walnut desk. Leaning over a stack of ledgers and invoices, his head bent, light from the desk lamp gleaming in his black hair, he worked, finally glancing up. "What?" His shirtsleeves were pushed over his forearms, leaving his dark skin bare.

An old ache settled in Tessa's heart. She stared at him a second, and she had trouble finding her voice. "Making yourself at home?" she asked finally. Though she tried to sound nonchalant, as if she didn't care one whit about him, there was a wistful ring in her words.

Denver leaned so far back in his chair that it creaked against his weight. Impatiently he stretched his arms, then cradled the back of his head in his hands. "I'm only staying a couple of weeks—to iron out a few things."

"Such as?"

"Back taxes for starters." His gaze shifted to a stack of unpaid bills. "Those next. And eventually the accounts with the feed store, hardware store—" He lifted a thick pile of paper. "Whatever it takes."

"To do what?"

His eyes narrowed. "To clean up this mess. According to John's lawyer, there have been all kinds of problems here—repairs that need to be made and haven't, bills unpaid, you name it!"

"Every ranch has . . . cash flow problems," she pointed out.

"What about that stallion that disappeared last spring—the best stallion on the place?"

Tessa cringed inside. She had hoped Denver hadn't heard about that. "Black Magic was lost. But we found him again—"

"He wasn't found. He just showed up."

Her voice was tight. "It doesn't matter. The point is, Black Magic returned and he's fine!"

Denver's lips twisted. "The point is that things are going to hell in a hand basket around here." He thumped his fingers on a stack of past-due bills. "This place is drowning in red ink."

"It's not that bad."

"Isn't it?" His eyes flashed.

She bit back a hot retort. "Things are just beginning to turn around, Denver," she said, ignoring the doubt in his eyes. "Tomorrow, when it's light, I'll take you around the ranch, show you the progress that isn't recorded in the checkbook."

His jaw shifted to the side, but he didn't argue.

"A ranch is more than dollars and cents, debits and credits, you know. A ranch is horses and cattle and machinery and people working together on land that matters."

One corner of his mouth curved up. "You haven't changed, have you?" he said, his voice husky. "Still a dreamer."

"I know what's valuable, Denver. I always have. And sometimes it doesn't show on a checkbook stub." She gazed directly at him, wishing the strain near his eyes would disappear.

"You've been wrong," he reminded her.

"I don't think so—not about the things that really matter."

His jaw clenched and he looked away—through the window to the dark night beyond. The desk lamp was reflected in the rain drizzling down the panes. "I should have talked to you a long time ago, I suppose."

"It would have helped," she replied, feigning indifference.

He looked as if he wanted to say more. For a second she caught a glimpse of him as he had been years before. His blue eyes turned as warm as a July morning. Then, as swiftly as the warmth appeared, it disappeared again. "It doesn't matter now," he said, clearing his throat. "It's all water under the bridge."

"Right," she lied. The entire room seemed filled with him, and, absurdly, she wanted to linger. "Can I get you anything? Make a fresh pot of coffee?"

The corners of his eyes softened a bit. "Don't bother."

"It's no bother."

"Tessa," he said quietly, "don't." Skin tightening over his

cheekbones, he added, "If I need anything, I'll get it. I know my way around."

Goaded, she quipped, "You're the boss," and was rewarded with a severe glance.

Reaching for the doorknob, she heard the sound of an engine in the distance and recognized the rumble of her father's pickup. She glanced out the window. Curtis Kramer's dented yellow truck bounced into the yard.

"Company?" Denver asked.

"Just Dad."

His eyes narrowed. "Good. He and I have to talk." He watched the beams of headlights through the rain-speckled windows, and his mouth compressed into a thin, uncompromising line.

The temperature in the room seemed to drop ten degrees. "What about?"

"Everything. We'll start with what he knows about all the money he's managed to lose for this ranch."

"Denver," she whispered. "Don't—"

"Don't what?"

Her eyes sparked. "Don't judge before you have all your facts straight."

"But that's what I'm here to do," he said, turning to her, his voice cold. "Get my facts straight. Curtis can help clear up a few cloudy issues."

"What's that supposed to mean?"

"He's been in charge a long time and things"—he gestured around the shabby room, to the scarred desk, the dingy walls and threadbare drapes—"haven't gotten any better. In fact, this place seems to be on the verge of falling apart."

"And you blame Dad."

"I don't blame anyone. Not yet. But there's got to be a reason, Tessa. I just want to know what it is."

The screen door banged shut and Tessa heard her father call out. "Tessa? You 'round? Milly?"

A satisfied smile crossed Denver's lips as he stood and started for the door. But she clamped her arm around his elbow, her fingers tight over his bare forearm. The feel of his skin shocked her. Hard muscles flexed beneath her hands, soft hair brushed against her fingertips.

Denver stopped, glaring at her fingers as if they were intruders.

"Dad didn't start the fire, Denver," she insisted. "No matter what Colton said. Dad wasn't behind it."

"Who said anything about the fire?"

"You didn't have to," she replied, meeting his seething gaze with her own. "It's written all over your face."

"Is it? How?" He shoved his face close to hers, so close that she saw the pinpoints of fire in his eyes, read his anger in the flare of his nostrils. "What is it you see when you look so closely, Tessa?" he bit out.

The scent of rain lingered in his hair.

Tessa could barely breathe. Though her senses were reeling, she wouldn't back down, not for a second. Her fingers dug into his arms. "What I see," she said evenly, though her heart was hammering out of control, "is a bitter man, hell-bent on extracting his own punishment for an imagined crime, a man whose irrational desire for retribution clouds his judgment."

"Is that right?" he mocked.

"And more! I see a man who's taking all his bitterness out on a tired old man and a woman who once thought he was the most important thing in her life!"

A muscle worked in his jaw. "Then you're a blind woman, Tessa."

"I don't think so."

"Maybe you'd better take a harder look."

"Don't worry, I will. You left this ranch and haven't stepped foot on it in seven years. *Seven years,* Denver. So what gives you the right to come back now?"

The cords in his neck tightened. "I own the place. Remember?"

"You and Colton."

"Well, he isn't around, is he?"

"Tessa? That you?" her father called through the study door.

"In here, Dad!" she shouted back.

"What in blazes are you doin' in here at this time of—?" Curtis Kramer shoved open the door and stepped into the dimly lit room. Color seemed to wash out of his weathered face. "Well, I'll be," he muttered, unconsciously smoothing his white hair with the flat of his hand. The scent of stale whiskey and cigarettes followed him as he crossed the room. His pale eyes focused more clearly. "I was wonderin' when you'd show up."

Unspoken accusations hung like cobwebs, dangling between them. Denver's eyes had turned so frigid, Tessa actually shivered.

Through tight lips, Curtis said, "I figured it wouldn't be long before you and Colton would want to check things out."

"I've already started." Denver's jaw was rigid, his eyes blazing with warning, but Curtis, whether bolstered by the whiskey or his own sense of pride, didn't back down.

"Good," he shot back. "About time you took some interest in things." Hooking his thumbs in the loops of his jeans, he turned to Tessa. "I'm gonna make me a sandwich. You want anything?"

"I'm fine," Tessa lied. Beneath her ranch-tough veneer, she was shredding apart bit by bit, and she wouldn't have been able to eat a bite if she'd tried. She heard her father amble down the hallway to the kitchen as she whirled on Denver. "What was *that* all about?"

"What?"

"You know what! You were baiting him, for God's sake."

"Was I?" He arched an insolent eyebrow. "All I said was that I was going to look things over."

"It wasn't so much what you said as how you said it. You implied something was going on here that wasn't aboveboard."

"You're overreacting."

"Just don't act like my dad's some kind of criminal, okay? Try and remember who stayed here and held this ranch together while you and your brother took off to God only knows where."

"I went to L.A.," he said, his voice cold. "Just as I'd planned."

She turned away. All these years she'd harbored some crazy little hope that he'd really cared for her, that he'd considered staying with her on the ranch, that she could have convinced him to stay in Montana with her if not for the fire. She hadn't really believed his words that their affair had meant nothing to him.

Her chin trembled, but she met his gaze. His eyes glared back at her without a hint of warmth in their cerulean depths. "So you said." She strode furiously down the hall to the kitchen. Her cheeks were flaming with injustice, and she felt her fists curl as tight as the hard knot in her stomach.

Her father was sitting in one of the beat-up chairs at the table. His cigarette burned in an ashtray, and a cup of coffee sat steaming on the stained oilcloth. "So he's back," Curtis grumbled, eyeing the local newspaper with disinterest.

"For a little while."

"How long?"

"I don't know."

"Humph."

"As long as it takes," Denver said from the hall. Leaning one shoulder against the doorjamb, he crossed his arms over his chest, the cotton weave of his shirt stretching taut over his shoulders.

"As long as it takes to do *what?*" Curtis asked.

Denver's expression was calculating, his features hard.

"I'm here to figure out why this ranch has lost money for the past five years."

"That's simple enough," Curtis said. "The silver mines were a bust."

"We made money before the mining."

Curtis took a long drag on his cigarette. "But John took out loans for the equipment. Besides, prices are down and we had two bad winters—lost nearly a third of our herd. It's no mystery, Denver. Ranchin' ain't exactly a bed of roses."

"So I've heard," Denver mocked.

Curtis squinted through the smoke. "Seven years hasn't improved your disposition any, has it?"

One of Denver's dark eyebrows cocked. "Should it have?"

Stubbing out his cigarette, Curtis shook his head. "Probably not. You McLeans are known for your bullheadedness."

Surprisingly, Denver's lips twitched. "Unlike you Kramers."

"Right," Curtis said, but he chuckled briefly as he pulled his jacket from a hook near the back porch. Squaring his stained hat on his head, he shoved open the back door and headed outside.

"You don't have to badger him, you know," Tessa said, keeping her back to Denver's lounging form.

"I thought he was badgering me."

"Maybe he was," Tessa decided. "But you deserved it." Through the window, she saw her father's old truck bounce down the lane. Rain ran down the glass, blurring the glow of the taillights. "Dad's just an old man whose only crime is that he's given his life to this ranch."

"And what's mine, Tessa?" he asked, his voice low.

She turned and caught him staring at her—the same way he'd studied her in the past. His face had lost some of its harsh angles, his expression had softened, and his eyes—Lord, his eyes—had darkened to a seductive midnight blue.

"You left me," she whispered, her throat suddenly thick. "You left us all—without a word of goodbye."

He glanced away. "I regret that," he admitted, shoving a lock of dark hair from his forehead.

"Why, Denver? Why wouldn't you see me in the hospital?"

His eyes narrowed and the line of his jaw grew taut again. "Because it was over. There was no point."

"You could have explained it to me."

"Unfortunately, I wasn't in tip-top shape," he said, his words cutting like a dull knife.

"Neither was I! You were in the hospital—I didn't know if you were going to live or die. My father was being accused of heinous crimes he had no part in, and no one would tell me anything! Good Lord, Denver, can you imagine how I felt?"

The corners of his mouth turned white. "And can you imagine what I was going through?" he said, his voice barely a whisper. "I was told I would never be the same, that I would probably never use my arm again. Both my parents were dead because of the fire, and a woman I trusted had set me up to cover for her old man!"

"No!" Tessa's eyes widened in horror. "You couldn't believe—"

"I didn't know what to believe!" Advancing on her, his eyes boring into her, he said, "I just knew that my entire life had gone to hell!"

He was so close that she could feel the heat radiating from his body, sense the anger simmering within him. "You could have given me a chance to explain before you set yourself up as judge and jury!"

"It was too late for explanations."

"Maybe it's never too late."

He gave a wry smile and some of his anger seemed to melt. Reaching forward, he brushed a strand of hair from her eyes, his fingertips grazing her cheek. "Still the dreamer, aren't you, Tessa?"

She swallowed hard, fighting a losing battle with the raw

energy surging between them. "I—I think I've dealt with the
past seven years realistically. At least I didn't run away."

Sucking in a swift breath, he dropped his hand. His eyes
blazed again. "Is that what you think?"

"That's what happened. And now you're back, sweeping
back in here like some sort of avenging angel—accusing my
father of everything from arson to involuntary manslaughter."

"I haven't accused him of anything."

"Not in so many words, maybe," she said, her temper flaring
wildly. "But it's obvious you blame him for the fire, just as you
blame me."

"When Curtis was here, we were talking about running
the ranch."

"Were we?" She strode across the room, tilting her head
back, forcing her eyes to meet his. "You could have fooled me."

"I don't want to talk about the fire," he snapped.

"Then leave it alone, Denver. Leave all of it alone. Because, believe it or not, we've been working our tail ends off
around here to save this place—a place you don't give a damn
about!" She strode out of the room, letting the screen door
slam behind her, then fumbled for the light on the porch.

"Mule-headed bastard," she muttered, tugging her boots
on before running down the back steps. The rain was coming
down in sheets, pounding the earth, turning the dust to mud.
Bareheaded, Tessa stalked furiously down the well-worn path
to the paddocks. She leaned against the wet fence, feeling
the wind tease her hair and toss the wet strands across her
face. She didn't care. This summer storm couldn't match the
tempest of emotions raging deep in her soul.

Damn! Damn! Damn! Her fingers flexed and curled. *Why
did he have to come back? Why now?*

Closing her eyes, she prayed the cool rain would wash
away the pain, dampen the fires of injustice that burned so
brightly in her heart.

"Tessa?" Denver's voice, so near, made her jump, her heart still fluttering at the sound.

"Leave me alone!"

"What do you think you're doing out here?" he asked so calmly she wanted to scream.

"Trying to put things in perspective."

Leaning over the top rail, his eyes squinting against the darkness, he stood so close that his shoulder brushed hers. She didn't move. Couldn't. Raindrops, reflecting the blue glow from the single outside lamp, collected in his hair and drizzled down his throat.

He hadn't bothered with a jacket, and his shirttail flapped in the wind. "Aren't you afraid of drowning?" he asked softly.

"In case you haven't heard, we're in the middle of a drought!"

His eyes searched the dark heavens. "Not tonight, we're not."

"The rain feels good." Why did she feel so defensive around him? Slowly counting to ten, she tried to control her temper. "Besides, we need every drop we get. The river's low and the fields are tinder-dry."

As the wind slapped against his face and the rain plastered his hair, Denver said, "This is crazy. Let's go inside where it's dry."

"I'm fine out here."

"Are you?" He tried to smother a smile and failed as he brushed a drip from the tip of her chin. His gaze shifted restlessly over her face. "You look like a drowned rat."

"I bet you say that to all the girls," she snapped, but couldn't help smiling.

"Only when I'm trying to impress them."

"So you're still the charmer you've always been."

He laughed, a low rumbling sound that warmed the cool night. "Low blow, Tessa."

"You deserved it. You haven't been pulling any punches yourself."

"I guess I haven't." The breeze snatched at his hair, ruffling it. "Come on inside. *I'll* pour *you* a cup of coffee." The determined line of his jaw relaxed, and he looked more like the young man she'd loved so fervently. He touched her lightly on the shoulder, his fingertips warm through her wet blouse. "Truce?"

She shook her head. "I don't know if that's possible, Denver." But she let him take her hand and told herself that the tingling sensation she felt in her palm was because of the storm. Hands linked, running stride for stride, they dashed through puddles in the backyard to the house.

In the kitchen he tossed her a towel, and Tessa wiped the rain from her face. As she sat in one of the chairs at the table, she studied him. His face had become lean and angular over the years, his skin dark and tight. But no amount of reconstructive surgery had been able to straighten his nose—a nose that had been broken when he fell from a horse at the age of twelve.

He'd changed. The lines of boyish dimples that had creased his cheeks had deepened into grooves of discontent, and his sensual mouth was knife-blade thin. A webbing of lines near his eyes indicated that he still squinted—but did he laugh and tease and smile as he once had?

After pouring the coffee, he handed her a steaming mug.

She took a sip, nearly burning her tongue. Cradling her mug in her hands, she leaned back in a chair and tossed the wet hair from her eyes. "I didn't really think you'd show up," she said. "I expected you'd sell your half of the place by phone."

He scraped back a chair, straddled it and leaned forward, blowing across his mug. "I wanted to, but it wasn't that easy."

So there it was. He admitted it. This ranch that she and her father had worked their bodies to the bone for meant nothing to him.

"As I said, there's a problem with back taxes," he said. "Seems they've been neglected."

"Money's been tight." A defensive note crept into her voice.

"So I've heard."

"And Colton?" she asked, wondering about Denver's brother. "Does he feel the same about this place?"

"I wish I knew." Denver glanced pensively into the dark depths of his coffee. "Since he owns half the place, I need to know if he wants to buy out my share or put the whole spread on the market."

"So, no matter what happens, you're going to sell."

"Right." He took a swig from his cup, without the slightest indication that he felt one second's regret.

"Just like that?"

"Just like that."

She leaned closer to him, placing her elbows on the table for support, her wet hair falling forward. "What would you say if I told you I wanted to buy you out?"

His features froze. "You?"

"Right. And not just your share, but Colton's, too."

Denver's mouth dropped open before he clamped it shut. "You don't want this ranch, Tessa," he said quietly. "You couldn't."

"Don't you presume anything about me, Denver McLean," she replied, her eyes serious, her voice surprisingly strong. "I've thought about it a long time. I've worked too hard on this place to have it sold out from under me."

"Tessa, this is crazy—"

"I'm not kidding, Denver. If you're going to sell McLean Ranch, I intend to buy it." Before he could protest, she added, "I've got some money of my own, livestock I could sell if I need to, and I've already done the preliminary talking to a banker in Three Falls."

"So you've got it all figured out."

"Most of it."

"Tell me," he drawled, "how do you expect to pull a ranch that can't hold its own back on its feet?"

"It can be done."

"With a huge mortgage?" He shook his head and finished his coffee. "I don't see how."

"That's the problem, Denver," she said evenly. "You've got your eyes wide open, but you can't see what's right in front of your nose." Feeling a hot lump forming in her throat, she whispered, "You never could."

Denver's fingers curled over his cup. Tessa was beautiful— *too beautiful*. He kicked back his chair, tossed the dregs of his coffee into the sink and tried to ignore the firm thrust of Tessa's jaw, the fire in her hazel eyes, the way her damp blouse clung to her skin. Her hair, though wet, shone beneath the dim wattage in the kitchen, and her face was flushed in fury, touching the forbidden part of his soul he'd hoped had smoldered to a cold death seven years before. "I think I'll unpack." He needed time to think, time to put everything into perspective, time to remind himself that she'd betrayed him and his family. Distance would help. Being in the room with her, feeling her accusing gaze still drilling hot against his back, wasn't good.

What was the old saying? That there was a thin line between love and hate? Convinced he was walking that line, Denver realized he had to be careful—or he was sure to fall.

"You can have the room at the top of the stairs," she said.

"*I* can have?" he asked, turning. She was still seated at the table, her eyes cool and distant, her face more beautiful than he'd remembered.

"It was John's room."

"*I* know whose room it was. I used to live here. Remember?"

She let out a little strangled sound, then cleared her throat. "Unfortunately, I could never forget."

To his disgust, he felt his guts wrenching, that same horrid pain that he'd felt when Colton had convinced him that Tessa was involved with her father in Curtis's scheme to fleece the ranch. To hide his weakness he leaned his hips against the counter and curled his fingers around the sharp edge. "What about my parents' room?"

"I'm using it."

"You?" he repeated. "You *live* here?"

"Yes." Standing, she shoved her fingers into the pockets of her jeans. "You can have any room you want, Denver. Just let me know, so I can move my things."

"Hold on a minute. Why are you living here?" he demanded, hot, fresh anger searing deep inside. Tessa had lived under the same roof as John before his death?

"It was more convenient."

"I'll bet," he muttered, imagining her with his uncle. A bachelor for life, John McLean had gained a reputation with the local women. But Tessa? Denver's insides knotted. Repulsed at the image of John and Tessa making love, he closed his mind and gritted his teeth. He wanted to discard the ugly idea, and yet he couldn't. He didn't really know Tessa, not anymore. Maybe he never had.

"What do you mean?" she asked before she caught the message in Denver's stormy eyes. "You're kidding, right?" she whispered, lips twitching. "You don't really think I was John's—"

"Were you?"

Laughter died in Tessa's throat. Denver was serious. Dead serious. And there was a possessive streak of jealousy lighting his eyes. "Think about it, Denver," she taunted, wounded once again. "You tell me." Her back so stiff it ached, she strode out of the room and ran up the stairs to her room.

How could he think that she would sleep with his uncle? The ugly thought made her sick! She threw open the closet and began stripping her clothes off hangers, hurling them onto the bed and kicking shoes into the center of the room.

One thing was certain, she thought furiously, she couldn't stay here at the house with Denver. She yanked her suitcase and an old Army duffel bag from the shelf and heaved both onto the bed. Cheeks burning, she began attacking the drawers of her dresser with fervor.

She slammed the top drawer. It banged hard against its casing, rattling the mirror. "Argumentative, insensitive beast!" she muttered through clenched teeth just as she caught sight of Denver's image, staring at her from the mirror over the dresser.

He surveyed her scattered clothes expressionlessly. "Don't let me stop you," he drawled.

"You won't!" She threw her clothes haphazardly into the suitcase and stuffed the remainder into the duffel bag. "Believe me."

Not everything fit. Corners of blouses and sweater sleeves poked out of the bag and she had trouble closing the lid of the suitcase. Finally it snapped shut. Lifting her head high, she said, "I'll be back for the rest in the morning."

With the suitcase swinging from one arm and the duffel bag tucked under the other, she strode across the bedroom and waited, the toe of one boot tapping impatiently, for him to move. "If you'll excuse me," she mocked.

"No way."

"Move, Denver."

"Not until you explain what you were doing in this room."

Her hazel eyes snapped. "I don't have to explain anything to you, do I? You left me without a word—*not one damn word!* I don't owe you anything."

His mouth tightened, but he was wedged in the doorjamb and she couldn't get around him.

"This is stupid, Denver."

"Maybe."

"Let me by."

"As soon as you tell me why your father lives down at the ranch foreman's house and you live here."

The truth was on the tip of her tongue, but her pride kept her silent. She glared up at him, willing her heart to stop beating like the fluttering wings of a butterfly, praying that he couldn't see the pulse leaping in her throat or notice that her knuckles had clenched white around the handle of her battered old suitcase. "As I said, Denver, it was more convenient. Think what you want, because I don't really care."

She attempted to brush past him then, but as soon as she stepped one foot over the threshold, his arm snaked forward and captured her waist. So swiftly that she gasped, he dragged her against him. Feeling every hard muscle in his chest, watching the fire leap in his eyes, she knew she was trapped—pressed tightly against his hard frame.

Outside thunder cracked. Rain blew through the open window. The curtains billowed into the room. Yet Tessa couldn't do anything but stare into Denver's eyes. "What do you want me to say?" she rasped, barely able to speak. "Do you want me to say that your uncle and I were lovers?"

A muscle leaped to life in his jaw, and his lips flattened over his teeth.

"Or do you want me to say that he was just one in a long line—a line you started?"

His arm dropped suddenly, and she nearly fell into the hallway. Disgust contorted his features, but she couldn't tell if he was revolted at her or himself. "You can stay," he said hoarsely. "I'll take the room at the end of the hall."

"I don't want to stay."

He plowed his fingers through his hair and leaned back against the old wainscoting in the corridor. But his face remained drawn, his muscles rigid. "It doesn't matter what happened. It's none of my business."

"You're right, but it is your place." Wrestling up her bags again, she said, "I'll go down to Dad's house." She dashed down the stairs before she could change her mind.

"Tessa—"

"I'll move back when I own the place." Shoving open the back door, she felt the rain and wind lash at her face. She took two steps toward the garage before she remembered she had no car. Her father had the pickup, the station wagon was in the shop, and her brother, Mitchell, had borrowed the old flatbed.

"Wonderful," she muttered, soaked to the bone almost before she started walking. If she cut through the fields, the trek was only a quarter of a mile—if she took the road, the distance tripled.

She glanced longingly back at the farmhouse. The windows glowed in the night—warm, yellow squares in the darkness. Setting her jaw, she shoved open the gate and started across the wet fields.

Before she'd gone ten yards, she felt a hand clamp on her shoulder and spin her around. "You little idiot," Denver shouted.

"Let go of me!"

"Not until you're back in the house!" He snatched her bags with one hand.

"I'm warning you—oooh!"

Hauling her off her feet, he threw her, fireman style, over one shoulder, one hand wrapped around her ankles in an iron vise.

"Let me down right now! This is ridiculous!" *Damn the man.* But he didn't heed her muttered oaths or flailing fists as she pummeled his back.

"Denver, put me down! I mean it."

Tightening his grip on her suitcase and bag, he strode purposefully back to the house. Mortified, she had to hang on to the back of his shirt for fear of sliding to the sodden ground. Her hair fell over her eyes, rain drizzled from her chin to her forehead, and she silently swore that when she was back on her feet again, she'd kill him. He hauled her up the steps and into the house.

"There you go," he said, depositing her unceremoniously on the floor, once they were back in the kitchen.

"Of all the mean, despicable, low and dirty tricks—" she sputtered, planting her fists firmly on her hips.

"And what were you planning to do—ford the stream?"

"There hasn't been a drop of water in the creek for over a month."

"Why were you walking?"

She didn't bother with an answer. Still fuming, she raked her fingers through her wet hair and hoped to hold on to the few shreds of her dignity that were still intact.

He glanced to the floor, where the duffel bag and suitcase sat in a pool of water on the cracked linoleum. As if noticing the Army bag for the first time, he bent on one knee and fingered the tags still tied to the duffel's strap. "Private Mitchell Kramer?" He stared up at her, his brows drawn into a bushy line. "Your brother is back?"

She nodded. The less she said the better.

"I thought he left after the fire."

"He did."

"So when did he show up?"

"Six months ago. You've been gone a long time, Denver. Mitchell's hitch was over last year. He's going back to school in a few weeks."

Frowning, he studied the name tags then straightened. "So where is he?"

She shrugged. "Around. Probably in town tonight. It is Friday."

"Still raising hell?" Denver asked.

Bristling, she snapped, "That was a long time ago, Denver. Mitchell's changed."

"Has he?" Denver asked sarcastically.

Tessa couldn't begin to explain about the mixed emotions she felt for her brother. He'd stood by her after the fire, when Denver had left her aching and raw—lost and alone. It was true that Mitchell had joined the Army soon after the blaze, but he was back, and for the most part, he'd straightened out. The hellion he'd been after high school had all but disappeared. "Mitchell's been through six years in the Army. He's grown up. If you haven't noticed, a lot of things have changed around here!"

"That they have," he said quietly, his gaze lingering in hers. "That they have."

Tessa's heart started thudding so loudly that she was sure he could hear it.

"Look, why don't you go upstairs, put those"—he motioned to the bags—"away. You said something about a hot bath earlier."

Tessa was chilled to the bone. A soak in a tub of warm water sounded like heaven. But she wasn't convinced that staying in the same house with Denver McLean would be smart or safe. "And what about you?" she asked.

"As I said, I'll move into the room down the hall."

"I don't think that would be such a good idea."

"This is my house," he reminded her. "And it's only for a week. Two at the most."

Knowing she was making a mistake, Tessa relented. Wet, dirty and just plain tired of arguing with him, she decided one night wouldn't hurt. In the morning, after the shock of seeing him again had worn off, she'd decide if she should move out.

"Just for tonight," she said, hoisting her bags.

"I can take those," he offered.

"No thanks." She hauled her bags up the stairs, and unpacked her nightgown and robe. Feeling like a stranger in her own home, she hurried to the bathroom, locked the door and stripped off her wet clothes.

Steam rose from the tub as she glanced in the mirror and groaned. Her hair was lank and wet, her face smudged with mud, her skin flushed from the argument. "This is crazy," she told herself as she stepped into the hot water. "Absolutely crazy!"

Denver poured himself a stiff shot. His second. Nervous as a cat, he paced the study, listening as the ceiling creaked. He knew the minute she dashed down the hall to the bathroom, heard the soft metal click of the lock, felt the house shudder a little as she turned on the water and the old pipes creaked.

Closing his eyes, he imagined Tessa stepping into the bath and wondered if her body had aged, or if it was still as supple and firm as the last time he'd been with her. Groaning, her image as vivid as if their lovemaking had been only yesterday, he gritted his teeth. "Forget it, McLean," he warned himself, tossing back his drink.

Swearing loudly, he dropped into the chair behind the desk and started working on the invoices. But he couldn't concentrate. Aware of the water running, he listened until the old pipes clanged and the hum of the pump stopped suddenly. Gripping his pen so tightly that his knuckles showed white, he leaned back and listened as she unlocked the bathroom door and padded softly to her room—his parents' old room.

Why the devil was she living in the house? He wanted to believe that she'd moved in after John died, to manage the old house and keep it running. But he knew better. She had admitted as much.

Had she been John's mistress? He doubted it. Yet uncertainty gnawed at him. She hadn't denied having an affair with the old man, but Denver wouldn't let himself believe her capable of making love to a man more than twice her age. He couldn't. Though, all things considered, it was none of his damned business. He'd given up any claims on her when he'd accepted the cold truth that she'd betrayed him.

He reached for the neck of the Scotch bottle again, intent on pouring himself another, then twisted on the cap. After shoving the bottle back in the drawer where he'd found it, he stood at the window and stared out at the night.

Lightning slashed across the sky, illuminating the ridge near the silver mine, the ridge where he'd first discovered how exquisite making love to Tessa could be. There had been women before and since, of course, but none of those brief experiences had been as soul-jarring as that one suspended moment in time when he'd made love to Tessa Kramer.

Angry with the turn of his thoughts, he yanked down the shade to blot out the picture, but it snapped back up again and the ridge was there again, knifing upward against the sky. He'd been a fool to return to this damned place; he'd known it and still he'd come back.

Tessa was just upstairs, lying in his parents' wedding bed of all places.

How, he wondered, fire burning hot in his loins, would he get through the night?

Chapter Three

A s the first streaks of dawn filtered through her open
bedroom window, Tessa tossed back the covers on the
old brass bed. She'd barely slept a wink. Because of Denver.

"You're a fool," she muttered to herself as she tugged on
a pair of jeans and buttoned her work shirt. Plaiting her
red-blond hair away from her face, she caught sight of her reflection in the mirror and grimaced as she snapped a rubber
band around the end of her braid. "You don't love him anymore," she tried to convince the hazel-eyed woman in the
mirror. "And he never loved you—so just get through the next
week and pray that he'll leave."

An old pain spread through her and she set her brush on
the bureau. Denver had left before. Without a word. She
could remember that night as vividly as if it had been twelve
hours before.

"I want to see him!" Tessa demanded, planting herself
squarely in front of the information desk of the hospital. For
five days she'd been thwarted by the hospital staff, but no
more. Though her letter had been returned unopened, her gift

of flowers sent back, her visits refused, she wasn't about to be put off. Denver was somewhere in this hospital and she intended to see him.

"I'm sorry, Ms. Kramer, but Mr. McLean is to have no visitors," the nurse said, her mouth compressed firmly, her spine as rigid as the crease in her white uniform.

"I know his brother has seen him!"

"Colton McLean is family."

"But so am I," Tessa lied, persevering despite the woman's uncompromising stare. "I'm going to be his wife. I'm his fiancée!"

The nurse glanced down at Tessa's ringless left hand. "I'm sorry, Ms. Kramer. Doctor's orders."

Desperate, Tessa said, "Then let me talk to the doctor."

The nurse hedged, then picked up the phone at the desk. A few seconds later, Tessa heard the page. "Dr. Williams. Dr. Brandon Williams to the main lobby."

"Thank you," Tessa said, unable to sit on one of the cold plastic couches that lined the reception area. She paced instead, walking a worn path between a potted palm tree and a magazine rack. "Come on, come on," she whispered, glancing at her watch.

The seconds ticked by, and finally a thin man with sharp features, wire-rimmed glasses and thinning gray hair swept into the lobby. Wearing a white doctor's coat and carrying a clipboard, Dr. Brandon Williams was the epitome of authority.

"I'm Tessa Kramer," Tessa said, extending her hand.

He shook it weakly, then crossed his arms over the clipboard. "I understand you want to see Denver McLean."

"I'm his fiancée."

Dr. Williams's expression clouded. "I didn't know he was engaged," he said slowly, obviously doubting her.

"It's, uh, recent."

He shifted uncomfortably from one soft-leather sole to the

other. "Listen, Ms. Kramer, you have to understand that Denver has gone through not only physical but emotional trauma," he said patiently.

"I realize that."

"He's very confused right now. Until the surgery—"

"Surgery!" she repeated, gasping.

"Cosmetic surgery," he assured her quickly. "But until he's convalesced completely, he doesn't want to see anyone."

"Anyone?" she asked, willing the horrid words over her tongue, "or just me?"

"This is difficult for him—"

"If I could just see him, talk to him. I know I could help," she insisted, glancing down the hall. She knew Denver was somewhere on the first floor, but had no idea which room.

"His brother and uncle are complying with his wishes— as I am. In a few weeks, after Denver's had time to deal with everything, he'll probably want to see you."

A few weeks. Tessa couldn't wait that long. It was a week since the fire, five days since she'd first tried to see him here, and now the doctor was talking about *weeks?*

Was it possible, as her father and brother had suggested, that Denver didn't want to see her? She swallowed back every ounce of pride she had. "Could you please tell him— right now—that I'm here. That I have to see him."

The doctor sighed, his thin face drawn. "It won't do any good."

"Why not?"

"Because I've spoken with him about you before. He doesn't want to see you."

"I don't believe it!" she said, stricken, her worst fears confirmed. "I won't. Not until I hear it from him!"

"I'm afraid that's impossible."

"Nothing's impossible!" she hissed, and started to half run, the soles of her boots muffled against the brown carpet.

The fear that had been with her since the night of the fire gnawed at her, tearing a greater hole in her heart. Something wasn't right—something more than the terrible tragedy of the fire.

"Hey! You can't go down there!" she heard someone behind her yell, but she didn't stop.

"Miss—miss! Stop her! Oh, hell! Someone call security," another man said.

Tessa had been in the hospital only once before, but she tore down the halls, looking into private rooms, scanning the signs at each junction of the corridors. *Where was he? Where?*

She rounded a corner and collided with Colton McLean. She fell against the wall, the wind knocked from her lungs.

Colton's gray eyes were cold as slate. "What're you doing here?" he demanded, catching hold of her arm as she tried to scramble past.

"I have to talk to Denver."

"No way."

"Let go of me," she demanded, jerking on her arm as her eyes peered into the surrounding rooms. "He has to be here. Where is he, Colton?"

"You don't get it, do you?" Colton said, ignoring her question. "He doesn't want to see you."

"I don't believe you! If I could only see him—talk to him—" She wriggled free and started down the hall again, only to be met by two burly security guards.

"I think you'd better leave," the larger man said.

"Not until I see Denver McLean," she insisted. She was so close! She had to see him—tell him how much she loved him!

"If you don't leave of your own volition," the shorter guard added, his kind eyes understanding despite the rigid set of his shoulders, "we've been told to call the police."

"That wouldn't be a good idea," Colton added. "Your family's in enough hot water as it is."

"My family had nothing to do with the fire!" She glanced yearningly past the shorter guard's shoulder, down the hall to a wing labeled ICU. Intensive care! Of course! Desperate to see Denver again, she turned to Colton. "Please," she begged, "please tell him to call me!"

Colton's gray eyes flickered with sympathy before turning stone cold. "I'll tell him you were here," he said tautly as the heavier guard clamped a beefy hand over her upper arm and dragged her toward the doors.

The next day, she'd gone back to the hospital only to be told that Denver had been flown to a hospital in Los Angeles. All her cards and letters had been returned and even John McLean had kept Denver's whereabouts a secret. If it hadn't been for her brother, Mitchell, she wondered if she would have gotten through those first long, lonely weeks.

Now, as she thought of those seven lost years and the fact that Denver was back for the sole purpose of selling the ranch, her blood boiled. He had a hell of a lot of nerve, she decided, hurrying downstairs.

The house was quiet as a tomb, aside from the ticking of the grandfather clock in the hallway.

Tessa assumed that Denver, wherever he'd spent the night, was still sleeping. Relieved that she didn't have to face him, she poured water into the coffeepot.

Last night she'd reacted to him much too violently. His appearance had surprised her, but now that she knew where she stood, she'd be able to face him more calmly. Somehow, some way, she'd have to keep a cool head.

She'd just poured herself a cup of coffee and was prodding strips of bacon with a fork when she heard a creak on the stairs. Her heartbeat instantly went wild. She tried to concentrate on the meat sizzling in the frying pan, but she knew the moment he walked into the kitchen.

"Hungry?" she asked, without turning around.

"Starved."

Dear God, he sounded so close, and she was reacting to him as stupidly as she had the night before. With an effort she asked, "Will bacon, eggs and toast do?"

"Sounds great." She heard him pour coffee from the glass carafe on the counter then listened as a chair scraped against the floor.

Carefully, she forked sizzling bacon onto a platter, pushed down the button on the toaster, then cracked eggs into the frying pan. She felt his gaze boring into her back. When she turned to place plates on the table, she met his eyes briefly and her heart thundered.

Sleep still hovered in his eyes. Startlingly blue, they touched a vital part of her she had hoped was long dead. His hair was rumpled, falling over his forehead in a thick black thatch that matched the shadow covering his jaw.

"Rough night?" she asked, unable to resist baiting him.

"Rough enough. How about you?"

"I slept like a baby."

The corners of his mouth twisted a bit. "Don't tell me you woke up crying every two hours."

She couldn't help but smile. The fleeting glimpse of tenderness she'd seen in his eyes lifted her spirits. She slid into a cane-backed chair at the table.

He took a sip from his cup and motioned toward the food. "I didn't expect this sort of hospitality."

"I guess you got lucky."

His lips twitched. "No arsenic in the jelly?"

She smothered a grin. "Not yet. But you'd better be on your best behavior."

"Always am."

"Hah! Last night you came charging in here like a bloodthirsty pack of wolves! Arsenic would've been too good for you."

His gaze touched hers, remaining for a second before it shifted back to his plate. "You weren't exactly all cordiality yourself."

"I get that way when my character is assassinated."

Pretending that he didn't affect her, that she didn't notice the seductive glint in his eyes, that her heart wasn't slamming against her ribs, she buttered a slice of toast.

"I guess I deserved that."

"And more," she said, remembering his remarks about his uncle. A bite of toast stuck in her throat.

"I'll try to keep that in mind."

"Do."

He watched her closely, studying her movements before finishing his meal and shoving his plate aside. "I thought you had a cook."

"Milly usually gets here around nine-thirty. She makes lunch and supper for the hands, then leaves about seven. I may as well warn you now, you'd better not tangle with her. You might own this place, but she definitely considers the kitchen her turf."

"I'll remember that." He stared at her again with that same stripping gaze that stole the breath from her lungs. "There's something else I wanted to say."

Here it comes. "Oh?"

"Last night got a little bloody."

"You noticed," she said dryly.

"I said some things I didn't mean."

She lifted a skeptical eyebrow, but let him continue, hoping he didn't notice that her pulse was doing somersaults in the hollow of her throat.

"I was out of line."

"Way out of line."

He grimaced. "Right."

"Forget it," she said, trying to sound casual, as if nothing he said had wounded her so deeply that she hadn't slept a wink.

"Then we can start over?"

Her heart skipped a beat and her hands trembled. *Start over.* If he only guessed that for years she had prayed for just that—to start all over—from the beginning. Before the fire, before the lies, before he had turned away from her forever. She couldn't answer, but nodded quickly, hoping to find her voice as she cleared the table.

Denver set his cup on the counter and Tessa saw his hand. A few dark scars webbed across from his wrist to his fingers, the difference in skin tone barely discernible.

He, too, noticed the ugly reminder of the tragedy and shoved the disfigured palm into his pocket. "It never lets me forget," he said, his jaw growing taut.

Instantly she pitied him, and the hard look in his eyes told her he must have recognized her pity for what it was. "Maybe we can't start over—not completely over," she said uncomfortably, avoiding his gaze. "But at least we can back up a little and ignore what happened last night."

"I doubt it," he ground out, shoving his hand under her face. "This"—he shook his palm under her nose—"won't let us." His eyes blazed, and any trace of tenderness had left his features. "I don't want your pity, Tessa. I don't want anything from you!" He shoved his hand back into his pocket and strode out of the room, his footsteps ringing up the stairs.

Stunned, Tessa decided to put as much distance as she could between herself and Denver. She slammed the back door as she strode through the porch and down the steps, away from that man and his mercurial temper. One minute he'd been kind and caring, the man she'd once loved—the next he'd once again become a bitter stranger.

Outside, the air was clean and clear. There wasn't a trace of the storm, not one solitary cloud to wisp across the blue

Montana sky. The hills seemed to gleam, and the grass smelled fresh with the earthy scent of dewdrops clinging to the dry blades.

In the pastures, spindly-legged foals frolicked near their mothers, kicking up their heels and nickering noisily. In the larger fields, cattle grazed, moving lazily across the lower slopes of the surrounding hills. Tessa breathed deeply, slowly counting to ten, willing her emotions under control.

She paused near the barn and leaned against the fence. Brigadier whistled at the sight of her. His eyes ablaze with mischief, he tore from one end of his paddock to the other, his fiery red tail unfurling like a banner behind him.

"Show-off," Tessa whispered. She watched as the sleek chestnut trotted to the fence and shoved his head into her empty hand. "I'm sorry, boy, nothing today."

Disgusted, Brigadier snorted against her palm, tossed his head and raced to the far end of the paddock.

"You'd sell your soul for an apple," she called after him.

Boots crunched against the gravel.

Denver!

"And what would you sell yours for?" he asked.

"That," she said through clenched teeth, "is my secret."

He touched her shoulder and she moved quickly away. "I'm sorry."

"For what?" She faced him then, saw the remorse etched across his features.

His jaw slid to the side. "I can't stand pity."

"Then you won't get any from me."

"Good."

She stared into his eyes, then forced her gaze back to the paddock. To change the course of the conversation, she pointed to Brigadier. "He's my pride and joy. And he's not part of your ranch. I bought him and paid for his upkeep here out of my own pocket."

"I'll remember that," Denver said tightly.

"He's part of a herd of six. Brigadier and two of the mares, Ebony and Red Wing, are special."

"Where did you get them?"

"At auction. From one of the neighboring ranchers. You remember Ivan Aldridge?"

"Ivan the Terrible—that's what Colton used to call him."

"Right." Tessa frowned and ran the tip of one finger along the dusty fence rail. "Ivan's had a few rough years himself. Most every rancher in this valley has. Anyway, he had to sell Brigadier. Two years later, I found Red Wing. Ebony and the rest came later."

Denver's eyes narrowed on the small herd of pregnant mares. "Were they Aldridge's, too?"

Shaking her head, Tessa said, "All the horses came from different ranches."

Denver's gaze shifted back to her. "How could you afford to pay for them?"

"I don't see that it matters."

"Just curious."

"Sure." Denver McLean always had an angle. "Not that it's any of your business," she finally said, "but I'd saved some of the money and I borrowed the rest." Gathering her courage, she met his eyes and decided to go for broke and tell him the truth. "Of course no bank would loan me any money. I was still going to school and working here."

"Of course."

"Fortunately, John saw Brigadier's potential. He loaned me the money to buy the stallion."

"And how," he drawled, eyeing her suspiciously, "did you pay him back?"

"Stud fees."

Blue lightning flashed in his eyes and a muscle jumped in his jaw. But before he could ask any more questions, a green station wagon rattled up the drive.

Mitchell climbed from behind the wheel. Squaring his hat

on his head, he approached Tessa and Denver. "So you really did show up," he said, his eyes narrowing on Denver McLean for the first time in seven years. He wedged himself between Denver and Tessa.

Denver returned Mitchell's cold smile. "Thought I'd better check on my investment."

"Investment?" Mitchell snorted. "I wouldn't be counting on retiring from this place if I were you."

"I'm going to sell it."

If this information surprised Mitchell, he hid it. His thin mouth didn't move beneath the gold-colored stubble covering his jaw. His gaze didn't flicker. He shoved a wayward strand of straw-blond hair from his face. "I figured you would."

"Your sister wants to buy me out."

"Does she?" Mitchell's brows shot up. He cast Tessa a questioning glance.

"Where's your father?" Denver asked. "I'd like to talk to him."

"He'll be here. He had to pick up some feed in town."

Tessa threw her brother a worried look. That was a lie. They both knew it. Tessa was going into town later for supplies, not Dad. She was about to correct Mitchell, but the look in his eyes warned her to stop, before she said something that would embarrass him or Dad.

Mitchell said, "When he shows up, I'll tell him you're looking for him."

"Do that." Denver shot a hard glance at Mitchell then strode into the house.

Tessa whirled on her brother. "Why did you lie?" she demanded.

"Because it's none of his business what Dad's doing." Mitchell started for the barn.

"He owns the place," she reminded him.

"How could I forget?" Mitchell threw open the barn door

and walked swiftly to the medicine cabinet. He grabbed a bottle of pills. "I'll be working with the calves—"

"Dad works for Denver," Tessa cut in. "We all do."

"Don't I know it," Mitchell grumbled, jamming the bottle into the pocket of his jacket. For years he'd felt it his duty to protect Tessa, and obviously he still did. "Don't tell me you're on McLean's side!"

"Of course not."

"He's not interested in the ranch, you know."

"He doesn't claim to be."

"Look, Tessa," Mitchell said gently. "From what I hear, McLean's had plenty of women—so don't get any ideas—"

"I don't have any 'ideas,'" Tessa protested. "Denver doesn't interest me in the least!"

"Tell that to someone who'll buy it," Mitchell murmured.

"You think I'm lying?"

"Nope. I think you're deluding yourself. Just like you always do with Denver McLean."

Tessa wanted to throttle her brother. Instead, she decided to change the subject before things really heated up. "What was all that baloney about Dad being in town? Where is he?"

"At the house. Sleeping."

"Hung over?"

Mitchell shrugged. "I suppose. When I came in last night, I found him on the couch, passed out."

"Wonderful," Tessa said on a sigh. She slit the twine on a bale of hay and forked yellowed grass into the manger. "Denver won't be as understanding as John was."

Mitchell asked, "What's all this nonsense about you buying the place?"

"It's not nonsense."

"Just impossible," Mitchell decided.

"And why's that?"

"Financing, for one thing. Who's gonna back you now that old John's gone?"

"I've already talked to Rob Morrison at the bank."

Mitchell let out a hoot. "That guy? He's still wet behind the ears. How old is he, twenty-two? Twenty-three maybe?"

"At least he was willing to listen to me," Tessa grumbled.

"Big deal. He was probably hoping to put the make on you."

"No way—he was interested in what I had to say."

"Or sneaking a peek down your blouse when you were signing the papers."

"Knock it off!"

Yanking the pitchfork from her hands, Mitchell gave her a knowing look. "He's been after you for the past six months."

"That has nothing to do with it."

"Of course it doesn't," he mocked, shaking some hay into the manger as he winked at his sister. A crooked smile slashed across his jaw. "But it just might work, you know. His old man does own the bank."

"That's enough!" she said, ripping the pitchfork from his fingers. "I don't have to take this abuse from you." *Or Denver McLean,* she added silently. She was tired of inquisitions. "Don't you have something more important to do than snipe at me? Maybe you could muck out the barn."

"Touchy this morning, aren't we?" he teased. "I don't suppose that has anything to do with the fact that Denver's here."

"Out!" she muttered, aiming the pitchfork at his chest and jabbing playfully.

Mitchell took off his hat in a sweeping gesture and bowed.

She poked at him again.

"I'm leaving already," he said, hands raised, backing toward the door. But as he reached the doorway, he added, "Just be careful, Sis. Denver's back. Don't let him walk all over you."

"I won't," she swore, lowering the pitchfork a little as he turned on his heel, opened the door and disappeared.

* * *

Denver snapped the file closed and rubbed his eyes. It was late afternoon, and he'd been studying tax forms, income projections, profit and loss statements and invoices for nearly six hours. The sandwich Milly had left him on the corner of the desk was still there, the bread dry, the filling oozing a little.

His stomach rumbled and he took one bite before tossing the rest back on his plate.

Tessa hadn't shown up at the house. He'd seen some of the crew assemble for lunch, staying only long enough to catch their names and tell a disappointed Milly that he couldn't join them.

Driven to check the figures and get out of this place with its painful memories, he'd worked until he saw several of the hands drive away. Though he listened all afternoon, he hadn't once heard Tessa's voice nor seen her through the window.

Also, Curtis Kramer hadn't bothered showing up at all. Not only had the old man avoided the den, but as far as Denver could tell, Curtis hadn't set foot on the ranch. Curtis could be anywhere, Denver told himself; the ranch was huge, and much of the spread wasn't visible from the house or this one solitary window. But still he felt uneasy. Something wasn't right, and it gnawed at him. He twisted his pencil between his fingers and glowered at the stack of unpaid bills lying haphazardly on the desk.

Frowning, he stretched, hearing his back crack. For the hundredth time he looked through the window. Where was Tessa and what the hell was going on here?

Tessa climbed a back fence. She ran through the fields to her father's house. He hadn't bothered showing his face all day, and his absence was glaringly obvious.

She opened the gate and sprinted along a weed-choked path to the back door of a small, rustic cabin. Originally this house had been built as a temporary shelter for the first homesteading McLeans. Little more than three rooms, the cabin had quickly been replaced by the main house on the knoll for the McLean family. Afterward, the cabin had become quarters for the foreman and his family.

Tessa had grown up here. She'd shared a room with her brother, Mitchell, until the age of seven, when Curtis had converted the back porch into a private room for his son.

She glanced around the yard. The grass was yellow and dry, but the old tire swing still hung from a low branch on the gnarled maple tree near the front porch. The screen door sagged, and the hinges were so rusty they creaked as she pushed open the door. "Dad?" she called as she strode into the living room. "Dad—are you here?"

"Back here," he growled.

She followed the sound of her father's raspy voice to the kitchen alcove where Curtis was scrambling eggs over a wood stove. A cigarette burned unattended in an ashtray on the windowsill and an open bottle of beer rested near the back burners.

"Milly's expecting you for supper," Tessa said softly.

"Guess I won't make it."

"You have to."

He shook his head. His face had become lined with the years, and the veins across his nose had broken. His hair, snowy white, had thinned, but he was far from bald. "Why?"

"You know why. Denver's back."

"Humph." Curtis snorted in disgust and drained his bottle.

Tessa noticed that the alcove reeked with the smell of stale beer. Empty bottles were stacked neatly back in their cases near the old refrigerator.

"What difference does that make?"

"A lot. He owns the place."

"Bah." Curtis scraped his eggs onto a plate and held up the pan, offering some of his haphazard meal to his daughter.

She shook her head and watched as he lowered himself into the same chair he'd used for thirty years.

"Dad, listen, Denver wants to talk to you, he expects you to run the ranch—"

Curtis reached for his beer and took a long draft. "So what's he gonna do? Fire me?"

"Maybe," she said, panicked.

"Doesn't matter. He's plannin' on sellin' the place anyway, isn't he?"

"Yes, but—"

"But nothing. The new owner isn't going to want a man pushin' seventy to run the place, not even if his daughter is the best horsewoman in the state." He smiled a little then, his faded eyes shining with pride.

"I wouldn't fire you."

He glanced up sharply.

"I'm planning to buy the place."

"You?" He held his fork between his mouth and plate. "How're you going to manage that?"

"I've already talked to the bank, and if I have to I'll sell part of my stock—Brigadier, Red Wing and Ebony."

Her father snorted. "That's the craziest thing I've heard yet," he muttered. "The reason you want the ranch is to breed horses, so if you have to sell Brigadier and the mares what would be the point?" He shoved a forkful of eggs into his mouth and swallowed.

"I'll still have the other mares," she said. "Besides, when I buy the ranch, I'll own the McLean stock. Including Black Magic."

"Magic doesn't mean half to you what Brigadier does."

"I know. But he's a great horse."

"I don't know, Tessa," her father said, leaning back in his chair to study her. "You love those horses you plan on sellin'. Seems to me you aren't thinkin' straight. But then maybe you can't when Denver McLean's around."

"What's that supposed to mean?"

"Just what I said. You seem to lose all your common sense when that man looks your way." Disgusted, he took another bite.

"So do you," she pointed out. "Denver won't like it that you're not working. Mitchell and I can't cover for you all the time."

"Don't bother," Curtis grumbled as he scraped his plate into the trash. "Denver McLean's no fan of mine. He wasn't before the fire and he sure as hell hasn't changed his mind in the past seven years." He found his now-dead cigarette, frowned and lit another. "Take my advice and stay away from him."

"He'll only be around a week or two."

"Long enough." Blue smoke curled to the ceiling. "Maybe you should move back here while he's at the ranch. I don't trust him."

Tessa laughed. "You don't trust him, he doesn't trust you— this is insane." Shaking her head, she walked to the back door. "Don't worry about me."

"Just be careful," he warned, his pale lips thinning. "Denver's not the man he was."

"None of us are the same."

"You know what I mean."

"Yeah," she said, yanking open the Dutch door and stepping onto the front porch. "I know. Try and show up tomorrow, okay?"

"Don't know why," Curtis said, coughing.

He was right about one thing, Tessa mused. Denver had changed. Gone was any sign of the soft-spoken young man with that special wit and genuine smile. In his stead was a cynical man, hard-featured and grim, who didn't trust anyone.

The wind, warm and moist, pushed the straggling strands of hair from her eyes. She squinted against the lowering sun, staring at the tall ranch house silhouetted against a blaze of lavender and pink. The house had been owned by generation after generation of McLeans, and now she intended to buy it.

If she could.

Gazing across the golden meadows of stubble, she watched the ruddy-hided Herefords, heads bent as they plucked at the dry grass. Calves mimicked their mothers, trying in vain to eat the tiniest scrap of straw. Maybe Denver was right. Maybe she couldn't handle this much land alone.

But she didn't like being beaten, especially not by Denver McLean. Pride thrust her jaw forward mutinously.

Halfway across the field, she saw him. Her heart somersaulted. Back-dropped by the fields and dusky hills, Denver looked again like the man she'd fallen in love with. He was still lean and trim, and his hips moved with the fluid grace of an athlete as he walked with quick, sure steps. His chest was broad, shoulders wide and he held his head high. The wind tossed his black hair away from his face, and his features, growing more distinct, weren't as hardedged as they had seemed the night before.

"Where've you been?" he asked as he met her.

"I thought I'd check on Dad."

"He didn't show up today." It wasn't a question.

"No, he, er, wasn't feeling well." Nervously, she avoided his eyes.

"Mitch said he went into town."

She couldn't lie. He'd find out the truth soon enough. "No. Mitchell thought he had, but I took the truck in and picked up the feed."

"I could have come with you," he said softly, and stupidly her pulse leaped.

"You were busy."

"Not *that* busy."

They were closer to the house now, near a thicket of oaks

at the corner of one field. The last rays of sun filtered through the branches, dappling the ground and casting luminous splotches on the few standing puddles that hadn't dried from the storm.

She glanced at him from the corner of her eye. "So, have you solved all the ranch's financial problems yet?"

"Hardly," he admitted, scowling.

"You could start by selling the place to me," she pointed out, placing herself squarely in his path. Overhead, leaves shifted restlessly in the wind.

"Not without Colton's consent."

"So get it."

"I will. Just as soon as I figure out where he is."

"Don't you have any idea?" she asked skeptically.

"Your guess is as good as mine. He's been undercover so long he's probably forgotten who he is." Denver felt the muscles in his jaw tighten, just as they always did when he considered his younger, reckless brother and his passion for danger. Since graduating from college, Colton had been traveling as a free-lance photojournalist, assuming fake identities to gain the most spectacular, honest camera shots of men fighting wars throughout the world. "Last I heard he was in Afghanistan. But that was a few years back."

"John never heard from him," Tessa said on a sigh. She reached up and grabbed one of the lowest branches of a small oak, and Denver took in the way that her upstretched arms pulled the cotton of her blouse taut over her breasts, showing all too clearly the pattern of lace on her bra and the dark peaks of her nipples.

Denver noticed everything about her. The way her hair shimmered gold in the fading light, the dusting of perspiration across her brow, the pensive pout of her lips and the provocative swell of her breasts. Beneath her tan, he noticed the small freckles swept across her nose and the flush to her cheeks.

Swallowing hard, he glanced away from her, concentrating instead on the cattle moving restlessly over the arid hills. "Why do you want this place?" he asked, his voice uncomfortably tight. The fragrance of her perfume caught in the breeze and swirled around him in a delicious cloud. "And don't give me some baloney about how hard you and your family have worked here. There's got to be more."

"There is. A lot more." She let go of the branch. The limb snapped up, leaves rustling. "I've never wanted to live anywhere else."

"You haven't been anywhere else," he reminded her, hoping to chase away her girlish fantasies, fantasies that could trap him as easily as they had her.

"I've been to Seattle, Dallas and Phoenix." Glancing over her shoulder, she added, "John thought I should see a little more of the world."

Denver's mouth thinned. "Did he?"

"Um-hmm. He liked showing me cities I hadn't seen."

"I'll bet."

"And of course, I went to college—not away to a campus, but I drove into Three Falls three times a week."

"Three Falls isn't much in the grand scheme of things."

"And L.A. is?" she taunted.

"Yes."

She arched one beautiful brow, saying more clearly than words that she didn't believe him.

"If you had ever gone there, you would have seen that Southern California is more than cars, smog, beach and Disneyland."

"I didn't get a chance, did I?" she said.

He moved quickly. One hand wrapped around her wrist and he pulled, yanking her to him. Her breasts crushed against his chest, her eyes were level with the determined line of his mouth, and she could barely breathe. "I thought we were going to put all that behind us," he growled.

She watched a muscle tighten in his jaw, smelled soap mingled with musk and wondered at the beads of sweat on his lip. "You're right. I shouldn't have said anything." He was too close—the pressure of his arms around her too possessive. Forbidden flames licked through her blood as she shifted her gaze to those blue, blue eyes.

"Why do you insist on taunting me?"

"Me, taunt *you?*" Her mouth dropped open, and in that second he groaned.

"It's more than that," he rasped. "It's as if you're deliberately fighting me."

"I only offered to buy the ranch. Nothing more."

"And you haven't meant to torture me?"

"What in the world are you talking about?" she asked, but her blood was already on fire, pulsing through her veins.

"This!" He covered her lips with his. They molded perfectly against hers, moving gently, the pressure bittersweet and familiar. Her knees buckled and she couldn't think, didn't let herself. His tongue was hard and wet and warm, pressing insistently against her lips.

She moaned softly, her mouth opening of its own accord. His tongue slid enticingly between her teeth to plunder the soft recess of her mouth. Her traitorous body wanted more. Seven years she'd waited for just this moment!

She drank in the smell of him, drowned in the power of his arms, felt the warm river of desire flow from deep within. She savored everything about him, tasting the salt on his lips, feeling as if she'd sampled a long-forbidden wine.

"Tessa," he whispered, barely lifting his head, his eyes glazed. "Don't do this to me."

"I—I haven't done anything."

He groaned and kissed her again, his lips stealing down

the length of her throat, past her collar, to the V where her blouse met over her breasts.

He still cares, she thought for a wondrous moment, ignoring the part of her that thought he might be using her. Her fingers laced through the coarse strands of his hair and she let her head loll back.

Nuzzling lower, he pressed wet kisses to the hollow between her breasts, and she arched closer to him, her braid nearly dragging to the ground, her arms twined around his neck.

Her breasts strained upward, through two thin layers of cloth, and his mouth closed over one rounded mound.

Tessa's mind whispered a thousand warnings. She refused to hear any. Eyes closed, feeling the coming night shroud them, she was conscious only of the play of his lips across her breast.

She felt her blouse open, knew tiny buttons were sliding free of their bonds. Fresh air touched her skin, and then his tongue, quick and sure, stroked against the lace of her bra, torturing her so that she pressed her hips urgently upward.

"Sweet Jesus," he murmured just as his mouth closed over her breast, suckling gently, teasing with his teeth, leaving a wet brand against the patterned lace.

Tessa's fingers dug into his shoulders, past his shirt, deep into the corded muscles hidden by rough cotton. "Denver, please—" she cried, trying to tame the desire running like a swollen river out of control. A small needle of pride pierced the rapturous splendor fogging her mind. *Don't let him hurt you again! This time you may never get over him.*

"Please—what?"

She struggled with the words clogging her throat. "Please, stop," she begged, her voice hoarse and rough. "For God's sake, don't do this to me!"

His head snapped up, and the hand at her back dropped so quickly that she landed on her rear near a puddle. His face was white and lined, his eyes smoldering hot and blue. "Don't do this to *you?*" he choked out, wiping a shaking hand across his mouth as if her kiss revolted him. "Don't do this to you? Oh, Tessa, if you only knew!"

Without another word, he vaulted the fence, landed on his feet on the other side and, hands thrust deep in his pockets, strode toward the house.

"Bastard," she hissed, though the delicious salty taste of him lingered provocatively against her lips. A small part of her had hoped that he couldn't stop, that he had been as caught in that roiling river of passion as she had been. But she'd been wrong. She was just a distraction for him. Whatever he'd felt for her had died long ago, and she had no recourse but to face it.

She buttoned her blouse, and her fingers grazed the tender skin of her breasts, still moist where he had so recently suckled. Tears sprang to her eyes, but she pushed them back. Standing, she dusted off her rump, squared her shoulders and shoved aside any trace of sadness. *It won't happen again,* she told herself. She wouldn't let Denver McLean tromp all over her pride again!

Denver shoved the back door open so hard that it banged against the wall.

"What in the world?" Milly asked, nearly jumping out of her skin. She was pulling a chocolate cake from the oven. "Mr. McLean, is everything all right?"

"Just fine," he snapped, his black brows pulled together in a single line of frustration. "And call me Denver."

"All right," she said nervously. "Will you be eating with us in the dining room?"

"I don't think so."

"But you didn't take time off for lunch," she pointed out, her lips pursing.

"I had a big breakfast."

"Did you, now?"

He didn't bother to answer her. With long strides he headed straight for the den and closed the door behind him. The sooner he dug through the mounds of paperwork on this damned ranch, the sooner he could take off for Los Angeles and the sooner he would leave Tessa to rot here if she wanted to!

Furious with himself and his stupid impulse to kiss her, he shoved his hand through his rumpled hair and was disgusted to find that his fingers were trembling. So that's how he reacted to her!

"Bah!" Grimacing, he dropped into the chair and stared at that damned, traitorous hand. He noticed the scars running across his skin, remnants from the fire.

"Damn it all to hell," he swore, thinking of the bottle of Scotch in the desk. He reached for the handle of the second drawer and pulled hard. There it was—half full, amber liquid sloshing against the clear glass.

But he slammed the door shut again. Alcohol was no answer to what ailed him. He needed a woman. And not just any woman. His blood ran hot, desire burning feverishly for just one woman—Tessa.

No, Scotch would dull his mind, but it wouldn't stop the burning ache that scorched through his brain and settled uncomfortably in his loins.

He shifted, painfully aware of the bulge straining against his jeans. His only relief would come from lying with Tessa again and making love to her. But he wouldn't succumb. Making love to Tessa was the one pleasure he would deny himself, no matter what the cost!

Chapter Four

The next four days were torture. Tessa avoided Denver like the proverbial plague, and fortunately he left her alone. The kiss they'd shared beneath the oaks had charged the air between them—changed the complexion of their relationship, igniting old emotions that should have long ago smoldered into ash.

"You're a coward," she told herself, glancing into the rearview mirror as the old Ford bounced down the lane. She and Denver had studiously avoided crossing paths, even missing each other at dinner. Most of the time he was holed up in the study, and Tessa kept herself busy outside. At night, she found excuses to go into town, only to return late and wonder where Denver was.

Not that she cared, she told herself as she parked the truck near the barn and switched off the ignition. She glanced at the house and sighed. Sooner or later, she'd have to face Denver again. If only he'd just pack up and leave, she thought angrily as she climbed out of the cab and glanced at the hazy sky. Tattered clouds floated high above the valley, and insects thrummed in the lazy afternoon. Overhead, swallows cried and vied for positions under the eaves of the barn.

Tonight, Tessa decided as she yanked open the barn door, she would talk to Denver and make a formal offer on the ranch.

She snapped on the lights then marched to the oat bin. Running her fingers through the grain, she didn't hear the door open again.

"Looks like the rats are havin' themselves a feast," her father said. He surveyed the bin with a practiced eye. "Maybe we should get another cat. Marsha doesn't seem to be doin' her job."

"Marsha's busy with four kittens," Tessa replied. The old calico had delivered her litter three weeks before. Hidden beneath the floorboards of the barn, the little kittens mewed softly. Even now, Tessa could hear their worried cries.

"Still—a good mouser is a good mouser."

"Tell Marsha that the next time you see her."

"Don't think I won't." He sat heavily down on an overturned barrel. "Denver cornered me today."

"Did he?" Tessa didn't look up. As if she had no interest in Denver whatsoever, she fixed her gaze on the dusty seeds running through her fingers. "What did he want?"

"The same old thing. I swear that man's a broken record." He shook out a cigarette and thumped it on the barrelhead. "He seems to think there's some reason this place has lost money—something more than what we've told him or what he can see in plain black and white."

"Meaning?" Tessa asked. Her hand stopped moving restlessly through the grain.

"He suspects me of mismanagement." Curtis's lips twisted cynically in the gloomy interior.

"He'll find out differently," she said.

"I doubt it. It really doesn't matter how hard we talk or what the figures say on paper, the man has it in his mind. It's that simple."

"So he's already convicted us." A heavy weight settled upon her shoulders.

"That's about the size of it. I guess we should be glad that he's only talking mismanagement rather than embezzling."

"Embezzling!"

"He claims some of the figures don't add up.".

"Hogwash," she snapped, furious again. Ever since Denver had returned, her emotions had been riding a rollercoaster that was climbing steep hills and plunging down deep valleys, running completely out of control. "He's wrong."

"He's also the boss."

Damn Denver! Embezzling? That was the craziest notion he'd come up with yet!

"Calm down. Like I said, he hasn't really accused anyone yet—"

"He wouldn't!" Tessa cried. "He—he couldn't! No one's taken a dime."

Curtis's old eyes warmed fondly at his spirited daughter. "Just remember, Tessa, that man's got a chip on his shoulder—a chip that's grown to the size of a California redwood in the past seven years." He straightened slowly, his old muscles tight from sitting too long in one position. "Stay away from him," Curtis advised.

"I have."

"Smart girl."

I wish, she thought ruefully, not wanting to count how many sleepless hours she'd spent thinking about that one, earth-shattering kiss she'd shared with Denver.

Curtis clicked his lighter over the tip of his cigarette as he left the barn. Tessa heard him shuffle down the ramp leading to the main field. A few minutes later an engine caught, and through the open door she saw his old yellow truck rumble down the drive.

She had no excuse to leave the ranch, no errand to run, no friend's home where she could escape. Tonight she was stuck at the house. With Denver. And later, once she'd thought through exactly what she was going to say, he was going to get a piece of her mind!

Determined not to make the same mistake as she had under the oak trees, she walked into the tack room and took down a bridle. The leather was soft in her hands and the bit jangled as she hurried to the paddock where Brigadier, his nostrils flared, glared at her from the far corner.

"Come on, boy," she whispered, digging in the pocket of her jeans for the small apple hidden there.

The chestnut snorted, his eyes rolling suspiciously as she approached. He pawed the dusty ground, but couldn't resist the tantalizing morsel she held in her palm. As he reached for the tidbit, Tessa slipped the bridle over his ears.

"Serves you right for being such a pig," she teased as he tossed his head and stomped, one hoof barely missing the toe of her boot. "Careful," she said, laughing as she climbed onto his broad back and swung her leg over his rump just as he sidestepped. "Come on." Leaning forward, she pressed her heels into his ribs.

He stopped at the gate and waited nervously as she leaned over and pushed it open. Then, just as she caught her balance again, Brigadier bolted.

He took the bit in his teeth and raced across the dry earth, his hooves pounding, dust clouding in his wake. Wind screamed past Tessa's face, tangling her hair and tearing the breath from her lungs. Her fingers clutched the reins and wrapped in his silky mane as they tore across the fields.

She rode as she had as a girl, bareback and carefree. She didn't think about the ranch, about the unpaid taxes, the low supply of feed or the painful fact that she might have to sell this magnificent creature running so wild and free beneath her. Tessa hadn't felt this rush of joy in years. Seven years.

Denver had forced her to grow up before she was ready.

"And you were more than willing to," she muttered angrily as Brigadier slowed near the creek—or what had been the creek. Now just a winding ditch with a bare trickle of water threading through smooth, dusty stones, the stream cut through the fields on its path to the Sage River.

Near an old apple tree, she slid off Brigadier's back, tethered him and stretched out on the dry ground. The sun was just setting over the hills in the west. Fiery streaks of magenta and amber blazed across the wide Montana sky.

Leaning her head against the tree's rough bark, Tessa studied the shadows lengthening across the valley floor. Insects buzzed near the water, and somewhere in the distance a night bird cried plaintively.

The bird's call echoed the loneliness in her heart— loneliness she'd denied until she'd seen Denver standing in the barn door, the sheeting rain his backdrop.

Her heart squeezed at the memory.

Clouds gathered over the hills, clinging in wisps to the highest peaks. She heard hoof beats and dragged her gaze away from the dusky sky.

Denver was riding toward her. Astride a rangy gray gelding, his hair tossed back from the wind, he reminded her of the last time she'd seen him upon a horse, the afternoon of the fire. Tessa's insides tightened and her heart did a stupid little flip. Though she'd wanted to avoid him, she couldn't stop the rush of adrenaline that flowed eagerly through her veins.

The gray slid to a stop at the edge of the creek. Denver swung his leg over the gelding's back and landed on the ground not ten feet in front of Tessa.

"What're you doing here?" she demanded, trying to ignore the sensual way his jeans stretched over his buttocks as he slid from the gray.

"Looking for you."

Her stomach knotted and her pulse jumped crazily. "Why? So you can accuse me of mismanagement and embezzlement?"

He grinned, that cynical slash of white she found so disarming. "You've talked to your father."

"Why don't you just leave him alone, Denver?"

"I will—soon." He stretched out beneath a tree opposite her, his legs so long, they nearly brushed her boots. "You've been avoiding me."

She shrugged. "I thought it was better this way."

He considered that. "Maybe," he allowed, his gaze drifting to the shadowy hills as he took a handful of dust and let it drift to the ground. "But I can't very well accomplish everything I need to without your help."

He needed her? Her heart constricted, but she ignored her leaping pulse. Wanting her help on the business end of running the ranch didn't mean he needed her. "What do you want?"

"Just some cooperation. Your father isn't too helpful."

"Do you blame him?" she asked.

"Maybe I did come on a little strong."

"The way I hear it, you practically accused him of embezzling."

"It didn't go that far."

"Didn't it?" she snapped. "Since the minute you set foot on this place, you've been insinuating that Dad's the sole cause for the cash flow problems here."

"I'm not blaming your father, Tessa."

"Sure. Just like you don't blame him for the fire!"

His lips tightened. "I thought we'd settled that."

"Far from it, Denver. Even though we're supposed to forget about the fire, none of us can because you never bothered to come back until you had to. We can try to ignore the fire, but it happened, Denver."

"Don't you think I know that?"

"Of course you do, but you don't have to wear your scars like war wounds, for crying out loud!"

He moved quickly. With the speed of a lightning flash, he rolled forward and caught her shoulders in his hands. She tried to scoot backward, but the apple tree wouldn't budge.

Rough bark dug through the thin fabric of her blouse and into her skin.

"If you want to know the truth, Tessa," he growled, "I wish I could erase that ungodly night from my mind forever."

"Do you?" Lifting her chin, she met the fire in his eyes with her own blazing gaze. "I don't believe you. I think you've been waiting to come back, savoring the day when you could point your finger at all of us. All the stories that you heard, all the lies, have built up in your mind. And now you, in all your self-righteous fury, have the power to destroy everyone!"

His eyes glittered fiercely. "Is that what you think?"

When she didn't answer, his fingers curled over her shoulders, pressing deep into her muscles. "Maybe you're wrong."

"No, Denver. I heard the rumors, the gossip. It ran like wildfire through town. Dad was to blame—your parents were dead and you were nearly killed because of his carelessness." She blinked hard, battling wretched tears of shame. "The fact that you wouldn't talk to me, to any of us, only made it worse. And you—you believed Colton's lies! You wouldn't even talk to me—hear what really happened!"

"My parents were dead!" he retorted.

"It was an accident!"

As their furious gazes locked Tessa felt his anger. Raw and wild, it surged through his muscles until the grip of his scarred fingers hurt her shoulder. "You tried and convicted my family without a trial," she insisted, still not backing down. "That's why Mitchell left for the Army—to get away. Dad tried to get me to leave too, to go away to college."

His eyes searched her face, his fingers relaxed a little. "Why didn't you?"

"Because someone had to stay! I love this place, Denver, and Dad couldn't face all the gossip, the speculation, the interrogation from the insurance company and the sheriff's department by himself."

"Noble of you," he mocked.

She felt as if she'd been kicked. Struggling against the lump in her throat, she whispered, "John believed in us."

"Good old Uncle John."

"That's right!" she shot back, tears drizzling from her eyes. "He was good!"

Denver saw her anguish. Guilt pricked his conscience, but his doubts, fueled by her tears over his uncle, tore at him. "How good?" he asked, eyes narrowing.

Gasping, she reacted—slapping him across his stubble-dark cheek. The sound of skin meeting flesh clapped loudly, startling birds overhead.

He sucked in his breath, then moved with lightning speed. Shoving her shoulders to the ground, he pinned her against the dry grass. His blue eyes flamed jealously as he straddled her. "How good?" he repeated. "Tell me about your relationship with John."

"Get off me, Denver," she said through clenched teeth, ignoring the warmth charging through her veins—the dizziness in her head. She couldn't feel like this, with him, not now. He'd insulted her so horridly, and yet a coiling desire deep within warned her that all too soon she'd lose her will and body to him again. All he had to do was kiss her—show her some trace of tenderness.

"I asked a question."

Was it her imagination, or was he rubbing suggestively against her, his taut jeans shifting slowly over her abdomen? He was on his knees, his weight evenly distributed so that he didn't rest on her, and yet she couldn't move. He placed the flat of one hand between her breasts, on the V of flesh exposed by the open collar of her blouse. His fingers spread lazily over her skin, grazing her bra. She began to ache inside and wanted to move with him. But she couldn't let him win, not this way.

Closing her eyes, she wounded him the only way she could. "John was the best."

Denver froze. He tried to tell himself that she was baiting him, but his fists balled and he saw red. Looking down at her, he shuddered. He wanted her as violently as ever, more with each passing day. He'd followed her to the creek with the express purpose of laying his cards on the table, telling her that he couldn't get her out of his mind, admitting that each and every moment without her had been torture. Just the night before he had opened the door to her room, had seen the moonlight playing on her rumpled hair, turning the blond streaks to silver, had watched in fascination as she'd groaned and turned over, her face innocent and unwary.

He'd used every bit of his energy to walk quickly back down the hall and stand for twenty minutes under the sharp needles of a cold shower.

Now, his legs holding her prisoner, her body warm against his thighs, his cheek still smarting, he shuddered, fighting the urge to undress her, make love to her—and suffer the consequences if she scorned him. Slowly he withdrew his hand.

Tessa willed her eyes open. Staring up at him, she caught a glimmer of pain in his eyes—or was it only her imagination? His face was in shadow and she tried to convince herself that he appeared sinister. But she knew better. Deep in her heart, she believed there was still some tenderness in Denver McLean. Buried beneath a charred layer of cynicism, this was the same man she'd loved with every breath in her body.

"Is this why you came out here, Denver?" she asked, her voice hoarse. "To prove that you're stronger than I am, to show me that you could have your way with me if you wanted to? To humiliate me?"

"What do you think?" he asked, but all the sarcasm had left his voice, and his jaw slackened.

"I hope to God that you didn't follow me to degrade me. I hope there's some shred of decency left in you."

He laughed hollowly. "Not much." But he swung his leg off of her and stretched out beside her on the grass.

She didn't move away. She didn't want to give him the satisfaction of thinking she was afraid of him. "That was a childish thing to do."

"And this wasn't?" he asked, rubbing the red mark on the side of his chin.

She sighed. "You deserved it."

"So did you."

"It wasn't the same thing. I just reacted."

"So did I."

"You tried to frighten me," she said. "But it didn't work. I'm not afraid of you, Denver, and you can growl and bluster and try to humiliate me all you want. I still won't be afraid of you!"

With a groan, he rolled onto his back and stared at the sky. The first winking stars blinked high in the heavens. "I don't want you to be afraid of me, Tessa," he conceded.

"You have a strange way of showing it."

Closing his eyes, he whispered, "I wasn't even going to come back, you know. John's attorney talked me into it." He shifted his gaze back to her face. "Then I thought I'd show up here, stay a couple of days and take off for L.A. again."

Tessa's heart began to pound so loudly it drowned the tiny gurgle of water in the stream. "And now?"

"God only knows," he muttered, staring at her as if he were memorizing her every feature. "Why aren't you afraid of me?"

"Because I know you, Denver."

"I've changed."

"Not as much as you'd like me to believe."

He eyed her skeptically, one dark brow arched.

"Okay, you've changed a lot," she admitted, "but basically you're the same man you were that afternoon on the ridge."

He sighed. "If you only knew," he muttered, picking at a dry blade of grass and watching it float on the breeze. "Nothing's the same, Tessa. Nothing will ever be." He sat up then, dusting his knees. "We both better face it."

But she wasn't through. She had to settle things with him. Reaching forward, she caught the front of his shirt, crushing the fabric in her fingers. "I'll never be afraid of you. You could have stripped off all my clothes and forced yourself on me, and I wouldn't have been scared."

His head snapped around quickly, his eyes filled with self-loathing. "Don't you know what just happened, Tess? Couldn't you feel it?" Trembling, he held up his hand, his finger and thumb close together. "I was this far from raping you."

"No!" She shook her head violently. "You would *never* force me."

His jaw set in revulsion, he muttered, "I guess we'll never know, will we?" Rolling to his feet, he reached for the reins dangling from his horse's bridle, then climbed into the saddle.

Digging his heels mercilessly into the gelding's sides, he leaned forward. The gray leaped away, leaving a plume of dust that sparkled in the moonlight as horse and rider disappeared.

Tessa wrapped her arms around her knees and refused to cry. What had happened to her? Why couldn't she tell Denver the truth about her relationship with John, that she'd only been his nurse after his heart condition had been diagnosed?

"Because he wouldn't believe you anyway," she whispered, kicking disgustedly at a clod of dirt with the toe of her boot. Denver didn't trust her. He wanted to believe the worst of her, and her pride had held her tongue.

She could argue her virtue until she was blue in the face and Denver wouldn't listen. "Think what you want," she muttered, as if he could still hear her. She grabbed the reins and swung onto Brigadier's broad back. "Go right ahead!"

By the time she'd ridden back to the ranch and cooled Brigadier, Denver was gone. His rental car wasn't parked near the garage and the house was empty. She should have been relieved, but she wasn't. There were still a few things she'd like to set straight with him, one of which was that she intended to buy the ranch. She'd already started the wheels in motion. She had an appointment with the loan officer at the bank the following morning, and she planned to stop by the Edwards ranch. Nate Edwards, the owner, had always been interested in Brigadier, and he'd once told her to contact him first if she ever wanted to sell the stallion. Tomorrow, she thought sadly as she climbed the stairs to the second floor, she'd take Nate up on his offer.

Once in her bedroom, she stripped out of her clothes and tossed her blouse and jeans into a hamper near the bureau. She caught sight of her reflection in the mirror, her lean, strong limbs, slender hips and waist, small, high breasts. Her hair was a wild cloud of untamed strawberry-blond curls that fell past her shoulders.

How did she compare to the women Denver usually saw, the sophisticated women in Los Angeles? she wondered.

"Who cares?" she muttered, angry at herself. She found her robe and dashed toward the bathroom. Intending to sit in a hot bath until the water turned tepid, she turned on the spigots and started brushing the tangles from her hair. With swift strokes, she tugged the brush through the twisted strands and tried not to think about Denver and how much she'd wanted him to kiss her—to make love to her. The urge had been undeniable, and even though he'd intended to degrade her, she'd wanted him.

"You don't love him," she told her hazel-eyed reflection. "You can't!"

Still arguing with herself, she lowered herself into the tub, sucking in her breath as her rear touched the hot water. Closing her eyes, she sank even deeper, still trying to convince herself that her feelings for Denver had died with the years.

Three Falls, Montana, wasn't much of a town in comparison with the cities and towns fanning out from Los Angeles. Denver drove down the main street, past a small college campus and into the business district. Most of the buildings were one or two stories, with neon lights blazing against the darkness.

The town had grown, he decided, noting a bank, motel, strip mall and two fast food restaurants that hadn't been around when he'd lived at the ranch.

He pulled into the rutted parking lot of a tavern on the south end of town. The weathered plank building looked the same as it had years before. Once a livery stable, it was now the local watering hole and boasted a live band on the weekends.

The interior was dark. A smoky haze lingered over the crowd despite the noisy attempts of an old air conditioner to recirculate and freshen the air.

"What'll it be?" the bartender asked. A burly man with a ruddy complexion, flat nose and world-weary expression, he stared straight at Denver, then grinned. "McLean?" he asked, his sandy brows lifting. "Well, I'll be damned!"

Denver recognized him as soon as he spoke. He'd gone to school with Ben Haley. "How're you?"

"Can't complain. And yourself?" Ben's gaze narrowed, as if he were looking for the scars from the fire.

"I'm all right."

"What'll it be?"

"A draft."

Ben poured quickly and slid the mug over to Denver. "On the house. I own the place these days." He swiped at the scratched bar with a white towel. "I heard you were back at the ranch."

"Just for a week or two."

"Rumor has it that you intend to sell."

"Soon as I can," Denver admitted, sipping from his glass. "Know anyone who's interested?"

"Just Tessa Kramer," Ben replied as he caught a shapely redhead's eye at the end of the bar. She signaled and he poured her another drink. When he'd finished refilling her glass, Ben returned.

Denver twisted his glass in his hands. "Did Tessa tell you she wanted to buy me out?"

"No," Ben said, pouring another drink. "Tessa's brother, Mitch, he comes in here quite a bit. He mentioned something about it."

"What did he say?"

"Nothing much," Ben hedged. "Just that John was gonna make some provision for Tessa in his will—make sure she could buy the place." He frowned and looked away, almost guiltily. "She was awfully good to him."

"Was she?"

Ben shrugged his big shoulders. "Maybe he changed his mind."

"Maybe," Denver agreed as Ben was called into the kitchen. Denver studied the foam dispersing from his drink. He felt the familiar coil of jealousy tighten in his gut and told himself it didn't matter. What Tessa and John had meant to each other was none of his business. Still the idea of his uncle and Tessa together stuck in Denver's craw. And no amount of beer could wash it away.

Chapter Five

S he heard Denver return. Lying on her bed, ears straining, Tessa heard the scrape of his boots on the stairs and listened as he stumbled at the top step, swearing loudly.

He started down the hall, but paused at her door.

Tessa sucked in her breath, her every nerve end tingling. *What now?* The knob turned, the door opened. Denver stood on the threshold. Light from the hall threw the lean lines of his body into stark relief. His broad shoulders nearly touched each side of the frame. His hair fell over his eyes and the smell of liquor wafted into the room. "Tessa?"

"I'm awake." Her nerves were stretched tight as bowstrings. Sitting up, she clutched the sheet to her breasts and shoved a handful of thick hair from her eyes. "What do you want?"

"I wish I knew, Tessa. I wish to God Almighty I knew." Rubbing one tanned hand tiredly over his shoulders, he expelled a long breath. "I made a mistake today at the creek."

"Is this an apology?"

"Of sorts." He frowned and leaned one shoulder against the molding. "This afternoon—I just wanted to talk to you. You'd been avoiding me, and I really didn't blame you, but I figured it was time we got a few things straight. I saw you ride to the creek, so I followed."

"To talk."

"Right. But I blew it."

As her eyes adjusted to the darkness, she could see that one side of his mouth had curved in self-mockery.

"What 'things' did you want to get straight?" she asked, wishing she had the nerve to throw him out.

His eyes bored into hers. "Us."

"There was no 'us.' Remember?" She couldn't help wanting to hurt him—just as he'd wounded her.

"I guess that's what I said."

"And you were right."

"Of course I was." Still, he didn't leave.

Her teeth bit into her bottom lip. Here he was in her bedroom, for crying out loud, in the middle of the night, trying to apologize. Her mind was spinning and she was caught in the trap between trusting him and knowing that he was lying. "Then why are you here? Have you changed your mind?" she whispered, dreading the answer. "I mean, about 'us.'"

"I don't know." His jaw tensed. "I've never been so damned indecisive in my life. I hate it."

"And that's what you wanted to tell me?" Convinced that he was holding something back, she arched an eyebrow skeptically.

"There was another reason," he admitted, his eyes narrowing on the bed.

Tessa's throat constricted. "And that is?"

"Because I want you, damn it!" he admitted angrily. His fingers curled into a tight, impotent fist. "God knows I've tried to fight it, but the truth of the matter is, I've wanted you from the first time I saw you in the barn."

"Because I'm here. Because I'm convenient," she bit out, angry with herself and with him.

"Because you're *you*," he said heavily.

If she'd expected anything, it wasn't this kind of confession, and though a part of her longed desperately to hear just those words, the more rational side of her mind told her it was the liquor talking—not the man.

Dropping the sheet, she slid to the side of the bed. His eyes followed her every move as she grabbed her robe and shoved her arms down the sleeves.

"Don't," he said, when she tried to tie the belt at her waist. "Leave it open."

Jaw taut, she cinched the belt as hard as she could and swept across the room. "What do you really want from me, Denver?" she demanded, wishing he were stone-cold sober. "An affair? A quick roll in the hay? A little more 'experimenting'—isn't that what you called it—like we did when we were younger?"

He winced. "Of course not." His gaze drilled into hers. "I just want you."

Tessa's heart beat a quick double time, but she didn't trust him—couldn't. Not after her humiliation at the creek. Not after seven years of being treated as if she didn't exist. "The way you wanted me earlier?" she asked, feeling a hot flush of indignation steal up her neck.

"I said I was sorry—"

"I heard you." She inched her chin upward. "But I don't trust you, Denver. You've come back here practically accusing every member of my family of trying to rob or steal from you. You think we're all a pack of arsonists, embezzlers and liars. And you think I was your uncle's mistress." She could feel the flames leaping to her eyes, the anger burning brightly in her soul. Just because he wanted her was no reason to believe that he had ever loved her. So furious that her breasts were heaving, she placed her palms firmly on his chest and pushed. "I think you'd better leave."

His hands flew from his sides, capturing each of her wrists.

They tightened possessively and his nostrils flared. "If you're through destroying my character—"

"Not quite," she retorted. "And now you have the audacity—the unmitigated *gall*—to think you can waltz into my bedroom, claim that you want me and think I'll fall into bed with you just because you're *sorry!*"

"Oh, no, Tessa. I've never thought you could be pressured into doing anything you didn't want to do." A furious muscle worked in his jaw, but his thumbs rubbed in slow circles along the insides of her wrists, and his smoldering gaze never left hers.

"Then what?" she demanded, trying to ignore the erotic feel of his gentle fingers.

"You've always given me a fight—a run for my money. But always before you've been honest with yourself."

"I am," she insisted, though her voice faltered a bit. If he'd only quit touching her, then maybe she could think!

"I don't think so."

"And what about you? Have you been honest with yourself?" she threw back, but his arms surrounded her and he kissed her fiercely. His lips were hard and sensual, and she could taste the liquor lingering on them. Her heart pounded erratically, beating like the wings of a frightened bird, thudding wildly against her ribs. All the taunts forming on her tongue disappeared into the shadowy corners of the room.

Though she tried to push away, he held her close, hands splayed across her back, forcing her to curve against him, hips and thighs pressed tight, the thrust of his desire hard against her abdomen.

"Get out," she commanded, but even as the words passed her lips, she'd circled his neck with her arms, her mouth returning all too eagerly to him. Heat, liquid and dangerous, began to curl within her, and she had trouble breathing, couldn't think. "Don't—"

"Don't what?" he whispered across her ear, and she shivered with the ache that was building out of control.

"D-don't touch me—oohh." She felt his hand move forward along her belt, untying the knot. The terry fabric parted and his hands delved inside, long fingers searching.

"You want me to stop?"

"Y-yes. Oh, Denver, *please!*" She shuddered when he touched the firm point of one hard nipple and could barely hold back a cry when he bent his head and took that hard little button, hidden in the folds of soft cotton, in his warm mouth.

Her fingers tangled in his hair, she held him close, and her legs seemed to turn to water. She felt each tiny button of her nightgown as it slipped through its hole, knew when the yoke had parted and the cool night air touched her breast. Still he toyed with her through the cloth, the fabric wet and hot as his tongue searched for and laved her nipple.

"Please?" he repeated, his voice hoarse.

Moaning softly, she tried to fight the tide of desire that kept pulling her under its warm, liquid depths. Her head was swimming, her breath trapped deep in her lungs, but one tiny scrap of her pride surfaced. "Please, *don't*—don't—try to humiliate me again. Don't use me."

He stopped then, his muscles instantly rigid. "Never," he whispered, straightening, his hands moving swiftly to her chin, forcing her to look deep into his eyes. "I *am* sorry, Tessa," he vowed, his voice filled with regret. "I've never meant to hurt you."

And yet he had. She'd died a thousand deaths all those years ago, just thinking that he'd used her—that she'd meant nothing to him. And again, when he'd seen her in the barn and denied loving her at all. Her throat was hot, her eyes luminous with unshed tears.

He brushed one solitary drop from her lashes and cursed under his breath. "What the hell am I going to do with you?"

His thumb caressed the curve of her cheekbone and she felt him tremble.

"I—I can handle myself," she murmured.

"I know you can, Tess." With a sigh, he swept her off her feet and carried her back to the bed. She buried her face in his neck, drinking in the clean scent of him, the powerful feel of his muscles. She kissed the warm crook of his neck.

"Stop it!" he rasped. "I'm trying to be noble here."

"Noble?"

Before she could say another word, he tucked her robe around her and drew the covers to her neck.

"You're leaving?"

"If and when we make love again—"

"Don't flatter yourself," she snapped, lashing back. He was rejecting her again!

His night-darkened eyes searched her face. "Next time, there will be no regrets."

She shoved the covers aside and sat up in the bed. "There won't be a next time!"

The cords in his neck protruded. "Stop pushing, Tessa. You're lucky I still have some self-control."

"Sure," she taunted, thrusting her chin forward defiantly. "Now just leave!"

His jaw worked and his eyes clashed with hers. Then, as if afraid he might change his mind, he turned on his heel and strode quickly out of the room. A few minutes later she heard the shower running.

The next morning Tessa didn't waste a minute. She'd spent most of the night laying plans, and today she intended to put them into action. If the night had proved anything, it was that she was still just as susceptible to Denver's charms as she'd ever been. Ignoring the traitorous part of her heart that had argued long and hard with her, she reasoned the sooner she sent him packing to L.A., the better.

She showered, then dressed in a wheat-colored linen suit and magenta blouse. Curling her hair, she twisted it into a thick braid at the back of her head before stepping into tan heels and adding color to her lips, cheeks and eyes. With a satisfied glance at her reflection, she decided that she was ready to face Rob Morrison at Second Western Bank. He'd indicated that he would loan her the money to buy the ranch. Now she had to make sure he was as good as his word.

Downstairs, Milly was already bustling around in the kitchen. Apple pies were cooling on racks by the windows and she was poking at the corners of the floor with her broom.

"I won't be around for lunch today," Tessa said.

"You skip too many meals, if you ask me." Straightening, Milly set the broom in the corner, then eyed Tessa up and down. "My, don't you look nice."

"Nice?" Tessa repeated, rolling her eyes. "I don't want to look nice. How about professional or sophisticated or chic?"

"All of the above," Denver said as he opened the door from the back porch. Unshaved, hair mussed, he was squinting, as if the morning light were much too bright.

Smothering a smile, Tessa realized he was suffering from a hangover. Good, she thought wickedly. Serves him right!

Milly took pity on him. "How about a cup of coffee?"

"And about two dozen aspirin," he said, forcing a smile as he fell into one of the table chairs and studied Tessa. "Where are you going?"

"To the bank." Placing the cup on the table in front of him, she offered him an emphatic smile. "I have an appointment with Rob Morrison."

"Isn't he a teenager?"

"He was, Denver. Not only has he graduated from high

school, but college, and now he works for his dad as a loan officer."

"I remember when he was still stealing hubcaps and shooting the hell out of mailboxes," Denver grumbled.

"No more," Milly said. "Rob's become a real straight arrow. Belongs to the city council and all. Time didn't just stand still, you know."

"So I've been told," Denver admitted, his gaze catching Tessa's. Lord, she was beautiful. "Over and over again."

"Guess you're a slow learner," Milly observed as she shoved the broom in a cupboard on the back porch.

"I guess so." Denver couldn't take his eyes off Tessa. Seeing her dressed as a lady—no, as a businesswoman—did strange things to him. She was fascinating enough in her jeans and work shirts, her attractive ranch-tough veneer. But dressed elegantly, in an expensively tailored skirt and jacket, she made him face the fact that she was truly the most captivating woman he'd ever met. The fire in her stormy hazel eyes, the proud lift of her chin and the confident set of her shoulders were potent and evocative.

Seven years ago he'd been attracted to her, maybe even loved her, but her innocence and spunk had been childishly intriguing. Now, he was faced with a full-fledged woman, a mature woman who knew her own mind, a woman he'd tried to humiliate the day before, a woman he'd nearly made love to last night.

The phone rang and he realized he'd been staring.

"I'll get it," Milly called out as she reached around the corner and picked up the receiver. "McLean Ranch," she answered brightly, then glanced sharply at Denver. "Yeah, he's here. Just a minute." She held the receiver toward Denver. "Long distance," she whispered. "Jim somebody."

"Van Stern," Denver said, placing his cup on the table. "My partner. I'll take it in the den." With a quick glance at

Tessa, he strode out of the room. A few seconds later Milly replaced the receiver.

"I wonder what that was all about?" the housekeeper muttered.

"He does have a business in L.A., you know." Tessa finished her coffee. "Maybe Van Stern wants him to go back to Los Angeles. Denver only intended to stay a few days." That particular thought should have been uplifting, but Tessa's spirits didn't soar. Quite the opposite. After she'd avoided him for days, swearing to herself that she didn't care for him, not one little bit, that her attraction to him was just chemistry, the thought that he would suddenly be out of her life was difficult to accept. Frowning, she reached for her purse and said, "I'll be at Second Western Bank this morning, then I'll stop over at Nate Edwards's place. I should be back in time to feed the stock, but if I'm not, tell Mitchell he can handle it."

Milly snorted sarcastically. "He'll like that a lot."

"I know, but he can just bloody well do it." With a wave she walked out the back door.

Second Western Bank was a two-story concrete structure on the corner of Main and First Streets. With its narrow, black-framed windows, the square gray building looked more like a jail than a financial institution. Only a few trees and shrubs planted between the bank and parking lot softened the sharp angles.

A security guard was posted in the front entrance, and inside, the main lobby floor was brick, shined to a glossy finish. If only there had been bars on the windows, the penitentiary decor would have been complete.

Rob Morrison was waiting for her in his office on the second floor. Less austere than the rest of the bank, his corner suite was decorated with a few oil paintings of rugged coastlines and high mountains, cream-colored furniture and thick burgundy carpet.

Rob rose from his chair when she arrived. A thin man with rust-colored hair, freckles and narrow features, he extended his hand. "Tessa! What a pleasure," he said, smiling and waving her into one of the side chairs near his desk. "What can I do for you?"

"Guess."

"The McLean Ranch, right?" He twisted his pen in his fingers.

"Right. I'd like to take out a loan and buy the ranch."

Still twisting his pen, Rob leaned back in his chair. "All of it?"

She nodded. "Unfortunately, no one's been able to find Colton, and he owns half the place."

"You don't think he'll want to buy out Denver's share?"

"Do you?" she asked.

Rob laughed. "It's doubtful. The last I heard, Colton was in Afghanistan or somewhere."

"Even if he can't be found, I still want to buy out Denver's share."

"He wants to sell?"

"In a hurry," she said, smiling dryly. The one trait that hadn't changed in Denver was his need to escape. He intended to leave Montana as quickly as he could, and though she tried to tell herself that his departure was for the best, that she'd lived well enough without him—she couldn't forget his words, loosed by liquor. *If and when we make love again, next time there will be no regrets.*

"Have you settled on a price?" Rob asked.

"Not yet."

"That's the first step. As soon as you and Denver and Colton work out an agreement, I'll go to work. I'll give you the loan application forms and you can take them with you. The land will be mortgaged, of course, but the bank will require a down payment. You can work that out with Denver."

Tessa wasn't sure she could work anything out with Denver, but didn't say so. A few minutes later, she was back in her car, driving south.

Nate Edwards's ranch was all that the McLean Ranch wasn't. The main house looked as if it were more suited to a Southern plantation than the windy hills of Montana. Rising three full stories, the shiny white exterior was punctuated with huge bow windows and cobalt-blue shutters. A porch, complete with an old-fashioned swing and wicker furniture, ran the length of the building, as did an upper balcony.

The ranch buildings and fences were all of gleaming white. A lake fitted with huge irrigation pipes forced water across the dry acres. Even in late August, the grass on Nate Edwards's property was healthy and green.

Tessa parked her car at the curve of a circular drive and mounted brick steps. She rang the bell and waited until Nate's wife, Paula, opened the door. Red-haired and younger than her husband by fifteen years, Paula grinned widely.

"Tessa! This is a surprise. Come in, come in," she invited, "It's about time you stopped by. Sherrie's been asking about you."

"I've been busy," Tessa explained, feeling a little guilty. She and Paula had been friends since high school, and Paula's daughter, Sherrie, was a child after Tessa's own heart.

"Who is it, Mommy?" a small voice called as Tessa stepped inside the cool interior.

Glancing up, she spied a dark-haired imp on the landing of the stairs. "Don't tell me you don't remember me," Tessa said.

The child squealed in recognition. "Tessie!" she cried, hurrying down the sweeping staircase and running into Tessa's outstretched arms. "You promised to take me riding!"

"That I did."

"Over my dead body!" Paula interrupted, wagging a finger

in front of Sherrie's pert little face. "You can't ride until you're five, remember."

Sherrie crossed her plump little arms over her chest. "I won't *ever* be five."

"Sure you will," her mother teased, touching the tip of Sherrie's nose with her finger and winking at Tessa. "Come out to the back porch. I've got a pitcher of iced tea in the refrigerator, and Sherrie and I baked cookies this morning."

"Apple squares!" Sherrie chimed in, scrambling from her mother's arms and making a beeline for the kitchen. "I'll show you."

The kitchen was as formal as the rest of the house. Gleaming pans hung from the ceiling, marble counters stretched around the room and every appliance sparkled. On the center island were two huge platters of warm cookies. Sherrie picked out the largest square in her plump little fingers and handed it to Tessa. "Try it," she commanded, her eyes bright, her pink cheeks flushed.

"Delicious," Tessa pronounced as she bit into the gooey confection.

"I know," the girl said proudly.

Paula promptly lectured her daughter on the virtues of being humble.

Hiding a grin, Tessa strolled outside. Paula joined her a few minutes later on the back porch. While Sherrie picked flowers in the garden, Paula and Tessa sat beneath a table umbrella and sipped from frosty glasses of iced tea.

"So where've you been this morning?" Paula asked, eyeing Tessa's suit.

"The bank. I'm trying to buy the ranch. That's why I'm here." Tessa shoved her hair from her eyes and watched Sherrie pick the petals off a budding rose. "I wanted to talk to Nate about Brigadier and a couple of mares. He was interested in buying them once."

"Still is," Paula said. "He's never forgiven you for buying that stallion right out from under his nose at the auction."

"I guess he has a chance to get even."

Paula studied the ice cubes dancing in her drink. "I hear Denver's back."

"For a while," Tessa replied, her eyes squinting against the sun.

"How's it going?"

"So far, so good," she said, knowing she was evading the truth. Paula was a trusted friend, but Tessa doubted she could understand the tangle of emotions that linked Denver and Tessa as well as drove them apart.

"You don't think you can convince him to stay?"

Tessa shook her head. "I couldn't before the fire, and now . . . a lot has happened. Besides, we have separate lives now. He loves L.A. I like it here."

"You've never been to L.A.," Paula reminded her gently.

"I know."

"Aren't you just a little curious?"

"About what?"

"The city. The beach. Why Denver lives there?"

Tessa blew a wayward strand of hair from her eyes. "A little," she admitted. In truth, she wanted to know everything about Denver. What he'd done the past seven years. Where he'd lived. With whom he'd shared his life.

"You loved him once," Paula reminded her.

"I was young—and foolish."

Paula, always the matchmaker, lifted a lofty red eyebrow. "So, if you're not still hung up on Denver, why haven't you married?"

One corner of Tessa's lips curved upward. "Maybe I haven't met the right man."

"Oh, you've met him, all right. And you're living under the same roof with him. If I were you, I'd use that to your advantage."

"It's not that simple."

"I don't know," Paula mused, her eyes crinkling at the corners. "Seems to me, life's as simple as you make it. You're not married. Denver's still single, and you used to be so in love with him that you couldn't think of anything else. Some things just don't change."

"I'll remember that," Tessa said, finishing her drink and finally turning the conversation away from Denver to Paula and her plans for Sherrie.

Two hours later, as she drove back to the ranch, the interior of her car so hot she had begun to perspire, Tessa considered Paula's advice then promptly discarded it. Denver had come back to the ranch to sell it. Period. His return had nothing to do with her—he'd admitted as much that first night when he found her in the barn. Any tenderness he'd felt for her had died in the fire. Even the night before, the gentle way he'd touched her had been because of the alcohol he'd consumed— nothing more.

Hands shoved deep in his pockets, Denver walked through the gloomy machine shed, eyeing each battered piece of equipment and remembering some of the older rigs. The combine, mower and drill were the same ones he'd used himself. Trailing his finger along the dented seat of the old John Deere tractor, he frowned. He'd spent more hours than he wanted to count chugging through the fields, dragging a harrow or hay baler behind. From the time he could first remember, he'd wanted out—a chance at another life. Years ago, before the fire, he'd thought he would claim that life, make a name for himself as an engineer, study for an M.B.A. and marry Tessa Kramer.

But, of course, things hadn't turned out as he'd planned.

And now, he wasn't so sure that he was ready to leave.

Scowling darkly, he dusted his hands, as if in so doing he could brush aside any ties that bound him to this land.

Though ranching wasn't what he'd dreamed of all his life,

he'd found a quiet peacefulness here that he hadn't felt in years; the slower pace was a welcome relief from the tension and stress in L.A. Even his condominium on the beach in Venice didn't interest him. Not without Tessa.

He hadn't really acknowledged his growing attachment to the ranch—or was it his fascination with Tessa?—until his partner had called, reassuring him that things were slow in the engineering firm and that he could handle everything for a few more weeks. Oddly, Denver found the extra time soothing.

He shouldered open the door and stopped suddenly. There, only forty yards directly in front of him were the charred ruins of the stables. The debris had been hauled away years before, but a few blackened timbers, now overgrown with berry vines, were piled near what had once been the concrete foundation.

Though the wind was hot, he shuddered as memories of the blaze burned before his very eyes. Once again, he was seven years younger—

Fire crackled high in the air. Smoke scorched his lungs as he ran to the stables. Horses screamed in terror, and fear thudded in his heart. Inside the heat was so intense, the roar of the flames so deafening, he couldn't see or hear. Throwing one arm over his mouth, he held his breath and moved by instinct, fumbling with locks on the stalls, hoping to set free a few of the scrambling, terrified animals. Stallions and mares squealed. Kicking madly, they bolted as soon as Denver tore open the gates.

He heard a cough, then a tortured cry, and he whirled toward the tack room. God, were his parents trapped inside? *Hold on,* he thought, *I'm coming. Just hold on!*

As he stepped forward, a blast ripped through the stables, throwing him off his feet. His hands scrabbled in the air, catching on the bit of a bridle still dangling from the wall.

The scorched leather snapped and he fell to the floor. In his last few seconds of consciousness he knew he would die.

"Denver?"

He whirled, the old memories fading as he stared into Tessa's worried eyes. Standing only inches from him, her golden hair catching in the breeze, a small smile quivering on her lips, she whispered, "Are you all right?"

"Fine," he muttered, praying silently that he would become immune to the fragrance of her perfume and the tenderness in her perfect features. The vision had been so real—so ghastly—that once again he remembered how she'd betrayed him. He swiped at his forehead with a shaking hand and noticed the beads of sweat lingering at his hairline.

"You . . . seem . . ."

"I said I'm fine!" he growled. If she would only go away so that he wouldn't notice the way the hem of her skirt flirted around her knees or the shapely length of her calf. Right now, when his emotions were still raw, he couldn't talk to her objectively, couldn't slow the thundering rush of adrenaline in his blood. As much from her nearness as from the horrifying memory, his heart was hammering crazily, pumping blood in a rush that echoed through his brain.

She glanced at the ruins of what had been one of the grandest stables in the county. "It's not easy," she said softly—her voice as gentle as a lazy summer breeze. "I know. But it's over. It was over a long time ago."

"I only wish to God it were," he said through clenched teeth. The memory of his parents seared through his mind until he willfully shut the agonizing thoughts aside.

Tessa swallowed hard. "I never said I was sorry," she said quietly. "About what happened. But I am. You know that I cared for your father and mo—"

"It wasn't your fault, remember?" His voice was like a whip cracking with sarcasm.

"Empathy has nothing to do with blame!" Her eyes blazed with gray-green fire and her small chin wobbled. "Hide it from everyone else and hide it from yourself, damn you, but don't try to hide it from me! I know you too well."

His eyes narrowed maliciously. "*Knew* me. Past tense. You don't know me at all anymore."

"You think not? You think I can't see past that hard shell you've covered yourself with? Think again, Denver. Think back to what we meant to each other!"

"I already told you what we meant."

Flushing furiously, she jabbed a finger at his chest. "So you did. You tried to hurt me, Denver, and you did one hell of a job at it. But I knew you then, and I can't believe—no matter what's happened—that you don't have one shred of the decency, one ounce of the kindness and moral fiber you once did. I won't accept that you have become a callous, jaded cynic who wants nothing more from life than enough money to keep him comfortable!"

His skin tightened menacingly. "You're deluding yourself, Tess."

"Am I? Then what about last night? Was that all my imagination, my *delusions,* or was that you?"

"I was drunk."

"Not *that* drunk."

"It was the booze talking."

"I don't think so," she said fiercely. "Tell me, is it just me or the world in general that infuriates you?" Tossing her head proudly, she turned and strode back to the house.

Denver's fists coiled. He watched her stomp up the steps to the back porch and heard the door bang shut. Swearing angrily under his breath, he slammed one clenched hand into the side of the machinery shed, sending splinters of siding flying through the dry air.

* * *

Flinging her skirt onto the bed, Tessa wondered why she bothered dealing with Denver. ". . . insufferable, arrogant bastard!" She kicked her shoes into the closet. Why had she even bothered trying to reach him? The man was the most temperamental, moody beast on the ranch!

One minute she thought he wanted to make love to her, the next strangle her. "Just the way you feel about him," she reminded herself angrily.

She'd found him standing near the ruins of the stables, his face drawn with pain, his eyes focused on some private horror that only he could see, and she'd been foolish enough to try to comfort him.

"That's what you get," she muttered, flinging herself on the bed, staring up at the ceiling and feeling like an utter fool. If only he would leave, end the turmoil, let her life return to its normal state.

But the thought of his actually packing his bags and walking out of her life again settled like a rock in her stomach. She threw one arm over her eyes and whispered, "You're out of your mind, Tessa!"

How much more humiliation would she let him inflict? "None," she promised herself, reaching for her jeans and tugging them over her hips. When Denver McLean left Montana again, she vowed silently to herself, she would wish him good luck, then pray that she never set eyes on him again.

Chapter Six

The phone rang. Without looking up from the papers strewn across the desk, Denver reached for the receiver. "McLean Ranch," he muttered.

"Denver?" Ross Anderson's voice boomed over the wires. "How's it going?"

"As well as can be expected, I suppose." He hadn't talked to Ross since he'd left the attorney's office nearly two weeks before.

"I thought you were heading back to L.A."

"I got side-tracked. Your advice." He leaned back in his chair and waited. Ross wouldn't be calling without a reason.

"I thought you'd like to know I may have a lead on your brother."

Denver sucked in his breath. *Finally!* "You're sure?"

"Nothing's sure until we see him," Ross replied. "But a private detective in New York contacted one of the magazines he works for, and I think we may have gotten lucky. Just three weeks ago, Colton was in Belfast."

"I'll be damned," Denver said, wondering if his luck were changing.

"You and me both," Ross said with a laugh. "The investigator is flying to Ireland tonight. We should know something in the next couple of days."

Denver sighed. "I guess I'll owe you one, Ross."

"Let's wait and see. But the editor seems to think Colton is still working undercover, posing as a member of the IRA."

Denver's stomach knotted. "He's lucky to be alive."

"If he still is."

"Let me know."

"Oh, I will. The minute I hear."

Denver hung up and wondered how Colton would take the news that he'd inherited half of the ranch and Tessa Kramer wanted to buy it. A slow smile spread over Denver's features. If nothing else could entice Colton back to Montana, the threat of selling out to Curtis Kramer's daughter just might.

Nate Edwards was a big, burly man whose dark hair was shot with gray. He'd been a horseman all his life, and his eyes gleamed as he leaned on the fence and watched Tessa lead Brigadier around the paddock.

"A fine-looking animal," he said, eyeing the stallion.

Brigadier's muscles quivered as Nate reached across the top rail and rubbed the stallion's muscular shoulder.

"I think he's the best in the state."

Nate smiled, exposing one gold-capped tooth. "I don't know if I'd go that far. What about Black Magic?"

Tessa considered the gleaming black stallion—John McLean's pride. "It's hard to compare," she said grudgingly. "But I'd still put my money on Brigadier."

Nate's gaze swung to the two mares, both pregnant, standing head to tail, and switching flies in the next paddock. "You're sure you want to sell all three?"

No, she wasn't, but she had no choice. For the past few years, she'd pinned her dreams on these animals, and the thought of selling the two mares and Brigadier hurt. But it was worth it, she told herself, for the ranch. "If I get the right price," she whispered, as her fingers caressed Brigadier's sleek neck. It seemed sacrilege to sell this horse. Aside from his value in dollars and cents, Brigadier had become a big part of her life. She enjoyed his feisty spirit and ornery streak. Now, Brigadier minced nervously, rolling his eyes until they showed white, as Nate opened the gate and slipped through.

"Careful," Tessa warned.

Running his hands over Brigadier's back, Nate moved slowly around the horse and had to jump out of the way when one back hoof lashed out, nearly connecting with Nate's shin. "Friendly, isn't he?"

"He can be," Tessa said wistfully and offered Brigadier a piece of carrot. "But he can be trouble, too."

"I'll remember that," Nate replied, giving the horse's rear end a wide berth as he eased back through the gate.

Tessa unsnapped the lead rope and gave Brigadier a slap on the rump. The horse whirled, then took off, his long, red legs flashing as he raced to the far end of the paddock, his ears pricked forward to the next field where Red Wing, Ebony and Tessa's other three mares grazed. The horses nipped grass and switched flies with their tails.

Tessa's stomach tightened and her heart grew heavy. Selling her favorite horses felt like selling a vital part of her family. She felt a traitor to her own kin. A hot lump formed in her throat as she watched the three horses, ears still flicking nervously, standing quietly in the shade of a solitary pine.

"Tessa?" Nate asked gently. "If this is gonna bother you—"

"I'll get over it," she said, though her eyes burned with unshed tears. She hurried through the gate and managed a wan smile.

"Okay. But if you change your mind, let me know." Nate turned toward his Jeep. "I'll call you in the next couple of days with an offer."

"I'll look forward to it," Tessa lied, her heart tearing a little. "And tell Sherrie I'm ready to give her riding lessons whenever she can convince Paula she's old enough to handle a horse."

"Don't hold your breath." Nate chuckled, his eyes bright at the thought of his daughter. "If Paula has her way, Sherrie never will get into a saddle."

Tessa nodded. "I'll bet Sherrie convinces her otherwise."

"We'll see. That chestnut mare—" He hitched his thumb toward the barn.

"Red Wing?"

Nate nodded and climbed into his Jeep. "I think Red Wing or that foal of hers will be perfect for Sherrie. Just give me a couple of days to convince my wife." He slammed the door and started the engine.

Well, Tessa thought unhappily as she watched Nate's Jeep disappear, the wheels were in motion. As soon as Nate bought the horses, she could make Denver a formal offer on the ranch. Kicking at a clod of dirt with the toe of her boot, she wondered why she didn't feel happy at the prospect. She glanced again at the paddock. Ebony was playfully nipping Red Wing's neck and was rewarded with a disgruntled kick. Tessa's eyes filled with tears. *Dear Lord, I'll miss them,* she thought, this small herd that had been the focus of her life until Denver returned.

Denver. He was behind all this. She squeezed her eyes shut and fought the urge to sag against the fence. Could she ever really trust him?

Two days later, Tessa was working with the most temperamental colt on the ranch. "Easy, now," she cooed, straining against the lead rope. An ornery roan yearling, appropriately named Frenzy, was on the other end of the leather strap, pulling and bucking and being a real pain in the backside.

As usual. The high-strung roan seemed to enjoy giving Tessa fits.

It didn't help that Tessa had been in a foul mood herself ever since seeing Nate. And her nerves had been on edge since she noticed Denver watching her every move. She'd seen him staring through the study window, known he was in the barn, felt his eyes on her when she was going about her chores. Though they hadn't said a word, the charged tension between them had been stretched as tight as piano string, ready to break.

Frenzy yanked hard on the rope, tossing his red head and whistling. The leather slid through Tessa's hands. "Calm down," she said, soothing the colt with her voice. She inched forward and Frenzy, wild-eyed, reared and bolted. The rope snapped taut and pulled her off her feet. She flew through the air and landed with a smack on the dry ground.

"Oof!" Her bones jarred. Lifting her head, she spied Frenzy at the far end of the paddock. "Ingrate!" Tessa whispered, standing slowly and dusting her jeans. "Stupid, miserable beast!"

Still muttering under her breath, she turned and found Denver standing in the shade of the barn. One shoulder propped against the weathered boards, his arms folded over his chest, he tried unsuccessfully to smother a smile. "I thought you saved all those endearments for me," he said, chuckling.

Tessa's temper, already worn thin, snapped. "No," she said, "I've got special names for you."

"I guess I should be honored."

She shot him a warning glance. "I wouldn't be so sure of that!"

"You're just mad because he"—Denver cocked his head toward Frenzy, who was standing in a corner of the paddock, the lead rope dangling from his bridle—"got the better of you."

"This time." She winced and rubbed her shoulder.

"Are you all right?" Denver walked quickly through the gate and touched her upper arm.

She flinched, gritting her teeth.

"Maybe I should look at that."

His touch was already playing havoc with her mind. "I'm fine," Tessa said, shifting away. "The only thing that's bruised is my pride."

"He didn't look so tough to me." Denver surveyed the feisty colt.

"No?" she said. "You think you could do better?"

Denver rubbed his chin thoughtfully. "Probably."

"Good. Have at it."

Denver's gaze returned to hers and his eyes had darkened. "Okay. But maybe we should make this more interesting," he drawled suggestively.

"It'll be plenty interesting. I guarantee it." She climbed onto the top rail of the fence for a better view.

"I was thinking in terms of a small wager—"

"I don't gamble."

One corner of Denver's mouth lifted provocatively. "Sure you do, Tess. Unless you've changed."

Her throat constricted for a second, and she looked away. "What's the bet?" she asked, hating the breathless tone to her voice.

"Simple. If I get him to accept the saddle and walk calmly, I win."

"And what's at stake?"

"Name it." His eyes glinted magnetic blue.

Tessa had trouble finding her voice. The heat in Denver's gaze was equal to that of the late-afternoon sun still warming the valley floor. "Okay," she finally said. "If you can get him to take the saddle and walk docilely around the ring, you win. But if he won't take the saddle, you lose."

"And my punishment?" he asked, squinting up at her, his sensuous mouth curving suggestively.

Tessa could barely breathe. "If you lose, I—I'll expect you to work on the ranch the next week—shoulder to shoulder with the hands."

"And if I win," Denver said slowly, touching the side of her jaw with his finger, letting his hand slide slowly along it, "I'll expect you to spend a weekend with me in California!"

"That's impossible," she said quickly. The thought of spending a weekend completely alone with him caused her heart to hammer. "I—I can't be gone that long and—"

"And you're afraid of what you'll find out about me and maybe yourself," he suggested, leaning lazily over the top rail of the fence, his elbow nearly touching her thigh.

"That's not it! I have work here! Who'll run the ranch if I leave?"

His face turned hard. "Your father," he bit out. "After all, Curtis *is* the ranch foreman. That's what I pay him for."

"Dad can't do it alone."

"He'll have Mitch and Len and the rest of the hands."

"*If* you win."

"Oh, I'll win all right." A slow smile spread over his face, and with the grace of an athlete, he strode across the paddock and started talking softly to the horse.

Tessa bit her lip and crossed her fingers. She couldn't lose—not after she'd promised to go with him to L.A. *Come on, Frenzy,* she silently pleaded, *don't let me down. Show him who's boss!*

As if he'd heard her, Frenzy reared and shrieked. Head high, nostrils flared, he galloped past Denver at breakneck speed. The ground shook.

Tessa wanted to whoop, but Denver, his eyes steady on the colt, kept after him, talking low, moving slowly. The lathered roan pawed the ground nervously and sprinted past Denver in the opposite direction.

"That's it—" Tessa said.

"Not yet." With the patience of a lion stalking prey, Denver kept walking, gradually making his way until he reached the dangling lead rope and slowly picked it up. Then, each move deliberate, he wrapped the leather around his hands, approached the horse and placed a calming hand on Frenzy's quivering coat.

To Tessa's mortification, he managed to lead the yearling to the fence where a blanket was folded over the top rail. Denver placed the blanket on Frenzy's quivering, lathered hide.

The colt shied. He minced away from Denver, but Denver persisted and finally placed the saddle gently on Frenzy's strong back. He tightened the cinch. The yearling, squealing, took off like a rocket!

Denver braced himself. The lead rope stretched tight, yanking hard on Denver's arms. "Damn you," Denver muttered as the colt dragged him forward a few feet.

Tessa grinned.

But Denver dug his heels into the ground. His shoulders flexed and strained. Frenzy bucked and reared, his hooves slashing as he tried to shake the horrid leather beast from his back, but he couldn't rip the strap from Denver's hands.

"You're only going to wear yourself out," Denver told the horse. Frenzy reared again, shrieking. Denver moved closer. "Come on, boy. Let's see what you've got." Clucking his tongue, Denver urged the colt forward.

Chagrined, Tessa watched as Frenzy began trotting around Denver. The colt was far from calm, his steps were nervous, his eyes rimmed in white, but he did, in fact, run at the end of the lead in a tight circle.

"How about that?" Denver said, gloating.

Tessa, grudgingly, conceded. "I didn't think it was possible."

Denver's face was covered with dust, but he was grinning from one ear to the other. When he finally pulled the saddle from Frenzy's back and unsnapped the lead, he couldn't help rubbing his victory in. "Easy as pie—if you know what you're doing," he said.

Tessa felt the perverse urge to ram Frenzy's bridle down Denver's throat, but she said instead, "Good job."

"So, how soon can you get packed?"

Her eyes rounded. "You're not serious."

"We had a bet," he reminded her.

"But I can't leave!"

"I thought we already discussed this." He wiped the sweat from his forehead and shoved a jet-black lock of hair away from his face. "I have some things I've got to take care of here, too," he said, "but then, you and I are going to L.A."

She fought back the urge to scream at him. For years she'd been able to hate the city where he'd run. It was easy to blame California for the pain he'd caused. But she'd never reneged on a bet in her life, and now, as she stared at his dust-streaked face, she found herself wanting to go to Los Angeles, to find out more about him, to know every tiny detail of his life. "Give me a few days," she said, hopping to the ground beside him.

"Okay. But since I have to wait, I think you owe me something."

"I don't owe you anything—"

He placed a finger to her lips. "Before you go flying off the handle, just listen. All I want is to spend a little time with you."

Her heart fluttered expectantly. "We're together all the time—"

"You've been avoiding me."

That much was true. "I thought you wanted it that way."

"Maybe I did," he admitted. "But since we're stuck here together, we should try to get along."

She laughed. "Impossible."

"Is it, Tess?" His voice was suddenly serious, his gaze far off, as he stared at the hills.

She swallowed against a lump in her throat. The tender side of Denver had always broken through her resistance. As she stared at him, his face grimy, his hair windblown, the hard edge to his features temporarily erased, she couldn't say no. "What do you want to do?"

"Come on," he said, taking her hand. "I'll show you."

"Wait—Denver—" But he was running across the yard, past the house. She had trouble keeping up with him, taking two strides to his one. "Where are we going?" she asked, gasping for breath, as they wound down a seldom used path to the small lake nestled in a thicket of oak and maple.

Blackberry vines crept through the underbrush and high overhead, beneath the tattered clouds, geese flew, their V formation seeming to float over the sun-dappled water. The old dock was gray and beginning to rot. It listed as it stretched into the lake.

"I haven't been here since I've been back," Denver said, eyeing the lake's smooth surface.

"It's low this year," Tessa remarked, conscious that her hand was still linked with Denver's.

Glancing down at her, he smiled, then led her to the small stretch of sandy beach. Taking a clean handkerchief from his pocket, he dipped it in the water, then gently wiped her face. "Evidence of Frenzy's victory," he chuckled, exposing her freckles and tracing the slope of her cheek.

Shivering expectantly, she took the handkerchief from him. "You, too." Though her hands shook a little, she pressed the wet cloth to his forehead and cleaned the dirt from his smooth brow. "That's better."

She tried to pull her hand away, but his fingers curled possessively around her wrist. His eyes turned dark blue. "You're a fascinating woman, Tessa," he said quietly, "the most fascinating woman I've ever met."

Slowly, using his weight, he tugged on her arm, pulling her down to the dry grass, half-lying beside her. She knew she should get up, stop this madness before it started, but she couldn't. Her heart thudded over the quiet lapping of the lake.

"You're not what I expected." His gaze delved deep into hers, so deep she was sure he could see her soul, that her love for him was painfully obvious. His fingertips moved leisurely over her wrist, as if they had all the time in the world to get to know each other again. The earth was warm against her back, the sky turning a soft shade of lavender.

"I thought you'd be the same as when I left."

Her lips twisted wryly. "I grew up."

"I noticed." His eyes drifted down her body, his gaze scraping against her curves.

"Sorry to disappoint you."

He traced her eyebrows with one finger and she had trouble concentrating on anything but the warmth in his touch.

"That's the problem, Tessa," he admitted, his eyes searching her face. "I'm not disappointed. I wish I was. Things would have been so much simpler." He pulled her into the circle of his arms and held her close, his lips brushing her crown, his breath stirring her hair. She shouldn't be this close to him, Tessa thought. She shouldn't let his kind words in.

"I didn't think you'd become so . . . determined. You always had a mind of your own but I thought you would change. That after the fire—" His breath fanned her ear and warning bells rang in her mind.

She couldn't let him do this to her! Not now. Not when so many things were unsettled. Not when his scars on the inside were more visible than those across the back of his hand.

She pushed against his chest. Half of her wanted to stay curled in the security of his arms, the other half knew that lying with him near the deserted lake was dangerous. "If you taught me anything, Denver, it was that I had to stand on my own two feet." The old bitterness returned; she struggled and failed to get away from him. "Fortunately Mitchell was around," she added, remembering those first excruciating weeks.

"Mitch?"

"He helped me pull myself together!"

"I thought he went into the Army."

"Not until he knew that I was okay," she said quietly, remembering back to the pain of Denver's rejection. It still hurt—that burning, gaping hole in her heart. "He was here when you weren't."

"And now he's back—hanging around, doing nothing."

"You just don't understand, do you?" she scoffed. "He came back here after the Army because he had a few months to kill before he started school. He's—he's been a big help."

"Doing what?" Denver asked skeptically.

"Making fence, feeding the stock, repairing the machinery. Just generally helping out."

"And all this time I thought he was just sponging off you."

Tessa's temper flared. "That's what happens when you live in California and make rash judgments!"

"Is that what I've done?" he mocked, refusing to release her.

Was he laughing at her? "Of course it is!"

"Tell me about life in L.A. As you see it," he goaded.

She rose to the bait. "I'd be glad to." Struggling up to one elbow, she shoved her hair from her eyes. "My guess is that you live in your chrome-and-glass apartment with a security guard at the door. Drive a sports car thirty miles an hour in bumper to bumper traffic. Spend vacations in Hawaii or Mexico or Catalina and for God's sake wear an imported Italian suit!"

He smiled, then, a secret, caring smile. "I live in a house near the ocean, Tessa, in Venice—and a lot of my work can be done at home. I drive an old Jeep and avoid the freeways when I can. This is the first vacation I've had in years, and I wouldn't know an Italian suit if it reached up and said, *"Lasciate ogni speranza, voi ch'entrate."*

One of her blond eyebrows raised quizzically. "It said what?"

"Literally translated, 'Abandon hope all ye who are foolish enough to plunge your arms down the sleeves of this overpriced imported jacket.'"

"No!" she whispered, but laughed.

"Well, not really. It means 'Abandon hope all ye who enter here,' but it's the only Italian phrase I know."

"So what's your point?"

"That I'm the same man no matter where I live. And you're the same woman whether you live in Three Falls, Montana, L.A. or New York City. You'll find out soon," he said, grinning. "And I can't wait."

"Why?"

"I think you'll love Rodeo Drive, Melrose Avenue and Wilshire Boulevard. I'll get you on one of those buses that tours through Beverly Hills and shows you the homes of the stars, and then we'll check out the movie studios—"

"Oh, save me," she whispered, groaning and trying to hide a smile.

"You'll love it. I promise."

She shook her head. "Maybe for you it works," she said.

"It does."

"But for me"—she glanced to the lake, where a wood duck was landing on the glasslike surface—"this is where I belong."

"I can change your mind," he whispered, his mouth pressing against her parted lips.

"Never," she replied, her voice caught somewhere between her throat and lungs. A voice inside her mind nagged at her, reminding her that Denver believed that she'd had an affair with his uncle—that her family had been involved in the fire. That the last time he'd been with her at the creek, he'd humiliated her. His words were as false as his love had been all those years before.

With all the strength she could scrape together, Tessa shoved him away and scrambled hastily to her feet. "It won't work, Denver," she said, breathing hard, seeing his expression turning from surprise to anger.

"What are you talking about?" he rasped.

Her eyes narrowed, though her heart was still beating traitorously. "I'm not about to give you the opportunity to humiliate me again."

"I wouldn't," he said slowly, standing.

"You're right," she said quickly. "Because I won't let you!" Then, before she could change her mind, she ran back to the house and took the steps two at a time.

Chapter Seven

She didn't see Denver until the next day at dinner. Seated across the table from Tessa and wedged between her father and Len Derricks, a ranch hand who had stayed with John after the fire, Denver did his best to appear amiable and relaxed. He complimented Milly on the meal and made small talk as if he'd never set one foot off the ranch—as if he'd never accused Tessa or her father of starting the blaze in which his parents had died.

His shirt was open at the throat, his jeans faded but clean, the worn denim hugging his hips. Black hair curled enticingly from beneath his collar. A dark shadow covered his jaw, making his smile, a rakish slash of white, brighter in contrast. His clear blue eyes had lost their hostile shadows, and his thick eyebrows moved expressively as he spoke.

Tessa felt foolish and cowardly. She should never have run from him, and she vowed that she wouldn't again. Unfortunately, she could barely drag her gaze away from the sensual curve of his lips, or the arch of a skeptical eyebrow.

"Delicious," Denver pronounced to a beaming Milly.

"It's only stew," she replied, blushing in pleasure.

"The best stew I've ever eaten."

Tessa's eyes narrowed on him as he placed his elbows on the table and turned to Len, asking his advice on purchasing more cattle for the ranch.

"If we add more head, we'll have to buy extra feed. We're already goin' through the hay we cut just two months ago."

"Can we get more?"

"Don't know," Len said, rubbing his chin thoughtfully. "Everyone around here is in the same fix. Except for Nate Edwards. He's been irrigatin' like mad, and from what I hear, he harvested more bales than he expected."

"Then maybe we can buy from him."

"Maybe," Len agreed, grinning at the prospect of adding to the herd.

"I'll give him a call. Now, tell me what kind of cattle you'd like to see on the ranch. We've got Herefords, right?"

"Ever since I can remember."

"So what about a new breed? Angus or Charolais?"

Len launched into his favorite topic, and to Tessa's horror, even her father and Mitchell added their two cents worth. Eventually everyone at the table was weighing the pros and cons of adding more beef to the stock. Why did Denver care? Tessa wondered. What was his angle? Wasn't he going to sell the ranch to her—or had he lied again?

"So when did you get so interested in ranching?" she asked, finally unable to hold her tongue. She felt her father stiffen beside her, but she glared at Denver. "I thought you were leaving."

Denver leaned forward, pushing his face across the table. "Until I actually sign on the dotted line," he said slowly, "I intend to take part in *all* the decisions that affect this ranch."

"From L.A.?"

"If need be." His eyes glinted wickedly at the mention of California.

"Tessa—" Mitchell warned.

"Do we understand each other?" Denver asked.

"Perfectly," she said, meeting the fire in his gaze with her own.

With a smile, Denver turned back to Len as if Tessa hadn't even interrupted.

Her temper soaring to the stratosphere, Tessa could barely listen. Though she pretended interest in the conversation around her, she couldn't concentrate. Not the way she should have. Not with Denver watching her through hard, calculating eyes. He wasn't actually staring—he feigned interest in the entire group of hands and household helpers seated around the table—but Tessa could feel his gaze follow her. When she reached for the biscuits, as she laughed over a joke Mitchell whispered to her, or even while she helped Milly clear the table, she could feel the weight of Denver's gaze.

"I'd add about fifty head of each," Len was saying, leaning back in his chair as Milly offered thick slabs of apple pie around the table.

"That's an increase of a hundred and fifty. I don't know," Curtis whispered thoughtfully.

Tessa couldn't stand the easy camaraderie, false as it was, a minute longer. "I thought you were going to sell the ranch lock, stock and barrel," she cut in, her eyes trained on Denver's face.

"I am. But not until the ranch is in better shape."

"And you think by spending money on cattle and feed that things will improve?"

"Couldn't hurt," he drawled, one corner of his mouth lifting.

He was actually enjoying her show of temper! "Then maybe it's my turn to make something clear. As I said before, I intend to buy this ranch, and I don't want the added expense of extra stock. Not yet."

Denver's eyes flashed. "And I told you I couldn't sell until the books were straightened out and I found my brother."

"That could take years!"

He did smile then, an infuriating grin that curved his lips

lazily and caused her heart to throb. "I've got all the time in the world. Don't you?"

Her jaw fell open. "I thought you couldn't wait to get to L.A."

"I can't," he drawled, and Tessa felt a telling flush creep up her neck. She knew in an instant that he was baiting her again—seeing just how far he could push. "I'm looking forward to California," he said, and for a minute she was afraid he'd tell everyone about their bet. His gaze flicked around the table. "Unfortunately, I might not be able to wait until the place is sold, so I've got to make some plans to get it back on its feet before I leave."

"And do what?" she asked, standing. "Run the ranch from a cell phone while you're getting a tan at Malibu Beach?"

Denver didn't react. "If that's what it takes," he responded calmly.

Tessa felt everyone's gaze on her, but she didn't flinch. Leaning over the table, she smiled sweetly and said, "Don't bother. I've already talked to the bank for the mortgage, and I can come up with the down payment. Now, all that has to happen is for you and me to come to some sort of an agreement. You won't have to worry about this place once you're back in L.A.!"

"You and I already came to an agreement," he reminded her. "About California."

Her jaw dropped, and she silently pleaded with him to keep their wager to himself.

"But do you honestly think it's possible for us to agree on anything?" he asked, returning to the question of the ranch.

Relieved, she said, "If we're both willing to cooperate."

"And what about the back taxes on this place?"

"Pay them—or make a provision for that payment in the sales agreement. Lower the price of the ranch by the amount of taxes owed, and I'll take care of them."

"And Colton?"

"Find him."

"Seems as if you've got it all figured out," he drawled, lifting his coffee cup and scrutinizing her carefully over the rim. His eyes became slits.

"Almost. Just as soon as you come up with a reasonable price." She felt the tension in the air. Everyone at the table had fallen silent. Not one fork scraped a plate. As if to break the charged silence, Milly coughed. Mitchell scooted his chair back, and Curtis fished nervously in his breast pocket for his cigarettes.

"You prove you're serious. Make a formal offer," Denver said deliberately. "Then, if you can come up with the money and I can find Colton, we'll have a deal."

Tessa couldn't believe her ears. "That's all?" she asked, waiting for the hitch—the strings that had to be attached.

"That—and a certain payoff."

"Payoff?" Mitch repeated.

"It's nothing," Tessa said quickly. She wondered if Denver were lying again—tricking her into believing he would sell. She had no option but to call his bluff. "I'll have everything ready as soon as possible," she said, her throat suddenly dry at the prospect of buying the place and thereby allowing him to leave. Now that he'd returned, the prospect of living without him again loomed in her future like a gaping black abyss.

Denver grinned, that easy, crooked smile that Tessa found wickedly irresistible. "I'm looking forward to it. Then maybe you could take a break from this place. Find some sun and sand and relaxation."

Tessa wanted to drop through the floor.

Denver shoved his chair from the table. "Thanks for the meal," he said to Milly, then he strode, whistling—*whistling* for crying out loud—down the hall.

Tessa snatched several plates from the table and carried them into the kitchen. Her entire body was shaking, and the china rattled in her hands.

"Careful now," Milly warned, eyeing Tessa's flushed features. "You're letting that man get to you."

"He's *not* getting to me!"

Smothering a knowing smile, Milly snapped an apron from a hook near the stove and tied it around her thick waist. "Whatever you say, Tess," she said, turning on the tap. Hot water began to fill the sink, steam rising to Milly's face.

"He's as changeable as a chameleon," Tessa sputtered. "One minute he's nasty as can be, the next he's sweet as pie, praising everyone, asking their opinions, when all he wants to do is get the hell out of here!"

"I wouldn't be so sure of that," Milly said, sliding a knowing glance Tessa's way as she began to stack rinsed plates into the dishwasher.

"What's that supposed to mean?" Tessa had been placing leftover stew into a bowl, but she paused.

"I just happened to walk by the den this morning—you remember, when he took that phone call from Jim what's-his-name, his partner."

"Van Stern."

"That's the one. Anyway, Denver was convincing this Van Stern character that he needed more time here; maybe another couple of weeks." Milly dried her hands on the edge of her apron and grinned. "The way he was talking, barking orders, trying to convince his partner that he didn't need to return to L.A. until certain things were just right, made me think he *wanted* to hang around here."

Tessa couldn't dare believe, not for a second, that Denver actually wanted to stay in Montana. All his life he'd never been interested in the land or the livestock. He'd been restless at the ranch. He was just waiting until she could break away and pay off her debt. *Damn him! Damn her stupid pride for taking that bet!* "He probably just wants the extra time to tie things up and get rid of the place."

"His lawyer could do that," Milly pointed out. "No, if you

ask me, that man has another reason for staying here." Her kind eyes met Tessa's and she winked.

"His decision has nothing to do with me."

"Oh no?" Milly's lower lip protruded thoughtfully. "Maybe not. But you'll never know until you take down your armor, now will you?"

"Meaning?"

"If the two of you could ever quit fighting long enough to talk sensibly, you might surprise yourselves."

"I don't think so. Denver made it very clear how he feels about me the first night he was back." But she couldn't forget yesterday at the lake. He'd seemed so sincere. So honest.

Milly's lips pursed pensively. "Well, maybe he was lying to save his pride. Did you ever think of that?"

Remembering how callously he'd told her he'd never loved her on the first night he returned to Montana, Tessa shook her head. "I don't think so."

"We'll see," Milly said. "We've got a couple more weeks of Mr. McLean. A lot can happen." She hung her apron on a hook near the door and reached for her old, plaid jacket. "I'll see you in the morning."

As Milly left with the few remaining ranch hands, Tessa decided to check on the horses and try to get her mind off Denver. She couldn't for a minute think Denver still cared for her. Though she wanted to believe that Milly was right, that Denver still felt something for her, she knew those hopes were only foolish fantasies. And even if Denver had loved her before the fire, too much had happened since for that love to rekindle. Never once had he suggested he loved her. *Wanted* her, yes, but love? Never. Even the other night, when his tongue had been loosened with liquor, he'd never mentioned love.

"Don't even think about it," she muttered to herself, shoving open the door of the barn and snapping on the lights. Though the only sounds she heard were the snorting of horses and rustling of hooves, she sensed someone else was inside. "Who's in here?" she called through the musty, dark interior.

"I am," her father's voice boomed.

"Dad?" Turning, she found him sitting on a bale of hay, a half-empty bottle dangling from his hands. "What're you doing here? I thought you were still in the house."

"I was. But I thought I'd better wait for you."

"Give me that," she said, afraid Denver might show up. She reached for the bottle, but her father yanked it away, twisted on the cap and stuck the flask behind the very bale on which he was seated.

"Don't trust him," he said flatly.

"Who? Denver?"

"Right."

"Hey! Whoa!" She pointed an accusing finger at her father. "Aren't you talking out of both sides of your mouth?"

"What do ya mean?"

"Was I mistaken, or were you the guy hanging on his every word at the dinner table? Weren't you chatting with him about the merits of an Angus over a Hereford?"

"He's the boss, damn it."

"I know, but the last I heard you weren't even planning to show up for work. You thought he'd fire you."

"He didn't," Curtis grumbled. "After that one lecture, he never brought up the fire again. I figured the least I could do was help out."

"So now you're telling me not to trust him? I don't get it, Dad." She leaned one hip against the manger, felt a soft nose nuzzle the side of her jeans and absently patted Brigadier's muzzle. "What's it going to be? Is Denver friend or foe?"

"That's a tough one," Curtis admitted, rubbing a trembling hand over his stubbled jaw. "Just remember that he's different from you and me. He's only here to sell this place. He doesn't give one good goddamn about it, and when it goes, we go."

"Not if I buy it."

Her father snorted, reached behind him and, as the hay stirred and dust motes swirled, extracted the bottle again. "I already told you what I thought of that fool notion—I'm not goin' to waste my breath again." He opened the bottle and took a long swallow.

"Stop it," she whispered harshly. "You just said you're getting along with Denver. Don't blow it with this!" She grabbed for the bottle again, grazing it. Spinning crazily out of Curtis's hands, the flask dropped onto the floor, crashing into a thousand pieces and spraying alcohol on the dry hay and old floorboards.

Tessa couldn't move. She stared at the glittering glass and pooling liquid and her stomach turned over. This is how it could have happened! Carelessly spilled alcohol, a dropped match that was still smoldering, combustible hay . . . Oh God! She remembered the horrid black smoke, the crackling flames, her desperate, haunting fear for Denver's life and her father's body being dragged from the inferno.

"You see anyone else in there?"

"I—I don't know," he mumbled, still coughing.

The paramedic glanced at the fire chief. "He wouldn't know. He's three sheets to the wind."

Tessa stood frozen, scared. The smell of alcohol and smoke had clung to her father that day and she hadn't cared. She had just been thankful that he was alive.

Now, as she saw the amber drops staining the floor, she said angrily, "Let's clean this up before Denver sees it."

"Too late." Denver's voice rang through the barn.

Tessa jumped and her father flinched.

Standing in the open door, his dark eyebrows drawn into an angry black line, Denver glared at the pitiful scene in front of him. "Accident?" he mocked.

"You could say that," Tessa said. She was shaking inside, her stomach quivering. *Please God, not Dad,* she silently prayed. *He couldn't have been responsible for the fire!*

"It's my fault," her father cut in, before realizing the irony in his words.

"Is it?" Denver's eyes narrowed on the old man and his jaw slid to one side. Every muscle in his body tensed. The back of his neck was flaming, his teeth clenched tight. "Go home and sleep it off," he advised slowly. "I'll take care of this mess."

Curtis hesitated.

"Have Mitch drive you," Tessa said softly, her insides wrenching. Was it possible? Could her father really have started the fire accidentally and lied about it to everyone? Everything she'd believed in had somehow crashed with that bottle shattering against the floor.

His arthritic shoulders stiff with pride, Curtis stood and walked tightly to the door. Denver moved enough to let him pass, but the coiled tension in his every muscle was as condemning as a public flogging.

"Don't you ever speak to my father like that again!" Tessa hissed, once Curtis was out of earshot.

"Open your eyes, Tessa, the man has a problem."

"Don't we all?" she snapped back, seeing him flinch a little. She found some towels and a broom and began cleaning up the spilled whiskey. Denver reached for a whisk broom.

"I can handle this," Tessa said coldly. "Don't you have something better to do?"

"Not at the moment, no." His eyes held hers for a second. Filled with accusations, they drilled deep. Tessa swallowed with difficulty.

"You can't keep covering for him, Tessa."

"I'm not covering for anyone!" Fury caused her heart to pound. She swiped at the floor with a towel and sucked in a swift breath when her fingers scraped over an invisible shard. "Damn." The prick was small but deep, and blood dripped from her hand.

"Let me take a look at that," Denver insisted, wrapping firm arms over her wrist.

"I'm fine. Just leave me alone!" She tried to yank back her hand, but his fingers were an unbending manacle.

"Hold it up," he commanded, reaching with his free hand into his pocket for a clean handkerchief.

"It's no big deal—"

"Not yet," he admitted.

"Really, just a small cut . . ."

"That could get infected. This place isn't exactly sterile, you know."

"I'd noticed," she said dryly, her gaze sweeping the long, hanging cobwebs, the dust collecting on the beams and the loose straw scattered in corners on the floor.

"Then you won't argue about going into the house to clean it up. I'll finish here."

"I'm not a cripple," she muttered, but saw the determined gleam in his gaze.

His fingers tightened over her wrist. "For once in your life, Tessa, just do as I say."

"Yes, sir!" she shot back, offering a mock salute with her free hand.

His lips, despite the hard set of his jaw, twitched upward, and he released her arm.

Marching stiffly out of the barn, she tried to calm down— count to ten—do anything to cling to her fleeing patience. She'd never considered herself irrational or quick to anger, but with Denver around, her temper flared as instantly as a match struck against tinder-dry kindling. Every time she attempted to be reasonable, he said or did something that pushed her world out of kilter—like clamping his hand over her wrist and barking an order at her while her stupid pulse raced crazily. Or like tenderly swiping her hair from her eyes and telling her that when he made love to her again, there would be no regrets—

"He's just a man," she reminded herself when she turned on the water in the bathroom a few minutes later. But as the warm water dripped over her hand, she caught sight of her reflection in the mirror and saw the color in her cheeks, the still-pounding pulse at the base of her throat, the fire in her hazel eyes. "Why do you let him get to you?" she demanded of her silly reflection and knew the answer. *Because, damn it, you've never stopped loving him!*

Sick at the thought, she wrenched the faucet closed, rubbed her finger with an antibacterial cream and wrapped her wound quickly with a small Band-Aid.

Walking out of the bathroom, she found Denver sitting on the banister overlooking the entry far below. His hands beside him for balance, he hopped off the polished rail as she entered the hall.

"Are you okay?" he asked gently.

That stupid part of her heart warmed at the concern in his eyes. "I told you I was fine."

"You don't need stitches?"

"Nor neurosurgery either, thank you very much!" She heard the bite in her words the minute they passed her tongue and regretted speaking so harshly. "Look, I didn't mean to snap, it's just—"

"Just what?" he asked.

She felt her shoulders slump a bit, but she looked him squarely in the eye. "It just seems that I can't do anything right when you're around. You're always trying to prove that you're the boss or that you know more than I do, or that—" She thought back to the day by the creek and cringed inside. "Or that you have some sort of power over me."

One corner of his mouth lifted. "I don't think anyone has any power over you, Tessa." His voice was tender, endearing. If she were to close her eyes, she could almost imagine that he was seven years younger and they were in love again. That same gentle tone she'd found so special still brought shivers to her skin.

When he touched her lightly on the shoulder, she wanted to lean against him, beg him to call back the hateful words he'd spoken when he first returned, plead with him to forgive her and her father for inadvertently causing him so great a tragedy.

"You were hard on Dad."

Denver was standing behind her, his hands on her shoulders. "He can't hide in a bottle forever."

"It's difficult for him, too."

His fingers gently pulled her backward until her shoulders met the firm wall of his chest and his breath fanned across her crown. Closing her eyes, she willed the waves of tenderness forming in her heart to recede. Although she yearned to tell him she loved him still, that deep in her heart her feelings had never wavered, she couldn't. He would only laugh at her confession, chide her for being the same silly romantic she'd been years before.

With all the effort she could muster, she tried to think clearly, to fight the magic of his nearness. Her fingers curled around the cool wood banister, her nails digging into the polished surface.

"It doesn't have to be this way," he said softly. "We don't have to keep lunging for each other's throats."

She could hear it then, the hard beat of his heart. Pounding in counterpoint to her own, it seemed to echo through the long, carpeted hall.

"Do you know you've been driving me crazy?"

"Is that what's doing it? It's my fault you've been acting like a madman from the minute you stepped onto the ranch?" she asked, wishing she could add some venom to her words, but her voice sounded breathless and hoarse—as if it belonged to a frightened young virgin.

He chuckled, gripping her tighter, forcing her against him

until her spine pressed tight to his chest and abdomen. His hands slid the length of her arms, to her wrists, then closed over her stomach, holding her so close that she felt the hard bulge in his jeans.

Bending a little, he placed his chin over her shoulder. His cheek was warm against hers, and she felt like moaning. Her fingers dug deeper, knuckles white, rigid in their grip of the railing as his lips, warm and inviting, soft and gentle, touched her neck, sweeping slowly from her shoulder to her earlobe.

"Denver, please," she said, trying to think. "Don't."

"You don't like it?" he teased, his fingers lacing under her breasts.

Was he crazy? "I-I just don't think it's wise . . . Oh!" His teeth nibbled on the shell of her ear and it was all she could do to hold on to the balustrade. Her knees went weak, her heart beating a wanton cadence. "Denver—" Turning in his arms, hoping to convince him that what they were doing was insane, she caught one glimpse of the passion smoldering in his eyes before his lips captured hers in a kiss that cut off any further protest.

His mouth molded against her skin, covering her parted lips anxiously. His tongue darted and flicked between her teeth. Bittersweet sensations raced through her body. Like wildfire through prairie grass, passion seared through her, until she couldn't think, and didn't want to.

Her arms lifted, circling his neck, holding him closer still as she returned his fever. Pulsing white-hot between them, the smoldering ashes of desire ignited.

His hand stole upward, strong fingers surrounding one breast. Tessa moaned softly, weak inside as he kneaded her flesh, causing her nipple to harden and protrude against the lacy confines of her bra.

Still he kissed her, his hips thrust hard against hers, her back now supported by the railing.

The front door banged open. "Tessa?" Mitchell's voice shattered their intimacy.

Tessa froze in Denver's arms and reluctantly dragged her mouth from his.

"Hey, Tess? Where are you?" her brother said, his voice booming up the stairs.

"Up here," she choked out. "I'll be down in a second."

"Good! I'll be in the kitchen. We need to talk." His footsteps echoed through the house and Tessa, forcing her unsteady legs and arms to work, pushed away from Denver.

"We're not finished," he insisted in a hoarse whisper that hissed through the upstairs hallway.

"I think we are."

His arm reached forward, jerking her around. "We're not finished by a long shot, Tessa," he said, his eyes glinting like newly forged steel. "Get rid of him."

"Just like that?" she mocked.

"Just like that."

She yanked her arm away and started for the stairs. "Don't hold your breath!"

He was leaning over the rail, watching her descend. "It's not *my* breath I intend to hold on to," he said suggestively.

Denver McLean had to be the most despicable man on earth!

And you love him.

"Fool!" she ground out, stalking toward the kitchen, her steps echoing through the old house with the same ring as Denver's amused laughter.

Chapter Eight

Mitchell was waiting. The heels of his boots propped on one chair, he leaned back in another and cradled a cup of coffee between his hands.

"Where's McLean?" he asked when Tessa entered.

Much as she wanted to, she couldn't lie. "He's here," she replied, keeping her voice low.

"In the house?"

"I think so."

Mitchell swore roundly, twisting so that he could see his sister.

Hoping beyond hope that Mitchell wouldn't notice her swollen lips or flushed cheeks, Tessa poured herself a cup of coffee with unsteady hands. "How's Dad?"

"How do you think he is? He told me what happened in the barn." Mitchell's green eyes darkened dangerously and deep lines grooved his forehead.

"Dad shouldn't drink so much," Tessa said, taking the chair across from her brother. Placing her elbows on the table, she sipped from her cup, but didn't taste the coffee.

"Who's gonna tell him? You?"

"Maybe."

"Why? You've tried before. Nothing changed."

"I know, but tonight was different. He dropped the bottle, the whiskey sprayed all over the floor. If he'd been smoking, God only knows what would've happened."

"Dad doesn't smoke in the barn."

Tessa gritted her teeth. "What if he forgets? If he's had one drink too many?"

"When has that ever happened?"

Tessa swallowed back the cold lump of betrayal that formed in her throat. "Maybe seven years ago."

Mitchell's feet dropped to the floor. "No way." His green eyes squinted indignantly as he scanned her face and his jaw became granite-hard. "Don't tell me McLean's got your thinking all turned around," he whispered. Shoving a lock of wheat-blond hair off his forehead, he let out a long, low whistle and shook his head. "Well, I'll be," he murmured sadly. "You're falling for him again, aren't you?"

"I am not."

"Oh, no?" His gaze dropped to her lips, so recently kissed, then traveled a knowing path to the scarlet creeping steadily up her neck. His jaw slackened. "Come on, Tessa, don't do this. Not again. McLean's no good. You and I both know it. I was there to pick up the pieces, remember?"

Tessa would never forget how good Mitchell had been, how he'd helped her battle the numbing cold that had settled upon her when she'd finally accepted the fact that Denver had left her. "If Denver's so bad," she asked, her spine stiffening, "why all the friendly talk at the table tonight?"

"He's the boss," Mitchell said simply. "I don't like it, but there it is."

Sighing, she leaned against the wall. "You sound just like Dad."

"I'm just trying to get through the next few weeks, then I'm out of here," he reminded her. "School starts the end of September. I may not like McLean, but I'm trying not to ruffle his feathers—which, by the way, was your advice." His lips tightened and sadness stole into his gaze. "Besides, I'm just trying to get along with the bastard—you're on the verge of having an affair with him."

"Don't be ridiculous." She wanted to slap him and shout that a love affair with Denver McLean was the last thing on her mind, but Mitchell had already guessed the truth. She cleared her throat. "Not that it's any of your business."

"I saw enough of his kind in the Army. A different girl in every city." She started to protest but he held up one hand, palm out. "Sure, you're here and available. So he's interested."

"I am not 'available.'"

Mitchell's face grew taut, as if he could read something new in her gaze. "Oh, God, Tess, don't tell me you've been saving yourself for him."

"I'm not telling you anything! What happens between Denver and me is between us."

Mitchell looked sick. "I just don't want to see you make a fool of yourself again. Don't you remember how much he hurt you? How he left without one word? How he and Colton accused Dad of murder? *Murder!*"

"No one actually said—"

"If it hadn't been for John McLean, Dad would have been strung up by his heels. Colton and Denver would have seen to it."

"But it didn't happen, did it? John gave Dad a chance."

"And now you're giving Denver one." Mitchell's hands were actually shaking when he shoved his hair from his eyes. "I can't tell you what to do, Tessa. I never could. But for God's sake, be careful. I wouldn't trust Denver McLean any more than I would a nest of rattlesnakes."

"I'll remember that."

Mitchell scraped his chair back. "While you're remembering, don't forget that McLean's been in L.A. a long time. You think he's been without a woman all that time?"

"I don't really care."

One golden eyebrow arched as Mitchell said, "No? Well, think about it, Tessa. All of a sudden, he's interested in you. So what happened to the past seven years? Why hasn't he called, written or stopped by? All that time while his uncle was dying, he didn't so much as write one goddamn note."

"He didn't know about John."

"He wasn't too interested, was he?"

Tessa wanted to defend Denver but didn't. What was the point? Mitchell's mind was set. He couldn't believe Denver capable of any kind of compassion or feelings. In Mitchell's opinion, Denver had abandoned his uncle. But John had kept the secret of his heart condition to himself and a few close friends, all of whom were sworn not to tell Denver or Colton. Keeping that secret vow had been easy. Colton seemed to have fallen off the face of the earth, and Denver hadn't been interested in anything or anyone on the ranch. So John had died alone. And Mitchell was condemning Denver.

"As I said, I can deal with Denver."

"I hope so, Tess. I hope to God you can!" He found his hat and jammed it onto his head. Turning on his heel, he was through the back door before she had a chance to argue.

Denver twisted a pencil between his fingers. Through the open study window, he heard the back door slam shut and Mitchell's boots stomping across the yard. A few seconds later an engine sputtered, caught and roared to life. Gears ground and gravel sprayed as Mitchell tore down the drive.

Denver knew that Tessa and Mitch had been arguing, probably over him. Snatches of their conversation had filtered through the old house, and he could guess the rest. Mitchell didn't trust him—didn't like him involved with Tessa.

Denver didn't blame Mitch. Hell, he didn't want to be involved with Tessa himself. But ever since setting eyes on her again in the barn that first night, he'd been compelled to be as near her as possible.

Night after night, he had told himself to forget that she was only a short walk down the hall, that if he played his cards right, she would eventually make love to him and that, if he could control his emotions, he'd be able to satisfy himself with her and walk away again.

His pencil snapped in two. Guilt tore a hole in his heart. He'd felt her respond, knew that it was only a matter of time before he could seduce her. And now, when he was certain of victory, he didn't want it, couldn't bear to see the hurt in her eyes when he left her again.

The other evening at the creek had been telling. He could have made love to her and been done with it, except that he couldn't hurt her. And now, he was looking forward to taking her back to Venice. For what? A day? A week? A lifetime? He didn't know. But he was sure of one thing. Tessa hadn't betrayed him all those years before—she couldn't have. She wasn't involved in her father's scheme to ruin the McLeans. Or else she was one hell of an actress. Her indignation and pain seemed real enough, and he believed her.

He wasn't so sure about Mitch or Curtis. But Tessa, he felt, hadn't been involved, even innocently, in the fire.

So now he wanted her—more fiercely even than he had seven years ago. Desire was running at a fever pitch, and he wasn't sure how much longer he could keep it in check.

Clenching his jaw so hard it ached, he reached for a new pen and stared down at the figures on the profit and loss statement lying open on the desk. But the typed pages couldn't hold his attention, and he wondered how he'd get through another long night just three doors down the hall from the only woman who could stir his blood to a fever pitch.

He heard her walking overhead, knew she was probably undressing for her bath. When the old pipes groaned loudly, he closed his eyes, envisioning her naked, her strawberry-blond hair spilling down her back, her skin pink from the hot water, her eyes glassy in relaxation. Her breasts would swell gently at the waterline, her nipples erect little buttons pointing proudly above the lapping water.

He could imagine his tongue stroking those proud little peaks, the hot water touching his lips as he suckled. Her fingers would twine in his hair and with one hand slowly dipping through the waves of warm liquid, sliding past the silky skin covering her ribs and the tight muscles of her abdomen, he'd ravish her slowly. Touching that private nest of fine reddish hair at the apex of her legs, he'd tell her of the nights he'd lain awake wanting her, the years he'd wished she had warmed his bed.

Smiling, Tessa would toss her head back, moaning softly, her hair floating around her as he gently parted her thighs, teasing that special little bud until she was writhing and wrapping her arms around his neck, dragging him into the water with her, begging him to make love to her and never stop.

A quiet rap on the door startled him. He had to stretch his legs and shift on his buttocks to ease the swelling that pressed hard against his jeans. "What?" Damn, but his voice sounded unnatural and husky.

Tessa pushed the door open and poked her head inside. Her fingers were wrapped around the edge of the wood, but she didn't enter. Denver used every ounce of control he possessed not to fly out of the chair and tear that silky pink wrapper off her body. Seeing the wet strands of her hair, knowing how soft and yielding her flesh was beneath the quickly donned robe, he could think of nothing more than giving in to the sweet temptation she was so innocently offering.

"I just wanted to warn you that we're out of hot water— I'll have the element on the tank checked in the morning."

"Thanks," he said, hoping to appear busy as he leaned over the desk. Then, unable to resist, he flashed her a lazy smile as he glanced up at her. "I think if I take a shower tonight, it should be cold, don't you?"

"Whatever you want." But she smiled.

He propped both elbows on the desk and rotated his pen between his hands. "What I want has nothing to do with the temperature of the water around here."

"Oh." She bit her lower lip and seemed about to leave when a mischievous light sparkled in her eyes. "Does this mean I should lock my door tonight?"

"Don't tease me, Tessa," he warned with a wicked grin.

"Wouldn't dream of it," she said, chuckling, her lips curving softly.

Denver's throat tightened and the heat in his loins grew. What was she doing here, flirting so outrageously with him? "It's a good thing I'm a gentleman," he said gruffly, and she had the audacity and lack of common sense to laugh, a merry tinkling sound in the old, creaky house.

"You? A gentleman? You couldn't prove it by me," she quipped before ducking back through the doorway.

Denver couldn't stop himself. Feeling as if he were seven years younger, he was on his feet in an instant. He fairly flew across the room, yanking open the door so hard it crashed against the wall and hearing Tessa's laughter ring through the house, he saw just the hem of her wrapper as she hurried up the stairs.

Knowing he was going to hate himself later, he took the steps two at a time and landed on the second floor just in time to hear a door close and a lock click soundly. So she thought she could tease him and get away with it, did she? he thought, smiling inwardly.

At the door to his parents' room, he knocked softly.

"Go away," Tessa said, but she couldn't stop the giggles that erupted from her throat.

"Open up."

"No way." She backed across the room.

"Do I have to break it down?"

"Don't be silly—"

His foot crashed into the door and she laughed. "Denver, don't—this is crazy. Be reasonable—"

Bang! The door wobbled, and he gave it one last shot, the wood splintering away from the casing as his boot crashed against it. His eyes gleamed, and a smile tugged at the corner of his lips. "Reasonable?" he repeated. "The original, 'insufferable, arrogant bastard'—wasn't that what you called me?"

"You deserved it."

"That and more, I suspect," he admitted, still smiling. Surveying the damage to the door, he asked, "Did you really think you could lock me out?" His voice was low and seductive, but his eyes crinkled at the corners.

Tessa swallowed hard. The backs of her calves met the mattress. "I—I didn't think I'd have to." He was teasing, she could see the amusement in his gaze. But, despite the playful glimmer in his eyes, his jaw was rock hard, the cords in his neck visible.

He took a step into the room, his silhouette dark against the light in the hall. His gaze slid slowly from her face to her throat and the wet ringlets that coiled at her neck, then to the delicate circle of bones at the base of her throat, and lower still.

Tessa's nipples hardened, thrusting against the thin wrapper, visible in the half-light. The lighthearted playfulness seeped out of the room, replaced by an electricity that seemed to crackle between them.

"What kind of game are you playing, Tessa?" he whispered hoarsely, moving slowly toward her.

Tessa's heart thundered, and she licked her lips nervously. "I'm not—"

"Like hell." He stopped mere inches in front of her. "Here we are alone, and you come down to tell me something stupid like we're out of hot water—"

"We are!"

"For God's sake, you could have worn something more than this!" He flipped two fingers under the lapel of her wrapper, his skin grazing hers. She sucked in her breath. The fun-loving light in his eyes had fled, but his hands didn't move. The seductive warmth of his fingertips pressed lightly against her skin. "Don't you have any idea what you're doing to me?" he rasped.

"Probably about the same as you're doing to me."

His fingers wound around her lapel. "Don't tease me, Tessa," he repeated.

"I'm not," she vowed.

His hand slid along the lapel, between her breasts to rest at the belt cinched around her waist. She melted inside. Liquid heat swirled deep at her center as his fingers rested feather light against her abdomen. "You want me?" he asked.

Closing her eyes, she leaned against him. "Yes."

A muscle throbbed in his forehead, but his fingers worked against the knot.

"I—I—only wish I didn't," she admitted as the robe parted. His gaze wandered recklessly down the gap.

"Why?" His hand caressed her abdomen.

"Because it complicates things—ooh!"

He slid his hand around her waist, pulling her against him as he lowered his head and his lips slanted over hers. His tongue slid easily between her teeth, touching lightly, exploring and plundering sweetly as she wound her arms around his neck.

"Sometimes the best things in life are complicated," he whispered, his breath as ragged as her own as he pushed against her. Tessa lost her balance and together they tumbled onto the bed. "Oh, Tessa," he murmured, kissing her lightly from her forehead to her lips, "why couldn't I forget you? Why the hell couldn't I forget you?"

Tears of happiness filled her eyes. "I—I don't know," she murmured.

His hands tangled in her hair and his lips brushed slowly against her throat, softly stroking her sensitive skin. Aching inside, she quivered beneath him as he pushed the robe from her shoulders and stared for a minute at her breasts, straining upward, inviting him with their rosy-crested peaks.

He stroked one gently. It puckered, and he groaned, moving his hand in sensual circles, staring down at her in fascination.

"Touch me," he whispered, shaping her mouth with his again.

She fumbled with the buttons of his shirt and quickly shoved the soft cotton down his arms to bunch at his wrists. He flung the unwanted garment across the room and lay over her, his bare chest rigid.

Swallowing against a desert-dry throat, she reached upward. Her fingers moved gently along the length of his ribs, tracing a path so slowly through his swirling black hair that he groaned and closed his eyes.

She hesitated at the waistband of his jeans, and he pulled her to him, slashing his mouth over hers, his hands splaying against her bare back as she fumbled with the zipper. Once the zipper was down, he kicked off his jeans and, naked at last, rubbed gently against her. He kissed her face, her cheeks, her throat, moving slowly downward, his lips teasing as he played with her nipple.

Her blood pumped furiously in her veins, and she writhed against him as he took one breast into his mouth, laving it with his tongue.

Heat roiled deep inside her. She kissed his shoulders and chest, tasted the salt from the sheen of perspiration coating his body. He kissed her again and again, whispering her name as his tongue touched and stroked.

I love you, she thought, aching with want.

He groaned and moved over her. "Is it safe?" he whispered into her ear.

"S-safe?" she murmured, not understanding.

"You know—safe." He took in a deep shuddering breath and levered himself up on one elbow. "Protected?"

"Protected?" she rasped. "As in against pregnancy?"

A muscle throbbed near his temple.

Tears filled her eyes. Hot little drops of shame. How could he think she'd been with other men? "There's never been anyone but you."

"No one?" His blue eyes stared down at her in disbelief.

Dying inside, crumbling apart bit by bit, she choked out, "And especially not John." Mortified, she tried to roll away from him, but he pressed her firmly back onto the mattress. His hands clamped over her wrists, holding her close.

"It doesn't matter," he vowed.

"Of course it does, Denver," she cried. "It matters a lot. To you. To me. Ever since you got here, you've been insinuating I slept with your uncle, for God's sake. Your *uncle!* How could you think, even for a second, that I'd—I'd—" She shuddered.

Denver wanted to believe her. She could see it in his eyes. Staring up at him from the tangled cloud of red-gold framing her face, her hazel eyes leveled on him, she knew he wanted to believe her.

"I think you'd better leave," she said slowly, trying to deny the want that still caused her limbs to tingle, her eyes to shine.

"It's too late for that, Tessa," he whispered, kissing her neck, letting his lips linger against her sensitive skin. "I can't go now."

"Then, please, Denver. Please trust me. There's never been anyone but you."

"You don't have to—"

"I would never lie! Not about this!"

"I believe you, Tess," he whispered hoarsely, releasing her wrists. His fingers slid up her arms, across her back, tracing the curve of her spine before he cupped her buttocks.

"I—I've only been with you."

He groaned, a deep, primal sound of pain and pleasure as he kissed her again, his lips crashing down on hers with a need so urgent she couldn't resist. Her hands moved across his shoulders, feeling each firm muscle before slowly sliding down his arms.

When Denver guided her fingers lower still, she didn't resist, and her feather-light touches stoked fires already raging deep in his loins as he moved easily over her and parted her legs.

"No regrets?" he whispered, poised over her.

She swallowed but shook her head and held his gaze. "No regrets," she vowed.

Slowly he plunged deep into the warmest part of her, sheathing himself in her womanhood.

Gasping, Tessa twined her arms around his neck. Her body moved in a magic rhythm with his and she couldn't stop. Not in her dreams had she felt this rapture, this soaring of her spirit. "Denver, oh, Denver," she whispered until she could no longer speak—could only feel. He pushed her higher and higher, upward to a sky as blue as his eyes.

"Denver!" she cried hoarsely as the sky seemed to splinter and her body jolted. He fell against her, breathing raggedly, drenched in sweat and whispering her name.

Tessa welcomed his weight. Her arms encircled his chest, and she pressed light kisses to his cheek. Unbidden tears formed in her eyes, hot little pools that drizzled down her cheeks.

Denver touched her lashes, wiping the silent drops away with his thumb. "Tears?" he asked.

"Tears, yes," she whispered, sniffing, "but no regrets."

He chuckled—a deep, rumbling sound—as he gathered her into his arms and held her. "Sleep," he murmured into her hair.

Closing her eyes, she nestled closer to him, listening to the breath moving in his lungs and the muffled beat of his heart. Tonight she would stay with him. Tomorrow she would face whatever the morning might bring. Even if it meant following him to Los Angeles.

Chapter Nine

Morning shadows played across the room. Tessa opened one eye and found Denver staring at her. His eyes were as blue as a clear mountain stream, his hair rumpled and black, the lines in his face less severe than they had been. He'd kicked himself free of the sheet, and he lay completely naked across the bed. Sunlight streaked his skin, gilding the firm ripple of his muscles.

"About time you woke up."

"Mmm." She stretched. "What time is it?"

"Early."

"And you're awake?" she teased, glancing at the clock.

"I wasn't. But this ravishing blonde kept kicking me and trying to push me out of bed."

She grinned impishly. "Maybe you didn't satisfy her."

White teeth flashed against his dark jaw. "Maybe I didn't," he growled, rolling over so quickly, she didn't have time to escape. "Maybe I should try again."

She giggled as his mouth descended on hers. "Denver, stop," she cried, gasping for air and laughing all at once.

"No way. You threw down the gauntlet, and I'm accepting the challenge."

Wiggling, she tried to squirm away from him, but the task proved impossible. Just when she slid one of her legs out from under him, he captured her again, pinning her against the sheets and grinning wickedly.

"Let me up!"

"Give?" he taunted.

"No—never," she gasped.

"Glad you haven't changed, Tess." With her wrists bound over her head by his hands, and her legs immobile under his weight, he touched the tip of his tongue to her lips, rimming her mouth leisurely.

"You're—"

"What?"

"Incorrigible!" she said, for lack of another word. Her mind was spinning and her blood had already turned molten. His tongue flicked in and out of her mouth quickly, darting and parrying, touching but not lingering. "We—we've got to get up," she whispered, but already her traitorous body was arching closer to his, her hips thrusting upward, demanding more of this delicious torment.

"Why?"

"Dad—and Mitchell. They'll be here any minute—"

"So you give, right?"

"No!"

His eyes darkened seductively. "Good."

She could see the cords highlighting his shoulder muscles, the washboard of his flat abdomen, the soft hair clinging to his legs. He touched first his tongue and then his lips to the tip of one breast and she groaned low in her throat.

Tessa writhed beneath him, but her struggle was not to break free, but to close the gap that separated their bodies. He rubbed against her, molding his hips to hers, letting her feel how much he wanted her.

Her throat was hot and swollen, desire a living thing, stalking through her blood, hungry and wild. Only this one man could satisfy her. She realized with sudden, time stopping clarity that she loved him more than she had all those years ago.

His lips found hers again and she knew that he'd lost all self-control. His hands slid down her arms, caressing her skin. The game of wills was over.

She sucked in her breath as he thrust into her. The lava within her roiled, spreading through her limbs, moving faster and faster, hot and liquid at her very center. Her soul seemed to burst in a glorious explosion of passion that rocked the earth.

"Don't leave me," she cried, arching upward to be closer to him, her fingers digging into the firm muscles of his shoulders.

"Right here, love," he vowed, his hands on her hips as he spilled himself in her. "Tessa, oh, God, Tessa." His arms surrounded her. His breath was ragged against her skin, his lips still moving as he murmured her name over and over.

If only nothing would ever change, she thought dreamily. *If only Denver and I could stay here, entwined, bound as man and woman forever. If only we could shut out the rest of the world.*

Slowly, as the minutes ticked by, Tessa shed her cloak of afterglow and the passion-dusted dreams of a woman desperately in love. "I have to get up," she said reluctantly.

Denver's arms tightened around her, but she slid quickly from his grasp.

"Why?" He glanced up at her from the bed, and she almost changed her mind. The rumpled sheets, the scent of lovemaking lingering in the air and the misty light of dawn stealing into the room were hard to push aside.

"One of us has to keep up appearances," she decided.

"We're adults—"

"I know." She was already braiding her hair. "And I'm not ashamed. But let's not announce the fact that we spent the night together—at least not yet."

"You'd rather hide like a teenager caught in the backseat?"

"I'd rather keep my private life private." She snapped the braid into place and pulled on a clean denim skirt and cotton sweater. "I'll deal with Dad and Mitch when I'm ready." Besides, she thought to herself, what would she tell them—that she'd fallen into bed with Denver McLean? That she was in the middle of an affair—a one-night stand—what? How could she explain that despite all the accusations and lies, regardless of the fact that he'd left her without a word, she loved him so desperately that she would rather have one night alone with him than salvage her pride?

"I wouldn't mind breakfast in bed," he said, watching as she tugged on her boots.

"In your dreams." But she laughed.

"Eggs Benedict, fresh grapefruit, sectioned of course—"

"Of course," she mocked.

"Toast with honey, coffee and—"

"And this!" Snatching a pillow that had fallen to the floor, she hurled it across the room and smack into Denver's chest. Before he could exact any retribution, she slipped into the hall. "Fresh grapefruit!" she repeated, laughing as she clambered down the stairs. "You wish!" She knew her cheeks were flushed and her eyes were sparkling outrageously as she entered the kitchen, but she didn't care. Though she half expected her father to be seated at the table with the newspaper spread in front of him, she squared her shoulders.

Luckily no one had arrived yet. She managed to put on the coffee, snap some toast into the toaster and melt butter in the frying pan by the time Denver sauntered down the stairs.

"I guess I should've waited," he said, standing behind her and slipping his arms around her waist.

"For what?"

"To be served, of course."

She cracked an egg in the pan and grinned. "And you would've waited till hell freezes over."

Chuckling, he drew her close, his hands familiar and warm as they spread across her denim-draped abdomen. "I suppose I would have."

"Right!" Dear God, she sounded as breathless as a sultry summer night. "Unless you have something better to do, you can pour the coffee and butter the toast."

"I do have something better to do." He kissed her throat and ear. "Something much more important."

Her chest constricted. "I think it'll wait."

"Slave driver," he grumbled, but unwillingly released her to search in the cupboard for coffee cups.

"Second shelf," she said, catching his glance. In that one heart-stopping moment, she read the love deep in his eyes.

"Thanks."

Swallowing a thick lump forming in her throat, she turned back to the bacon sizzling noisily in the skillet.

They were just finishing the meal when Milly walked in, her arms laden with two sacks of groceries. "You found somethin' to eat, did ya?" she asked, glancing at the table.

"Plenty," Denver replied.

Tessa helped Milly unload the sacks. "By the way," Milly said, stacking two loaves of bread in the bread box, "that attorney called yesterday afternoon."

Denver's head snapped up. "Ross Anderson?"

Milly nodded. "He said that he was sure they'd found your brother."

Tessa's heart nearly stopped. "Colton?"

"Where?" Denver asked.

Milly shrugged. "Said you knew about it."

Dumbfounded, Tessa stared at Denver. Why hadn't he mentioned that Colton had been located?

"I knew some private investigator *thought* he might have found Colton in Northern Ireland. But since I hadn't heard anything in days, I figured he was wrong."

"Doesn't seem that way," Milly said, glancing from Tessa

to Denver and back again. "He said he'd call back tomorrow. He's in court today."

"Great," Denver grumbled, his countenance changing. "Did he say if Colton was returning?"

"Nope. That was it."

The phone jangled, and Milly answered it, then handed the receiver to Tessa. "Nate Edwards."

Tessa's nerves tightened. "Good morning," she said, forcing a smile into her voice.

"Same to you. I've been thinking, and I've decided I want the stallion and those two mares—the black and the chestnut."

"Both?" she repeated.

"If you're willing to sell."

She swallowed back the urge to tell him no, that she wanted to keep all three. "I am," she said, though a pain slashed deep into her heart.

"Good. Now, I know the mares are both with foal, and I'll buy 'em as such and keep the offspring, but if you'd rather, you can have the foals after they're weaned. I'll sell 'em back to you at a fair price."

"I'd appreciate that."

"I'll give you fifty thousand for the whole lot. I figure the stallion's worth twenty-five and the mares in their condition are between twelve and thirteen apiece."

She couldn't argue. She'd already decided that she wouldn't take less than forty; the extra ten thousand was a godsend.

"I'll give you a couple days to think on it."

"What was that all about?" Denver asked as Tessa slowly replaced the receiver.

"Nate Edwards has offered to buy Brigadier and the mares. It's enough money for the down payment on this place."

"And the rest?"

"The bank will loan the difference, I think," she said, sitting carefully in the nearest chair. Now that her dream was so close, almost in hand, she was scared.

"And Colton's been found." Denver didn't smile as he stared at her. "It looks, Ms. Kramer, as if you're on your way to owning a ranch." The words were said without malice, but there was an empty note in his voice. Denver finished his coffee, placed his dishes in the sink and turned toward the door. "I think I'll get cleaned up and drive into Helena. Maybe I can catch Ross when he gets out of court."

"I don't suppose you'd want company?" Tessa asked boldly.

His eyebrows shot up. "Don't you have things to do around here?"

She lifted a shoulder. "Mitch and Dad can handle everything. We may as well give them a trial run, don't you think?" she added, ignoring the quizzical look on Milly's face.

He grinned and drawled, "That might not be a bad idea. I'll be ready to go in about twenty minutes."

"I'll be waiting."

"And I'll tell your brother and father they're in charge," Milly said.

While Denver showered and changed, Tessa walked outside. The morning air was brisk, the grass still covered with dew. From his paddock, Brigadier whistled softly, tossing his head. Sunlight gilded his red coat as he hoisted his tail high in the air and raced around the fence with long, sweeping strides.

"You know this is killing me, don't you?" Tessa asked, delving in her pocket for a bit of apple. As the big stallion nipped the morsel from her palm, she wrestled with her conscience. Caught in a vicious circle, she found no answers. If she didn't sell her best horses, she wouldn't have money to buy the ranch, and if she couldn't buy the ranch, someone else would. Then she and her animals would have to find a new place—a place they could afford, a place that might not be big enough to support her growing herd. Besides, Nate Edwards was a good horseman and he'd treat her horses well.

But the crux of the problem was Denver. As it always had

been. If she bought the ranch from him, he'd surely leave. If she didn't buy the McLean place, he might stay longer, but only for a while. Then he'd be forced to return to L.A. For good. Without her. She had agreed to a weekend trip to California, but not a lifetime in L.A., which, she reminded herself, he hadn't asked her to share.

Her brows drew together in vexation. "Damned if you do, damned if you don't," she murmured, eyeing Brigadier fondly. There was just no perfect answer.

"Ready?" Denver called as he crossed the yard.

Tessa whirled and her breath caught in her throat. Clean-shaven, his hair neatly combed, he was dressed in a gray business suit—no longer the man she loved, but a stranger—an engineer who owned a firm of his own in Los Angeles.

"As ready as I'll ever be," she quipped. She walked to Denver's rental car just as her father and Mitchell drove in.

Mitchell was out of the cab before the truck had rolled to a complete stop. "Going somewhere?" he asked.

"Into Helena. It looks as if Colton's finally surfaced," Tessa explained.

"Has he?" Mitchell's lips tightened. "I suppose he's coming back here, too?"

"We don't know yet," Denver cut in.

Tessa caught the anger in her brother's eyes, and she understood it. It had been Colton McLean's horrid words that had turned Denver away from her. Colton hadn't held his tongue after the fire. In his outrage and fury, his false accusations had cut deep, wounding everyone in her family.

She didn't blame Mitch for hating him. But soon it would be over, and soon the McLeans would be out of this part of Montana. At that particular thought, her stomach churned. After these past few weeks, she wondered if she would find any joy in life without Denver. "We'll work things out," she said to Mitch.

Shoving his hat on his head, he muttered, "I wonder."

Denver's lips drew tight. "Let's go."

Tessa slid into the passenger side of the car, turning a stiff shoulder to the anger smoldering in her brother's gaze.

"When Colton gets back here, the fireworks are really going to start," she predicted, slanting a glance at Denver as he drove down the long lane and turned onto the main road.

Denver's answer was a grimace.

By midmorning the rolling hills had given way to the city of Helena. Denver drove toward the heart of the city and past the copper-domed capitol building before parking near the courthouse.

"You're going to wait for Ross here?" she asked, eyeing the building.

"Maybe. But first we'll check with his secretary; find out when he's supposed to be out of court. Then we'll have lunch."

He linked his fingers through hers and started across the street. A few minutes later they were standing in front of a huge oak desk in the reception area of a steel-and-glass building. The names of O'Brien, Simmons and Taft were mounted on the wall in chrome letters, and a petite woman with shining copper hair and a wide, friendly smile had waved them into the high-backed chairs in the waiting room; "Mr. Anderson's in court, but his secretary is in."

Within minutes a tall svelte blonde with striking dark eyebrows and a midnight-blue dress swept through the doors. Her glossy lips curved at the sight of Denver. "Mr. McLean," she said, extending her hand, her silver bracelet jangling a little. "I'm sorry but Ross isn't in right now."

Denver took her hand for a second, then let it fall. "This is Tessa Kramer," he said quickly.

"Nancy Pomeroy," the blonde replied.

"Nice to meet you," Tessa said woodenly.

Denver explained, "Tessa runs the ranch."

If that surprised Nancy, she managed to keep her face expressionless.

Denver added, "Yesterday Ross called and said he'd located my brother. I wasn't at the house and didn't get the message until this morning."

"And you're anxious to know what's going on," Nancy guessed. "I don't blame you."

"When will Ross be back?"

"Not until late afternoon."

Denver scowled, but there wasn't much he could do, Tessa realized. "We'll be back," he said, taking Tessa's hand again. "Don't let him slip away."

Nancy nodded, her brown eyes twinkling behind thick, mascara-blackened lashes. "I'll tie him to the desk if I have to."

"I'd appreciate it," Denver said with a lazy smile.

Inwardly, Tessa groaned. She saw the look of playful longing in Nancy's eyes and the easy response of Denver's grin. How many other women did Denver smile for? How many pairs of eyes had gazed longingly into his? Los Angeles was a big city—much larger than Helena—and so near Hollywood, it was practically oozing with beautiful women, actresses and models.

"Something wrong?" Denver asked as he shouldered open the glass door and squinted against the sunlight reflecting on the sidewalk and windows of the buildings lining the street.

"Nothing serious," she replied, fighting to repress the jealousy that coiled around her heart when she considered the fact that Denver might have a dozen women waiting for him in Los Angeles.

"You're worried about Colton, aren't you?"

"That's part of it, I suppose." It wasn't really a lie. Facing Colton wasn't going to be a bed of roses.

"And the rest?" There was a break in traffic and he pulled gently on her hand. They jaywalked across the street to a park.

"I was just wondering about your life in L.A."

"What about it?"

"I won't fit in. Not even for a weekend."

"Sure you will." They were walking more slowly now, the branches of the shade trees stirring lazily in the warm summer breeze. The noise of the traffic faded away. Children scampered down the worn paths to a playground and dogs bounded across the grass. She had to ask the question that had been with her ever since seeing Nancy Pomeroy's response to him. "Isn't there a woman in L.A.?"

"Thousands of them."

"You know what I mean."

He laughed loudly, startling a bird in the lacy branches overhead. The jay flapped noisily away. "A woman," he repeated, amused, "as in a lover?"

It sounded so childish. She couldn't meet his eyes. "It doesn't matter," she lied.

"Or mistress? Or fiancée?" he prodded.

"It was just a question," she retorted, angry with herself. "Don't make a federal case of it."

One side of his mouth curved upward, and he pulled on her wrist, tugging her off the path and around the broad trunk of a maple tree. "What do you think?" he asked, pinning her against the scratchy bark, his eyes delving deep into hers.

"I think it would be stupid of me to believe that an attractive man, who's not quite over the hill—"

"Over the hill?" he hooted, his blue eyes filled with mirth. "Me?"

"I said 'not quite over the hill'. Anyway, it's very possible that there's some woman waiting for you back in L.A."

"Not one," he corrected, touching the line of her jaw familiarly. "Dozens."

"You're impossible!"

"That's why they all love me." His arms were on either side of her head, effectively imprisoning her against the bole while the wind sifted through the leaves overhead.

"Be serious!"

"I am." His lips, thin and sensual, twisted in amusement. "Don't you know me better than to think I'm ready to bed any woman who shows some interest?"

"I used to think so."

"Don't you still? Didn't last night mean anything?" he asked, his smile fading as he touched the end of her braid with his fingers.

"It meant a lot. To me."

"And to me." His breath was warm against her face, his gaze sincere. She could see the pinpoints of light in his eyes, the perspiration beading on his brow.

She swallowed hard, and he noticed the movement, his gaze shifting to her throat. "I can't lie and say there haven't been other women, Tess. Seven years is a long time. But there haven't been all that many, and none of them, *none,* can hold a candle to you."

Absurdly, she wanted to cry. But she fought her tears. His lips rubbed lightly over hers. She wrapped her arms around his neck, mindless of the mothers with young children in strollers, the adolescents on bikes, the older men and women sitting together, shoulders touching, on park benches.

His arms circled her and he held her close, the kiss deepening, his lips as hot and hungry as they had been the night before. When he finally lifted his head, his breathing was ragged, but a smile tugged at the corners of his mouth. "Not that your jealousy isn't flattering," he said.

"Jealousy?" she retorted, wanting to deny what was so patently obvious.

"Admit it, Tess, you were jealous!"

"I hate jealous women."

"And I love them." He laughed again and dragged her from the relative privacy of the trees. "How about some lunch?"

"You're changing the subject."

"I'm hungry."

Cajoled out of her worries by his good mood, she laughed. "I am, too."

"Good. If things haven't changed too much, I remember a great little café with a view of Mount Helena."

The café was long gone. But they did find a small Italian restaurant not far from the courthouse. As the waiter brought pasta and Chablis, Denver sat across from Tessa at the table and clinked his glass to hers. "Here's to . . . a long and successful business arrangement."

Tessa almost choked. "Business arrangement?"

"Umm. You said you wanted to buy the ranch."

"I do."

"Well, now that Colton's been found and you've sold your horses—you have sold them, haven't you?"

Swallowing with difficulty, she set down her glass. "Nate's made a generous offer," she admitted.

"Then all that's left is to draw up a contract, sign it and take it to the bank. Right?"

Suddenly feeling depressed, she nodded. "If Colton agrees."

"And if he doesn't—you still want my half?"

"Yes," she said firmly, though inside she was dying a little. All her dreams of owning the ranch, of being mistress of the McLean spread, seemed to shrivel in front of her very eyes. Without Denver, the ranch meant so little. She shoved her fettuccine around on her plate and tried to eat. Her appetite had disappeared.

"But first you have to pay off your bet," he reminded her.

"And then what happens? When everything's signed, sealed and delivered, will you just head back to California?"

"What else?" He eyed her quietly, sipping his wine, his jaw thrust forward.

"Nothing, I guess," she whispered, then gave herself a quick mental kick. She wasn't about to let go without a whimper.

"You said last night was something special," she said, meeting his gaze again.

"It was."

"But it doesn't have to go on forever, is that it?"

"I didn't say—"

Her anger sparked. "Were we just 'experimenting' again, Denver? Seeing if it was as good as when we were kids?"

"What're you getting at?"

"Last night was more than a one-night stand. At least for me. I didn't wait seven years just to be used and tossed aside again!"

A muscle jumped in his jaw. "I never intended to use you."

"But it happened." She felt her cheeks flame, but she couldn't control the rage and hurt deep inside. "I don't want another affair, Denver," she snapped. "I had enough trouble living through the last one."

"You were only nineteen."

"And now I'm twenty-six, but my values haven't changed," she said angrily, tossing her napkin into her plate and stalking out of the restaurant. Outside the sun was blinding. She marched down the street, but Denver caught up with her on the second block, grabbed her hand and whirled her around.

"What do you want from me, Tessa? A marriage proposal?" he fumed.

Yes! "I'm not trying to manipulate you, Denver."

"Aren't you?"

She wanted to slap him and tell him to take his hands off her. But her dignity wouldn't allow this fight to be aired to all the good citizens of Helena. "Leave it alone, Denver," she said between clenched teeth, wrenching her arm away from him.

"That's the problem, Tess," he said, sighing. "I can't leave it alone. Just like I can't leave you alone. But, by the same token, I can't lie to you or promise you things that just won't happen."

"Look, you don't have to go on about this. I didn't ask you to marry me, did I?" She started up the street again and he kept up with her, stride for stride, until they reached the car. At that point she had to stop. The car was locked and there was nowhere she could run—no place she could hide.

"We need to talk," he growled, shoving his scarred hand through his ebony hair.

"Maybe we should've done more *talking* last night!"

Tense as a panther ready to strike, he paced from one end of the car to the other. "I just don't know what you want from me—"

"Denver?" Ross Anderson's voice boomed over the sound of traffic.

Denver's head jerked up. He watched in mild surprise as the wiry young attorney, briefcase tucked under one arm, dashed down the courthouse steps. "We'll discuss this later," he said from the corner of his mouth.

"Right." Tessa was disbelieving.

"Later!" Then, forcing a tight smile onto his face, he observed Ross zigzagging through the traffic.

"I called the office and Nancy said you were waiting for me," Ross said as he extended his free hand, "but I didn't think you'd be camping out on the courthouse steps."

"We weren't—we were just having a . . . discussion. Ross, I'd like you to meet Tessa Kramer. Tessa—Ross."

Ross grinned, his narrow face cracking with a smile. "I've heard a lot about you, Ms. Kramer. John McLean was one of your biggest fans." He offered his hand and Tessa shook it. But her gaze traveled past the expensive weave of his jacket to clash with the anger in Denver's eyes.

"John was good to me and my family. We miss him."

"Don't we all?" Ross shot a glance at Denver, whose lips had tightened until they were white.

"Have you heard anything else about Colton?" Denver demanded.

Ross reached into his pocket and withdrew a long, thin cigar. "Is that what this is all about?"

"Ms. Kramer, here, wants to purchase the ranch—all of it. We need to talk to my brother, then work out a purchase agreement. Since you're involved in the probate of his estate, I'd like you to iron out the details."

"If Colt agrees." Ross snapped his lighter over the end of his cheroot and puffed furiously, sending up a stream of small, blue clouds.

"Even if he doesn't, she wants my half."

Ross squinted thoughtfully through the smoke. "Unless Colt wants the entire place. There's a provision in John's will, you know. If one brother doesn't want his share, the other has the option to buy him out at fair market value."

Tessa's heart sank. Not only was she losing Denver to the bright lights of Los Angeles, but even if she did sell her horses and the bank approved her loan, Colton might want the place! Though he'd been overseas for years, he might want to quit his dangerous job, give up his wanderlust and settle back in the valley where his family had lived for generations.

"Colton won't want the ranch any more than I do," Denver said tightly. "He left right after the fire, too. Hasn't been back since."

"A man could change his mind when he owns the land."

"I didn't." Denver stared pointedly at Tessa.

"You're not your brother. Come on, we can talk more comfortably in my office."

Puffing smoke like a steam engine, Ross led the way, and

within minutes they were seated around his desk. "So you're here about Colton."

"Have you heard from him?" Denver asked, leaning back in his leather chair and eyeing the attorney.

Ross shook his head. "Not Colton himself. But the P.I. called again. He's sure the man he's seen is Colton—though his looks have changed. He just hasn't gotten close enough to talk to him yet. It's touchy, you know."

"Touchy?" Tessa asked. "How?"

"Dangerous. No one wants to blow Colt's cover," Denver explained, drumming his fingers on the arm of his chair.

"You make it sound like he's a spy."

"Close enough," Denver muttered. "Close enough."

"I don't know when we'll actually hear from Colton," Ross said, "but the investigator's supposed to call back in a few days. Hopefully he will have contacted him by then."

Denver's face muscles were tight. "Tell your man I want to talk to my brother."

"I'll try."

"And if by some fluke Colton himself calls, let him know what's going on; explain about John and the land. Let him know we have a buyer."

Ross scribbled himself a note and Tessa's name leaped off the clean yellow page.

"Maybe you shouldn't tell him who wants to buy," Denver decided, surveying Ross's notes.

"Why not?"

Denver glanced at Tessa. "He and the Kramers have never seen eye to eye."

Tessa's mouth went dry. Dealing with Denver's accusations had been bad enough. She couldn't imagine what Colton would say if and when he returned. No amount of arguing had changed his mind before he left Montana. She doubted anything would now.

Secretly Tessa had wondered if Colton had been behind
the accident. Though he was supposed to have been in town
with John when the blaze started, he hadn't been. John had
admitted as much later. And Colton had arrived at the ranch
quickly—just as the explosion had rocked through the stables.
However, she'd kept her thoughts to herself. Pointing fingers
without proof was a McLean trait, and she wasn't about to
lower herself to that level. But the thought of seeing Colton
again hung like a pall over her. First facing Colton—then
watching Denver leave for Los Angeles. Deja vu, she thought
wearily.

"—I'll let you know the minute I hear anything," Ross
was promising Denver.

"Good. Just make sure we don't put Colt in any jeopardy."
Denver stretched his arm toward Ross.

"I'll give it my best shot!" The wiry attorney shook
Denver's hand, but looked at Tessa. "Nice meeting you, Ms.
Kramer."

"You, too."

On the way home, she barely said a word to Denver. They
stopped for dinner at a restaurant owned by a young couple
who served "family-style" meals. The room was crowded,
the table big enough to hold four couples, which it did, but
there wasn't one bit of intimacy.

Tessa ate the chicken and dumplings and didn't taste a
bite. She couldn't think of anything save the fact that Denver
was planning to leave her again. Not that he'd ever promised
anything else, she knew. And there was some time left—time
to be shared here and in California. But the prospect of living
the rest of her life without him was more depressing than
she'd ever imagined. The past seven years she'd known that
somewhere, sometime, she'd see him again, but now it
seemed that once he left for Los Angeles, the only contact
she would have with him would be quarterly statements

about the ranch—property tax statements, income taxes and such—until he was completely bought out.

And what then? Would he return to the ranch whenever he wanted, to check up on her? Take her to bed for one night only to leave the next day? Her head was swimming, her eyes hot. She could barely breathe.

Shoving her chair away from the table, she scrambled to her feet. "I need some fresh air," she explained, not waiting for Denver's reaction. She struck out through the restaurant's front door and didn't stop until she was in the parking lot, breathing in huge gulps, mentally kicking herself for loving him.

She heard his footsteps thudding on the boards of the front porch. Before she could turn around, she felt his arms surround her waist, his breath on her nape. "I've been an ass," he decided, and she clenched her fists impotently.

She couldn't agree more. "This is all coming down too quickly. The ranch, Colton, you. It's not turning out like it was supposed to."

"No fairy-tale ending?" he mocked.

"I suppose I deserved that."

"What is it you want, Tessa?"

You, her heart thundered. *Just you!*

"If you want the ranch, I'll sell it to you. If you want Colton's share, I'll convince him you're the right buyer. If you need money, I'll loan it to you. Whatever it is that will make you happy . . ."

She tried not to shake, Her heart wrenched. "The ranch is all I've ever wanted," she whispered, her tongue tripping on the lie. *Tell him! Tell him you love him!* a part of her cried, but pride kept her silent.

"Then there's nothing to worry about. Let me handle Colton." He kissed the nape of her neck. A shiver darted quickly up her spine to linger at the spot where he'd brushed his lips across her skin.

"Let's go," she murmured.

Denver yanked viciously on the tie still knotted at his throat, then threw his jacket into the back seat. After rolling his sleeves over his forearms, he helped Tessa into the car, then slid behind the wheel.

For most of the drive, they didn't speak. The late afternoon sun descended slowly behind the rocky peaks to the west, streaking the sky in a blaze of pink and gold.

Tessa closed her eyes. She pushed her worries aside and leaned back in the seat, letting the heat of the day settle around her as Denver drove steadily north. Dusk had just shaded the sky when they passed her father's cottage and the lane to the McLean Ranch came into view.

"Almost home," Tessa murmured.

"Not yet." Denver said quietly. He stepped on the throttle, passing the lane.

"What're you doing?" Tessa asked, surprised.

He smiled crookedly. "I thought we deserved a detour." A quarter of a mile past the lane, he cranked hard on the wheel. The car responded, lurching onto the old silver mining road. Barely more than twin ruts in the bleached grass, the tracks curved, snaking along the banks of the Sage River and the Aldridge property before climbing the gentle slope of the surrounding foothills.

"Where're we going?" Tessa asked, though she had already guessed. This road led not only to the abandoned mine, but to the ridge where she and Denver had first made love. Nervously she reached for the handle of the car door, wrapping her fingers around the armrest.

The little car bumped and spun, leaving a cloud of dust. Denver had to flip on the lights as shadows lengthened stealthily through the trees. "I just wanted to see this place again."

"Nothing's changed," she said, her stomach knotting, her palms beginning to sweat. She'd been up to the ridge more times than she wanted to count, remembering how wonderful that afternoon had been before the smell of smoke and the crackle of flames had clouded the clear air and altered the course of their lives forever.

The road gave way to a clearing, and he parked, switching off the lights. Only the moon and stars illuminated the night, turning the dry grass opalescent. Two small shacks, sagging now from disuse, were the last reminders of the silver that had existed only in John McLean's dreams.

Denver climbed out of the car and stretched, rubbing his shoulder muscles.

Tessa joined him. "What is it they say about never going back?" she asked, hoping to sound lighthearted though her heart continued to beat unevenly.

"If *they're* talking about L.A., *they're* wrong." He strode swiftly through the stubble, ignoring the rambling blackberry vines and weeds clutching at his pants. He made his way up a short path to the ridge.

She scrambled after him. "I was talking about coming back here." A bramble pulled at her skirt, a branch tugged at her hair, but she closed the distance, catching Denver just at the edge of the cliff.

Majestic pines towered high overhead, their long needled branches soughing in the soft summer breeze. And the valley floor, in contrast to the dark trees, shifted restlessly under the moonlight. Cattle dotted the landscape, dark lumbering shapes against the moonlit grass. Its windows glowing with square patches of light, the main house was visible, as was the winding Sage River, a moon-washed ribbon reflecting a

wide canopy of twinkling stars. Far in the distance, the lights
of her father's house shone gold in an otherwise silvery night.

"How can you leave this place?" she wondered aloud.

He stared down at her. "It's not the land I'm leaving," he
said quietly. "Nor the work. Leaving the ranching life behind
is easy." His fingers were gentle on her arms. "What's hard
is leaving you."

Tessa's breath expelled in a rush. She could barely believe
her ears. And she wouldn't. Words were easy. Too easy. She'd
heard them before. "You don't have to leave."

"What I don't have to do is repeat a conversation we had
a long time ago."

Her heart squeezed wretchedly at the memories of their
arguments, long dead. Now, as before, nothing she could say
would stop him. He was willing to sell her this part of his
past, the dust, the trees, the stream and buildings, but he
couldn't, wouldn't, give her the one thing she wanted most—
his love.

Angry with herself for loving him when he didn't care,
she turned, unable to face him. She stared across the valley
floor. But he placed one finger under her chin and pushed it
upward, forcing her gaze to meet his. Her pulse trembled in
her throat, and before she could say a word, he lowered his
head and kissed her. Long and hard and hot, the kiss touched
the very deepest part of her soul. His tongue slid familiarly
past her teeth, his hands unwound her braid.

Her hair tumbled free in a twisted cloud that fell past her
shoulders.

She knew in her heart that she should stop him, but the
night and her senses were against her. She couldn't pull away
from him any more than she could stop breathing—or still
the wretched pounding beat of her heart.

Just once more, her mind screamed, drowning all her
doubts. *Just love me once more.*

As his weight pulled her downward, onto that very patch of ground where they'd made love so long ago, she didn't protest, but fell willingly, accepting his passion for what it was and meeting that delicious desire with her own driving needs.

For as long as he stayed, she would be with him. And she would cherish each moment even as she knew that as surely as the sun would come up in the morning, Denver would leave.

Chapter Ten

"I saw it happen," Mitchell said, as he and Tessa examined Brigadier in his stall the next day. The stallion's head hung low and he favored his right front leg. "He picked up a loose piece of gravel in the yard."

Tessa's brows drew into a worried frown. "Poor baby. Let's take a look." Tessa lifted the hoof, then moved quickly when Brigadier tried to nip her. "Hey, watch it!"

"I'll hold his head," Mitchell offered, stroking Brigadier's sleek neck. "I hope he doesn't turn up lame. That could spoil your deal with Nate Edwards."

"It doesn't matter," Tessa said sharply, her fingers running expertly along the edge of the stallion's tender hoof. Brigadier rolled his eyes and his ears flattened as she worked. "Looks like a bruised sole," she thought aloud. Brigadier snorted and jerked hard on the lead rope. "Find the toolbox and help me get this shoe off."

Together they removed the shoe and Tessa pared out the bruised area of the inner hoof. "I'll pack it with a poultice, but we'd better call Craig Fulton and have him take a look at it," Tessa said quickly.

Craig was a young veterinarian who lived on a ranch

nearby. He operated a clinic for large animals and house pets that was located on the outskirts of Three Falls.

"I'll call him," Mitchell offered.

"Good. I'll finish here."

Mitchell left the barn to phone the vet while Tessa cleaned the bruised area of Brigadier's hoof then packed it with a poultice. Once assured that the stallion was comfortable, she rubbed his jagged white blaze and handed him a piece of apple. The fruit was whisked out of her open palm before she had time to blink.

"Thank goodness you still have your appetite," she said, patting his soft muzzle before closing the gate to his stall behind her.

The barn door squeaked open and Tessa, expecting Mitchell, glanced over her shoulder. Denver! She'd left him less than an hour ago in the study, but her heart tripped at the sight of him.

Tall and masculine, he winked at her. "I thought I'd find you here."

Her pulse leaped.

Dressed in a gray sport coat, black slacks and a crisp white shirt, he was dashing and handsome and, unfortunately, looked as if he belonged in a high-rise office building in some huge city.

She, on the other hand, was wearing dusty jeans and a checked blouse. Not exactly haute couture.

"Brigadier's favoring his right foreleg. I think it's a bruised sole," she explained.

"I know. Mitch was on the phone in the kitchen."

"Eavesdropping?" she teased.

"About horse ailments? Hardly. I'm on my way back to Helena. Jim Van Stern called. He has some legal papers he wants Ross to draw up." He reached her and wrapped his arms comfortably around her waist. "I thought you'd like to join me." He flashed her a devilish grin and his blue eyes danced irreverently.

"I'd love to," she admitted. She wanted to be with him every minute of every day.

"Then do it," he whispered into her ear. "Just this once, indulge yourself. We could spend the night, order room service for dinner and never leave the hotel again."

"Now who's the dreamer?" she quipped, though she tingled inside.

He kissed her neck, his lips warm and inviting. "Come on, Tess."

More than anything she wanted to go with him. "You know I can't, not with Brigadier lame."

"The vet will take care of him."

She shook her head and toyed with the buttons on his shirt. "How about a rain check?"

One side of Denver's mouth lifted engagingly. "You've got it. How about tomorrow night?"

"You're willing to drive all the way to Helena again?"

His blue eyes twinkled. "For a night alone with you? You bet."

"We're alone here at night."

"It's not the same. Any minute I expect your dad or brother or Milly to show up and interrupt us." His lips pressed against her forehead. "I'd like to be alone with you where no one could find us for days."

A shiver of anticipation swept up her spine. "Sounds wonderful," she whispered. Denver lowered his head and kissed her softly on the lips. Responding, Tessa wound her arms around his neck just as Brigadier stuck his head over the stall gate and shoved her.

She lost her footing and fell heavily against Denver, who laughed in surprise.

"Someone's jealous," Denver observed. "Be careful, my friend," he said to the stallion, "this one's mine."

Brigadier tossed his great head, and Tessa felt a lump fill her throat. She rubbed the stallion's nose fondly. "I'm going to miss you," she said, her voice low.

"Then the sale is final?"

She nodded. "Nate plans to pick up Brigadier and the mares tomorrow."

As if understanding the conversation, Brigadier whinnied plaintively.

Denver's arms tightened around Tessa's waist. "You don't have to sell him, you know."

"I don't want to talk about it." She tried to extract herself, but Denver wouldn't let go.

"I know how fond you are of your horses."

"They're like family," she admitted.

"That's why you should keep them."

"Is this a way of getting out of selling the ranch to me?"

"I didn't say that. But maybe we could come up with some other way of financing the sale."

"I don't see how."

"I could waive the down payment—in effect loan the money to you without interest."

"And how would Colton feel about that?"

Denver's jaw hardened. "I'll deal with Colton, *if* I ever see him again."

Tessa considered her alternatives. Leaning against the power of Denver's chest, hearing the steady beat of his heart, feeling his breath stir her hair, she was just about willing to do anything he suggested. Except become beholden to him. "I don't think I should borrow money from you," she said softly. "People might get the wrong idea."

She felt him stiffen, saw a flash of anger in his eyes. "You mean the way some people might have gotten the wrong idea about you and John."

Her emotions, already strung tight, snapped. Tessa scrambled out of his arms. "That was different and you know it!"

"How?"

"I wasn't sleeping with John!" Bristling with injustice, she gave her hot temper free rein. "I thought we settled this."

"We have," he said tightly. "I just don't understand why you can work a deal with John and not with me."

"Because you and I—we're . . . *involved*."

"All the more reason to help each other."

"Not like this," she said. "I can't accept gifts from you, Denver, or loans without collateral."

"Why not?"

"Don't you know?" she asked in wonder. "Don't you realize that I don't want to be obligated to you—that I wouldn't want you obligated to me? You're the one who doesn't want any strings attached in this relationship. You're the one hell-bent to run back to L.A."

"I thought you were coming with me," he said slowly.

"That would only make it worse! I can't borrow money from you and then follow you like some moon-eyed calf to California! I no more belong on Rodeo Drive than—"

"*I* do in a hick town the size of Three Falls, Montana," he cut in, the edge in his voice sharp.

"You were born and raised here!"

"An accident of my birth."

She sucked in a swift, disbelieving breath. "Do you hate it here so much?"

He bit back the urge to say Yes! I hate this goddamned ranch and all the memories it brings—memories of pain and suffering and thick yellow smoke and flames. Instead he sealed his mouth shut. He didn't hate this valley or this ranch. His aversion to it was long over. But it wasn't the land that beckoned him. It was Tessa.

"I've got to leave," he said quietly, his face a mask. "You coming?"

Shaking her head, she said, "I'd better stay. The vet's probably already on his way."

"Then I'll see you tomorrow." He turned and walked quickly down the concrete corridor between the rows of stalls. Nearly colliding with Mitch in the doorway, he muttered a curse under his breath without breaking stride.

Mitch stared after him. "What was that all about?"

"Don't ask me."

Mitch frowned. "I am asking you. And you'd better tell me what's going on between the two of you."

"Nothing, Mitch."

"Sure."

"I told you—it's just business."

Mitch scowled, raking stiff fingers through his hair. "Okay, you win, Tess. Play it close to the vest. If you want Denver McLean, there's nothing I can say that will change your mind." His mouth compressed into a crooked smile. "I just hope he'll make you happy."

"I am happy," she said, turning back to Brigadier and changing the subject. "Did you call the vet?"

Mitch nodded. "Craig's busy. But his assistant's on her way."

"*Her* way?"

A slow grin spread across Mitchell's stubbled jaw. "That's right. Cassie Aldridge. Remember her?"

"How could I forget?" Tessa smiled faintly. Cassie was a couple of years younger than Tessa, and rumor had it, seven years before, that young Cassie had thrown herself at Colton McLean, making a fool of herself over Denver's headstrong younger brother much the way Tessa had made a fool of herself over Denver.

"Good thing Colton isn't back yet," Mitch remarked.

"It's been a long time," Tessa said. "Cassie's probably changed a lot."

"Well, she isn't married yet—or if she is, she hasn't changed her name."

Tessa turned back to Brigadier and scratched him fondly under the forelock. "It doesn't matter if she's married or not. Let's just hope she can take care of our boy here."

An hour later, Tessa realized that Cassie Aldridge had changed a lot in the past seven years. No longer a teenager with a wild crush on one of the McLean brothers, she was a full-grown woman with shiny black hair and intelligent gray eyes. Thin and athletic, she handled Brigadier expertly as she examined his hoof.

"Doesn't look too bad," she announced, once she'd closed the stall gate behind her. "The poultice should work. Just make sure he rests for a week and keep the hoof clean."

Relieved, Tessa walked with Cassie out of the stallion barn. Outside, the sky was hazy. Low clouds hung over the ridge surrounding the valley floor. The air was still and hot.

"Brigadier's a good-looking stallion," Cassie said. She opened the door of her beat-up truck but paused before climbing into the sunbaked cab.

"The best. But you should know that. I bought him from your father."

"That's right," Cassie replied, her smooth forehead creasing a little. "Call me if Brigadier gets any worse—or better. I like to know the good news with the bad."

"Will do," Tessa promised.

Cassie hopped into the cab of her dusty old Dodge truck, ground the gears and took off.

The next day Tessa opened the door of the barn and was greeted with an excited whinny. Brigadier pawed the straw on the floor of his stall. His eyes were clear, his ears pricked and he barely favored the sore leg.

"A medical wonder, aren't you?" Tessa teased, scratching

his ears fondly before giving him a carrot, which he ground noisily between his teeth.

Relieved, she brushed his rust-colored coat until it gleamed like polished copper. While she ran the currycomb across his hide, her thoughts drifted, as always, to Denver. Ever since he left the day before, she'd replayed their argument over and over in her mind. The fight had been silly and pointless, as arguments usually were. Still she was angry with him.

"He looks better," Mitchell said from somewhere behind her head.

Tessa nearly jumped out of her skin. "You scared me," she said with a nervous laugh.

"Didn't you hear me come in?"

She shook her head. "I . . . was thinking."

Mitchell poured oats into the manger, then walked outside with his sister. "Let me guess, you were thinking about Denver McLean." His green eyes were shadowed with worry, and deep grooves tightened the corners of his mouth. But he held his tongue and Tessa was grateful for that. She'd done enough soul-searching without having to be reprimanded by her brother. She wiped the sweat from her forehead and rinsed her hands in the cold water from a spigot near the barn. "I'm gonna run into town for some more wire for the fence bordering the Aldridge property. Want to come along?" he asked.

"I can't."

"Why not?"

"I've got things to do."

"Like wait for Denver to show up?"

"Like work on the invoices."

"Oh, come on. Lighten up a little. The bills aren't going anywhere."

"True, unfortunately."

"I'll buy you a hamburger." He offered her a smile and a wink. "Or I'll let you buy me one."

"And why would I do that?"

"Because I'm such a great brother."

She laughed. "Give me a break. Look, I can't go now. Nate Edwards is supposed to show up this afternoon."

Mitch's smile turned sad. "So this is it. You're really going to sell part of your herd. Unbelievable."

"It is hard to believe, isn't it?" she said, her voice gone rough at the thought. She shrugged her shoulders. "But it's almost done. Nate'll be good to them."

"Just make sure it's what you want," Mitch said before ambling toward the machine shed. "And if you change your mind and discover you can't live without a double-cheese bacon burger, let me know."

"I will."

She heard the sound of Nate Edwards's truck before she saw the big rig lumbering down the drive, a long horse trailer in tow, dust clouding behind.

Forcing a smile she didn't feel, Tessa waved as Nate ground the truck to a stop. He hopped out of the cab, and his daughter, Sherrie, unbuckled the straps from her car seat and jumped to the ground. "Tessie!" she squealed delightedly as she ran pell-mell into Tessa's waiting arms.

"How're you, sugarplum?" Tessa asked, hoisting the spirited child into the air.

"I want to see my new horse! Where is he?" she demanded. Her plump arms were crossed firmly over her chest.

"She," her father said, laughing. "You get one of the mares, remember?"

"Where is *she* then?"

"Over here." Tessa carried Sherrie to the fence beyond which Red Wing switched her tail, her body already round with the foal growing inside.

"I want to ride her!"

"You will."

"Right now!"

"Not on your life," Nate said, grinning widely as he plucked Sherrie out of Tessa's arms. "Maybe later, when we get home."

"But Tessa promised she'd teach me how to ride!"

"I will," Tessa vowed. "When your mom and dad say it's okay."

"That'll be never," Sherrie grumbled, her lower lip protruding unhappily.

"'Never' has a way of coming back to haunt you," Tessa said. "Sometimes when you least expect it or don't want it." *How many times had she promised herself she would* never *fall in love with Denver McLean again?*

Sherrie regarded Tessa mutinously, as if her special friend had turned coat and joined the enemy camp.

"I should have called you," Tessa said to Nate. "Brigadier's got a bruised sole. Cassie Aldridge looked at the hoof and told me it would be fine if we kept up the poultices and let him rest, but if you'd rather wait—"

"No way. Just let me take a look at him."

Tessa's heart nearly dropped to the ground. Until this moment, she hadn't realized how much she wanted Nate to change his mind—or at least put off his decision.

In the stallion barn, Nate examined the rather spirited Brigadier and laughed when the stallion tried to nip him.

"He looks fine to me," Nate drawled as they walked outside and stood near the fence next to Sherrie. He reached into his inside jacket pocket and withdrew a check. "Have we got a deal?" he asked.

Tessa felt numb inside, but shoved her worries out of her mind. "We will as soon as we sign the papers. Everything's in the house."

"I want to stay out here," Sherrie declared as her father turned toward the front door. "With my Red Wing."

"All right, dumplin'," Nate replied. "Just make sure you stay on *this* side of the fence."

"I will." Clucking her tongue softly and calling to Red Wing, Sherrie climbed the rails and peeked through. Aside from the flick of her pointed ears and the swish of her tail against a few bothersome flies, the mare didn't move.

The house was cool inside. Tessa led Nate to the study and sat behind the desk so recently vacated by Denver. She could smell his after-shave in the air.

Nate scribbled his signature on the bill of sale for each horse. "So where's McLean?" he asked, pushing the paperwork across the desk.

"In Helena," Tessa replied. "He should be back soon."

"How much longer is he planning to stay around here?"

"I—I don't know," Tessa answered quickly.

"Probably not too long. He couldn't wait to move away from here before. The fire just gave him a head start."

"I suppose," Tessa said woodenly.

"Well, this should make it easier for him," Nate said, thumping the paperwork with one thick finger. "Now that you've got the down payment on the ranch, he can take off for the bright lights of L.A."

"Right." Tessa wasn't about to think of impending departure. Not today. Not when she was giving up Brigadier and the mares for the sole purpose of buying a ranch Denver had no use for.

By the time she and Nate returned to the paddock, Len had loaded the mares into the trailer and Brigadier was being led across the yard by one of the younger hands. Brigadier nickered when he noticed Tessa and tossed his magnificent head as he pranced up the incline to the trailer. He barely favored his right foreleg.

Tessa's throat grew hot and thick and her eyes misted. Feeling like a traitor, she turned toward Sherrie just as Curtis hobbled across the yard.

"Howdy, there," he called to Sherrie. He tipped his hat and his weathered face cracked into a broad smile.

Sherrie squinted up at him. "Who're you?" she demanded.

Curtis chuckled. "Well, now, I could be askin' you the same question, couldn't I?"

"I'm Sherrie!" the little sprite said proudly, folding chubby arms across her chest.

Curtis glanced up at Nate. "You must be proud of this one."

"I am," Nate agreed, his gold tooth flashing as he scooped Sherrie from the ground.

"I want to ride Red Wing!" Sherrie cried.

"Later," her father said.

"That's what you always say," Sherrie pouted, staring longingly at the mare.

"You'll have plenty of time." Nate turned to Tessa. "You come and visit the horses anytime you like."

"And teach me to ride!" Sherrie commanded.

"I will," Tessa promised.

"Thanks a lot," Nate said, clasping Tessa's hand, "and good luck."

"You, too. Take good care of them," Tessa replied, despite the fact that the back of her eyes burned and her throat seemed nearly swollen shut with hot tears.

"I will." He nodded at Tessa's father. "See ya around."

Nate climbed into the cab of his truck and rammed it into gear.

Standing in the middle of the yard, Tessa watched as the rig carrying her precious horses rolled slowly down the lane in a plume of dry dust.

"You didn't have to sell them," Curtis said softly.

She refused to cry, though she felt a part of her had left in that trailer. "Of course I did. How else was I supposed to pay for this place?" she asked, dashing back the lingering tears in her eyes. Sniffing, her eyes red-rimmed, she faced her father.

"No one put a gun to your head, Tessa. Neither Mitch nor I—nor Denver McLean for that matter—expected you to buy the ranch." He slung an arm across her shoulders and hugged her. "I'm proud of you, y'know. But you shouldn't carry the world on your shoulders."

"I don't."

"Don't you?" He cocked his head toward the lane and Nate's truck and trailer. "You could take a lesson or two from Paula Edwards."

"Meaning?"

"Meaning being mistress of your own house—raising me a passel of grandkids."

Tessa thought about the baby she might be carrying. What would her father say? Surely he would figure out that the child was sired by Denver. She steered her thoughts clear of such dangerous ground and said, "So where were you during the women's movement?"

"Right here watchin' 'em burn their bras and what-have-you, protestin' and carryin' on. And all the time I'm wonderin' why they don't have the sense to know a good thing when they see it."

"I guess it depends on your perspective," Tessa said, squinting. Nate's rig turned away from the lane and rumbled out of view.

"All I know is that I'm almost seventy and haven't got one grandson to ride on my knee."

"Talk to Mitchell," she advised.

"I already have. But you—you're the one who should be thinking about settlin' down."

"I'll remember that," she said dryly, her lips pressed together.

"And I'm not talking about Denver McLean."

"Give me some credit, Dad. I know how you feel about Denver, and I know how Mitch feels about him." *Besides,* she thought, *he hasn't asked me.*

"And what about you?" her father asked gently, touching her shoulder. "How do you feel about him?"

"Denver's an enigma," she whispered, her voice catching.

"You think you're in love with him again," her father deduced, sighing loudly. "And don't deny it. I can see it in your eyes."

"I don't hate him, if that's what you mean."

"That's not what I mean and you know it, Tess. But there's just no reason for you to go pining for the likes of Denver McLean."

"I'm not *pining* for anyone."

"Good," he said, sounding unconvinced. He swatted at a yellow jacket buzzing near his head. "I guess I'd better see if Mitch needs some help with the combine."

Relieved that the conversation was over, Tessa walked through the back porch and into the kitchen, which smelled of spices and simmering meat. Milly was busy ladling gravy over pot roast.

"Denver with you?" she asked, without looking up.

"He's still in town."

"Well, if he gets back after I leave, tell him to call that partner of his."

"Van Stern?"

"Right. He called a half hour ago. Left a message. Denver's to call him immediately." She paused to look over her shoulder. "He sounded real upset."

"About what?"

"Didn't say, but I gathered it was important."

Great, Tessa thought, frowning to herself. *Now what?*

Chapter Eleven

Tessa flung off the covers, snatched her robe from the foot of the bed and glared at the clock. Four-thirty. She'd gone to bed at eleven and hadn't slept a wink.

Where was Denver? she wondered. *Still in Helena?* Cinching her belt tightly around her waist, she walked to her open window. Streaks of gray rimmed the mountains surrounding the valley floor, casting the buildings of the ranch into black shadows. In a few days, she realized, these old buildings, the equipment, the acres of land and the cattle and horses would all be hers.

If the bank approved the loan.

If Denver located Colton.

If she could stand to stay here without Denver.

"If, if, if," she said to herself as she hurried downstairs and thought about her future—a future without Denver.

She heard Marsha mewing at the back door. "I'm coming," she called, unlatching the lock and opening the door a crack as the old cat trotted to her milk dish. "So where're your babies, hmm?" Tessa asked as the calico rubbed against her bare leg. "Still hidden?"

Marsha mewed loudly again and followed Tessa into the

kitchen. After starting coffee, Tessa poured some milk into a clean dish and set it on the back porch. "There you go, girl," she whispered, petting the cat's arched back.

The sound of a car's engine cut through the early-morning stillness. *Denver!*

Clutching the lapels of her robe together, Tessa hurried outside. Denver parked the rental near the garage, and Tessa ran down the path barefoot. She reached the car just as he opened the door and stretched out.

He looked as if he hadn't slept in the two days he'd been gone. His jaw was dark with shadow, his eyes sunk deep into his head and the lines near his mouth seemed to have deepened.

"I thought you'd be asleep," he said when she flung her arms around his neck.

"I couldn't. I missed you," she said in a rush, glad just to be in his arms again.

His hands clasped behind her back and he held her close, his breath fanning across her hair. "I missed you, too," he admitted. "Maybe I should leave more often."

"Maybe you should stay." She could hear his heart drumming, feel the warmth of his body surround her. A slight breeze, cool from the night, played with her hair and ruffled his.

"Van Stern caught up with me. He needs me in L.A."

"He called here, too."

"I know. There's a problem with a project at work."

"So that's why you came back," Tessa said, disappointed.

"That, and the fact that I couldn't let you off the hook. You owe me, Kramer."

Cocking her head to look up at him, she asked, "Owe you what?"

His teeth gleamed in the dark. "A trip to L.A."

Tessa groaned. "I hoped you'd forgotten."

"No way. A bet's a bet." His arms tightened around her. "I've come to collect."

"Now?"

"Now. Get ready. *We're* leaving in"—he checked his watch—"less than an hour."

"But I can't—" she said, suddenly panicked. Though she longed to go with him, this was too soon. She couldn't just abandon the ranch—a ranch she'd worked so hard for. Nor could she leave her family for the sake of a whim . . . or a bet.

"Sure you can. I've already bought the airline tickets. Come on, Tess, it's only a few days." He took her face between his hands, forced her to stare up at him, and the laughter died in his eyes. "Come with me, Tessa. See how I live—stay with me."

Her throat closed. Hadn't he asked her once before to leave this ranch and follow him to Los Angeles? On the afternoon of the fire, he'd begged her to go with him, and then seven years later he'd told her that the love they'd shared, the love she'd cherished, had meant nothing to him.

"I have responsibilities," she said, her voice husky. She tried to take a step backward, but his arms were strong and unmoving, his features set.

"So do I. In L.A."

"But—"

"I'm not asking for a lifetime commitment," he reminded her, and her heart wrenched. *If only you were, Denver.*

His gaze delved deep into hers and she felt herself drowning in the liquid warmth. "It's payoff time, Tessa."

"Why now? What's this all about?"

The teasing light disappeared from his eyes. His skin tightened over his cheekbones, pulling taut, stretching over now-invisible scars. She sensed something had gone wrong—horribly wrong. She felt suddenly cold inside.

"Colton gave the P.I. the slip. He's not in Northern Ireland—

or at least he's not where Ross's private investigator thought he was." He squinted against the rising sun. Golden rays touched his face, but his features remained strained. "The investigator thinks he's in trouble. Big trouble."

"Isn't he always?"

Denver shrugged. "Probably. But I've got a bad feeling about this," he murmured, almost to himself. "If Colton needs to reach me, he'll try to get hold of me in L.A."

"Why would he want to get in touch with you now?"

"Because of the private investigator—because of John's death—"

"He didn't care about John."

"It's just a feeling I have," Denver whispered, and a shiver darted down Tessa's spine. "There's been a lot of trouble in Northern Ireland—a lot of unrest."

"There has been for years."

"But lately—" He shrugged, as if to shake off a sense of foreboding.

"What good would it do for me to come to L.A.?" she asked.

"I need you," he said, wincing a little, as if the words actually hurt. Exhaling slowly, he added, "Besides, you and I are at an impasse, Tessa. I think it's time we found out a little more about each other."

"And we have to do that in California?"

"Yes."

She studied the tired lines of his face, the tiny inflexible lines near his mouth, his black hair, falling fetchingly over his forehead. "And who will run this ranch?"

"Your father."

Inside, Tessa panicked. Though she was loath to admit it, she was afraid to leave the ranch in Curtis's hands. What if something went wrong? What if there were another accident? Dear God, what if he really had caused the fire all those years before? "I just can't."

"Mitch will be around to help him."

"Mitch is getting ready to go to college in Seattle."

"He's not leaving for a few more weeks. I'm only talking about a couple of days." He touched her tenderly on the cheek. "I need you, Tess," he said again, and he didn't have to say another word.

Within twenty minutes, Denver had showered, shaved and changed. Tessa threw a couple pairs of slacks, two cotton sweaters, a pair of shorts, T-shirts and a skirt into her old suitcase, then dressed in a billowing white skirt and pink sleeveless blouse. She plaited her hair into a French braid and snapped on small gold earrings and a matching necklace before meeting Denver downstairs.

"Do I look So Cal?" she asked, her dimple showing a bit.

"If that stands for sensational."

"Southern California," she said, laughing. There was something exhilarating and carefree about taking off with Denver and leaving the worries of the ranch behind. Even Denver's concerns for his brother seemed far removed. "Come on. We don't want to keep the Beach Boys waiting." With a wink, she breezed out the back door.

Denver locked it behind him. "You're enjoying this, aren't you?" he accused, tossing her suitcase into the trunk of his rental car as she slid into the passenger seat.

"Enjoying what?"

He grinned as he climbed behind the wheel and shoved the key in the ignition. "Harassing me at every chance."

"Me?" she asked innocently. "Never." But she couldn't stop the giggle that bubbled in her throat.

"Sure."

"You ask for it," she said as the car bounced down the lane. She relayed the message from Van Stern, then felt her lighthearted mood dissipate as they neared the foreman's house. Denver turned off the engine and she stared at the dark little cabin. "Dad won't like this," she thought aloud.

"Does that bother you?"

"A little."

"Enough to change your mind?"

She stared at him then, studied the crease furrowing his brow, the narrowing of his eyes, the way his fingers drummed against the steering wheel. "No," she whispered, touching his hand before climbing out of the car. When he reached for the door handle, she shook her head. "Let me handle this."

Brittle yellow grass brushed her ankles as she crossed the yard, rounded the corner and rapped on the back door. "Mitch?" she called through the panels. "Mitch?"

"What the hell?" her brother mumbled, stumbling to the door and poking his head through the crack. His hair stuck up at odd angles from his face and he had to blink a couple of times. He was bare-chested and wore nothing but jockey shorts and a wrist watch. "Tess? What're you doing here?"

"Saying goodbye."

"What?" He rubbed a tired hand across his face and focused. "Good Lord, where're you going?" he asked, before glancing at his watch. "It's barely five-thirty."

"I know. But I've got a plane to catch."

"A plane?" he asked, cobwebs of sleep still fogging his mind as he stretched, yawned and leaned against the doorframe for support. "What're you talking about?"

"I'm going to California. With Denver."

A half a beat passed. The sleep faded from Mitch's eyes. "To California," he repeated. "You're kidding, right?"

"Wrong."

For the first time he seemed to notice her clothes and hair. He rammed stiff fingers through his hair, only adding to the spikes already sticking straight up. "Why?"

"For a vacation."

"A what? Oh, no, Tess. This is wrong. All wrong."

"Why?"

"Why? Because you're trying to buy the place from McLean.

Because you just sold your horses to Nate Edwards. Because Dad'll never be able to run the ranch without you—"

"You can help him."

"I know, but—" His shoulders slumped, and he suddenly seemed to age ten years. "Are you sure this is what you want?"

"Positive."

Mitch frowned, his green eyes sad. "You've got it bad, haven't you, Tess?" he whispered. "You never really got over him, did you?"

"It's not a question of—"

"Just be careful. Don't let him hurt you again."

"He won't," Tessa said, wondering at the conviction in her words.

Mitchell's entire body flexed. "He'd better not," he growled, his lips thinning. "Because if he does, he'll have to answer to me!"

Tessa nearly laughed. "I'll tell him," she said, smothering a smile.

"Do that. I'd love to have a crack at McLean."

She couldn't help laughing then, eyeing his shorts and wristwatch. "I'll warn him. You just take care of Dad."

"I'll try," Mitchell said, crossing his arms over his bare chest as Tessa dashed back to the car.

"So how did he take the news?" Denver asked, once Tessa was in her seat and he'd rammed the car into gear.

"As well as can be expected."

"That well?" Denver asked dryly.

"Actually, he implied that he'd do you bodily harm if you hurt me."

"Did he?" Denver's crooked smile stretched across his face. "Protective bastard, isn't he?"

"Maybe he just doesn't want to pick up the pieces again," she said softly.

"He won't have to," Denver swore. He turned the car onto

the main road and slipped a pair of aviator sunglasses onto his nose. "I won't hurt you, Tessa. Never again."

A lump swelled in her throat when he linked his fingers with hers. "Don't worry about it," she whispered, blinking back hot tears. "I won't let you."

The California sun blazed hot in a hazy blue sky. The fronds of tall palms moved in a whisper-soft breeze as Tessa and Denver pushed open a courtyard gate and walked together along a flagstone path to the front door of his Spanish-style condominium. Vines, laden with fragrant purple flowers, climbed across the overhang protecting the door.

"It's beautiful here," Tessa commented, wishing she could hate the place.

"It's home." Shoving open the door, he carried her bag inside.

The interior was bright and airy. A staircase curled upward on one side of the entry, while two steps led to an expansive living room. The western side of the building was walled in two-story high panes of glass that offered a panoramic view of the sun-washed Pacific Ocean. "This isn't anything like I'd imagined," Tessa remarked, walking across the gleaming hardwood floor to French doors. A redwood deck stretched across the back of the condominium with steps leading down to the beach.

Tessa kicked off her shoes and grinned as she felt sand between her toes. "How did you find this place?" she asked, when Denver joined her. The tide lapped around her toes, frothy water swirling around her ankles. Salt spray misted in the air, carried inland on a warm Pacific breeze.

"I bought it from a friend of mine—a guy I went to school with. He and his wife divorced and he wanted to sell it fast. I'd been living in an apartment and this place seemed more permanent."

"And that was important?"

Unconsciously he rubbed the back of his scarred hand with the fingers of the other. "It seemed to be at the time," he whispered. "I'd been out of the hospital about six months and was working for a big firm not far from here. I decided it was time to grow some roots."

"So you'd never have to go back," she guessed, her heart constricting.

"There wasn't a reason to go back. Mom and Dad were dead, Colton was God only knew where, and you—" He sighed loudly, then gazed deep into her eyes. His own were shadowed with an intense pain that sliced to the bone. "I couldn't deal with you," he added.

"Why not?"

"Everything was too fresh, I guess." Frowning, he stared at the ocean, watching as sailboats, dark against the horizon, skimmed along the smooth surface of the sea. "Colton had convinced me that you were part of your father's scam."

"My father's *what!*"

"His embezzling."

"My father never took one dime from the ranch that didn't belong to him!" she hissed, instantly infuriated. She couldn't believe that after everything she and Denver had shared, he would still believe the lies—the horrid, hateful lies! "He's not an embezzler, or a thief, or an arsonist! As for the fire, you don't know that Colton wasn't behind it," she said, her mind spinning. "He was supposed to be in town with John during the blaze, wasn't he?"

"Yes, but—"

"Yes, but nothing. He wasn't with John. He didn't have an alibi. Said he'd been riding, but he showed up in a pickup. For all anyone knows he could've been in the stables, started the blaze and managed to escape!"

Denver's eyes narrowed. "Why, Tessa?"

"I don't know. Maybe for the same reasons he uses to blame Dad. Maybe he was skimming money off the top—"

"No way!"

"Maybe he didn't mean to start the fire," she went on, her thoughts ahead of her tongue. "It was probably an accident—he didn't intend to hurt anyone."

Denver's hands tightened over her bare forearms. "Do you honestly think he would accuse you, accuse your father, blame you for something he'd done!"

"Maybe," she accused. "He didn't stick around too long afterward, did he?"

"But he had no reason—"

"Neither did Dad! But you seem to think it's all right to accuse him! Think about it, Denver. Think about it long and hard. Why was Colton so adamant, so damned insistent that my family was involved!"

Turning, she tried to escape from the manacle of his hands, but he wouldn't let her go. "You're forgetting something, Tessa," he said, his eyes as dark as midnight.

"What?"

"Your father was found drunk at the fire. He really couldn't remember what had happened. Colton, on the other hand, had been riding the back fields—"

"He claims."

"His horse was still saddled."

"But he drove up in the truck. Isn't that odd? Just because his horse wasn't in the barn isn't any proof he wasn't involved."

"And it doesn't get your father off the hook!"

Gasping, Tessa arched her hand upward intending to slap him, but she didn't. She stopped just before her palm connected with his cheek. "I knew I shouldn't have come here," she said, fighting the urge to break down completely.

A gamut of emotions contorted his features—hate, anger, sadness, love?

To her surprise, he folded her into his arms. "Shh. Of

course you should have," he said, his face becoming gentle. "Let's not argue about it. Not now."

"But you don't trust us."

"I trust you."

"And Dad?"

"I'm not sure about him, Tessa. Face it. Your father has a problem—a serious problem. We have to do something about it."

"We?" she whispered, disbelieving. Denver wanted to help Curtis Kramer? She couldn't believe it—wouldn't.

"There are places he could go—hospitals and clinics. But first he's got to admit he has an alcohol problem."

Tessa swallowed back the urge to argue. "I—I'll talk to him when we get back," she said. She'd come to the same conclusion herself, but hated discussing her father's private life with Denver. "Mitchell seems to think he drinks to block out the fire."

Denver's lips twisted. "It doesn't work," he said. "I should know. I tried to pour myself into a bottle the week after I got out of the hospital."

"Why?"

He let out a long breath. "To forget you, Tessa," he said. "To forget you, the fire, everything." He glanced down at the scars on his hand and his mouth tightened. "Unfortunately I couldn't, and alcohol didn't make a damned bit of difference. So I gave myself a swift kick, picked up the pieces as best I could and threw myself into my work." He kissed her crown as the ocean breeze snatched at her skirt. "And I did my best to forget you."

"I didn't have anything to do with the fire," she said slowly. "I would never, *never* have done anything to hurt you."

His arms slid upward and he took her face between his palms. "I know that now," he whispered, his eyes shining as he slanted his mouth over hers.

His arms tightened and she fell against him, tilting her

face upward, her lips eager for his. He pulled her against him, the length of his body protection against the stiff ocean breeze. "Make love to me, Tessa," he whispered against her hair.

"Here?" She quivered inside. The beach was deserted, but houses and condominiums curved along the shoreline.

He grinned wickedly. "Inside." He scooped her into his arms and carried her up the few steps to the deck. She had to cling to him to keep from slipping as he shouldered open the door and climbed the stairs to a loft that shared a view of the ocean with the living room below.

"Here," he said, tossing her onto a huge bed with a patterned spread of forest green and pearl gray. Twining his fingers through her hair, he leaned over her, his weight causing the mattress to sag. "You don't know how many nights I've dreamed of you," he said. "Wished that you were here in my bed." His voice was low and throaty, his breath hot against her ear. Lying beside her, he guided her hand to the buttons of his shirt. "Make love to me, Tessa."

She slid the first two buttons through the holes, then pressed the flat of her hand to the hard muscles of his chest. She could feel his heart pounding wildly, knew its erratic cadence matched her own.

He moaned softly and his lips crashed down on hers, stealing the breath from her lungs and forcing liquid fire through her veins. She tingled expectantly and felt his hands slide beneath the elastic waistband of her skirt, slowly sliding the soft cotton down her legs and calves.

The bed creaked as he finished undressing her and rolled onto his back, guiding her to rest atop him. He watched the gentle sway of her breasts, nipples dark, above him. "Now," he said, letting his tongue rim her lips.

She moaned, wanting more. Heat coiled deep within.

Denver slid lower, capturing the tip of one breast with his lips then circling the firm bud with his tongue. "Make love to me, Tessa," he whispered. His breath was hot against her wet, taut nipple. "Make love to me all night long."

She had no choice.

The next morning Tessa was up before Denver and had dashed down to a local market for groceries. She'd already poured beaten eggs into a pan and grated cheese for an omelet before she heard his familiar tread on the stairs.

"What's going on?" he asked, poking his head into the kitchen. Sleep still clouded his eyes, his chin was dark with beard and his jeans hung low on his hips. His chest was bare and muscled and she had trouble dragging her gaze from him.

"When in California . . ." she said, motioning to the table, where fresh slices of oranges, melons and berries filled fruit cups and warm muffins were piled high on a small plate.

She was working at the stove. Slowly he sauntered over to her, slid his arms around her waist and clasped his hands over her abdomen, pressing her buttocks into his hips. She felt the bulge in his pants and her throat went dry.

"You should wear shorts more often," he growled into her ear, his hands reaching upward to cup a breast through her T-shirt. The scent of recent lovemaking still clung to him and she felt like a bride on her honeymoon.

"Not very practical on the ranch."

"Maybe you should stop being so practical," he rasped.

"Maybe I already have."

Twisting her in his arms, he slid his hands down her ribs, feeling each small indentation and watching as her T-shirt stretched across her breasts, displaying beneath the cotton fabric the hard buttons of her nipples.

"Hey, wait," she breathed, her mind swimming under his magical touch.

"Breakfast—"

"Can wait." He turned off the burners and hoisted her

upward, balancing her back against the wall, forcing her legs to wrap around his hips. Her arms circled his head as he pressed his mouth over her T-shirt and suckled, wetting the fabric and drawing on the sweet nubbin hidden deep in the cloth.

"Denver, please—ooh—" she gasped as his hands cupped her bottom and she felt her shorts being dragged over her hips. Together they tumbled to the floor and she forgot about breakfast as he stripped them both of their clothes and made love to her with a passion that tore through her soul and left her trembling in its wake.

For two days, Tessa learned the secrets of Denver's life in Los Angeles; she saw the wonder of Western sunsets blazing magenta and violet as the sun settled into the ocean. She smelled the salt of the sea and felt the ocean's spray against her face. They walked hand in hand through the streets of Venice, exploring the shops and boutiques, sipping drinks in shaded patios or walking barefoot near the ocean, playing tag with the waves.

"You love it here," she finally said as they trudged through the warm sand and up the steps to his deck.

"It's peaceful." One black eyebrow cocked. "Though some people have the impression that I live in a pressure cooker—that my life in Southern California has to be hectic."

"Okay, okay," she said, laughing and holding up her palms. "I'm guilty."

His arms circled her waist and he kissed her eyelids. "Guilty and beautiful," he whispered. His lips promised so much more.

The phone rang. "Go 'way," Denver growled.

The ring seemed more shrill the second time.

"You'd better answer it," Tessa said, pushing him away. "It might be Colton." *Or Mitch—or Dad.*

Grumbling, Denver threw open the French doors, crossed

the room and picked up the living room extension by the fourth ring.

Tessa strolled to the far end of the deck and placed her palms against the railing as she stared for one last moment at the sea. Salt air pushed her hair from her face and she breathed deeply of the tangy air.

Her flight back to Montana left in three hours.

"Second thoughts?" Denver asked as he reached her. From behind, he wrapped his arms around her waist and balanced his chin on her crown.

"Second and third and fourth and so on," she admitted.

"California's not so bad, is it?"

"It's wonderful." *As long as I'm with you.*

"You could stay longer."

Torn, she shook her head. "I have to go back. Everything I've ever worked for is there." She smiled wistfully. "But you could come with me."

He sighed, his breath stirring her hair. "Not for a while. That was my partner on the phone. He needs help on a project that's hit some snags. And then there's Colton."

"You really think he'll call you here?"

"I don't know."

"It's been so long," she pointed out before she wondered if waiting for Colton was just an excuse for him to stay. "If he really wanted to find you, he could. My guess is that he doesn't."

"Probably," Denver whispered, his voice barely audible over the roar of the sea. Placing his hands on her shoulders, he turned her, forced her to look in his eyes. "I'll fly back to Montana next week—then we can settle everything."

Her lungs constricted. "Such as?"

"You still want to buy the ranch, don't you?" he asked and her spirits dropped. "I'll call Ross and tell him to find some way for me to sell my part of the ranch to you."

"I thought you couldn't do that without Colton's consent."

Denver frowned. "There's got to be some provision—some loophole. Ross is a lawyer. It's up to him to figure it out. That's what he gets paid to do."

"Of course," she said sadly. "Well, I guess I'd better make sure I've packed everything," she said, her heart sinking at the thought of leaving.

"Or you could stay," he invited, leisurely tracing the column of her throat.

She shuddered, torn. All she'd ever wanted was Denver— on any terms. But now she realized he'd have to meet her halfway. One-sided love always died.

"No, Denver," she finally said, meeting his gaze dry-eyed, though the prospect of separating from him loomed dark in her horizon. "I have to go back."

Chapter Twelve

Mitchell was waiting at the airport. Shaved and dressed in clean slacks and a cotton shirt, a crisp Stetson pushed back on his head, he waved to Tessa as she pulled her suitcase from the baggage carousel. "I'll take that," he offered, eyeing her closely. "You okay?"

"I'm fine," she said, struggling with a smile.

"You don't look fine." Mitchell took her bag and slung one arm familiarly over her shoulders.

"Thanks a lot." She blew a strand of reddish-blond hair from her eyes as they wended through the crowded terminal. Mitchell showed her the way to the old pickup and held the door for her. "What's going on?" she asked suspiciously.

"Why?"

"The last time you opened a door for me was in high school. You wanted me to write a report on *Macbeth* or something."

"You're a jaded woman, Tessa Kramer," he said, his green eyes glinting in the afternoon sun.

"And you're holding out on me." She tapped her fingers on the sunbaked dash until he climbed into the cab, flicked on the ignition and threaded the old truck through the traffic in the parking lot. Tessa stared out the dusty windshield. "What's been going on while I've been gone?"

"Denver called."

"Today?" She snapped her head around, eyeing her brother.

"Just before I left. He thought you'd be home. He didn't know your flight was delayed in Salt Lake."

"And you did?"

"I called the airport and found out there were mechanical difficulties with your connecting flight." He grinned at her and winked. "I'm smarter than I look."

"Good thing," she teased, trying to keep the mood light, though she sensed something was wrong. "What did Denver want?"

"To talk to you. He said he probably won't come back here as soon as he'd originally planned."

"No?" Dread stole into her soul. Deep in her heart she'd feared that he would leave her again. Maybe their weekend in California had been a diversion for him and nothing more. But she hadn't expected his rejection so quickly. The force of it washed over her in an ice-cold shower of reality. Her hands curled into fists and she tried to drive the ugly thoughts aside. "Why not?"

"He didn't say," Mitchell said, driving through town and stepping on the gas. "I guess something came up."

"He must have told you something."

Mitchell frowned. "He said he'd call back as soon as he could."

Relief chased her fears away. "Did he say when?"

Mitchell's lips compressed and his fingers tightened over the wheel. "The conversation wasn't all that long."

"Why not?"

Mitchell stared through the dusty glass to the road ahead. "You may as well hear it all, I suppose. Dad answered the phone."

"So?"

"He wasn't in very good shape, if you know what I mean."

"He was drunk."

Mitchell's jaw clamped shut. He didn't look at Tessa. "He'd had a few. And he told McLean just what he thought of you going to California."

Tessa groaned. "How bad did it get?"

"Bad. Dad wasn't crazy about you flying off to L.A. with Denver, or any man for that matter, I suppose. The fact that it was McLean only made things worse. By the time I got on the phone, Dad had told Denver what he thought and then some. Dad was red in the face and Denver wasn't very communicative."

"Great," Tessa murmured.

"He'll call back," Mitchell said without much conviction. "And when he does, just make sure you answer the phone."

"I will." Leaning her head against the window, she sighed and said, "We've got to talk to Dad, you know."

Mitchell's shoulders stiffened. "About what?"

"You know what. His drinking. He needs help."

"I've talked until I'm blue in the face. It doesn't help."

"Something's got to. Not only is it unhealthy, but it's dangerous." She swallowed against a lump forming in her throat. "It won't be easy, but we've got to help him."

"He drinks because of the fire, damn it! Everyone blamed him, the town was against him, Colton and Denver all but accused him of murder."

"He drank before the fire, Mitch. We both know it. When they pulled him out of the stables, he was out cold, and it wasn't just from the smoke."

Mitch tossed her an angry glare. "You're beginning to sound like a McLean."

"I'm not—"

"A few days in California and Denver's got you convinced that Dad started the fire, Dad's got a drinking problem and Dad was ripping off the ranch," he grumbled, the back of his neck dark with rage. "Just remember who stuck by you, Tess. When you were torn apart. Where was McLean?"

Tessa clamped her mouth shut and seethed in silence.

Mitchell cranked down the window. Cool air swept into the warm cab. "The only other things that have happened on the ranch are that one of the tractors broke down—the clutch went out, and there are a couple of calves that turned up sick. I think they might have gotten into something—probably turpentine poisoning. Several branches from a pine tree near the barn blew down and the calves got into the needles. I called Craig Fulton and he said he'd be over as soon as he could."

"How serious?" Tessa asked.

"Not too bad, but I can't tell." He glanced at her. "Look, I'm sorry I got on you about McLean, but that guy has a way of getting under my skin."

Mine, too, Tessa thought, sighing. *Mine, too.*

Before she changed, Tessa thought she'd check on the two sick calves. She found them in a corner of the barn, lying on straw, rolling eyes up at her as she entered. "How're you?" she asked, rubbing her hand along one ruddy hide.

The calf bawled, his head drooping, but he struggled to his feet. As well as she could, she examined him, noting that though he was listless, he seemed sturdy. The other calf, a heifer, was worse. She barely moved when Tessa examined her. "Come on," Tessa said, rubbing the heifer's white face. "Hang in there."

Dusting her hands, Tessa walked toward the south end of the barn, but stopped as the odor of stale liquor filtered through smells of horses, cows and dust.

Then she saw him. Lying facedown on a bale of straw, an empty bottle dangling from the fingers of one outstretched arm, her father, dead to the world, snored loudly.

"Oh, no!" Tessa whispered, swallowing hard. "Dad, no." She touched him gently on the shoulder.

He didn't move.

"Wake up, Dad," she said, shaking him. Why couldn't she help him? Why couldn't he help himself? What demon possessed him that forced him to seek comfort in a bottle of Scotch?

Her stomach tightened painfully.

He snorted.

"For God's sake, Dad," she muttered, hauling him to a sitting position before shaking his shoulders so that his eyes rolled open and he coughed.

"What the devil?" he growled, rousing a little. He shoved her hands aside. Wincing and squinting one eye, he grumbled loudly. "Wha—what's goin' on?"

Tessa sat on the edge of a nearby bale. "My guess is that you passed out."

"What time is it?"

"About eight-thirty."

Curtis let out a long whistle and winced a little as he sat up. "I just came in to feed the stock . . ." he said, but avoided her eyes and dropped the bottle in an empty oak cask that had been shoved against the wall. His grizzled jaw hardened and he rubbed his chin. "Looks like I overdid it a mite."

"More than a mite."

"Maybe." He rubbed his forehead, then pinched the bridge of his nose between his thumb and forefinger as if to ward off a tremendous headache. "It's McLean's fault. He called and got me all riled." Blinking rapidly, he fixed his eyes on his daughter. "So now you're back from California." Sighing loudly, he asked, "What's gotten into you, Tessa? Taking off for three days and nights with Denver McLean. Living with him just like you were married! It's a good thing your mother's not alive."

She inhaled sharply, wounded by his words. "My relationship with Denver has nothing to do with you."

"I'm the one that raised you—taught you right from wrong."

"I haven't done anything wrong," Tessa said.

Curtis squinted. "That's probably a matter of opinion. Look at you." He wagged a finger at her linen skirt, silk blouse and leather pumps. "You already look different—like those damned mannequins you see on a Hollywood game show."

"I haven't changed, Dad, and I didn't come in here to fight about Denver," she said slowly, biting back the urge to scream that she loved Denver McLean. "I came to talk about you."

"Me?"

Tessa sat on the bale next to him. "You've got a problem, Dad. With this." She reached into the oak cask and withdrew the bottle.

"A problem? Me?" He barked a short, uncomfortable laugh. "No way. Sure, I have a drink now and then—"

"Every day. And it's not just one drink." She saw the pain in his eyes, the despair, and she had to fight to keep talking. Her own insides were shredding. This man had raised her and Mitchell alone, had done everything he could to give them a good life, had provided for them and cared for them when their mother died. He'd been mother, father, provider and friend—at least he had been until that horrid night when the stables were engulfed in flames.

Curtis's already flushed face reddened, his watery gaze drifted away from hers. "So now you're tellin' me how to run my life," he whispered, running one work-roughened hand over the worn denim covering his knee.

Tessa's eyes burned. "I only want to help," she said, placing her hand on his shoulder.

He flinched. "You've been listening to McLean."

"No—"

"Then why now, Tessa? Huh? Why now—right when you're fresh off the plane from Los Angeles and Denver McLean!" He eyed her speculatively. "And just when is he coming back here? Let's hope it's soon. Then he can sign the papers and we can all be rid of him."

"It's not that easy," Tessa said.

"Why not?"

"No one's heard from Colton."

"Bah! If you ask me, Denver's just stringin' you along. If he wanted to sell his part of this ranch, he'd be on the phone to his lawyer in a minute. Where there's a will, there's a way."

"Denver's already called Ross."

"Has he now? Does that mean he is or isn't coming back here?"

"I don't know," Tessa said. "Maybe you can tell me. He called, and you talked to him."

"It wasn't much of a conversation." Curtis shook his head, then reached into his jacket pocket, searching for cigarettes. He pulled out the pack, found it empty and crumpled it in his fist. "All he said was that he's been delayed. There was some kind of emergency."

"Emergency? What happened?"

"He didn't bother sayin'. If ya ask me, it was an excuse— a way to avoid comin' back here." His gaze turned sad and some of the fire left his eyes. He looked suddenly old and weary. "You know, Tess, there's a chance McLean's double-crossing you."

"Double-crossing me?"

"I'm just pointing out the facts," he said, his weathered face softening. "Doesn't it seem strange that he showed up just after John's funeral, stuck around long enough to find out what was going on—just to make sure the ranch was on its feet—and then took off?"

"He had work in California—"

"Sure he did. But my guess is that he found out you'd turned this ranch around, that it's making a profit, and he's decided there's no reason to sell."

She wouldn't believe it. "I went back with him."

"And now you're here alone," he pointed out. "Denver's

called, already made up an excuse about not bein' able to come back here."

Her lungs felt tight and some of her old fears took a stranglehold on her heart. "You think he used me."

Curtis's eyes shifted to the hay-strewn floor. "It wouldn't be the first time."

"No!" Her small fist clenched. She wouldn't believe that Denver had so callously and calculatingly seduced her! They had shared too many wonderful days and nights for it all to have been a lie. "Denver lov—cares for me."

Tears filled the corners of her father's eyes. "If you say so, Tess," he said, his voice raw. He touched her hair and sighed. "You're too good for him, you know. Too damned good."

"Denver doesn't want this ranch," she pointed out, trying to come up with reasons, explanations, excuses, *anything* to refute her father's accusations. Denver loved her—though he'd never said it. He had to!

"Maybe he changed his mind," Curtis said. "I checked the books—we're not in bad shape. In fact, this ranch is in the black. Think on it, Tessa," her father whispered, his old eyes squinting thoughtfully. "Why should he sell to you, when he could probably run the place from L.A. and make a handsome profit?"

"Because he gave me his word!"

The door to the barn swung open and Mitchell, his hands and shirt black with grease, entered. "The clutch is shot on the John Deere. I think we'll need to—" As if seeing Tessa for the first time, he stopped and glanced from his sister to his father. "What's going on here? Why haven't you changed?"

"We were just discussing Denver McLean," Curtis said.

"So we're back to him again, are we?" Eyeing his sister cautiously, Mitch leaned casually against the manger. "Don't tell me—you're defending McLean and Dad won't buy it?"

"Something like that."

"Well, you know where I stand."

"Stay out of this, Mitch," she warned. "We've been over it before."

Mitchell wiped a grimy hand over his brow, leaving a streak of grease. "Maybe someone should remind you that McLean doesn't have what you'd refer to as a sterling track record."

"Enough!" she shouted. She wouldn't listen to these lies a minute longer.

Her father sighed. "Mitch's right. Now that Denver knows this place is worth more than he originally thought, why wouldn't he try to sell it to a higher bidder?"

"Because we had an agreement," she said testily.

"In writing?" Mitchell asked.

"No, but—"

"Don't tell me," Mitch cut in. "He promised to sell the land to you, convince Colton to do the same, and then, once his brother was out of the picture, he'd come back, marry you and hand you your money back."

"Of course not!" she blurted, though deep in her heart, Mitch's scenario was just what she'd hoped for.

"Tessa," Mitch said softly, spreading his hands. "Open your eyes."

"I have!"

Pity stretched across Mitch's features. "Oh, Tess—"

Tessa wanted to run from the barn. Her words sounded strangled and forced. "Don't 'Oh, Tess,' me—okay? Things are going to work out just fine!"

"I hope so," Mitch said fervently. "I just don't see how. You know, there's a chance Denver won't locate his brother. Or that Colton won't come back here. He's got himself a hot-shot photography job all full of glitter and danger. He won't want to come back."

"But he might sell."

"And he might not."

Tessa's world was breaking apart. If only Denver were

here! If only her brother and father could see the real Denver, the man hidden deep beneath his scars from the fire. And yet, her family's accusations held a ring of truth. Inside, her heart was shredding. Hot tears clogged her throat. "You two are as bad as Denver and Colton," she accused, her voice a whisper. "You don't trust them, and they don't trust you."

"So whose side are you on?" Mitch asked.

"Believe it or not, there don't have to be sides."

"Oh, Tess, grow up. This isn't some female fantasy." She gasped, feeling as if she'd been kicked in the stomach. Hadn't Denver said just the same thing—hadn't he accused her of being a dreamer, a hopeless romantic? Sick inside, she ran from the barn, leaving her family and their horrid accusations of Denver behind. She'd call Denver, and if he didn't answer, she'd call his office. If that didn't work, she'd call Jim Van Stern. Once she heard from Denver everything would be all right.

Desperate, she ran into the house and dialed Denver's number in Venice. The phone rang twelve times before she hung up. It was late, but she called Denver's engineering firm. A tape machine answered on the third ring. She left a message for Denver and told herself not to worry. She'd hear from him in the morning.

"I'm sorry, Ms. Kramer, but all I know is that Denver took off in a hurry. He left a message on the recorder and said that he'd call in as soon as possible. I assumed he was in Montana," Jim Van Stern said over the hum of the long distance connection.

Tessa's heart sank and the headache behind her eyes began to throb.

"Have you called his attorney in Helena?" Jim asked. "I

don't know all the details, but he was hell-bent to sell the ranch. I just assumed this had something to do with the sale."

"I've spoken with Ross Anderson," Tessa said, remembering her telephone conversation with the young lawyer. "He hasn't heard a word."

"It's not like Denver," Van Stern remarked.

Tessa knew she was grasping at straws, that the possibility that Denver had heard from Colton was remote, but nothing else made any sense. She asked, "Could he have left because of his brother? He said he wanted to stay in L.A. until he heard from Colton."

"Maybe, but I doubt it. I don't think they've seen each other in years. Ever since that fire."

"Right," Tessa said, sick with worry. She stared out the kitchen window and wondered where Denver was. Why hadn't he called again? "If he phones you, please ask him to call me."

"Will do," Van Stern said before hanging up.

Tessa leaned against the wall. Her stomach rumbled. Her head was pounding, she ached all over. She hadn't slept well. She'd only dozed, and her dreams, when she had drifted off, had been filled with Denver. They'd been lying on the sand, the sea breeze ruffling his hair, the water lapping at her skirt, and he'd kissed her, long and hard, only stopping to vow that he loved her—

"Tessa?" a female voice called, accompanied by pounding on the front door.

"Coming!" Tessa hurried down the hall, swung open the door and found Cassie Aldridge standing on the front porch.

"Hi. Mitch called Craig yesterday."

"He did?" Tessa said before remembering.

Cassie nodded. "He had a couple of calves he wanted me to check out."

"Oh, right. They're in the barn. I'll come with you."

"I can find my way," Cassie offered with a smile. "Isn't that where I examined Brigadier?"

"Yes."

Cassie's black hair gleamed in the afternoon sun. "I was at the Edwards ranch the other day," she said as they walked toward the barn. "Brigadier's as good as new."

Tessa's heart turned over. "Ornery as ever?"

Cassie laughed. "He tried to take a bite out of my back side. Fortunately, I'm quick."

Chuckling, Tessa opened the door and snapped on the lights. The two calves were still in the stall, but they were both on their feet. At the sight of Tessa, they began to bawl.

"Hungry?" she asked.

Cassie opened the gate and caught the first calf. He tried to struggle free. The heifer, too, backed away. "They look good to me," Cassie said, examining first one calf, then the other. Both animals tried to escape, running into each other and nearly knocking Cassie down. "Mitch said he thought they'd eaten pine needles."

"No one said they were Rhodes scholars," Tessa replied, and Cassie smiled—a wide feminine smile.

"Well I don't see any reason to keep them penned up any longer."

"Good."

Together, they herded the rambunctious calves outside. The ruddy heifer and steer took off, tails switching, galloping through the dry field toward the rest of the herd.

"Thanks for stopping by," Tessa said as she walked Cassie back to her truck.

"No problem. I'll send you a bill." Cassie's hazel eyes gleamed and her mouth curved into a feminine smile. She climbed into the cab and leaned out the window. "Is Denver around?"

Tessa rammed her hands deep into the pockets of her jeans. "I don't know where he is," she admitted, wondering at the ease with which she confided in a woman she barely knew. "He was in California, but he left."

Jamming her key into the ignition, Cassie asked, "Has he heard anything from Colton?"

"Not a word," Tessa said.

"I guess that's not a big surprise." Cassie slid a pair of sunglasses onto her nose. Her mouth twisted wryly. "I don't think there's enough adventure or danger in this world to keep Colton McLean satisfied."

"Probably not," Tessa agreed, her thoughts with Denver, wherever he was.

"I'll see you around. Let me know if those calves relapse." Cassie stepped on the throttle and waved as she drove away. Tessa watched the white truck ramble down the drive and wished she had some inkling about Denver. Where was he? Frowning, she walked back to the house.

Get up! she told herself nearly a week later, but couldn't find the energy. She hadn't heard a word from Denver. Not one lousy word! "A lot he cares," she grumbled as she tossed off the sheets, then gasped when she felt the overpowering urge to vomit. She barely made it to the bathroom where she retched for a full ten minutes.

Sweat collected over her brow and the sensation slowly passed. She cleaned her mouth with water, then leaned against the sink. She'd suspected for two weeks she might be pregnant, this morning nearly confirmed it. She smiled wanly at her white-faced reflection in the mirror. Maybe she and Denver would never be together, but at least, God willing, she would have his baby.

Her heart bled at the thought of Denver. He hadn't wanted a child. Hadn't he asked her if she were protected on the first night they made love? Since then, he'd forgotten about birth control, but she knew in her heart he wouldn't want this baby. Nor did he want her.

Why else would he avoid her?

If Denver had wanted her, he would have called. If he had intended to sell the ranch, he would have returned to Montana to meet with the bank. And if he had loved her, he never would have left. Aching inside, she glanced at her reflection. Her eyes were shadowed with dark circles and her skin had paled. She looked every bit as miserable as she felt.

"Idiot," she accused, yanking the brush through her hair until the golden-red strands crackled. How could she have been such a fool—*and for the second time*? She tossed her brush onto the bureau, changed into clean jeans and a T-shirt and muttered, "Some people never learn."

By the time Milly arrived a half hour later, Tessa had convinced herself that Denver had conned her. Though part of her wanted desperately to trust him, the reasonable side of her nature wouldn't let her fall for his lies all over again.

"Trouble?" Milly asked as she entered through the back porch.

Tessa felt like a fool. She poured herself a glass of orange juice. "A little," she admitted grudgingly.

"Let me guess. This has to do with Denver, doesn't it?"

Tessa nodded. "You could say that. He had no intention of selling this place to me."

Milly's eyebrows raised a fraction. "And just how have you figured this out?" She tucked her purse in the pantry, hung up her jacket and whipped on an apron. "Didn't he try to call you?"

"Yes, but who knows why?" Tessa asked.

"At least give him the chance to explain."

"I will—if I ever hear from him again." She drank one sip of juice and her stomach revolted. Carefully, she set her cup on the counter.

"Oh, bah!" Milly started chopping onions. "Say what you

want, that man loves you. Any fool could see it when he was here."

"That's just the point. He's not here anymore, is he?"

"He'll be back."

"When?"

"Hasn't anyone told you patience is a virtue?"

"Over and over again," Tessa mumbled, unconvinced that Milly knew what she was talking about. "As soon as I'm finished around here, I'm going over to the Edwards ranch. If Denver calls—" Mentally kicking herself, she snapped her mouth shut. Denver wouldn't call. Nor would he return. He was gone again. Tears threatened her eyes and clogged her throat.

"I'll give him the number," Milly said, "right after I give him a piece of my mind!"

"I thought you were just singing his praises, telling me to be patient."

Milly's eyes glimmered. "Haven't you ever heard the old expression, 'Do as I say, not as I do'?"

"Too many times to count. But I always thought it was a crock," Tessa said, forcing a wan smile despite the stone-cold feeling that she'd lost Denver forever.

She went through the motions of doing the chores, but her mind was on Denver. Where was he? Why hadn't he called? If he loved her, and that was looking like a bigger "if" as each second passed, why had he left her? "It's over—face it!" she told herself, feeling positively wretched as she tossed hay into the manger. *And now you might be pregnant. What will you do? How will you tell him?* "I won't," she said aloud. She couldn't. Denver would twist things around, think she'd tried to trap him into a marriage he didn't want.

It hit her then with the force of a northern gale. Denver had used her, hurt her intentionally, lied to her. And he was probably now enjoying the fact—he'd gotten back at the family that had ruined his.

Dropping onto a bale of hay and drawing her knees to her chest, she let the tears that had been building for weeks fill her eyes. "No," she whispered, denying even now what was so evident.

Trust him. Give him time, one part of her argued.

Why? So he can drag out your heart and stomp all over it again? another part screamed.

Dropping her head to her arms, she cried from the depths of her soul. Deep racking sobs convulsed her small frame, and she sat rocking alone in the dark barn, the musty smell of hay mingling with the moist, fresh scent of her tears. Desperation ripped through her heart, and all her faith in love died as quickly as the flame of a candle in the rain. "Never again," she whispered, the words strangled, her voice raw with pain. "Never again."

"Tess? Is that you?" her brother called as the barn door creaked open.

Not now, she thought wildly. *I can't let him see me like this—not again!*

"I—I'm just leaving," she said, wiping her eyes and ignoring her quivering insides.

"Where're you go—" Mitchell rounded the corner, took one look at Tessa and groaned. "Oh, no, Tess. Don't tell me—"

"I'm not telling you anything."

"What happened?"

"Nothing. I, uh, just decided you were right about Denver." Refusing to meet the pity in his eyes, she swept past him. "But it's okay," she lied, "I'm going to straighten things out right now."

"How?"

I don't know! "I—I'm going to start with Nate Edwards," she said, then, before he could ask any more questions, she raced out of the barn, climbed into the pickup and shoved the old rig into gear. The truck lumbered out of the drive, lurching through potholes, kicking up dust and roaring loudly because of a hole in the muffler. Tessa didn't mind. Setting her jaw, she slid a pair of sunglasses on her nose and decided just how she was going to get her life back on track—without Denver McLean!

She drove to the Edwards ranch as if her life depended upon it. Knowing that Denver had left her as he had before—without a word or explanation—clarified things. The fact that he had called once didn't change things. He'd stripped her of her most precious possessions, then abandoned her. Well, she wasn't going to lie down and die! And maybe she'd get back at him. She'd never tell him about the baby—*if*, indeed, she was pregnant.

She coasted to a stop at the yard, then pulled hard on the emergency brake.

Her heart squeezed at the sight of Brigadier, prancing proudly in one small paddock, his ears pricked forward, his tail raised like a banner as he stared over the top rail of a whitewashed fence to a pasture of mares grazing nearby. He nickered softly, intent on the small herd, and ignored Tessa's repeated attempts to get his attention.

"Traitor," she murmured, dusting her hands as she approached the huge white house.

Nate answered the door in his stocking feet. "Tessa! Good to see you," he exclaimed. "You just missed Paula and Sherrie—they're in town doing the grocery shopping."

"That's okay," she said, though she would have liked to have a heart-to-heart with Paula and had hoped to give Sherrie the riding lesson she'd promised. "Actually, I came to see you."

"Me?" he asked, smiling. "I'm flattered. Come on in." He led her into the kitchen where the smell of coffee lingered in the air. "What can I do for you?" he asked as he motioned her onto a bar stool and held up the coffeepot. "How about a cup?"

"I'd love one."

She accepted a brimming mug. The coffee was strong and

black and hot. It warmed her throat but couldn't take away the frigid cold that had settled so deep in her soul.

"What's on your mind?" Nate climbed onto the stool next to hers.

"Business, I'm afraid. I came over to offer to buy back my horses. I was hoping you'd sell Brigadier and Ebony back to me. I'd like Red Wing, too, but since she's Sherrie's horse . . ."

"You want the horses back?" Nate scowled as he took a long swallow of coffee.

"Yes. But I'm willing to pay you more than you paid me— for all your trouble."

"I just can't help you, Tessa," he said, confused.

She had expected to haggle. Nate was a businessman. Leaning closer to him, she said, "This is very important to me."

"I know."

"Name your price."

"I can't."

"You *can't*?"

His eyebrows drew together over his eyes and his mouth turned down at the corners. "I already sold the horses, Tessa. I thought you knew about it."

Tessa's heart fell so far she was sure it would hit the floor. "You didn't," she whispered, feeling betrayed. She had no reason to feel Nate had deceived her. She'd sold him Brigadier and Ebony with no strings attached. And yet . . . "I—I just saw Brigadier out in the paddock."

"I'm keeping him and the mares until the trailer comes. Sometime today."

Sick inside, her world spinning, Tessa had to set her cup on the counter. It took all of her concentration to stay upright on the stool. "Wait a minute," she whispered. "You thought I'd know about the sale? How?"

"I sold the horses through Ross Anderson."

"Denver's attorney?"

Nate met her eyes. "Right. Denver bought the horses from me, Tessa. Even Red Wing. He paid top dollar, too. I made fifteen thousand on the deal, and he promised to sell me another horse for Sherrie."

Tessa grabbed the edge of the counter. She could barely breathe. "You spoke to Denver?" she whispered, her thoughts jumbled and confused.

"No—just Anderson. But believe me, Denver wanted your horses. I had no intention of letting them go, but I'm not fool enough to turn down a quick fifteen grand."

"Of course not," Tessa replied, blinking.

"Look, Tessa, I'm sorry—"

She waved off his apology. "I guess I'll just have to talk to Denver," she said, forcing a calm edge to her voice, though her mind was burning with accusations, her insides tied in knots of betrayal.

"He's not around."

"Don't worry," she vowed, as much to herself as to Nate. "I'll find him." *If I have to chase him to the ends of the earth. I'll find him, demand answers and then nail his handsome, lying hide to the wall!*

Chapter Thirteen

Furious, though her heart was breaking into a thousand pieces, Tessa drove back to the McLean Ranch. She stomped on the throttle, dying to tell Denver just what she thought of his crooked, underhanded dealings. How could she have been so stupid as to trust him again?

Not only had he reneged on the ranch deal, but he'd stripped her of her horses, her means of support—the animals so dear to her heart. Her fingers clenched around the wheel, knuckles showing white. Brigadier meant nothing to Denver except as a source of profit for the ranch.

"Black-hearted, vengeful son of a—" Downshifting, she wheeled the old truck into the lane. The pickup bounced and jarred. Tessa barely noticed. If she ever saw Denver again, she'd personally wring his neck!

And then what! Denver had all the cards. He owned the ranch, owned the horses, owned her own foolish heart. She had nothing, *nothing,* to fight him with. She'd lost everything, she realized as she drove past the acres of summer-dry ranch land—*McLean* Ranch land. Except, perhaps, the baby. And if she stayed here, let Denver know he might become a father, there was a chance, just for the sake of vengeance, he'd want the baby, too.

Tears drizzled down her cheeks. She couldn't stay here a minute longer. Without Denver, without the horses, she had no reason to stay at all.

Her gaze swept the surrounding hills, foothills she'd seen every day of her life. Mountains she'd naively believed would someday be hers. Pain welled from deep inside. She ached to belong, to be a part of this land, to be a part of Denver's life.

She blinked hard against the horrid tears. Even this damned beat-up old truck, she realized angrily as she cranked on the emergency brake, belonged to Denver. "He can have it," she murmured, hoping to sound strong though she was dying inside. Wiping her face, willing the red blotches to disappear, she jumped out of the cab and strode across the yard to the house—Denver's house.

"Something wrong?" Milly, elbow-deep in flour, asked. She was kneading bread at the counter, while Curtis, smoking and sipping coffee, sat in a chair at the table, a newspaper spread in front of him.

"Something? Try everything," Tessa said, pride lifting her chin, though her throat was still swollen. Her father stubbed out his cigarette. "Everything?"

She braced herself for another lecture. "Everything. You were right, Dad. About Denver. About this ranch. About me. This place belongs to the McLeans. Always has, always will!" Tessa met her father's worried gaze and fought the overwhelming urge to break down and cry all over again. "It's over, Dad." Stripped bare, her very soul raw and aching, she whispered, "Just like you knew it would be. I don't belong here."

"Hey, slow down," her father said. "Start at the beginning. Of course you belong here. More than anyone. You run this place."

"That's right," Milly agreed, wiping the flour from her hands on the hem of her apron.

"Not anymore."

She was shaking all over, and she had to battle a fresh flood of tears. "I'm leaving, Dad," she said, half apologizing. "I thought I could hold this place together—make something of it. But I was wrong."

"Now hold on—"

"Don't try to talk me out of it," she said firmly. Her mind was made up, her eyes glittering fiercely with standing tears. "It's time."

"Just because—"

"It's time," she said again. She turned on her heel before her emotions got the better of her. Willing the sobs in her heart to stop, she took the stairs two at a time and dashed into her room—Denver's parents' room.

She dragged out her old suitcase, the same suitcase she'd tried to pack on that humid summer night—the night Denver had returned. The very suitcase she'd taken with her to California.

Dear God, how did I let this happen?

"Don't," she told herself, refusing to think of aquamarine water, white beach and Denver. Always Denver. "He's not worth it!"

As she banged open the bureau drawers, she caught a glimpse of her red-rimmed eyes, her straggling hair, her pale cheeks. Furious with herself, she tossed her clothes recklessly into the tattered old case.

"Tess?"

Oh Lord, not now. She couldn't stand her father's pity. "I'll be down in a minute," she called, her fingers fumbling with the locks on her case.

He pushed open the door. Wearily, he surveyed the room. "Where you plannin' to go?"

"Doesn't matter."

"Sure it does."

"Alaska, then. Or Brazil. Or Singapore. I really don't know, and I sure as hell don't care!" she lied.

He sat heavily on the edge of the bed. It groaned beneath his weight. "It's not like you to quit."

"I'm not quitting, Dad. I was defeated." She held her palms out, silently pleading with him. "Don't try to talk me out of this."

"That's exactly what I'm gonna do." Offering her a gentle smile that would have broken her heart if it hadn't been broken already, he said, "You didn't give up on me, did you?"

"Of course not. But what—"

"I haven't had a drink in three days." He frowned and rubbed the back of his neck. "Though, I got to admit, it feels more like three hundred. I'm goin' to my first A.A. meeting on Tuesday."

She swallowed hard and blinked against fresh tears. Would she ever stop crying? "Good for you," she murmured. "I knew you could do it."

"Not without you I couldn't."

"I had nothing to do with it."

He stared at her old suitcase. "You know, if you leave, I might just reach for the nearest bottle."

"Nah." She shook her head, sniffing. "Not you. Not when you set your mind to something."

"That's what I thought about you."

"Oh, Dad, I'm just so tired of fighting." Her throat clogged even tighter when she witnessed the naked pain in her father's eyes. She had promised herself she would never cry for Denver again, but she couldn't seem to stop.

"What happened?" he asked.

"Denver bought the horses, Dad. He bought Brigadier and Ebony and even Red Wing. Right out from under my nose! He plans to use them here, on this ranch, for his own profit. You were right. Denver never intended to sell this place to

me. Never. I was stupid and crazy and just plain dumb to
have listened to him."

She heard the screen door slam downstairs. Yanking her
bag from the bed, she said, "I don't want to explain this all to
Mitch, all right? He wouldn't understand." She started for the
door, but her father caught her wrist in his gnarled fingers.

"You can't just run, Tess."

"Watch me."

"At least stay at my place for the night. You're upset. You
need time to think things through. Sometimes things are a lot
clearer in the morning."

"That's the problem, Dad. Things are too clear already."
She heard the sound of footsteps on the stairs and yanked her
hand from her father's grasp. She had to get out now, before
she changed her mind.

She took two steps just as he strode in.

"Look, Mitch, I've got to—" Her eyes clashed with Denver
McLean's curious blue gaze. Big as life, his expression
guarded, he blocked the door. "Oh, no," she whispered, wanting to shrink away from the magnetism in his blue eyes, from
the handsome angles of his face. He looked tired and drawn,
his hair long against his collar, his features more gaunt than
she remembered. Despite the pain, despite the anger, despite
the fact that he'd wounded her shamelessly and she was
still bleeding deep inside, she felt an overwhelming urge to
run to him, to suffer any ridicule, to feel his arms wrap around
her again.

Denver's gaze darted from Tessa to Curtis and back again.

"What're you doing here?" she whispered, her pride surfacing. "Don't you have some horses to steal, some old men
to beat down or a woman to stomp on?"

His gaze fastened to the fury in hers. "What's going on
here?" he asked, his voice so low, she barely heard it.

"You tell me."

"It looks like you're leaving."

"I am."

His eyes narrowed. "I don't think so." Dressed in a wrinkled shirt and slacks, his jaw dark with three days' growth of beard, his eyes sunken, he looked as if he hadn't slept in a week. Tessa told herself she didn't care. It didn't matter what he'd been through. He'd betrayed her, and any pain or remorse he might have suffered wasn't enough. It couldn't match the wretchedness slicing wickedly through her own heart.

"Why don't you start over," he suggested, "and tell me what this"—he motioned to her bag—"is all about?"

"It's simple. This place is yours, Denver," she replied coldly. "All of it. The horses, the machinery, the house and even the ridge! I don't want any part of it." Holding her chin rock solid, swallowing back hot, tormented tears, she tried to breeze past him, but he blocked the door.

"Wait a minute—where're you going?"

"Singapore or Brazil, wasn't it?" Curtis interjected, standing, trying to place himself squarely between his daughter and the man in the door.

Tessa said firmly, "I can handle this on my own, Dad."

"Just tryin' to help out."

"Thanks, but this is my problem."

"*What* problem?" Denver demanded, scowling savagely. "What the hell's going on here?"

"Move, McLean," Curtis said.

Denver refused to budge. His hard gaze landed on Tessa. "You and I have to talk."

"Too late."

"I don't think so."

"I'm leaving, Denver. There's not much to chat about!" She tried to squeeze past him.

He caught her wrist in his hard fingers, stepped quickly out of the door and met Curtis's gaze. "I'd like to speak to Tessa. Alone."

"Whatever it is you have to say, McLean, you can say to me."

"This is private."

Tessa's heart somersaulted. Denver's fingers tightened possessively over her wrist. "I can handle this, Dad," she said, her eyes as bright and furious as Denver's.

Curtis hesitated at the door, eyeing them both and shifting restlessly from one foot to the other. "I don't think—"

"I'll be fine," Tessa insisted. Now was her chance to tell Denver what a bastard he was, and she might not get another.

"All right," Curtis said reluctantly, his old face grim. "But I'll be in the kitchen." His lips pressed together until they showed white and he jabbed a gnarled finger at Denver's chest. "You've got fifteen minutes, McLean. Then I'm back up here and you're through with my daughter for good."

He pulled himself to his full five foot eight and glared up at Denver. "Fifteen minutes." Scrabbling in his breast pocket for his cigarettes, he turned and left the room.

"Okay, Denver, what is it?"

"You tell me. Why the hell are you leaving?"

"Why the hell do you care?"

"You're the most infuriating woman I've ever met."

"Good!"

With a growl, Denver kicked the door closed. It banged shut. Windows rattled in their casings and the whole house jarred. Tessa jumped. He clicked the lock into place. "I don't want to be disturbed," he said, when she started to protest.

His face muscles were tight, strained with leashed fury that sparked like blue flames in his eyes. Wrenching her arm, he nearly threw her into a chair and stood only inches in front of it, his arms crossed over his chest, his shirt stretched so tight at the shoulders the seams threatened to split. "Now, Tessa, you tell me just what's going on here."

"What does it look like?"

"It looks like you're taking a hike."

"I am."

"Why?"

"Why?" she repeated, incredulous. If nothing else, Denver had gall. She'd give him that much. But no more. "Because of you, Denver. Because of all the things you are and most certainly because of the things you aren't!"

"And what's that?"

"Honest."

"*You're* talking about honesty?" he said. "What about you? I spend the past week and a half going through hell for you and you're ready to walk out on me."

"Me walk out on you!" She leaped to her feet, tilting her head upward to meet the fury in his eyes. "Me walk out on you?" Laughing brittlely, she said, "You're the one who left me. You didn't call, didn't write, and now you're buying back my horses, *my* horses behind my back."

"Hold on a minute—"

"Why haven't you called?"

"I tried."

"Once."

"It was difficult," he hedged.

"I'll bet. And why didn't you show up, if for no other reason than to sign the papers at the bank?"

"I had problems. That's why I called. There was an emergency."

"Emergency? What? Did you find some other woman to put through an emotional wringer—accuse her and her family of horrid deeds and then buy her most precious possessions behind her back?"

"Is—is that what you think?"

"What else?" she jeered, wanting to hurt him as much as he'd wounded her. "Did you have to take a trip to Disneyland?"

His eyes narrowed angrily. "A little farther away than Disneyland."

"I don't really care!"

"By several thousand miles."

"Save it, Denver."

"I went to Ireland, Tess. Northern Ireland."

"Ireland?" she repeated dubiously, but some of her anger was already weakening as she guessed the answer. An icy chill ran down her spine. *Colton! Denver had gone looking for Colton!*

"That's right," he said, as if reading her thoughts. "I wanted to find my brother and convince him to come back here and sign the papers."

"No way."

"I just got a little sidetracked," he said.

"I'll bet."

Every muscle in his body coiled, and his lips thinned angrily.

She couldn't help goading him. "You expect me to believe that you flew all the way to Ireland to ask Colton to sell this place to me, when you didn't even call, didn't send a note, didn't so much as leave a message?" A traitorous part longed to believe him, wished that he could take away the pain of the past few weeks, that they could pick up where they'd left off, but she wouldn't let him fool her—not this time. Too much was at stake.

"That's what happened."

"I—I don't believe you."

"And just what do you think went on?"

"I think you've been conning me, Denver. This was all just a game to you. You don't have to deny it, because it just won't work. I'm done listening to your stupid lies."

"Lies?" he bellowed, sweeping her into his arms furiously, every muscle straining. He yanked her close against his rock-hard body, his nose nearly touching hers, his breath fanning her face, his eyes narrow slits. His fingers dug into her forearms. "The only lies I've told are to other people—people like my brother—to protect you!"

"Save it for someone who'll believe it."

His grip tightened. "I'm not lying, damn it!" Raw energy flowed from his body to hers—she could feel the anger coiling deep within him.

Tessa glared at him. "You never intended to sell this place to me! If you wanted to reach me, you could have. Instead you called Nate Edwards and bought my horses back so you could use them here."

"Why would I do that?" he growled.

"You tell me."

"Okay, I will!" Blue fire sizzled in his eyes. "Just after you left, I got a call from the private investigator."

"In Northern Ireland."

"Yes. He was worried about Colton. He'd spoken to him once and knew he was in trouble."

"So you flew over there?" she asked, doubting him.

"Yes, damn it. I went to Northern Ireland to find him and bring him back here to sign the papers. The trouble was, we didn't get that far because someone strolled into this cozy little bar and started taking potshots!" His eyes had grown cold, his face white beneath the black stubble of his beard.

"Don't lie, Denver!" But she'd begun to believe him, despite the voice in her mind that reminded her how often he'd lied.

His fingers clenched and he gave her a little shake. "That's what happened, Tess."

"I can't believe—"

"Because you won't!" The fingers digging into her flesh suddenly gave way.

"Why should I?" she demanded.

"Because it's the truth. Oh, hell." He shoved his hair out of his eyes impatiently and closed his eyes, as if trying to control his temper. He seemed weary and wrung out.

Seconds ticked by. Tessa edged toward the door.

When he spoke again, his voice was low—almost gentle.

"You and I both know the kind of work he does, how he thrives on danger."

That much was true.

"Someone was trying to kill him."

She felt numb inside. "Why?"

He shook his head, his broad shoulders slumping. "I'm not really sure. No one would tell me the whole story and I don't think the authorities have everything pieced together—at least not yet. I had a hell of a time leaving the country." Denver stretched wearily, shoving his shirtsleeves over his forearms as he did.

"Go on," she said, disgusted with herself for even listening. He was a liar, a cheat, a man who had found her pride and stomped all over it—

"As Dunkirk—he's the private investigator Ross hired—figured it, someone must have blown Colton's cover. Colton was in pretty tight with the IRA and had managed to take a few photos they wouldn't want published."

"So the IRA had him shot."

"Or the other side, posing as revolutionaries—"

"I don't want to hear this," she whispered, holding up her palms and shaking her head. "This is too bizarre." She reached for her suitcase. Denver kicked it across the room. It slammed against the wall, springing open.

"Just hear me out, Tessa," he said, blue eyes flaming again.

She set her jaw, eyeing her suitcase dolefully. "Get on with it." She couldn't let herself believe him—not again. Not ever. But inside she was wavering. She had to get out fast—before he worked his treacherous magic on her all over again. She noticed the muscles flexing in his face and had to tear her eyes from his strong profile. Unnerved, her breath already whispering through her lungs, she clenched one fist around the molded brass of her bed and with her back to him, stared out the window. "I don't have all night," she reminded him.

"Right. You're on your way out."

She swallowed back a hot retort.

He stepped closer to her. The floorboards creaked. Tessa's every nerve ending fluttered as he spoke so quietly she had to strain to hear.

"The upshot is that one side—God only knows which—decided to use him for target practice. Probably as an example."

"While you were there?"

He didn't answer, but she understood from his silence that he had witnessed his brother being gunned down.

"If you don't believe me, you could call St. Mary's Hospital in Belfast."

"Oh, God—" She felt as if she might be sick. Denver wouldn't lie about this. He couldn't. She could find out the truth too easily. Images swam before her eyes—Colton McLean, a handsome if bitter man, stretched out in a pool of blood. Denver crouching over him—in danger himself. Her hands shook, her insides roiled, and she forced herself to gaze up at Denver. "Is—is he all right?" she asked.

"He'll live."

Nauseated, she sank onto the edge of the bed. Her entire body was trembling. She could tell from his harsh expression, the tension radiating from his rigid muscles, that he was reliving that awful moment. Remorse tore at her soul. She felt like an utter idiot for a whole new set of reasons. "How badly was he hurt?"

"His shoulder will give him some trouble for a while."

"I'm sorry," she whispered, her voice trembling with genuine regret. If only she could call back the ugly words—if only she had trusted him more! How could she have stood there so damned self-righteously accusing him?

"We all are."

"Will he come back here?"

"As soon as he's released from the hospital and able to travel. My guess is that he'll show up in the next week or two."

"I owe you an apology," she said, her chin wobbling. "But you should have called."

"I couldn't. The authorities were highly suspicious of me. They grilled me for days."

"Why?"

"Because someone tried to kill my brother, as well as anyone else who happened to get in the way, only a few hours after I showed up. It looked a little too coincidental."

"I see."

"You believe me?"

Her throat so tight it ached, she whispered, "Yes—well, almost."

"Thank God for small favors." He dropped onto her bed, then sagged against the pillows. "I haven't slept in days." Rubbing the bridge of his nose, he let out a long sigh and closed his eyes. Black lashes swept the hollow circles over his cheeks.

Realizing that he might drift off, she had to ask a question that still nagged at her. "You managed to get through to Ross Anderson, but you didn't call me."

"I called Ross before I left for Belfast."

"So why didn't you tell me?"

"I tried to call. You weren't here. No one was." Blinking slowly, he forced his eyes open. "Besides, I wanted to surprise you."

"You managed that," she admitted, her fingers quivering as she brushed his hair from his eyes and tried to smooth the wrinkles from his brow. "I wanted to kill you."

"You and that idiot in Ireland."

"Did they catch him?"

Denver shook his head. "I don't know. I don't think so." He took her hand in his. "I guess I really blew it, handled the horse deal all wrong. I just didn't want you to sell stock. Those horses mean too much to you."

"I can't believe this," she murmured. Recognizing the

lines of strain around his mouth, the weariness in his eyes, she almost trusted him again. Slowly, she pressed her lips to his cheek.

"Believe, Tessa."

"I want to—" Oh God, was she baring her soul to him again?

"Did I hurt you that badly?" he asked softly as he draped one arm around her waist, holding her close. The nearness of him, his smell and touch, caused her skin to tingle, her heart to race. "After the fire—did I hurt you that badly?"

Shuddering, she shut her eyes. "I was okay."

"Were you?" Levering himself onto one elbow, he pushed gently on her shoulder. She fell back against the pillows.

"I did this all for us, you know. I bought the horses and told Ross I wouldn't sign any real estate papers because I thought I'd come back here and marry you. I thought we could straighten everything out."

Her heart lurched, missing a beat. "How?" she asked, her palms beginning to sweat. She couldn't risk believing him again. Not completely. Not when it came to matters of the heart. She was too vulnerable. Just because he mentioned marriage wasn't any reason to run back to him, believe anything he said.

"I already talked to my partner. I'm thinking of splitting off—maybe starting a consulting firm in Helena."

"You'd hate living here."

"Maybe not. I had a lot of time to think things over in Northern Ireland. I did some serious soul-searching."

"And what did you find out?"

He cocked his head to the far wall, where her suitcase had landed. "That I want to be with you. No matter where you are."

She sniffed, her pulse leaping, her eyes shining.

"This ranch is only important if you're here. If you're leaving—so am I."

"And if I'm not?" she asked, twisting to face him. Her long hair fell over his arm, red-gold tresses spilling over wrinkled white cotton.

One corner of his mouth lifted. "Then I stay."

She swallowed hard. "Is—is this some kind of a proposal?"

His gaze flicked from her eyes to her lips and back again. Tessa's breath lodged deep in her throat.

"What do you think?" he asked, pushing up on his elbows, placing trembling lips against the side of her neck.

Her pulse played hopscotch. "I think I'm crazy to even consider it." But she leaned back, twining her arms around his neck, feeling his thick dark hair brush her fingers.

"Let me be the judge of that." His breath whispered across her face.

"What about the fire?" she asked quietly.

His grin twisted wickedly. "It's getting hotter by the second." Lazily, he kissed her. As if they had all the time in the world. Maybe they did.

"That's not what I'm talking about."

"I know." He covered her mouth with his and all thoughts of the past escaped her. Once again she was caught in the feel of him, the here and now, the promise of the future. The past, the fire, were but a distant memory.

A hungry warmth, deep and primal, uncoiled deep inside of her, spreading in radiant waves to her limbs.

She moaned, moving anxiously against him.

"Don't you want to see your horses? They're probably on their way," he said, kissing the tip of her nose and grinning.

"I'll wait."

"What about your father? Curtis should be back here any minute."

"Don't remind me," she groaned, moving reluctantly away from him. He caught her arm, yanked her back and pressed hot, eager lips to hers. Immediately, she turned liquid.

"That's just to remind you that I missed you."

"I missed you, too."

"And I love you, Tess," he said, his words husky and raw. "I always have."

"Oh, Denver. I love you, too!" she cried, letting her tears flow as she held him close, blinking rapidly and wishing this moment would never end.

A hard rap sounded on the door. "Tessa?" her father asked, his voice heavy with concern. "You in there?"

"I'm okay, Dad."

"You sure?"

"Positive." She glanced into Denver's eyes.

"She'd better be, McLean!"

Tessa smothered the urge to giggle. "Maybe we should go wait for the horses," she whispered. "I wouldn't want my father to get the right idea about us."

Denver's grin slashed across his face. "Not until you promise to marry me."

"Oh?" she asked, her eyebrows shooting skyward, the gloom in her heart disappearing. "And what are you going to do if I don't?"

"Hold you prisoner until you beg for mercy."

"Sounds interesting," she teased.

"Doesn't it?" He gazed deep in her eyes. "But I don't think your father would approve."

"Probably not, but he won't approve of the marriage either."

"Maybe I can change his mind."

She laughed. "If you can, you'll be the first."

"Watch me." He slapped her fondly on her rear.

"I will." She rolled off the bed and landed lithely on her feet. Denver was right behind her.

She unlocked the door, but before she could open it, he slammed it shut with the flat of his hand.

"One more thing," he said.

"What's that?" She turned and regarded him through a veil of gold-tipped lashes.

"About the fire."

Here it comes, she thought frantically, bracing herself. *This was too good to be true!* She leaned heavily against the cool panels of the door. "I thought we were through discussing the fire."

"Almost. But I thought I should explain."

"You don't have to—"

"Shh." He placed a finger to her lips, tracing her pout. "Just listen. I put everything into perspective in Ireland," he said. "I had a lot of time, sitting around hospitals and talking to the authorities. I thought things through, and I finally realized that I should never have blamed you for the accident."

"The accident?"

"Right. No matter what happened, the fire was an accident. It was no one's fault. Not yours. Not your father's."

"It was someone's."

"No. Let's not try to fix any blame."

Her throat closed around itself. Tears threatened to fill her eyes.

"I wanted to blame someone, Tessa. Mom and Dad were dead, I was in the hospital, and I thought there had to be some reason it happened—some person to blame. Your father was an easy target. So were you." His eyes were bright with unshed tears. "Can you ever forgive me?"

Blinking, she forced a quavering grin. "I think I can find a way."

"I'll talk to your dad and make it up to him."

"You'd better," she teased. "I expect him to give me away at the wedding. You'll probably have to do some fast talking. He's not too fond of McLeans. Neither is Mitch."

"When Colton gets here—"

"Oh, Lord, I hadn't even thought about that. He hates me!"

"He just doesn't know you." Denver shoved open the door.
"I think it's time to start mending fences—and fast."

His fingers closed over hers and he pulled her downstairs.
How, she wondered, would they ever mend the old rift between the two families? Time was supposed to heal all
wounds, but the past seven years had only deepened the gap.

Her father would be easy. If Curtis saw how happy she
was, he'd forgive Denver. And when they had the baby,
Curtis Kramer would glide around this ranch on cloud nine.
The baby! Should she tell him? She slid a glance at Denver
and couldn't ruin the moment. She had to wait—at least until
she was sure.

Besides, she and Denver had other hurdles. Mitchell and
Colton would be more difficult to convince that she and
Denver loved each other than would Curtis. Her brother
and Denver were just too bullheaded and too much alike.
Heaven help us, she silently prayed. God only knew what
would happen when Colton McLean stepped back on
Montana soil.

Chapter Fourteen

The sky was overcast, heavy with the threat of rain. Tessa glanced through her bedroom window to the shifting dark clouds and wished that the storm would hold off, if only for one more day.

Tomorrow she and Denver would be married. In a private ceremony in the Edwardses' rose garden, finally, she would become Mrs. Denver McLean.

If only rain didn't spoil the nuptials.

"I'm still not sure I approve," her father said. Standing stiffly in front of a full-length mirror in her bedroom, he surveyed his reflection with a jaundiced eye. His tuxedo fit perfectly, the white shirt in sharp contrast to his tanned skin. "I used to call these things monkey suits, and that's what I feel like—a damned circus monkey."

"You'll get over it." She adjusted his bow tie and grinned. "I know you don't want to hear this, but you look rather dashing and distinguished."

"Bah!" His fingers scrabbled across the front of his stiff white shirt for a nonexistent pocket. "Damned fool things," he muttered.

"It's only for one day."

Curtis's eyes grew sober. "You're sure about this marriage?"

"Positive."

"Mitch is fit to be tied."

Tessa remembered Mitch's volatile reaction. "That's Mitch's problem, isn't it?"

Her father smiled crookedly. "I suppose it is." He eyed the mirror harshly. "Can I take this thing off now?"

"As long as you promise to put it back on tomorrow." She breezed out of the room on the same cloud that had carried her, floating in happiness, for the past week. Never once in that time had any of the old doubts surfaced, and Denver had been wonderful. In only seven days, he'd rented an office building in Three Falls, had Ross Anderson draw up the papers to sell off his half of the engineering business to Jim Van Stern, straightened things out with her father and even planned a honeymoon in the Caribbean. The only glitch had been that the activity within the house at all hours while planning the wedding had left little time for them to be alone. But tomorrow that, too, would change. And then, she thought smiling secretly, she'd tell him *her* news.

If Mitchell was still harboring grudges, he'd have to work them out himself, she decided.

The kitchen smelled of cinnamon and chocolate and fruit. Milly had decided a bakery wedding cake wasn't enough and had taken it upon herself to make enough pies, cinnamon rolls and fudge for the entire Third Battalion. All neatly wrapped for the next day, the spicy confections were spread upon the counter of the kitchen.

The first drops of rain began to spatter the windowpanes, but Tessa told herself she didn't care. If it rained, the guests would just have to suffer a few cool drops drizzling down the back of their necks. Nothing could spoil her wedding day.

"You think this is enough food?" Denver mocked, startling her. Turning, she saw him standing in the archway between hall and kitchen, one shoulder propped against the wall as he gazed at the overladen counters.

"Maybe."

"Maybe, my eye. We'll have to raffle off pies at the reception. Each guest will win five."

"You're exaggerating," she teased.

His smile was slow but suggestive as he sauntered across the room, rested a hip against the edge of the table and drew her into his arms. "Maybe a little." Placing his forehead against hers, he sighed. "One more night. And then three weeks of warm water, hot sun and white sand."

Her eyes sparkled. "Hard to believe, isn't it?" She heard her father's footsteps on the stairs.

"I can't wait!"

Curtis walked into the room dressed in his dusty Levi's, checked shirt and boots.

"More comfortable?" Tessa asked.

He snorted and lit a cigarette. "You'd better take some pictures tomorrow, because it's the last time you'll catch me in one of those damned suits again."

The back door creaked open and Mitchell tossed off his jacket before flopping into the nearest chair. "Don't you think you could cut your trip down to one week?" he grumbled.

"Too much work for you?" Tessa asked.

"I hate to admit it," Mitch said, offering an off-center smile to his sister, "but for a little thing, you do pull your weight around here."

"I'll be back," she reminded him.

"I'm going to run into town for a while—"

"You need to try on your tux," she reminded him.

"It'll fit."

"Let's find out tonight."

"Okay, okay. I'll be back in a couple hours. Don't get all bent out of shape. Just remember who's filling in for you while you're busy playing baccarat and drinking mojitos on the beach."

"I won't forget," she said as he left again.

"I'd better be shovin' off, too," Curtis said, eyeing his daughter fondly. "Big day tomorrow."

"The biggest."

Curtis glanced up at Denver. "I thought Colton might show up."

"So did I." Denver checked his watch. His forehead was grooved with worry. "He's still got a few hours."

"Not many," Curtis said tightly, and Tessa wondered if the bad blood between her father and Denver's brother could ever really be cleansed. Colton had been released from the hospital two days before, and Denver had hoped his brother would make it back for the wedding.

Colton, Denver had warned her, hadn't been thrilled at the prospect of Denver's marriage. Tessa figured there was nothing she could do to change his mind. That would take time.

"See ya tomorrow," Curtis said, waving as he shoved open the back door.

Tessa watched through the window. Her father ambled down the path and hunched his shoulders against the rain. "Do you believe in bad omens?" she asked as Curtis's old pickup drove away, the taillights barely visible through the zigzagging drops trailing on the glass.

"I've never thought of a summer storm as a bad omen." He wrapped his arms around her waist and kissed her neck. "In fact, I take it as a good sign. You know, a fresh start—that sort of thing."

"I don't know," she whispered leaning against him heavily. His arms were so strong, so protective.

"Don't borrow trouble." He turned her to face him. "Here we are, finally alone, the night before our wedding, and you're worried." He smoothed the lines furrowing her brow with one finger. "How about a toast?"

"A toast—with what?"

"A bottle of champagne." He eyed the pantry, where two cases of effervescent wine were stacked near the door.

"Milly will kill you."

"Milly will never know." Grinning devilishly, he strode into the pantry, pulled a jackknife from his pocket and deftly sliced the top case.

A conspiring smile twisted her lips. "I guess it is our wedding—our champagne."

"I doubt if we'll find many parched throats tomorrow. Not with this much champagne. We can spare a bottle, don't you think?"

"Well, maybe just one."

He poured them each a drink, clinked his long-stemmed glass to hers and said, "Here's to the most gorgeous bride in Montana."

"And California?"

"Most definitely California." His blue eyes danced. "And probably all the states west of the Mississippi."

"How about east?" she teased.

"Don't know about that." He wrapped one arm around her. "There might be one or two girls who are prettier than you."

"I'll remember that," she said with a laugh, sending him a wicked, provocative look.

Together they sipped champagne and shared chaste, wine-flavored kisses on the living room couch. After a week of self-imposed celibacy, Denver was about to go out of his mind. "I could carry you upstairs," he said, his eyes moving slowly down her neck to rest at the hollow of her throat.

"Then why don't you?" she teased. Half-lying across him, she poured the last of the bottle into each of their empty glasses.

"Because that damned brother of yours said he'd be back."

"He probably forgot. And he's not my 'damned brother,' he's your damned brother-in-law," she reminded him.

"Well, whoever he is, he'll show up the minute we go upstairs—"

Headlights cut through the night, flashing against the rain-spattered windows.

"What did I tell you?" Denver asked, his lips twisting wryly. "Right on schedule."

They heard boots clatter against the porch steps. The back door squeaked open. Footsteps paused in the kitchen and the refrigerator door clicked open.

"In here," Denver called over his shoulder.

"We thought you'd be back," Tessa said. She peeked over the back of the couch just as Colton McLean, one arm supported by a sling, his free hand clenched around the neck of a beer bottle, appeared in the hallway. Tall and lean, with suspicious gray eyes, an unruly beard and a rain-speckled suede jacket, Colton walked into the room as if he owned the place. Which he did. Or, at the very least, half of it.

Denver's muscles became rock hard as he slowly straightened. "Well, you finally made it! About time," he drawled, clapping his brother fondly on his back. "And from the looks of it, you're not too much the worse for wear."

Colton's glance slid to Tessa. "So tomorrow's the big day," he said without inflection. Grimacing a little, he twisted off the cap of his beer.

Tension crackled in the air. Tessa sat up quickly, smoothing her denim skirt and feeling very much like a sixteen-year-old virgin caught in the backseat of a car. Reminding herself that Colton was just Denver's brother, nothing more, she forced a smile. "I'm glad you made it. We were worried you might not get here in time for the ceremony."

"Oh, I wouldn't miss it for the world," Colton drawled,

sweeping his gaze back to Denver. "The day that Tessa Kramer finally traps you into marriage is a red letter day for the McLeans."

"No one trapped anyone." Denver's eyes became slits, and his affable smile tightened into a thin line of frustration. Crossing the room, he draped his arm possessively around Tessa's waist.

Tessa, thinking of the baby within her, wanted to die. Would Denver think she'd tried to trap him? Colton would surely hammer the point home.

"So you've said," Colton replied, his gaze drifting through the house where he'd grown up.

There was a fight brewing—as intense as the storm outside. Tessa could feel it in the tightness of Denver's muscles, see it in the pulse throbbing at his temple. She tried to intervene. "How's your shoulder?"

"Just great," Colton muttered. He leaned against the windowsill, staring at the black night beyond. His gray eyes were dark, his lips drawn tight. "Anyone else around?"

Denver shook his head. "Just us."

"So where's the rest of the Kramer clan?"

"Why do you want to know?"

"It's been a long time," Colton said slowly. "I just wanted to talk with my new *family*."

"Leave it alone, Colt," Denver commanded.

Tessa was in no mood for Colton's snide insinuations. She tilted her chin up proudly. "Dad's down at his place and Mitchell's due back anytime."

"Good."

"You know," she said, watching as he crossed the room, dropped into a chair and rested the heels of his boots on a coffee table, "my family wasn't too thrilled about this marriage."

"I'll bet."

"But they came around."

He lifted skeptical dark brows. "And why's that?"

"For the same reason you came all the way back here," she said, "because they care about me. Just as you care about Denver."

Colton took a long swallow of beer. "I didn't come here just to give you a wedding present," he said, wincing a little as he shifted in the chair. His face grew taut and white from pain. "I want to know how you can reconcile yourself to all this, Denver. How you can give up your life in L.A. and marry a woman you can't trust?"

Denver stepped between Tessa and Colton. "It's simple."

"Is it?"

"We love each other."

"Bah! Love?" Colton laughed. "You? Give me a break!" His insolent gaze moved to Tessa. "You conned him again, didn't you? He's always been weak where you're concerned."

"Leave it alone, Colt," Denver growled.

But Colton's mouth curved into a cynical smile. "At least she's smart enough to get what she wants, isn't she? She always wanted this ranch, Denver, and now she'll have it."

Tessa's chin inched upward. "Believe what you want, Colt. I'm sure I can't change your mind. But just to set the record straight, I'm marrying Denver because I love him."

"Sure you do." He took another long swallow. His eyes slid to his brother. "Have you ever explained what happened the afternoon of the fire?"

Denver crossed the room and loomed, huge and furious, over his brother. "It's a closed subject."

"Not with me." He took another long swallow, ignoring the storm in Denver's eyes.

"If you just came here to cause trouble, you may as well leave. Now."

Beneath his beard, Colton grinned roguishly. "Now that's not very hospitable of you, Denver. I traveled all this way—"

"To mess things up."

Colt's smile faded. "To straighten things out. I owe you one, and I'm paying you back right now."

Denver's voice was low, threatening. "I appreciate your concern. Now, either you're here with good wishes or you're history—if I have to throw you out myself."

"Stop it!" Tessa intervened. Outside, thunder cracked. "If you two want to fight like a couple of twelve-year-olds, for God's sake, wait until after the wedding—after Colton's recovered."

She heard the whine of an engine and her heart dropped. Glancing through the windows, she saw the truck roaring up the lane. So Mitchell was back. Maybe he could stop the fight simmering between the two brothers.

"God, Denver, open your eyes, for crying out loud!" Colton said just as the back door banged open. His voice had taken on a slight Irish accent—as if he were used to slipping into brogue. "The woman's been playing you for a fool from the first time she set eyes on you."

"That's enough!" Denver growled. "Tessa is going to be my wife and nothing you can say—"

"What the hell's goin' on in here?" Mitchell asked. Standing, dripping, in the front hall, his wheat-colored hair plastered to his head, he surveyed the room with surprised green eyes that landed with an almost audible thud on Colton.

"Well, if it isn't Denver's future brother-in-law," Colton drawled.

"Colt?" Mitchell whispered, eyeing the bearded man. All the color drained from his face.

"In the flesh." Colton stood and ignored the fire in Denver's eyes. "Tell me, what do you think about Denver and Tessa tying the big one?"

"I figure it's Tessa's life."

"And my brother's," Colton added.

"Knock it off, Colt," Denver warned.

"Not until I get to the bottom of this. Not until I convince you that the woman you're planning to marry betrayed you and the whole family. Don't you remember the fire, Denver?" he asked, clutching Denver's scarred hand and raising it high in the air like some sort of medal.

Tessa took one step toward Denver, wrapped her arm through his.

"It's over." Denver yanked his hand back.

"It'll never be over, Denver. How can you forget all those days in the hospital—all the surgery?" Colton spit out. "And the fire. You remember that, don't you? And Mom and Dad didn't make it out of there, for Christ's sake! All because Tessa, here, and her old man, were ripping us off!"

Mitch's face washed with horror. "Don't—" he rasped.

But Denver moved as quickly as a cat. He shoved his brother against the wall and pinned him there.

Colton's shoulder slammed against the wall and he winced.

Face set, Denver curled his fingers around the sodden lapels of Colton's jacket. "You want to settle this, Colt, then let's settle it. Between us."

"A fight?" Colt drawled, his face tight with pain but his hard smile flashing beneath his beard. "How chivalrous!"

"No!" Aghast, Tessa wedged herself between the two brothers. "Stop this right now! I had nothing, *nothing* to do with that fire—"

"Like hell!" Colton hissed.

"But maybe you did," she went on defensively. "You didn't have an alibi—"

"Are you crazy?" Colton asked incredulously.

"Leave her alone!" Mitch commanded.

Denver gave Colton a shake. "And get the hell out."

"Not until she admits what she and her father planned—"

"No!" Mitch cried, shaking. "She had nothing to do with it!"

"Then who—" But the question died on Colton's lips, and Tessa, horrified, met Mitch's tortured gaze.

"No—Mitch—"

Denver swung around, staring at Tessa's brother.

"It—it was my fault." Mitch's voice cut through the anger simmering in the air.

Tessa couldn't believe her ears. Wouldn't. "No, Mitch—"

"It's the truth, damn it!" Mitchell's face was pale, his eyes clouded with self-loathing.

"What the hell?" Colton said as Denver dropped his hands.

"I altered the books," Mitch admitted slowly, "I—I was ripping off the ranch."

"No!" Tessa cried, walking to him. "Don't—"

"It's true."

"I won't believe it."

He turned pleading eyes to Tessa. "I'm sorry, Tess. So sorry."

"Don't even say it," she whispered, disbelieving. Not Mitch—not the brother who had helped pull her out of her own emotional rubble.

"It's true, damn it!"

Colton's eyes fixed on Mitchell.

"I was in trouble—gambling debts—and so I started taking some money, a little here and there. Denver's father was catching up to me. I didn't mean to start the fire—it was an accident."

"You bastard! You lying, cheating, murdering bastard!" Colton growled, starting across the room.

Denver held him back. "Let him finish," he said, but his voice was harsh, his blue eyes frigid.

"Don't do this," Tessa whispered, "You don't have to—"

"I do, Tess," he said, his eyes pleading with her to understand. "It's been too long. I should have told everything right up front, but Dad insisted that it would only be worse for me." Mitch's body was shaking. "God, I'm sorry!"

"Curtis was in on this?" Denver hissed.

"Not really."

"What the hell is that supposed to mean?"

"He didn't know. I'd been stealing from the petty cash in the office, and I knew old man McLean was on to me." His eyes turned dark with the memory, his breathing irregular. "I—I was going to rip the ranch off one last time and take off. But something happened, I don't know what."

"Oh, God," she murmured.

Colton tried to break away from Denver's grip. "You were paying off gambling debts, and it cost my family their lives?" he roared. "Christ, what kind of man are you?"

"And you 'accidentally' caused a fire that consumed the whole damned stables and everything in it?" Denver hissed.

"Stop it! Please, all of you," Tessa commanded. "Stop it!"

But Mitch wasn't finished. "I used to smoke," he said. "I was nervous, and I guess I must have dropped my cigarette in the straw in the stables before I went up to the office. By the time I took the money and changed the books the downstairs was already in flames. I opened all the stalls I could and left."

"You bloody bastard!" Colton lunged again, but Denver held him back.

Tessa's eyes were bright with tears, her insides ripping apart. Her world was out of kilter on its axis, spinning crazily out of control. "You could have told me," she whispered.

"You were already destroyed because of Denver!" he spit out, then lost some of his fire. "Dad thought it best if no one said anything. I'd already had a couple of scrapes with the law—Oh, hell, Tess, why do you think Dad drinks so much? Why do you think it's been worse since the fire? Because he took the rap for me, damn it!"

Denver released Colton. "Two people died in that fire, Kramer!" Colton thundered. "Two people!"

"I know it."

"What kind of a miserable bastard are you, Kramer?" Denver demanded, his temper exploding. "My parents and seven horses burned to death! And all this time, you knew. Your father knew! Why the hell didn't you say anything?"

"Denver," Tessa whispered, seeing the anguish in his eyes, the throbbing of the arteries at his temples.

"Oh, God, I don't know," Mitch whispered, his eyes red. "I'm sorry, I'm so sorry."

"Sorry?" Colton bellowed. "Sorry?"

Denver's teeth clenched. "Why the hell didn't you tell anyone? And don't give me that baloney about doing what your father wanted! That's just plain crazy. You ran because you were scared. Because you were a coward."

"Yes!" Mitch choked out, his eyes swimming in tears of remorse.

"Just listen to him!" Tessa yelled, defending her brother. "Can't you see how hard it is?"

"Harder than this?" Denver asked, stretching his fingers wide, his webbing of reddish scars more visible than ever before.

Mitchell was shaking. "Dad was sure that I'd be sent to prison for . . . involuntary manslaughter. He told me to join the Army—to get away. Let things die down."

"And so your dad poured himself even deeper into a bottle," Denver accused. "All because of you!"

"You miserable, lying murderer!" Colton hissed. He lunged at Mitchell, drawing back his fist. He connected with a right cross. Mitchell's head snapped back, and he reeled backward to land against the wall. His skull crashed into the wainscoting and he slid to the floor.

"Stop this!" Tessa screamed, running to Mitchell's side.

"Get out, Colton! Just get out!" She dropped to her knees as Mitchell, holding his jaw, struggled to a sitting position. "It's over! Can't you see it's over?"

"It'll never be over," Colton snarled, as he kicked at an end table, sending it crashing against a far wall, then stalked out of the room.

Tessa's eyes flew to Denver. His face was taut, his eyes filled with accusations. He stood poised over Mitchell, muscles coiled, nostrils flared, as if he, too, would like to beat the living hell out of her brother,

"So that's it, Tessa," Denver said. "Your brother is a murderer and your father a drunk. Hell of a family I'm marryin' into!"

"No one's twisting your arm," she threw back at him.

His lips thinned furiously before he turned, shoved open the front door and stalked outside into the driving rain.

All the pain of the past—the lies, the treachery, the mental anguish of the days after the fire—burned bright in Tessa's mind. Denver had walked out on her before. And now she, because of Mitch, was linked to the fire. No doubt he blamed her. No doubt he thought she had known the truth all along.

"I'm sorry, Tess," Mitch said, biting his lip and rubbing a hand over the bruise already showing on his chin. "I should've told you a long time ago. I should've gone straight to the sheriff. God, it's been hell."

She saw him more clearly then, the relief that seemed to wash away his scowl, the pride that held his chin upward. Obviously Mitch had suffered every day since the accident.

"It's all right."

"It's not, Tess! Two people died. People Denver loved." He blinked rapidly. "It cost so many people so much. But it's over. Thank God, it's finally over." Standing, he forced pride back into his shoulders. "I think I've got a few phone calls to make."

"Can't you wait till morning? Give yourself time to talk to an attorney."

His green eyes were calm when they met hers. "I've waited seven years. It's time to face the music." Wincing, he reached for the phone.

But Tessa snatched the receiver from his fingers and slammed it back in the cradle. "Just stop and think a minute—call Ross Anderson."

"Forget it, Tess. This time I do what I should've done seven years ago. Don't you have a few things to do, to get ready for tomorrow?"

Tomorrow—the wedding!

"I don't know if there will be a wedding," she whispered, shaken to her roots. She ran quivering fingers through her hair while her mind spun out of control, trying to sort out everything that had happened in the past ten minutes—as well as the past seven years. "Denver and I have a few things to iron out," she said shakily. She forced her shoulders square, took in a deep breath and told herself it was now or never. "Will you be all right?"

Mitch smiled tiredly. "Better than I've been for seven years."

"I'll be right back," she said. "Don't do anything foolish."

"I can handle it, Tess." He reached for the phone and waved away the protest forming on her lips.

"Okay, Mitch, do it your way."

"You just worry about McLean."

"That I will," she vowed, thrusting open the front door and dashing down the rain-slickened steps. Wind tore at her hair. Rain drizzled relentlessly from the sky to run down her neck and cheeks. Squinting, she scanned the yard. Denver was nowhere in sight.

Maybe he's already left, she thought, her heart thudding painfully.

Then she saw him. Tails of his shirt flapping in the wind,

his hair ruffled, he sagged against the bole of an old apple tree near the burned-out remains of the stables. She took off running, her heart in her throat. This time she wasn't afraid. This time she would force the issue. This time, come hell or high water, she was going to put out those last smoldering ashes of the fire no matter how long it took!

"What're you doing here?" he growled as she dashed through the wet grass.

"Looking for you."

"Why?"

"Because we need to talk."

His face was lined and strained, his shoulders set. He didn't look at her, just glared at the ugly black timbers. "What did you know about the fire, Tessa?"

"Nothing more than I told you."

"Your brother didn't fill you in?" he asked sarcastically.

"Not until tonight."

"You expect me to believe that?"

Wind howled through the valley, chilling the air. In the distance, thunder rumbled across the hills.

"You can believe what you want to," she said, shivering. "But you'd better listen to what I have to say. I've taken a lot from you, Denver. More than I should have. And I've done it for only one reason. Because I love you. I've let you humiliate me, degrade me, use me and accuse me, but I won't take it anymore."

She saw him flinch, but still he didn't look her way.

"Go back to Los Angeles, Denver. Run away. It's what you're best at! But don't expect me to be here if you return, because this is the last time I'll let you walk away from me, the last time I'll ever let you drag my heart through these damned ashes!"

His jaw worked angrily. His fingers clenched and flexed only to clench again.

She wanted to drop to her knees and beg him to love her,

to forget the past, but she stood ramrod stiff, letting the rain and wind lash at her face and hair, bracing herself for the worst. "This is it, Denver. Either you love me forever, or you walk away. It can't be anything else."

"You've always been a dreamer," he said cuttingly.

"And you've always been in my dreams."

He blinked rapidly. Rain slid down his face and neck, past his wet collar. "And you've been in mine, Tessa," he admitted. "But maybe that's all we had. Dreams. Ashes. Nothing solid."

With a boldness she'd never felt before she planted herself in front of him and poked one long finger at his chest. "You listen to me, Denver McLean, we can make our dreams come true. And it doesn't matter what Colton or Mitch or the whole damned world thinks or does. All that matters is here and now. Me and you. What's it going to be?" She steadied herself, ready for the rejection she felt hanging in the air. *So be it,* she thought, *there's no going back.*

His throat worked. "What I want," he said, his voice as rough as the stormy night, "is you. Nothing more. Nothing less. But it has to be forever."

Tears burned behind her eyes. She could barely believe her ears. "You're sure?"

"Yes," he whispered, his voice nearly lost on the wind.

"Well, it can't just be us."

His jaw tightened, his features twisting in torture. "Why not?"

"Because I'm pregnant, Denver. I found out for sure this morning. You're going to be a father."

For a second he didn't speak. "You're sure?"

"Positive."

"Oh, God."

"You can have me and the baby—or you can take a walk and never look back," she said, her heart frozen at the thought, though she loved him enough to let him go. "I won't tie you down."

"Like hell," he murmured, his lips curving into a smile of wonder. "You're never getting away from me again."

"But the baby—"

"Makes it all the better," he said, blinking rapidly. "A baby?" Rain slid down his collar and his arms wrapped securely around her. "Marry me, Tessa. Be mine the rest of my life."

"I wouldn't have it any other way," she vowed, just as his rain-soaked arms tightened around her; strong, possessive and warm.

His lips crushed hers hungrily. "Neither would I."

"Welcome home, Denver," she said with a sigh.

A shudder ripped through him. Thunder cracked in the dark sky. "I don't think I ever really left."

"You may kiss the bride," the preacher announced, and a whisper of approval swept through the guests standing on the wet lawn behind Nate and Paula Edwards's manor.

"Amen," Denver murmured. He lifted Tessa's ivory veil and stared deep into her wide hazel eyes. His lips covered hers in a familiar warmth, and for a minute he was lost in her, aware only of her fingers on his shoulders, his arms circling her waist, the eager promise of her mouth molding to his.

"I love you," she whispered, when at last he lifted his head. Her eyes were bright with wonder, her cheeks flushed.

"Let's leave."

"Soon," she promised as they strolled among the guests, arms linked, smiles wide.

Denver caught his brother's eye and winked. It had taken long hours of convincing, but finally Colton had agreed to attend the wedding, albeit reluctantly. Even Mitch had decided to attend, though earlier he'd spent hours with the county sheriff and insurance people. Things would work out, though, Denver decided, glancing again at his gorgeous bride. Mitchell might have to do some time. But then again, maybe not. No one, not even Colton, was pressing charges. As for Colton, he was trapped in Montana, at least until his arm healed.

"You take care of her," Curtis said as he approached.

"I can take care of myself." Tessa laughed.

"Lord, am I tired of hearin' that!" Curtis grinned at Denver. "Now maybe you can listen to it."

"I'll take care of her," Denver said, his eyes glinting mischievously. "In more ways than one."

"Talk is cheap," she quipped.

"Just you wait, Mrs. McLean," he replied, but he laughed just the same. For seven years he'd carried a burden deep in his soul, and now, beneath a cloudy sky, he felt as if he were finally free.

"Come on, let's get out of here," he said.

"And where will we go?"

"How about Brazil? Or maybe Singapore," he mocked and she jabbed him playfully in the ribs.

"How about the Caribbean and then Three Falls, Montana?" she suggested, as her new brother-in-law, looking uncomfortable and stiff in his formal suit, approached.

"Congratulations," Colton said, forcing a smile. "Isn't it a custom to kiss the bride?"

Denver's lips twisted. "I'm not too keen on tradition."

Colton raised his eyebrows, then touched the boutonniere pinned to Denver's black tuxedo lapel. "You could've fooled me," he said with a genuine smile that slashed white against his beard. He glanced at Tessa. "When you get tired of this guy, maybe you should give me a call—"

"Don't even think it," Denver warned, but he laughed when he caught the teasing glimmer in Colton's gray eyes.

"The man's incorrigible," Denver decided as his brother strolled uncomfortably through the crowd.

"A McLean family trait," she observed. "Let's just hope it's not passed on to the next generation." She smiled then, a knowing smile that caused his heart to lurch.

A warmth spread through Denver like none he'd ever felt before. "No regrets?" she asked, cocking her head coyly.

"No regrets."

Tender Trap

Chapter One

"**D**amn it all to hell!" Colton McLean growled, kicking at the straw and slamming the stall gate so hard the timbers of the old stable rumbled. Several horses snorted nervously. "Where's Black Magic?" Colton whirled to face Curtis Kramer, the ranch foreman.

"Gone."

"I can see that."

Curtis rubbed his silver-stubbled chin. "I already checked the paddocks and the south pasture."

"What about the other barns? Maybe someone put him in the wrong place."

Squinting at the younger man, Curtis slowly shook his head. "Nope. Len searched all the buildings and the paddocks. Black Magic's nowhere in the yard."

"He couldn't disappear without a trace!" Colton strode out of the stallion barn, ignoring the restless grunts of the other horses. Black Magic was the single most valuable asset of the McLean Ranch. And he'd vanished into thin air. "I knew I should never have agreed to stay here," he muttered, thinking unkind thoughts of his older brother, Denver, who, with his wife, Tessa, had left Montana three weeks before in order to "tie up some loose ends" of the engineering firm he was moving from L.A. to the nearby town of Three Falls. This ranch was Denver's business as well; Colton didn't want any part of it.

Outside, the night was as dark as Colton's black mood. Rain from the vast Montana sky fell relentlessly, bending the grass in the surrounding fields and turning the ground to muck.

Curtis had to run to keep up with Colton's long strides. "If ya ask me," he said, catching his breath, "this is all the doin' of Ivan Aldridge."

Jolted at the mention of a sworn enemy, Colton turned on the older man. "Aldridge? What's he got to do with this?"

"He's stolen Black Magic, sure as I'm standin' here!"

"Bah!"

Curtis lifted his chin. "As sure as he stole that horse last spring, he's taken him again."

"Last spring? What the devil are you talking about?"

"Didn't anyone tell you?"

Colton's patience snapped. He was cold and wet, and the last thing he wanted to do was stand in the driving rain and discuss Ivan Aldridge. "No one knew where I was last year," he reminded the older man.

"Well, while you were getting shot up in Northern Ireland, Black Magic disappeared for nearly two weeks."

Colton didn't want to think about the bar in Northern Ireland where, six months before, someone—Colton didn't know who—had witnessed him snapping pictures, taken offense and turned his gun on him. Colton was lucky to have gotten away with his life. "The horse escaped last spring?"

"I think he had help. No one could prove it, of course, but the way I figure it, Ivan Aldridge stole the horse, used him to service some of his mares, then let him go before anyone was the wiser."

"That's crazy,"

"Yeah, that's what everyone told me last year. And then when the horse showed up, everyone got busy again and conveniently forgot that he'd been gone. No one dug very deep. The insurance company and the rest of us were relieved."

"So what's this got to do with Aldridge?"

"Old Ivan always swore to get even."

Colton scowled. He knew better than anyone just how deep Ivan Aldridge's hatred ran.

"No way. The horse hasn't been stolen! And as for the feud—let's not bring it all out in the open again, okay?" Colton suggested, irritated. Just the mention of Ivan brought back memories of Cassie—memories he'd sworn to destroy.

"Suit yourself." Curtis delved into his shirt pocket for his cigarettes. "But it's not my neck on the line. When Denver finds out the most valuable stud in the state of Montana is missing, there'll be hell to pay."

"Maybe he never should have left me in charge."

"Maybe you never should have agreed."

"Don't remind me," Colton bit out. He needed a drink— a hot drink. Irish coffee.

Curtis cupped his hands around a cigarette and lit up. "You're the boss," he said, plucking a piece of tobacco from his tongue. "But if I were you I wouldn't let my feelings for Ivan's daughter get in the way."

Colton took a menacing step toward the older man. "I don't have any feelings for Cassie Aldridge."

Curtis shrugged. "Eight years ago—"

"Eight years is a long time," Colton cut in, closing the subject.

Curtis knew when to quit. "Okay, okay. Forget about Cassie."

"I have," Colton lied.

"So what should we do about Black Magic?"

"Find him!" Colton rubbed the back of his neck. It was wet. "We'll split up, go over every field. Len and Daniel can check the western fields, you check south and I'll take the north."

"Fair enough. Just be sure to check the property butting up to Aldridge's place."

"I will," Colton promised as he climbed into his Jeep and headed north. He'd check every inch of fence line, every square foot of the northern corner of the property, if for no other reason than to prove Curtis wrong. He and Curtis had a tenuous relationship at best. For years Colton had thought Curtis responsible for the fire that had cost his parents their lives. However, he'd been wrong, and in the past few months he had discovered just how much Curtis knew about ranching. The old man, once he'd given up the bottle, was loyal, true-blue and Denver's father-in-law.

Now, with Denver in California, they had to work together—at least for a few more weeks. Then, once Colton's shoulder healed from the wound he'd received while on assignment in Northern Ireland, he'd take off. Colton couldn't wait to leave Three Falls, Montana. As soon as his doctor gave the word, Colton McLean was history in big sky country.

Two hours later Colton hadn't found any trace of the horse. His shoulder throbbed and his muscles were cramped from the cold. Angry with Black Magic and the world in general, he squinted past the rain-spattered windshield.

"That's what you get for letting your brother talk you into sticking around and looking after things," he jeered, glancing at his reflection in the rearview mirror. Two gray eyes glowered back at him. He turned his attention to the acres of Montana ranch land stretching past the beams of the headlights. "Damn horse."

Colton yanked on the steering wheel, guiding his Jeep along the fence line. Maybe he'd get lucky and find Black Magic. But maybe not. The chronic pain in his shoulder reminded him that his luck had run out some six months before.

The wipers slapped the rain off the glass as he studied the

sagging wire. Easing up on the throttle, he slowed near a thicket of oaks in the northeast corner of the property. The Sage River cut through Aldridge property on the far side of the fence.

Colton was about to give up, but a gaping hole between two fence posts caught his eye.

Jaw clenched, Colton yanked on the emergency brake, let the Jeep idle, then hopped out. His boots sank into an inch of mud. His eyes never left the fence—or what was left of it.

Sure enough, the fence wire had been cut, all four strands neatly snipped. The rusted wires sagged, leaving more than enough room for a horse—or an entire herd—to slip through to the stretch of land between the fence and the river.

Fingering a clipped end, Colton noticed a clump of ebony hair—probably from Black Magic's tail—clinging to a barb. Beneath his beard, Colton's jaw grew rigid. Rain and wind lashed at his face. "Son of a—"

Thunder cracked over the hills.

Colton swung the beam of his flashlight over the ground. Hoofprints and bootprints were clearly imprinted in the soft earth. A cigarette butt had been tossed on the wet stones flanking the river. Thick, heavy-treaded tire tracks followed the jagged course of the Sage. Swollen by spring rains, the river rushed by, shining silver, roaring so loudly he barely heard the next clap of thunder.

Colton glared at the swift current. The Sage was a natural dividing line between the McLean Ranch and the Aldridge spread—as deep and wide as the feud that had existed between the two families for nearly a generation.

So Curtis had been right. Black Magic hadn't just disappeared, he'd been stolen! Again. This time from under Colton's very nose. Transported to heaven-knew-where by a truck that had been waiting on Aldridge land.

With all the proof he needed, he strode swiftly back to the pickup. He ignored the rain pouring down the collar of his jacket and the sharp jab of pain in his shoulder as he yanked open the door and crawled into the battered old rig.

Ramming his Jeep into gear, he stared through the windshield toward a scraggly thicket of oak and pine, beyond which stood the Aldridge ranch house. The house where Cassie still lived.

Colton's fingers curled over the gearshift. Cassie's image swam before his eyes. Impatiently he shoved the vision aside. Eight years had passed since he'd last seen her. If he had his way, he would never lay eyes on her again, never stare into her luminous face nor touch the lustrous sheen of her blue-black hair.

Stomping on the throttle, he turned the Jeep toward the road leading to the Aldridge ranch. He hoped Ivan was home. Tonight was as good a time as any to drag the truth from the old man.

Cassie twisted off the faucet and stepped out of the shower. Through the bathroom window she heard Erasmus, her father's crossbred collie, barking and growling loudly enough to wake the dead.

"I'm coming!" she called. "Hold your horses!" Muttering to herself about Erasmus's particular lack of brains, she snatched her favorite robe from a hook on the bathroom door and stuffed her arms down the sleeves.

She was so tired she wanted to drop. After spending the past twelve hours at the Lassiter ranch, trying to save some of George Lassiter's heifers from a serious case of milk fever, she was beat. Two animals had survived. Three had died. Veterinary work wasn't for the fainthearted, she decided as she cinched her belt around her waist.

She dashed down the threadbare red runner on the stairs. Outside, Erasmus was going out of his mind. Barking gruffly and snarling, the old dog paced the porch and scratched at the front door.

"What's gotten into you?" Cassie asked, flinging open the door. Fur bristling, teeth bared, Erasmus streaked past her and dashed around the corner to the kitchen. "What the devil?" Cassie whispered.

"Down!" a male voice commanded from inside the house.

Cassie froze.

Erasmus quit whining.

"Miserable beast," the voice muttered again.

Cassie's heart slammed against her rib cage. Who was in the kitchen? Her throat cotton-dry, she silently crossed the worn living room carpet, opened her father's gun closet and cringed at the soft click of the lock. Quickly she withdrew her old .22. It was unloaded, of course, but the intruder, whoever he was, wouldn't know that.

Did Erasmus know the man? she wondered wildly, disturbed that the dog had obeyed the rough command. She clenched her fingers tightly around the stock and barrel and padded noiselessly to the kitchen. Lifting the rifle to her shoulder, she stepped into the light.

"What's going on here?" she demanded, then stopped dead in her tracks. She nearly dropped the .22.

There, in the middle of the room, was Colton McLean—the one man in the world she detested. Big as life, his wet Stetson low over his eyes, he straddled one of the chipped maple chairs and scratched Erasmus's ears. The traitorous dog whined in pleasure.

His gaze, as cold as silver, clashed with hers. "Cassie," he drawled. "It's been a long time."

Chapter Two

Cassie's heart nearly dropped through the floor. "What're you doing here?"

Tipping his Stetson back, Colton surveyed her through slitted silvery eyes. "Waiting."

"For?"

"Your father."

"He's not here."

Colton merely shrugged. His gaze narrowed on her, his expression murderous. His face was rugged, craggier than she remembered it. A full beard covered his jaw, and his features were lean and jaded with the added years. His denim jacket, stretched taut across his shoulders, was wet from the rain. His attention drifted to the rifle. Its barrel gleamed blue in the dim light from a single low-watt bulb mounted high on the ceiling.

"What're you going to do, Cassie? Shoot me?"

"I haven't decided yet." She lowered the rifle.

"I've been used for target practice before." His teeth flashed beneath his beard, and her stomach knotted as she remembered the rumors she'd heard about the shooting in Northern Ireland—how he was lucky he hadn't been killed.

"How'd you get in?"

"The door wasn't locked."

"So you just waltzed in and made yourself comfortable?"

His lips twisted. "Believe me, Cass, I'm not comfortable."

"But you had no right—"

"Probably not." His cold gaze slid slowly up her body before resting on her face. She felt stripped bare.

Several heart-stopping seconds ticked by before she found her voice. Her hands were clammy; her voice threatened to shake. Colton McLean was the last person she'd expected to find in her kitchen. Though he'd been back in Montana for nearly six months, he'd been reclusive and, according to the rumors circulating in town, hadn't been seen much. Cassie hadn't run into him once. "Don't you believe in knocking?" she asked.

He glanced at the open door and the unlatched screen. "Don't you believe in locking your doors?"

"Dad lost his key—oh, never mind!"

"I knocked. Twice. No one answered."

"I was in the—"

"I can see where you were. I heard the shower running."

Suddenly aware of her damp hair, her towel-buffed skin and her naked body protected only by a ragged terry robe, she clenched the rifle more tightly. She wasn't afraid of Colton McLean, not really, but the sight of him brought back too many memories—dangerous memories—of a love affair she'd rather forget.

"You knew I was upstairs taking a shower? And you came in anyway?"

"I knew the water was running. That's all."

"Nervy of you."

He sighed and rubbed his jaw. "When's Ivan coming back?"

"I don't know, but you can't wait here for him."

"Why not?"

"Take a wild guess," she invited, her temper flaring.

"I couldn't begin to," he drawled.

"Try." At first she'd been surprised that he'd landed, dripping and ready for battle, in the middle of her kitchen, but as she slowly recovered, her shock gave way to anger. It had been over eight years since she'd seen him, eight years since he'd walked out the door of this very house! And now he had the nerve to straddle one of her kitchen chairs as if he owned the place!

"Why don't you just tell me?" he drawled.

"Because I don't want you here! I've had a long day and all I want to do is curl up in bed with a good book!"

"Don't let me stop you," he taunted.

"I'm in no mood for games, Colton."

"Neither am I."

"I'll tell Dad you stopped by and he'll call you."

"Sure he will."

She clenched her teeth. "Hasn't anyone told you it's dangerous to bait a woman holding a rifle?"

He laughed, a short derisive sound that conjured up half-forgotten images of a warm summer filled with young love. "I remember how good a shot you were, Cassie. You couldn't hit the broad side of a barn."

"I've improved."

He cocked one dark brow, and his eyes glinted. "Have you, now?" he asked, his voice low, almost seductive.

"Get out, Colton!"

"You haven't even heard why I'm here."

"I'm not interested."

"No? Not even if I told you Black Magic was missing?"

"Black Magic?" she repeated.

"You've heard of him?"

"Of course I have—the whole county has," she said, remembering the fiery charcoal stallion with the jagged white blaze running the length of his nose. "I treated him once last year."

"Oh, that's right, you're a veterinarian now," he jeered, his lips twisting.

"And you're a famous photojournalist, right?" she threw back at him, agitated. He had no reason to mock her career, no right to barge into her house and badger her! He'd left her life in shambles, and she'd managed to pull herself back together. Alone. "So what are you doing hanging around here?"

"Marking time," he replied, never taking his eyes off her. She set the rifle against the wall and forced a thin, impatient smile.

Colton watched her. "I just want to ask Ivan a few questions."

"About Black Magic?"

"Yes."

Cassie frowned. "You think Dad might know where your horse is?"

"Denver's horse," he shot back.

"That's right. You're not into ranching, are you?"

"Never have been."

"Neither was Denver. He changed," she flung out, hoping to wound him a little, though any hope she had that Colton had mellowed over the years died when she noticed the hard angle of his jaw.

"I won't." His eyes were steely gray as he scrutinized her. She saw the room as he did—peeling paint and scratched counters, worn, overwaxed flooring, blackened kettles hanging from dusty ceiling beams. His eyes were restless, and there was a wariness about him, a hard edge she didn't remember.

"Why're you here? Why not your brother?" she finally asked.

"Denver and his wife are in Los Angeles."

She remembered now. In her work as a veterinarian, she'd

overheard snatches of conversation at the surrounding ranches. Denver and Tessa would be away for another few weeks. "And you're stuck with the ranch," she taunted, unable to resist goading Colton. "So how did you manage to lose the most valuable horse on the spread?"

"I didn't lose anything. He was stolen."

Finally she understood why he was sitting in the middle of the Aldridge kitchen, his expression hard with unnamed accusations, his bearded chin jutted in fury.

Her voice, when she found it, was barely a whisper. "You're not here to suggest that Dad had something to do with Black Magic's disappearance, are you? Because if you are, you can just haul your self-righteous backside out of here right now!"

He didn't move.

Cassie advanced on him. "Dad would never—"

"He's made threats."

Her lips twisted. "That was a long time ago, Colton."

"Feuds have a way of smoldering—then flaring when you least expect them."

"Not this one!" She poked a finger at his chest. Her skin collided with rock-hard denim-clad muscles. "You'd better leave. Now! Just get in your truck or Jeep or car or whatever it is you've got parked outside and take off, before *I* decide to start the feud all over again by strangling you!"

"Strong words, Cass," he chided.

"Strong accusations, Colt."

He eyed her speculatively. "You've changed."

"Thank God."

His gaze lowered to the hollow of her breasts displayed all too vividly by her gaping robe. "But in some respects, you're still the same—"

"Get out, Colton."

"Not until I talk to Ivan," he said with infuriating calm.

"He may not be back tonight."

"I'll take my chances."

"You can't."

Colton didn't budge.

Emotions, old and new, roiled deep within Cassie. She hated him—hated the very sight of him. Or at least that's what she'd been telling herself for eight years. "Dad doesn't want you here—don't you remember?"

His eyes narrowed. "How could I forget?"

"Then take a hike and do it fast! Or I'll call the sheriff's office."

"Go ahead." With a jaded half grin, he motioned toward the phone. "I know a deputy there, Mark Gowan. You've probably heard of him."

She had. Mark was one of the best the sheriff's department employed.

"Go ahead. Call him. When Gowan gets here, I'll explain about Black Magic and the fact that the fence was cut—the fence between your property and mine. Then I'll repeat every threat Ivan's made against the McLeans to the good sheriff!"

Cassie blanched.

"And if that isn't good enough, I'll tell my tale to the local press—I've got connections, you know. Friends in high places. It comes with the territory."

"You bastard!"

He winced a little.

"You wouldn't!" she whispered, grasping at straws. "You'd look like a fool!"

"And your father would look like a criminal," he growled.

He was bluffing! She knew it. He couldn't risk another scandal with the McLean name. Not after the last one—when John McLean had seduced Cassie's mother! She reached for the phone, but he caught her wrist. The receiver clattered against the wall. "This would be a whole lot easier, you know, if you let me take a look around myself."

His fingers were hot and hard against her flesh. "Dad's never stolen anything in his life!"

"So prove it."

She glared at him indignantly. Why bother explaining? The stern set of Colton's jaw told her he'd already tried and convicted her father, just as he had her, years before. "Let go of me, Colton."

He didn't.

She tried a new tack. "This happened before—right? Last year. I heard it from Milly Samms, Denver's housekeeper. The horse was missing, then just showed up. This is probably the same kind of mistake."

"This is no mistake, Cassie. Someone took Black Magic. I want to know who." His grip tightened, the warm pads of his fingers playing havoc with her pulse. She tried yanking her hand from his, but he wouldn't let go. "Come on, Cassie. Here's your chance to prove me wrong."

Her gaze burned into his. "One of your ranch hands just got careless."

He dropped her hand. "Then you won't mind if I walk through the barns and stables?"

"Are you crazy? I'm not going to let you go poking around, disturbing the animals—"

"After I see what I came to see, I'll leave."

She wavered. She wanted him to leave, and the opportunity to prove him wrong and put him in his place was tempting. "Okay—but this isn't going to take all night. We check out the stables and that's it."

He nodded.

"It'll take me a few minutes to change."

"Don't bother. I can find my way around—"

"No way!" she sputtered. "You can't march over here with

ridiculous accusations and then start tearing the ranch apart board by board! Your stallion is probably just lost, and I'm not about to let you turn this place upside down just because you 'suspect' Black Magic was stolen. If that's the case, go to the sheriff! If not, just give me five minutes to change."

He spread his palms, and an ingratiating smile stole across his bearded chin. "By all means . . ."

Goaded, she stomped out of the room and took the stairs two at a time. Her mind was spinning as she tied her hair away from her face and yanked on a pair of jeans. Cassie didn't believe Black Magic had been stolen—not for a minute. The cut wires were just an accident. Most likely someone had been repairing the ancient fence earlier in the day. As soon as she spoke with her father, the downed fence would be explained. And Colton McLean would have to eat crow!

Smiling at that thought, she pulled a wheat-colored sweater over her head and hurried back to the kitchen.

Colton was leaning against the door, one booted foot propped on the seat of a chair as he stared impatiently through a rain-spattered window. Thick brows converged over his eyes, and his face was a hard, rough-hewn mask. He'd matured in the past eight years. Living a dangerous life as a photojournalist who snapped pictures of war-ravaged political hot spots had stolen any trace of boyishness from his face. Even his coffee-colored hair had a few strands of gray at the temples, and his skin was lined near the corners of his eyes.

"You won't see anything from here," she pointed out.

He swung his gaze back to hers, and for just an instant she remembered him as he had been, handsome and warm. He'd smiled often then, his irreverent grin spreading from one side of his tanned face to the other. There had always been a dangerous side to him—his temper was infamous—but there had been a kind side, too, and she'd loved him with all of her naive young heart. There had been a few other boys she'd had crushes on while growing up, but deep in her heart, from the time she had turned fourteen, she'd harbored a love for Colton so deep it had kept her awake at night. But that was years ago, she reminded herself.

"Let's go," he said gruffly.

Without a word she swept past him. On the back porch she snatched her faded jacket and a flashlight from the cupboard, then tugged on her boots.

Outside, the wind slashed at her face. Rain peppered the ground and slid down Cassie's collar as she followed her flashlight's unsteady beam. She half ran to keep up with Colton's long strides.

"Don't upset the horses," she warned.

"Wouldn't dream of it."

"Good." She reached for the door. "Several mares are due to foal, and I don't want anything disturbing them."

He slanted her a hard glance. "I'm not interested in your mares. I just want to find Black Magic."

"Then you're going to be disappointed."

"It won't be the first time," he said, his gaze locking with hers. For an instant she hesitated, lost in his stare. Her throat felt suddenly swollen and hot.

Giving herself a mental shake, Cassie strode inside. The familiar smells of oiled leather, warm animals and horse dung mingled with the dust. She snapped on the lights.

Cobwebs clung to the rafters, and a fine layer of grime covered the windows. Horses snorted and rustled the straw scattered over the floor of their stalls. Inquisitive dark heads poked over the top rails, and a few mares nickered at the sight of Cassie.

"It's okay," she murmured, petting each velvet-soft muzzle thrust her way.

Colton's gaze swept the boxes, taking in every detail, each swollen-bodied mare and shifting, nervous stallion. One wild-eyed gray pawed anxiously in his stall, tossing his head at the unfamiliar scent of Colton. "Friendly guy," Colton observed dryly.

"Like you," she shot back.

Colton's boots echoed against the concrete floor. "Black Magic's not here," he muttered under his breath. His face was drawn, his expression clouded.

Cassie felt like smirking. "Satisfied?"

"Not yet."

"Come on, Colton," she jibed, unable to hide the sparkle in her eyes. "Admit it. You were wrong."

"Aren't there any other barns?"

"Just for the cattle—"

"Let's check them."

"No!" She reached for the door, wrenched it open and flipped off the lights in one swift motion. "I put up with this—this stupid idea of yours, just to prove that you were wrong about Dad. But I'm not about to let you rip apart every blasted building on the ranch just to prove my point!"

He moved swiftly, curling his hand around her upper arm. "I'd like to think that your old man is as honest as you claim he is," he said slowly, his eyes glittering dangerously in the darkness. "But I've got to be sure. Your family has a history of lying."

She thought her heart would break. Though she'd told herself he could never hurt her again, she'd been wrong. Struggling against the old wounds, she whispered, "I never lied to you, Colton."

"Ha!"

As she tilted her chin up defiantly, her gaze collided with the naked cynicism in his. "Believe what you want, but I swear by everything I believe in, that I never lied to you."

A muscle worked in his jaw, and for a second, indecision flashed in his eyes. His expression became gentler as he gazed down on her, and Cassie sensed he was wrestling an inner battle. "Maybe you just twisted the truth."

"And maybe *you* did," she whispered as his breath, warm and familiar, filled the air between them. Her throat went dry at the nearness of him.

If only she could forget how much she had loved him, how much she had cared. . . .

Then, as suddenly as it had appeared, his uncertainty vanished. His jaw slid to the side, and he surveyed her through narrowed eyes. "I played the fool for you once, Cassie," he admitted, his lips thin as he tossed her arm away in disgust. "Believe me, it won't happen again."

"You arrogant bastard," she cried, stepping away from him. "You've got a lot of nerve. . . ." Knowing she was fighting the inevitable anyway, she led him to the barn across the yard. She barely felt the rain and mud as she marched into the tall building and switched on the lights. A few white-faced Herefords lowed and shoved their heads through the manger, hoping that she would toss some more feed in the trough.

Colton followed her inside. He noticed the challenge in her eyes and the pride that stiffened her slim shoulders as she waved her arm in a wide arc. "Be my guest," she invited caustically.

"I will." He strode through the building, searching it from one end to the other and found nothing, not one bloody trace of Black Magic. Swearing under his breath, he wended his way through the bins of feed, oats and loose bales of hay to the door where Cassie leaned insolently against the dusty frame. Her arms were folded under her breasts, and her generous mouth was curved into a fair imitation of a smirk. "Find him?" she asked, pretending interest in her nails.

"No."

"You're sure?" she drawled.

"Positive."

She cocked her head to one side and glanced toward the ceiling. "Better check the hayloft," she suggested sweetly, savoring her revenge. "Dad could have used the grain elevator to lift your precious horse up there."

Unexpectedly Colton grinned. He eyed the loft, a platform built some ten feet above the wooden floor. Tightly stacked bales were piled to the apex of the roof, where a small round window reflected the beam of Cassie's flashlight. "You've made your point, Miss Aldridge."

"About time." Shoving open the door, she shined her flashlight on his dented Jeep. "Now, if you're done accusing my family and searching this place from stem to stern, I think I'll go into the house. It's been a long day."

"It's not over yet."

"Oh, yes it is!" she said succinctly. "At least for me." Her eyes blazed. "The next time you go around accusing innocent people of crimes they didn't commit, you'd better get your facts straight."

"You're a good one to start talking about the truth, Cass."

The words cut deep, stinging like the bite of a whip. "As I said, Colton, I never lied to you. You just weren't man enough to trust me!"

"Trust you?"

"Yes. You didn't even have the guts to let me explain!"

"Explain what? That you were trying to trap me into marriage by imagining a baby that didn't exist?"

"No!"

"Don't, Cassie," he whispered, his voice low, his eyes dark.

"Get the hell off my land, McLean!" she ordered. Spinning on her heel, she took off for the house.

Colton watched her sprint across the yard. Her black hair streamed behind her; her hips moved gracefully as she hurried up the back steps and slammed the door in her wake.

Seething, his jaw clenched so hard it ached, Colton strode to his pickup and climbed inside. What was it about her? She was a liar—a woman who at seventeen had tried to trick him into marriage—and yet there was something captivating about her tantalizing smile and wide hazel eyes.

He jammed the old truck into gear and stomped on the throttle. He'd known women before and since his brief affair with Cassie, but none had been able to get under his skin the way she had.

"Never again," he told himself as the old Jeep whined and he shifted into second. "Never again."

Chapter Three

"**Y**ou're an idiot!" Cassie muttered, kicking off her boots as she heard Colton McLean's Jeep drive away. Angry with herself as well as the whole lot of McLeans, she marched through the kitchen and upstairs.

She had, over the years, convinced herself that she was long over Colton. But tonight, after seeing him again, she wasn't quite so sure. The hate she'd sworn to harbor was tangled up with an emotion she'd rather not examine too closely. Their love affair, long dead, seemed closer than it had in years.

"What love affair?" she taunted her reflection as she yanked a brush through her wet hair. Love had never been a part of that summer.

A familiar ache, an old feeling she'd buried along with her foolish notions of love for Colton, wrenched her heart. Sinking unsteadily onto the edge of the mattress, she clenched her fists around the edge of her quilt. Her memory tortured her with vibrant images of a young man unjaded by the years. It seemed that it was just last night when she'd been seventeen and hopelessly in love. . . .

* * *

It was a summer to remember, a beautiful hazy time when anything was possible. Cassie sprinted playfully along the edge of the lake. The lapping water tickled her toes, and sandy soil squished under her bare feet. The summer sun had already settled behind the western hills. Vibrant slashes of magenta and orange streaked the wide Montana sky.

"Bet you can't catch me," she called, glancing over her shoulder.

"Why would I want to?" Colton asked. His back propped against the scarred trunk of a pine tree, he plucked a twig from a low-hanging branch. He lifted one side of his mouth lazily as she waded ankle-deep.

"Figure that one out for yourself," she teased.

He tossed the twig into the water, then shoved his hands deep into the pockets of his cutoff jeans, as if he didn't care what she did. But she noticed the gleam in his eyes, the involuntary flexing of his thigh muscles, the tension in his stance. Though he attempted to appear nonchalant and uninterested, Cassie knew he was only fighting her—and fighting a losing battle.

Bending forward and running her fingers through the cool water, she grinned. She'd loved him for so long, and now he was finally returning those feelings. For the past six weeks they'd been seeing each other, on the sly, of course. Her father would kill her if he thought she was dating a McLean.

Today her heart soared as high as the hawk circling distantly overhead.

Feeling Colton's gaze searing her backside, she turned. He had moved from his spot near the tree and was sauntering closer to the lake.

"Maybe we should go," he suggested restlessly. His voice had grown husky, his eyes dark.

Cassie's heart somersaulted. "We just got here." She

moved deeper; the cool water lapped against the hem of her shorts.

"Isn't your father expecting you?"

"He's in town. Won't be back for hours." Tossing her hair over one shoulder, she wiped her hands on her shorts.

"Ivan wouldn't like it if he knew you were here with me."

"Ivan doesn't have to know."

He arched one of his dark brows insolently. "Don't use me to rebel against your father."

"I'm not!" she vowed, her throat swollen as she gazed at him. Colton was everything she'd ever dreamed of—and more. Against a backdrop of pine and cottonwood, he stood at the water's edge, his tanned chest bare, corded muscles visible beneath a swirling mat of black hair. His jaw was lean and sharp, less boyish than it had been the summer before, and his eyes glinted like newly forged steel.

Colton moved closer, rippling the water's surface. Cassie's heart hammered so loudly she could barely hear the gentle thrum of insects or the lapping of the lake.

"I don't like sneaking around."

"Neither do I."

"Think about it, Cass. We both know your father would skin us alive if he found out we'd been meeting behind his back."

"I have thought about it."

"Have you?" he asked distractedly. His eyes slid from hers to the halter top that covered her breasts in pink gingham. The fabric was stretched taut, and she could feel a slow trickle of sweat on her skin, the tangle of damp curls against her neck.

He swallowed hard. "What do you think my dad would say?"

Cassie's carefree mood faded.

"And then there's Uncle John. He'd kill me."

She cringed at the mention of Colton's uncle. She didn't want to think about John McLean, nor of the affair he'd had with her mother. That time, so long ago, still caused a horrid aching in her heart—an aching she didn't want to experience. Not today. She'd heard the rumors—knew that her mother had abandoned her long before because of John McLean. "Because I'm Vanessa's daughter?" she asked, thrusting out her chin.

"Because you're Ivan's."

Bravely, for she'd never dared mention the feud to him before, she said, "What happened between your uncle and my mother is in the past." A love affair that had soured. A love affair that had cost Cassie her mother and her father his pride.

"Tell that to your dad."

"I have."

His head jerked up, and his gaze, bright and seductive, drilled into hers. "And what did 'Ivan the Terrible' have to say?"

"Nothing." She hated it when Colton referred to her father as if he were a monster; and yet she understood why. Ivan had never gotten over his wife's betrayal, and he'd blamed John and anyone else cursed with the surname of McLean for ruining his life. That curse included Colton.

"You're lying. Ivan's made no bones about the fact that he blamed John and everyone related to him. Vanessa never came back, did she? She just left your dad to take care of himself and you. You really can't blame the man for being bitter!"

Cassie's throat constricted as painful memories clouded the otherwise perfect day. "I—I don't want to talk about Mom."

"Do you ever hear from her?"

"Of course," she lied, avoiding Colton's eyes.

"Sure."

"Besides, it doesn't matter. You and me—that's what's between us. What we have doesn't have anything to do with Dad or Mom."

"Cassie," he whispered. He was so close she noticed the shadows of suspicion clouding his gaze. He touched her shoulder and lifted the tiny strap that was knotted behind her neck. "It does matter."

She swallowed hard. "Dad lives in the past, Colton. There's nothing we can do or say to change that. We can't worry about it."

His lips curved sardonically. "And when he finds out?"

"He won't," she said mutinously, thrusting out her chin. "I'm seventeen and I've already graduated from high school! I can make my own decisions."

He sucked in a swift breath and let his hand fall to his side.

She wanted to kick herself for bringing up her age. For some reason, he thought her a child, though he was only four years older than she.

"Come on," he said hoarsely, "I'll take you home."

"But we've got all night." Never before had she been so forward, but she'd never been with Colton before—not alone.

He swore violently, his gaze sweeping the swell of her breasts peeking from beneath her halter, to her flat, tanned abdomen and the curve of her hips. "We do *not* have all night."

He wrapped strong fingers around her wrist as he started back for the shore, dragging her through the water quickly.

"You just think I'm a kid," she pouted as she tried to negotiate the slippery bottom.

"You are."

"Colton, I love you!"

"Oh, Cass, no!" He stopped then, and she ran into him, her legs giving way. She started to fall, but he caught her and lost his balance. They plunged into the ice-cold depths. Water swirled over them both, and she sputtered as he hauled her to her feet. "Love?" he repeated, his chest heaving. Drops of water clung to the dark hair from his chest to the waistband of his wet cutoffs. "What do you know about love?"

"I know that I can't think straight when I'm around you, and when I'm not, I can't wait to see you again!"

"You've been *in love* with half the boys around—"

"I have not!"

"What about Dave Lassiter?"

"We had one date—and he's just my best friend's brother," she said, thinking Dave was just a boy. Colton, on the other hand, was so mature. Then she smiled to herself. Obviously Colton had been keeping track.

"And Mike Jones?"

"He asked me to the prom." She forced her eyes to his. "I've had dates, Colton, sure. I've even thought I liked a couple of the boys. But it's not the same as I feel about you."

"Oh, Cass, no. Don't—" His gaze appeared tortured.

"Why won't you believe me?"

"Because it *can't* happen. You're too young and I—I have plans for my life. I can't be stuck in this Podunk town, feeding livestock and talking about property taxes. . . ." He clamped his mouth shut, and for a moment she thought she saw a flicker of love in his eyes. "Oh, hell, what's the point?" he growled, swearing roundly.

Cassie flushed, feeling incredibly young and naive. But the hand over her wrist never let go, and Colton's gaze lingered before dropping.

Glancing down, she saw the wet fabric of her halter top hid very little. Her raised nipples pressed intimately against the sheer scrap of gingham.

"Oh, Cassie, what are you trying to do to me?" he groaned.

"Nothing—I—"

He jerked her forward quickly, capturing her lips with his. Her breath was lost somewhere in her lungs. She couldn't breathe, could only feel the dampness of his muscled chest, his hair tickling her skin, and his lips, hard and sensual, moving anxiously against hers.

The driving beat of his heart was matched only by her own.

She leaned against him, and he stepped back, his eyes narrowing to hide the desire smoldering in his gaze. "Nothing, my eye. You know exactly what you're doing to me. I should never have agreed to meet you here!"

"But you did."

"It was a crazy idea."

"Why?" Hope swelled again. "Colton, believe me, I know how I feel!" she whispered, throwing all of her pride to the wind. "Ever since last summer I've dreamed about you, waited for you."

"You don't know what you're saying! Before the summer's over you'll change your mind."

A hard, tight ball filled her throat. "You don't love me," she accused.

He took her face between his hands. "We barely know each other." His hands dropped. "Besides, you're just a—"

"Kid," she finished, mortified. "That's what you think, right?"

"You're more than a child," he said slowly, his gaze moving meaningfully to her breasts. "But you just don't know what you're getting into. You're playing with fire, Cass."

"I love you—"

"Stop it," he commanded roughly. "You don't know the first thing—"

Wrenching her hand away from his, she fought the urge to break down and cry. She'd bared her soul to him, and he'd as much as laughed in her face. To save what little pride she could still claim, she started running out of the lake and across the sandy strip of shoreline to the woods. Intent on walking barefoot all the way back to her father's house, she struck out through the trees.

"Cassie, wait!"

"Leave me alone!"

But Colton caught her at the forest's edge and circled her waist with his strong arms. He tugged her kicking and clawing against him. "Where do you think you're going?"

"Home!"

"Like this? Barefoot?"

"Yes!"

"But it's almost dark."

"I don't really care. Let go of me, Colton. I think I've suffered enough embarrassment for one night, don't you?" she accused, trying to deny the weakness in her knees, the constriction of her lungs. She struggled to get away from his musky male scent and the coiled power of his arms.

"I'll take you home." His voice sounded rough.

"I'll walk!"

"No way." His eyes seared hers, and the protest on her lips died a quick death.

Wrapped in the strength of his arms, feeling the heat of his body, the raw sensuality of his wet skin rubbing against hers, she couldn't find her voice or the self-righteous anger that had flared so quickly only seconds before.

She knew that he intended to kiss her. As he lowered his head, she tilted hers up eagerly. His lips covered hers and stole the small whisper of breath in her lungs. Moving slowly, expertly, his mouth molded against hers. His tongue gently prodded, sliding easily between her teeth, exploring and plundering.

All thoughts of leaving him fled into the shadows of the towering pines. Cassie slid her arms around his neck, and she leaned against his muscular chest. Her body responded easily to Colton's kiss; her skin tingled when he splayed his hands against her bare back, shifting slowly, sensually, fanning the forbidden flames of desire that heretofore she'd only dreamed of.

"Stop me," he whispered hoarsely.

But she couldn't. She felt one of his hands slide around to caress the burgeoning fabric of her halter. She gasped when his palm covered her breast, and the wet gingham slid erotically against her nipple. "Don't stop," she breathed. "Colton, please, don't stop."

He groaned a deep primal moan of surrender that turned her blood to fire. Heat swirled deep inside her as he untied the thin straps and bared one soft breast to the night. He gulped as he gazed at her. "You're too young to look this way," he protested, but let one thumb graze her nipple, watching in fascination as the stiff peak responded.

"Just love me," she murmured.

"I can't—"

"Please. Colton, oh, please—"

Groaning, he lowered his head. His lips moved gently along the column of her throat, and one hand became tangled in her hair as he dragged them both to their knees. "This is dangerous," he rasped.

"No—"

"And so are you."

Instinctively she let her head loll back and arched her neck as he kissed her slowly, sliding downward until his mouth was poised over her breast.

"You're so beautiful," he murmured, his hot breath fanning her nipple before he took all of that rosy button into his mouth and suckled hungrily.

She wound her fingers in the thick strands of his hair, and the warm ache within her, a new and frightening passion, stretched and yawned deep·within. She didn't protest when his weight forced her back against the sand, where her halter fell completely away.

She kissed his head and smooth shoulders as he laved her breast, teasing and tormenting with each supple stroke of his tongue. Cassie shuddered, unable to think beyond the delight of his body molding to hers.

His muscles were rigid and hard. Sweat beaded his brow. He lowered the waistband of her shorts. Her abdomen flattened expectantly.

"This is a mistake," he whispered.

"No, Colton, it's right. So right. I *love* you."

He squeezed his eyes tight for a minute, as if he was trying to get a grip on himself. For a heart-stopping second, Cassie thought he would tear himself away. But he didn't. And when his lips found hers again, they were hot and hard and hungry. All his self-control fled. His fingers worked feverishly on the snap and zipper of her shorts.

He stripped them from her so quickly she gasped. His hands ran anxiously along her thighs, smoothing her skin, parting her legs easily, stroking her panties until she began to writhe anxiously, her blood thundering wantonly, throbbing with desire.

"I want you, Cassie," he murmured against her hair. "Damn me to hell, but I want you."

Somewhere in her passion-drugged mind she knew she should stop him, that lust didn't mean love. But she didn't care. In time he'd learn to love her just as she loved him.

"Touch me," he breathed, guiding her hand.

Hesitantly she reached for the top button of his cutoffs. Her fingers flitted against his abdomen, and he drew in a swift breath, his own fingers delving, searching.

He groaned when she touched him, his muscles flexing. "Oh, Cassie." Lips, full and hungry, captured hers, and he kicked off his clothes, his body in all its young, virile glory straining over hers. "I—I don't have anything for protection—"

"I don't need anything but you," she whispered, watching him through glazed eyes.

Shuddering, he parted her legs with his own. He moved quickly then, thrusting into her, past the thin barrier of her virginity.

She gasped with the searing pain, a white-hot burst that

he assuaged with his gentle, rhythmic movements. Cassie closed her eyes, and the sounds of the night faded. She could no longer hear the gentle drone of crickets, the quiet lapping of the lake, the wind soughing through the pines. She heard only the beating of her heart and the thundering cadence of Colton's, felt only the liquid heat within her building with each joyful, binding thrust.

She dug her fingers into his shoulders as his tempo increased. Moving with him, she arched upward, her spine curving, her breasts full against him.

"I can't hold back," he cried, just as the first spasm sent her rocketing into a new, wondrous world. Light splintered before her eyes, and she heard him cry out lustily, the sound echoing through the trees.

"Cassie, Cassie," he whispered, hoarse and clinging, his body fused to hers. He gazed down at her, and regret darkened his gaze. "Oh, God—"

"Shh . . ." She pressed a finger to his lips and smiled, but he closed his eyes and clung to her, as if blocking out an image he couldn't bear.

"I'm sorry," he said.

"For what?"

"You—you were a virgin."

"Of course I was!" She held his face between her hands. "There's no reason to be sorry."

"Oh, God, Cass, there are a thousand reasons," he whispered, levering himself on one elbow and gazing down on her.

His eyes moved over her slowly, and his expression turned pained, guilt-ridden. "This wasn't the right time," he muttered, his muscles still glistening with sweat.

"It was perfect."

"That's the trouble, Cassie. You see things the way you want to see them. I see them for what they are."

"And what was this?" she asked, almost afraid to know.

"This . . ." He smiled wistfully for a second before he swallowed hard. "This was—a mistake."

"No!"

"Cassie, you're not ready for any of this."

"I know what I want."

"You couldn't," he said, looking up to the darkening sky as if searching for answers.

"Colton? Talk to me."

He ran a hand through his still-wet hair, and his fingers trembled. "I-I think we'd better get dressed."

"So soon?"

"For God's sake, Cassie!" he exploded. "Think about it." Muttering under his breath, he yanked his cutoffs on.

"I'm not ashamed."

His head snapped up. "Good. You shouldn't be," he said quickly.

"Neither should you."

He pinched his lips together. "Forget it."

"Colton, it was beautiful! I love—"

"Don't!" he said, rubbing the back of his neck nervously and biting the corner of his lip. "I care about you, Cass. Hell, you know that. But you're so young. . . . I just think we should slow things down a little."

"What do you mean?" she asked, crushed.

"That we're moving much too fast."

Reluctantly she stepped into her panties and tried not to cry. Tears formed in the corners of her eyes, but she forced them back. Maybe Colton didn't love her now, right this minute, but he would! She knew it! Surely he couldn't have touched her so intimately, caressed her skin so fondly, if he didn't—

"What the hell do you think you're doing?" a strong, familiar voice demanded.

Cassie froze, grateful for the shadows cast by the trees.

Colton, lifting his head, scrambled to hide her from his brother's incriminating gaze.

Astride a rangy bay gelding, Denver McLean glared down at them. His face was lined with disapproval, his brows drawing into one thick black line. "Have you lost your mind?" he demanded harshly.

Colton coiled, his muscles flexed as if he was about to leap up and drag his brother from the saddle. "I think you'd better leave!"

"So you can go back to bedding Ivan Aldridge's daughter?" Denver sneered. "Not on your life."

Cassie wanted to die! She struggled into her halter and shorts.

Standing, Colton snapped the closure of his cutoffs. "It's none of your business!"

"No? And what happens if she turns up pregnant? What do you think her old man will say?"

"I swear, Denver, if you don't leave . . ." Colton warned, still using his body to shield her.

"Come on. Take your best shot." But Denver didn't slide to the ground. He glanced at Cassie and sighed. "Hell, Colt, she's only a child!"

"I'm seventeen," Cassie insisted, her clothes finally intact even if her pride was shredded to ribbons.

"Sweet Mary! Seventeen?" Denver exclaimed, his furious gaze ricocheting back to Colton. "Ivan Aldridge will personally nail your hide to the wall!"

"That's my problem," Colton retorted, standing next to Cassie, one hand curved protectively around her waist.

"That's everybody's problem," Denver pointed out. "There's still a lot of bad blood between the two families. If Ivan finds out that you and his daughter are lovers, there'll be hell to pay."

"I'm warning you," Colton ground out.

"It's none of your business," Cassie cut in, her temper flaring.

"Isn't it?" Denver's blue eyes glinted. "I hope to God that

you're old enough to protect yourself," he said furiously. "I don't know how your dad would feel about becoming a grandfather to a McLean."

"Protect myself?" Cassie repeated.

"It hasn't come to that, Denver," Colton lied, his jaw tightening.

"But not far from it."

Colton bristled. "I can handle myself."

"Just use your head."

"Oh, like you do whenever you're around Tessa?"

Denver's face became a mask of iron. "Leave Tessa out of this," he warned in a low growl. "You'd better get back to the house. Dad wants to talk to you. And you, Cassie—"

"I'll take care of her," Colton bristled.

"If you haven't already." Yanking on the bay's reins, Denver swore furiously. The horse twirled on his back legs and took off in a cloud of dust.

"Come on," Colton said gently, "I'll take you home."

"I don't want to go home."

A muscle tightened in Colton's jaw, and his silvery eyes sparked. "Denver's right, you know. This'll only cause trouble." He took her hand in his and guided her to the truck.

"But all I want is you! I want to marry *you*!"

"Oh, God, Cassie. Marry me?"

"Yes."

He shook his head violently. The fading light was reflected in his eyes. "You'll change your mind a dozen times before—"

"Don't tell me I'm too young to know what I want," she said, tears flooding her eyes as he helped her into the dented Ford pickup. She hated being only seventeen—hated it!

"Okay, I won't. But I'll tell you what I want. I want to finish college. I want to travel. I want to be the best photographer in the newspaper business." He ground the old gears, and the truck lurched forward. "And I'm not interested in a wife—at least not now."

He couldn't have wounded her more if he'd taken a knife to her throat. Huddled miserably on the passenger side of the pickup, Cassie wondered how she could change his mind. He'd wanted her, and there was more to their relationship than simple lust, she thought wretchedly. There had to be. Somehow she'd prove it to him.

The next morning Cassie was working out her plan to see Colton when her father cornered her in the kitchen. "You were out yesterday," he said. Seated at the battered old table, he sipped coffee from his favorite chipped mug.

"Umm." She kissed her father on his crown. "But I wasn't late."

"Who were you with?" he asked.

"Just a friend." She reached into the cupboard and found a cup for herself.

"Boyfriend?"

"Yes," she said, naively thinking she could end the feud right then and there. "Colton McLean."

Her father's head snapped back and a steady flush crept up his neck as he glared at her. "I thought I told you the McLean boys were off limits."

"And I thought that it was time to start mending fences,"

The back of her father's neck turned scarlet. "Some fences are never meant to be mended. Don't you remember what the McLeans did to us? To our family?" He shoved his plate across the table.

"That was John."

"I never want to hear that name in this house!" he warned. "And you may as well realize all the McLeans are the same— cut from the same bolt of rotten cloth. Especially Colton. He's wild and irresponsible, that one!"

"You just don't know him."

"Don't I?" Ivan's hands were shaking. He rolled his fingers into his palms, and his jaw clenched and relaxed several times before he found his voice. "Use your head, Cassie. Colton McLean doesn't care for you."

"You don't know anything about him!" she cried.

Ivan cocked both eyebrows. "I know this—you're not to see him."

"You can't stop me!"

"You're still a minor, Cassie. You're living under my roof, by my rules."

She clenched her fingers tight around the cup, her knuckles white. She swallowed hard. "I love him, Dad," she admitted, cringing a little when she saw his shoulders slump.

"You're too young to know about love."

"Mom was seventeen when she married you."

"And look what happened. She ran off with John McLean. Then, when he was through with her, she didn't bother coming back."

"And so you blame everyone with the McLean name."

"The same blood runs through their veins." He stood and jammed his hat onto his head. "You're not to see Colton McLean again, hear?"

"And what if I do?"

His old eyes saddened. "Don't be forcing the issue, Cassie. It's a mistake to choose between family and a man who doesn't want or need you."

"You're wrong about Colton!"

"Am I?" Ivan paused at the door. "Then if he wants you, he'll have to court you. I won't have you sneaking off behind my back!"

Colton didn't call. Not that day, nor the next, nor any day that week. Her father never mentioned his name again, but Cassie thought of him constantly. She rode along the fence line, hoping to catch a glimpse of him working on the ranch, and she spent hours in town with her friends, hoping to run into him. Once in a while she'd see him and he'd be staring at her, but guilt would change his expression and he'd quickly look away.

Two weeks later she was seated in a corner booth in Jerry's, a local burger hut. Cassie had purposely chosen this booth near the window facing Main Street so that she could stare outside and watch the traffic, just in case Colton or someone from the McLean spread drove into Three Falls.

She sat there for fifteen minutes, sipping cola, pining for Colton, when Beth Lassiter, her best friend, breezed through the front door.

Spying Cassie, Beth waved, dashed to Cassie's booth and slid excitedly onto the red plastic seat. "I'll have a Coke and onion rings," she said to Bonnie, the waitress, then trained worried blue eyes on her friend. "Guess what?" she whispered, her brown ponytail falling forward, her cheeks flushed.

"What?" Cassie swirled her straw in her drink, watching the ice cubes dance.

Beth bit her lower lip. "Colton McLean's dating Jessica Monroe."

Cassie gasped, her stomach turning over. Her hands began to shake, and she hid them beneath the table and tried to appear as calm as possible. "No—"

"I didn't believe it, either, but I got the word from Ellen."

Ellen was Jessica Monroe's younger sister. There were three Monroe sisters in all. All blond, blue-eyed, petite and gorgeous. Jessica was the oldest and probably the prettiest.

"That's impossible," Cassie said, finishing her Coke. She wouldn't believe that Colton had betrayed her—couldn't. Already she suspected that her lovemaking with Colton had cost her more than her virginity. Her period was late, and Cassie was certain that she was pregnant.

Beth rolled her eyes. "Look, Cassie, I know you've got a major crush on Colton, but you may as well forget it. He's only got a term or so left in college in California and then he's history. He won't be coming back here."

"You don't know that—"

"Sure I do. He's as much as told everyone he's met that he's going to be some hot-shot journalist. Face it, this town *bores* him."

"Maybe he's changed."

"Are you kidding? Cass, what's gotten into you? He's more like his Uncle John than the rest of his family and— oh, jeez, I'm sorry," Beth said, grimacing. "I—I forgot about your mom."

"It's okay." Cassie forced a smile that threatened to fall from her face. The back of her eyes burned when she thought of her mother and especially when she thought about making love to Colton McLean. "But you're wrong about Colton."

Bonnie, a heavyset woman with a once-white apron strapped around her thick waist, deposited onion rings and Beth's drink on the table.

Beth handed her a couple of dollars, then poured a thick glob of catsup into her paper-lined plastic basket. "If I were you, I'd forget about Colton," Beth advised. "There are other fish in the sea."

"So I've heard."

Beth sighed. "Colton's just not for you."

Cassie didn't believe her. She'd seen the way he'd looked at her, felt the electricity charging the air between them, known the ecstasy of lying in his arms.

But another week passed and she didn't hear from Colton. Because she loved him with all of her heart and she felt she was carrying his child, Cassie thwarted her father. Though he'd ordered her not to chase after Colton McLean, she couldn't stop herself. Not with a baby on the way.

Lying on her bed, listening to the sounds of the night through her open window, Cassie waited until her father was asleep, then sneaked down the stairs and hurried outside.

Erasmus yipped at the sight of her, and Cassie jumped.

"You scared the life out of me!" she whispered. "Hush!"

Shoving her hands into the pockets of her jean jacket, she crossed the yard, letting moonlight guide her into the barn.

She couldn't chance starting the engine of the truck, so she slipped a bridle on Tavish, her favorite chestnut gelding, then led him outside. Not bothering with a saddle, she swung onto the chestnut's broad back and dug her heels into his sides.

The gelding bolted; his hooves thudded against the dry fields as he fairly flew over the hard ground. The dry summer wind streamed through Cassie's hair, and she blinked against the tears collecting in her eyes.

She knew what she was doing was dangerous. The horse could trip in the darkness, throwing her. Or her father might wake up and discover her gone. But she had to talk to Colton.

Closer to the edge of the property, she pulled back on the reins and slowed Tavish so he could pick his way through the pines near the river. She heard the roar of the rushing Sage.

Tavish stepped from between the pines, and Cassie saw the river in the moonlight, the turbulent white water splashing over stones and slicing through the dry earth.

The horse shied near the edge of the river. Cassie talked softly to him, patting his sleek neck. "Come on, boy. We can do it. We have before."

Tavish tossed his head before stepping into the river. The dark water swirled around his legs and belly. As she twisted the reins in her fingers, the first icy touch of the Sage brushed against her bare legs. Tavish stepped deeper, then began to float.

Cassie felt his legs stretch as he swam, carrying them across the current and toward the opposite shore. "That's it," she said, encouraging, soothing, though her throat was dry, her lungs constricted. "Hold on—just a little more . . ."

Finally his hooves struck bottom. Scrambling over the

rocks, Tavish lunged from the river. Once on land, he shook, snorting and blowing, the bridle jangling loudly.

"Good boy!" Cassie cried, climbing off his back and tying him to the sagging fence separating McLean property from Aldridge land. "Wait for me."

Her canvas shoes squished as she slipped under the barbed wires. She ran through the fields by instinct. Her heart was pounding, and though her shorts were damp from the cold water, she began to sweat. What if Colton wasn't home? What if he wouldn't see her? What if, God forbid, he was there with Jessica?

"Don't go borrowing trouble," she told herself as she approached the center of the McLean Ranch. The stables, barns and outbuildings loomed ahead, glowing eerily beneath the security lamps. Beyond the buildings and across the yard, lights gleamed in the windows of the McLean house.

Cassie nearly lost her nerve as she climbed the final fence and started across the yard. She was sure someone would look out the window and see her. And then what?

She was almost to the front door when a car approached. Headlights bobbing, engine whining, the sports car sped up the hilly lane leading to the house. Cassie's heart sank, and she ducked behind a tree, silently praying she wouldn't be seen.

The car screeched to a stop not far from the tree. A car door banged open.

"I never want to see you again!" a woman screamed, and Cassie recognized the voice as belonging to Jessica Monroe.

"Don't you?" Colton drawled.

Cassie's knees gave out. She leaned against the rough bark for support. So it was true. He was seeing Jessica! After he had made love to her. Her stomach roiled, and she thought she might throw up right there on the lawn.

"You're a lying, two-timing bastard, McLean."

"I didn't call you," he reminded her.

"It's that Aldridge girl, isn't it?" Jessica charged.

"Leave her out of this," Colton warned.

"God, Colton, she's barely out of diapers! And her father would murder you if he ever got wind—"

"Stop it!" Colton cut in, his voice low.

"Don't I mean anything to you?" she wheedled, and a long silence followed.

So Colton didn't care about Jessica! Cassie, flattened against the tree, heard her heart slamming against her ribs.

"You're a fool, Colton McLean!" Jessica charged.

"Probably."

Cassie heard footsteps crossing the gravel driveway and the sound of a car door slam loudly. She peeked around the tree trunk just as the convertible roared to life again and tore down the drive. Jessica's long blond hair waved like a moon-dusted banner behind her.

Cassie turned her gaze to Colton. He was standing in the middle of the yard, but he wasn't paying the slightest attention to the disappearing car. Instead, an amused smile curved his lips. His hands on his hips, he stared straight at Cassie.

"See enough, Cass?" he taunted.

Cassie swallowed hard. She wanted to run as fast as her legs would carry her back to the fence where Tavish was waiting, but she forced herself to step forward. She felt young and stupid and incredibly naive. "I heard you were dating Jessica," she admitted, forcing her head up to meet the questions in his eyes.

"Not much of a date," he said sarcastically. "It was her idea."

Cassie managed a poor imitation of a cynical smile. "Seems like you have all sorts of women chasing you down."

"Not many. Some are girls."

She bristled. "How can you say that? After . . . after—"

Colton sighed, plowing his hands through his hair. He closed the gap between them and grabbed her arm, drawing her into the shadows away from the house. "You are a girl, damn it," he ground out, more exasperated than angry.

"Seventeen, for crying out loud!" He dropped her arm and swore. "I don't know what to think of you, Cassie."

"We made love."

He sucked in a swift breath. "I haven't forgotten."

"Then why haven't you called or stopped by?" she asked, her heart pounding wildly with fear—fear that he would reject her, fear that he wouldn't want the baby.

"Oh, God, Cass," he whispered, his voice rough, "if you think this has been easy—"

"Don't you want to see me?"

His jaw worked. "More than I should."

"Then, why—"

"Because I don't want to make the same mistake twice."

"Mistake?" she whispered, her throat closing. "Mistake?" Unbidden, tears filled her eyes. "How can you call what we shared a mistake? I love—"

He held up one flat palm. "I don't want to hear it!"

"Why not, Colton? Because you're afraid?"

"Yes, damn it! I *am* afraid." He grabbed for her again, his hands clamping over her forearms. "I'm afraid of what's happening to me—to you—to us. What about the rest of our lives, Cassie? You have dreams, don't you? Didn't you tell me you want to become a veterinarian?"

"Yes, but—"

"And I want to finish school, get a job with the best goddamn paper in the country."

"You can—"

"With a wife?" he mocked. "Because that's what you're after, Cassie. You as much as said it before." He stared down into her eyes and groaned. "You're beautiful, Cass, and loving and smart, and you've got your whole life stretched out in front of you. You can have anything you want."

"Except you."

Colton swallowed hard, and his eyes searched hers. For a

split second she thought he might kiss her. "Give it time," he pleaded, his voice rough.

"Maybe we haven't got time," she whispered.

"Of course we do. . . ." He stared down at her, as if noticing for the first time how pale she was, how pinched the corners of her mouth had become. "What do you mean?"

"I'm pregnant," she whispered, her voice raw.

His arms dropped to his sides, and he leaned one shoulder against the house, sagging. "Pregnant?" Stunned, his face chalk-white, he asked, "You're sure?"

"Of course I am."

"You've been to the doctor?"

She shook her head, fighting against tears. "Not yet."

"Then maybe——"

"I'm positive, Colton. It's not something you guess at. I've been around a ranch for years. I know the facts of life."

"But until you've seen the doctor, you really don't know," he protested.

Cassie was firm. "I'm nearly two weeks late, and I've already started throwing up before breakfast."

"Oh, God," he muttered. Pinching the bridge of his nose between his thumb and forefinger, he squeezed his eyes shut.

With a sinking heart Cassie understood just how little he wanted the baby, how little he cared for her. She hurt all over. "Look," she finally said, her voice barely audible, "this isn't your problem. I—I can handle it." She started walking, faster and faster, away from him, before the tears burning behind her eyes began to fall.

"It's as much my fault as yours."

"It's no one's *fault*, Colton. It just happened."

He let out a long breath. "I'll marry you."

She stopped short, barely believing her ears. "You don't have to——"

He caught up with her, and every muscle in his face was

hard and set. "I won't run away from my responsibilities, Cassie. You're pregnant, the child's mine, and we'll get married."

"There's no need to be noble."

He snorted. "Oh, this is far from noble."

If only she could believe him! "What about your career?"

His eyes searched the heavens, and a wistful smile curved his lips. "There's time. It'll wait. We'll live here until we get on our feet, then we'll find a place of our own. When we can afford it, we'll both finish school."

It sounded so clinical, so hollow. Where was the happiness? The joy? The love everlasting? The earth-shattering knowledge that this love—their love—would bind them together always? "I don't want to get in the way, Colton," she whispered, suddenly feeling as if she'd made a big mistake in telling him about the baby. "You have your plans—"

He grabbed her again, his fingers tightening over her arm. "We'll make it work, Cassie," he vowed, "but it won't be easy. You've got to understand that."

"I'm willing to work at it."

"Good. So am I." He glanced up at the moon, smiling wearily. "This isn't what I'd planned," he admitted, "but maybe it's just what I, we, need."

"Of course it is!" she cried, forcing their happiness.

He held her then, wrapping his arms around her waist and kissing her full on the mouth. Warmth spread through her, and she clasped her hands behind his neck, dragging them both to the ground. "I love you, Colton," she whispered over the pounding of her heart, "and I always will."

"Shh, Cass, I know. I know," he said, sighing.

So he hadn't said he loved her. But at least he wanted her. She saw it in his eyes, felt it in the urgency with which he cast their clothes aside. Cassie gazed up at him, filled with the wonder that this virile man would soon be her husband.

* * *

Two days later, Cassie squirmed in the hard, plastic chair.

Dr. Jordan, a man in his fifties with glossy white hair and small, even features, stared at Cassie over the tops of his glasses. He was seated behind his desk, his fingers toying with the edge of her medical chart. "The lab results are back. You're not pregnant."

Cassie froze. "Not pregnant?" she repeated, disbelieving.

"Your test was negative. This should be good news," the doctor said, though obviously from his expression he could see the disappointment on her face.

"There must be some mistake—"

"No mistake, Cassie."

"But I've been sick and my period is late!"

"You probably had the flu, and sometimes that can affect your cycle."

"No . . ."

The doctor smiled. "You've got plenty of time."

Did she? She felt as if all the sand in her hourglass had just slipped through her fingers.

As she walked outside, a warm summer breeze caressed her face and tugged at her hair. Overhead, leaves turned in the wind and squirrels chattered and raced nimbly through the branches. The air felt fresh and clean, but she felt cold inside. What would happen now? How could she tell Colton that she'd been wrong?

She wrapped her arms around her waist as she walked along the dusty sidewalk. She tried not to notice young mothers pushing strollers or a happy couple, obviously in love, sneaking kisses in the park.

Walking past a boutique, she eyed a lace wedding dress in the window. Would Colton still want to marry her? Two doors down she paused at the only children's store in Three Falls. Her throat went dry. Rattles and blankets and sleepers in a rainbow of pastels were strewn around a bare wooden rocking horse with glass eyes and a hemp mane and tail.

"Maybe someday," she whispered, her fingers trailing over the glass. She strolled into the store and touched the soft clothing and adorable stuffed animals until she could stand the self-inflicted torture no longer.

"Fool," she whispered to herself as she drove home, squinting against the lowering sun. Knowing she had to tell Colton the truth, she drove straight to the lane leading to the McLean Ranch, but at the last minute she changed her mind and sped past the gravel drive. What would she say? What if Denver answered the door? Or worse yet, Colton's parents or his uncle John? No, she had to wait until she got Colton alone.

She was still lost in thought, worried sick about breaking the news to Colton, when she parked the pickup near the barn.

"Where ya been?" her father asked as she raced through the back door. Seated at the kitchen table, working the crossword puzzle in the morning paper, he glanced up at her.

"In town."

"Get anything?"

Just bad news. "Nope—nothing caught my eye." She forced a smile she didn't feel.

Ivan turned his attention back to the open newspaper pages, and she ran upstairs and changed, feeling miserable.

She considered calling Colton, but couldn't risk it, not until her father was away from the ranch. If Ivan heard her end of the conversation, he'd go through the roof. And she couldn't chance another midnight ride; she might get caught by the McLeans or her father.

A little voice in her mind nagged at her—told her she was just putting off the inevitable, but she wouldn't listen. She had time, she assured herself. Besides, it was better to be safe than sorry.

* * *

In the next few days her father never left the ranch. And, unfortunately, he expected her to help with the hay and wheat harvest—so she was in the fields as much as he. Cassie spent nearly twenty-four hours a day with him. If Colton had called, she'd been out and missed him.

One evening while her father was doing the chores, she forced herself to take a chance. Her insides churning, she reached for the phone, dialed, and waited.

"Hello." Denver McLean's voice rang over the wires. Was it her imagination or did he already sound hostile?

"Hello?" he said again. "Hello?"

Cassie swallowed hard.

"Is anyone there?" Denver asked, his voice angrier than ever.

"Cass?" her father called.

Whirling, Cassie hung up.

"Don't let me bother you," her father said, nodding toward the telephone.

Shaking her head, Cassie mumbled. "I was finished anyway."

"Who was it?"

Cassie thought fast. "Just Beth," she lied, hating herself for the deception.

Her father chuckled. "You two would tie up the lines around here all day if you had the chance," he said, and Cassie felt worse than ever.

Her father grabbed his cap from a hook near the door, then disappeared outside again.

Cassie sagged against the wall. Somehow she had to find Colton and tell him the truth—in so doing, she would relieve him of his obligation and set him free to do what he really wanted with his life. Sooner or later they had to talk.

As the next few days passed, she felt more and more guilty. And there was a tiny part of her that kept hoping that even when he knew that there was no baby, he would smile and say, "It's all right, Cass. I love you. We'll get married anyway."

By the end of the week she'd gathered all her courage and found an excuse to go riding alone. The sun was just setting over the western hills, and Cassie knew that it was now or never. She followed the same path she'd taken the night she'd told Colton she was pregnant. Tavish streaked across the fields to the river, where, after snorting his disapproval, he eventually swam with Cassie clinging to his neck.

Her heart was pounding, her hands sweaty, as she tied Tavish's reins to the fence, ducked under the sagging barbed wire and ran through the bleached stubble of the McLean pasture.

Please, God, let him be home, she silently prayed. Climbing the final fence, she nearly lost her nerve. The yard was empty, but she saw Katherine McLean in the garden near the house.

Cassie combed the tangles from her hair with her fingers, squared her shoulders, and ignoring the fact that the hem of her denim skirt was damp, she forced herself down an overgrown path to the garden.

"Mrs. McLean?"

Katherine, bent over a row of bush beans, cast a glance over her shoulder. From beneath the brim of her straw hat her blue eyes widened a bit. But if she thought it strange that Ivan Aldridge's daughter was standing in the middle of McLean property, she didn't show it. "Cassie! How're you?"

"Fine," Cassie said, her fingers twisting nervously in the folds of her skirt. She could feel the flush in her cheeks, knew her heart was slamming a million times a minute. "Is— is Colton here?"

Katherine dusted her hands, and her dark brows drew into a thoughtful frown. "No, he left over an hour ago. He was going into town, and then I thought he said he was stopping by your place. He should be there by now."

Cassie swallowed hard, and the color that had invaded her face drained. "I must've missed him," she whispered, a thousand horrid scenarios flitting through her mind. What if at this very minute Colton was talking with her dad, explaining about the baby, telling Ivan he intended to marry her? She started backing up. "Well, uh, maybe I'll catch him there."

Katherine winced and rubbed the small of her back. "Are you sure? You look pale. Maybe you should come into the house for a drink. I know I could use a break. There's sun tea in the refrigerator—"

"No—no thanks," Cassie said quickly, feeling miserable. She hated turning down Colton's mother and this chance to help bury some of the bad feelings lingering between the Aldridges and McLeans, but she couldn't take a chance that Colton might be telling Ivan that he was going to sacrifice himself by marrying Cassie—all because of a baby!

She fairly flew across the arid fields, her hair streaming behind her in the wind. At the fence she ducked quickly, snagging her blouse, feeling the prick of one sharp barb on her back. She didn't care.

Her fingers fumbled with the reins. The wet leather had partially dried, tightening the knot. "Come on, come on," she whispered, finally yanking the reins free and jumping onto Tavish's broad back.

Digging her heels into the gelding's sides, she urged him into the river, not even noticing the Sage's icy water against her calves and thighs.

Tavish scrambled up the bank, and Cassie leaned forward. "Come on, boy—now!" As his hooves found flat ground, she slapped the reins against his shoulder and he bolted, streaking down the path through the trees and across the open, windswept fields. Grasshoppers flew out of Tavish's path.

Jackrabbits scurried through the grass to the protection of brambles. The chestnut's strides reached full length, and tears blurred Cassie's vision.

"That's it," she whispered, riding low, her legs gripping Tavish's heaving sides,

She yanked on the reins at the stables, and the gelding slid to a stop. Not bothering to walk him, nor take the bridle from his head, she looped the reins over the top rail and scrambled over the fence only to spy Colton's Jeep parked in the yard.

"No . . ." she cried. Her throat closed, and for a minute she had to stop and lean against the rough boards of the barn to catch her breath. Maybe it wasn't too late. He couldn't have been here long, though the lavender streaks of coming dusk told her that time had passed, perhaps too much time.

With as much dignity as she could muster, she climbed up the steps to the back porch, flung open the door and stepped inside.

Ivan and Colton were in the living room, both standing, surveying each other as if they were mortal enemies. Colton's back was to the fireplace, where the old clock on the mantel ticked softly near the faded pictures of Cassie's mother.

"I—I didn't know you were coming here," she whispered, her voice barely audible. She felt Colton's gaze on her, knew he could see the tangles in her hair, the flush on her cheeks, the dampness discoloring her skirt.

"I should have called," Colton said tightly, and she knew instantly that he was furious. His face had whitened under his tan, and his mouth had thinned to a hard, cruel line.

"What in blazes is going on here?" Ivan demanded, hooking an insolent thumb at Colton. "McLean here says he wants to talk to you—alone. When I told him you'd gone riding, he said he'd wait."

Cassie's heart dropped through the floor. "It's—it's okay, Dad."

Ivan scowled. "Whatever you have to say to my daughter, you can say to me."

"I don't think so," Colton replied.

"Please, Dad—"

"You know how I feel about this."

"It won't take long," Colton told him.

Ivan hesitated, glanced at Cassie and swore under his breath. "I need a drink," he said, his eyes narrowing on Colton before turning to Cassie. "I'll be on the back porch." With one last disparaging glance at Colton, Ivan strode stiffly into the kitchen, rummaged in the cupboards until he found his favorite bottle of rye whiskey and a glass, then stomped loudly outside. The screen door slammed behind him.

"Is—is something wrong?" Cassie asked, not knowing how to break the ice.

"You tell me," he said flatly.

"As a matter of fact, there is," she admitted. "I—I was just over at your place looking for you."

"Were you?"

She could feel the loathing in Colton's gaze. His nostrils flared angrily, and disgust curled his lips. Why was he so angry? she wondered . . . and then it hit her. He knew. Somehow, some way, he'd found out! Frigid desperation settled in her soul. "There—there is no baby," she admitted.

"And you weren't going to tell me." His voice sounded flat, lifeless.

"Of course I was. I just wanted to wait until we were alone." She turned pleading eyes up at him, begging him to understand.

The anger in his eyes died for just an instant, and Cassie's hopes soared. "When—when did you find out?"

"Last Monday," she answered, watching in dread as his features hardened to stone.

"Last Monday! A week—nearly a week ago! And you

didn't tell me? When were you planning to give me the news, Cass? *After* the wedding?" he demanded, his hushed voice growing louder, a vein throbbing in his neck.

She reached for his arm. "No, Colton, I swear—"

"Don't bother," he muttered, yanking his arm away from her in disgust.

"But I called—I was just at your house, looking for you—"

The back door flew open, and Ivan raced into the room. "What the devil's going on?" he demanded, his eyes darting anxiously from Colton's stiff spine to the tears rolling soundlessly down Cassie's cheeks.

Colton's face turned to stone. He started for the door, but Cassie ran after him, catching him just as his fingers curled over the knob.

Throat knotted, tears streaming from her eyes, she clutched Colton's sleeve. "Wait—I can explain—"

"I just bet you can!" He yanked open the door. Hot night air streamed into the room. "How do you think I felt when I told a friend of mine you and I were going to be married?" he demanded.

"But—"

"That's right, I let Warren Mason know. Warren just happens to work at LTV labs. He was congratulating me all over the place, then asked who the lucky girl was. When I mentioned your name, he got real quiet, I mean *real* quiet."

"Oh, no—"

"I asked him what was wrong, and he told me—reluctantly, mind you—that he'd seen your pregnancy tests. I was stupid enough to think he was going to congratulate me on becoming a father, but he didn't. Instead he let it slip that the test was negative."

"Oh, God," Cassie whispered.

"There never was a baby, Cassie, and you knew it."

"Then why would I have the test done?"

"To convince me," he growled.

"No—"

"Then why didn't you tell me *last Monday*?"

"I wanted to—"

"Did you?" Seeing her fingers curled into the folds of his denim jacket, Colton snarled, "Let me go, Cassie."

"I can't—I love you."

"It's over!"

"I didn't mean to—"

"Didn't mean to what? Lie to me? Deceive me? Trap me into marrying you?"

"I never—"

Slowly, he peeled her hands off his jacket. "Save it, Cassie. Save it for someone who'll believe it. Maybe the next guy you seduce!"

She shrank back at his cruelty. "I can't let go," she whispered pathetically.

"You don't have a choice."

Wounded beyond words, she felt her shoulders begin to shake, her body droop heavily against the wainscoting.

"Get out, McLean!" Ivan commanded, his voice a deadly whisper as he stalked into the entryway. His face was purple, his eyes bright, his fists clenched at his sides. "I don't know what the hell's going on here, but I don't care. You get out and leave my daughter alone! If you ever so much as step one foot on this property again, I swear, I'll kill you!"

"Dad—no—"

Colton's gaze moved slowly from Cassie to her father and back again. "Like father, like daughter. Always swearing something that doesn't mean a damn thing."

"No!" she cried, colder than she'd been since that devastating night when her mother, her eyes red with tears and her coat billowing behind her, had left through the very same door. "I love you!" she cried, and saw Colton's shoulders stiffen.

"Don't, Cassie," he rasped, shaking his head as if convincing himself that he didn't care. "Just don't!" His jaw set, he strode out of Cassie's life.

"Okay, Cassie," her father whispered, his lips tight, "I think you have some explaining to do."

"What do you want to know?" she whispered.

"Everything."

"Oh, Dad—"

"Come on, now," his voice was gentle, but firm. He wrapped one arm around her shoulders. "It can't be that bad."

"You don't know."

"Whatever it is, we'll get through it," he said as they listened to Colton's Jeep racing out of the driveway. "Didn't we before?"

"This is different."

"Not so much. You're hurt again, and I'm here to help."

Her heart felt as if it had broken into a thousand pieces. The sobs burning deep in her throat erupted, and she clung to her father's neck, burying her face against the rough cotton of his work shirt. "I love him so much," she sobbed, unable to stem her tears. "I'll never love anyone else."

"Sure you will," Ivan predicted, "sure you will."

But she hadn't. No man had ever touched her as Colton McLean had. No boy in high school or college had been able to break through the barriers Colton had built, stone by painful stone.

Now, eight years after he'd left her alone and miserable, silly, futile tears slipped down Cassie's cheeks to fall on to the eiderdown quilt. Regret filled her. Regret for a love that hadn't existed, regret for memories tarnished by Colton's hard heart, regret for the pathetic, lovesick fool she'd once been.

She blinked, then squeezed her eyes shut tight, willing away her tears. She wouldn't cry for him—she wouldn't!

Ignoring the hot lump in her throat, she braced herself for the future. No matter what happened, she'd be strong—stronger than she'd ever thought possible. Because, like it or not, Colton had walked back into her life.

Chapter Four

Colton stomped on the throttle. The old Jeep leaped forward, its wheels spinning on the gravel ruts that comprised the Aldridge's lane. What had possessed him to drive here? And why, when he'd learned that Ivan wasn't around, had he stayed?

Cassie. Always Cassie. Damn, but he wished he could forget her. She'd changed, of course. Her innocence and optimism had matured with her. Though not worldly-wise, she now had a sophistication within her that she hadn't possessed at seventeen. She knew her own mind, said what she thought and had developed a hard-edged sense of humor.

All in all, she'd caught him off guard. He hadn't expected to be attracted to her. In fact, he'd hoped that with time, he'd developed an immunity to her—that his infatuation at twenty-one would seem a simple schoolboy crush.

Unfortunately he'd been wrong. Seeing her now as a beautiful young woman who seemingly could stand up to anyone, he'd been trapped by her beauty. Trapped. Again.

"You've just been cooped up too long," he rationalized, cranking the wheel as he nosed the Jeep onto the highway. The pain in his shoulder flared, and he gritted his teeth. "You need to get out more." *And away from this godforsaken scrap of scrub brush.*

From the time he'd been a child, he'd known he would leave—that he wanted more than ranching could offer. But for the past six months he hadn't had many options. His wound had required several surgeries to repair the damaged joint and ligaments.

"Soon," he muttered, comforting himself with the thought that he could leave as soon as Denver and Tessa were back.

Unless, of course, this problem with the horse was unresolved. And unless he could not get Cassie Aldridge out of his system.

To change the direction of his thoughts, he snapped on the radio, only to hear a song from the past—a love song that had hit the charts that summer he'd been involved with Cassie—a song that reminded him of her.

Angrily he punched a button for another station and contented himself with listening to the news. The windshield wipers slapped the rain away. The mailbox signaling the turnoff to the ranch flashed in the headlights. Colton slowed, then gunned the engine past the lane. He was too keyed up to go back to the blasted ranch.

He needed a drink, and it was about time he showed his face in town again, anyway. Remembering a local watering hole, he drove down the main street and past a rainbow of flickering neon lights.

The Livery Stable, a weathered plank building named for its original purpose, stood on the far end of town. Colton wheeled into the parking lot, braked, then cranked on the emergency brake and shouldered the door open. Ducking his head against the rain, he plowed through puddles to the front door.

Inside, the interior was hazy with smoke. Customers lined the bar and filled most of the booths. Pool balls clicked, people chatted and laughed, and video games buzzed erratically.

Colton strode straight to the bar and recognized Ben Haley, an old classmate of Denver's, who owned the place.

"Well, look who finally showed up," Ben commented. A stocky man with flat features and a cynical smile matched only by Colton's, he motioned to the nearest stool.

"I thought it was about time."

"What'll it be?"

Colton eyed the glistening bottles arranged in front of a ceiling-high mirror. "Irish coffee."

Ben's thin lips twitched. "Irish coffee," he repeated, glancing at Colton's shoulder. "Don't you have enough reminders of that place?"

"I guess I'm just a glutton for punishment." Colton eyed the other patrons as Ben mixed his drink. "Has Ivan Aldridge been in?" he asked.

Sliding a mug across the scratched surface of the bar, Ben nodded. "A couple of hours ago."

"Alone?"

"No—Monroe and Wilkerson were with him. They come in for a couple of beers once in a while."

"Hey, Ben, how about another?" a young, curly-haired man at the end of the bar called.

"Right with ya." He glanced back at Colton. "Glad to see ya around, McLean. Just give me a yell if you need anything."

"I will." Colton stared into the depths of his mug, swirling the hot murky concoction and wondering why, no matter what he did, he couldn't erase Cassie's image from his mind.

"So McLean's lost his horse again?" Ivan asked the next morning. He kicked out the chair next to him and, cradling a mug of coffee in his palms, grinned widely. "Too bad." Propping his stocking feet on the other chair, he leaned back and eyed his daughter.

"That's what he says," Cassie replied. She flipped pancakes onto a huge platter and watched her father from the corner of her eye. His once-black hair was now steel-gray and thin, his tanned face lined from hours in the sun, and his light brown eyes a little less bright than they had been. Wearing a faded red flannel work shirt and dungarees held in place by red and black suspenders, he warmed his back near the wood stove.

"Serves the whole lot of them right!" Ivan settled back in his chair as Cassie placed platters of pancakes, bacon and eggs onto the gouged maple table.

"You're glad he lost the horse?"

Ivan's grin faded. "I'm glad he's havin' some trouble. No reason for him to be back in Montana as far as I can see."

"He was wounded."

"Yeah, right, got his ass shot up in Northern Ireland—"

"His shoulder."

"Doesn't matter. It's time he took off again. That's what he's good at, isn't it?"

Cassie, feeling a hot flush climb up her neck, sat at the table and stacked hot cakes onto her plate. "I suppose."

"You *know*!" Ivan waved his fork in front of Cassie's face. "He can't be tied to anything. He's been back here six months, and no one in town has seen hide nor hair of him."

"I guess he's been recuperating," Cassie said, wishing it didn't sound as if she was making excuses for a man she detested.

"Yeah, well, he can do it somewhere else."

Cassie smiled wryly. "I'm sure the minute he can, he'll make tracks out of here so fast, all we'll see is dust."

"Can't happen soon enough to suit me!" Ivan declared, spooning two fried eggs onto a short stack of cakes and pouring maple syrup over the whole lot.

"So what do you think happened to Black Magic?"

"Don't know and don't care."

"Dad . . ." Cassie cajoled, probing past the crusty facade of Ivan's surliness. "What do you really think?"

"How the hell should I know? He probably just ran off. The horse isn't dumb, you know." Ivan chuckled. "Maybe Black Magic got tired of Colton McLean and took off for greener pastures."

"Be serious."

"Okay, my best guess is that the stallion was randy, saw some mares and jumped the fence."

"The wires were cut."

Ivan's brows inched up. "Cut?"

"Snipped—just on the other side of the Sage. Where our property butts up to the McLeans'."

"So from that, Colton thinks I had something to do with it?"

"That and the fact that there were tire tracks on the wet ground."

"Big deal."

"Colton seems to think it is. He came over here with his guns loaded!"

"Did he now?" Ivan's old eyes sparkled. "I hope you gave him hell."

"Well, I tried to throw him off the property, but that didn't work." She cocked her thumb toward a worn spot under the table where Erasmus lay hoping for a fallen tidbit. "Our watchdog here barked his head off, then turned over and whined for Colton to rub his belly."

Ivan chuckled, though the features of his face had tightened. "I'm sorry I wasn't here," he said. "I'd have given McLean a piece of my mind and saved you the trouble."

"I handled it."

His gaze darkened. "He's a bastard, Cassie. Always has been. Always will be. I haven't forgotten what he did to you."

Cassie's chest grew tight. "Let's not talk about it."

Tenderness crept into the old man's features. "Okay—it's over and done with."

"Right." But Cassie could feel his gaze searching hers.

"Maybe the fence was just broken."

"He didn't seem to think so. I thought I'd go check it out this afternoon when I get back from town."

Ivan shrugged. "Suit yourself. But if I were you—"

"I know, I know. You'd stay away from Colton McLean."

"All the McLeans," Ivan clarified, his expression hardening. "But especially Colton. He's as bad as his uncle was." Then, as if he, too, didn't want to dwell on a past filled with pain and betrayal, he turned his gaze to his plate and tackled his breakfast with renewed vigor.

They finished the meal in silence, Cassie still trying to dispel all thoughts of Colton. "You're on for the dishes," she reminded her father as she set her plate in the sink. "I still have to get ready."

"This is women's work," he grunted, but as Cassie cleared the table, Ivan grudgingly started rinsing the dishes and stacking them in the portable dishwasher that Cassie had purchased with her first paycheck from the veterinary clinic.

"You'll survive," she predicted. "It's time you got yourself out of the fifties."

"I've been out of the fifties longer than you've been alive."

She laughed, glad that the subject of Colton McLean had been dropped. "I have to stop by the Lassiter ranch to look at a couple of lambs, then I'll be at the clinic. I'll be home around six unless there's an emergency."

"I'll be here or over at Vince Monroe's. He's havin' trouble with his tractor and wants me to take a look at it."

"You should've been a mechanic."

"I am," he said, offering her a gentle smile. "I just don't get paid for it."

"I don't know how smart that is," Cassie called over her shoulder as she dashed upstairs. In her room she changed into a denim skirt and cotton T-shirt, dabbed some makeup on her face and ran a brush through her hair. Yawning, she tried not to think about Colton. He'd already robbed her of a night's worth of sleep, she thought angrily, remembering how she'd watched the digital clock flash the passing hours while she'd tried and failed to block Colton from her mind. But his image had been with her—his steely eyes, beard-covered chin, flash of white teeth.

"Stop it!" she muttered at her reflection. She had work to do today, and she couldn't take the time to think about Colton McLean or his missing horse!

"So what did Aldridge say?" Curtis asked, matching Colton's long strides with his own shorter steps as Colton strode across the wet yard to the stallion barn. Sunlight pierced through the cover of low-hanging clouds.

"He wasn't there."

"So you don't know any more than you did last night?"

"I talked to Cassie," Colton muttered, throwing open the door and frowning as he noticed Black Magic's empty stall. A few soft nickers greeted him, and the smell of horses and dust filled his nostrils.

"Did you now? And what did she have to say?"

One side of Colton's mouth lifted. "Not much. She held a rifle on me and ordered me off her place."

"Friendly," Curtis murmured.

"Hardly."

"So you didn't find out anything?"

"Once I convinced her that I'd had enough bullet wounds to last me a while, she finally showed me around the place."

"And?"

"Nothing," Colton said quickly, dismissing the subject of Cassie. He'd thought of little else since he'd seen her, but he wasn't going to get caught up in her again. Not that she wanted him. She'd made it all too clear just how much she loathed him. "Not one sign of Black Magic."

Curtis frowned as he measured grain into feed buckets. "So you think Ivan wasn't involved?"

"I don't know what to think," Colton admitted, climbing a metal ladder to the hayloft overhead. *Damn* the horse. *Damn Denver! Damn, damn, damn!* He kicked a couple bales of hay onto the cement floor and glowered at the empty stall from high above. Why did the damn horse have to disappear now? Using his good arm, he swung to the floor, then slit the baling twine with his pocketknife. "I still have to talk to him."

"What about the sheriff's department? Maybe we should call and tell them what's been going on," Curtis suggested, grabbing a pitchfork and shaking loose hay into the mangers.

"Later—when we know more," Colton said. He'd been an investigative photojournalist for years—lived his life on the edge. He was used to doing things his way and he didn't like the complications of the law. "Not yet. First we'll talk to the surrounding ranchers—see if anyone saw anything. There's still the chance that the horse'll show up like he did before."

Curtis's lips thinned. "If you say so."

"I just think we should dig a little deeper," Colton said. "Give it a couple of days. If we don't find him by the end of the week, I'll call Mark Gowan at the sheriff's office."

"And Denver?"

"Let's not phone him yet," Colton decided, knowing how his headstrong older brother would take the news. "It'll wait until he gets back. There's nothing more he or Tessa could do." He sliced the twine on the second bale. "Besides, I still intend to talk to Ivan Aldridge."

"I don't envy you that," Curtis muttered.

Colton grimaced. He wasn't crazy about facing Cassie's

old man again—but it had to be done. As soon as he checked this place again, he would confront Ivan Aldridge and see what the old man had to say for himself.

And what about Cassie?

Colton sighed loudly and rubbed the back of his neck. Oh, yes, what about Cassie? There had to be some way to get her off his mind. All night long he'd dreamed of her, imagined the scent of her lingering on his sheets, envisioned the soft, blue-black waves of her hair tumbled in wanton disarray against his pillow, pictured in his mind's eye the creamy white texture of her skin and the soft pink pout of her lips.

Whether he wanted to or not, sooner or later he'd have to face her again.

Cassie slipped the bridle over Macbeth's broad head. A rangy roan gelding with a mean streak, he snorted his disgust and sidestepped as she climbed onto his wide back.

"Come on, fella, show me what you've got," she whispered, leaning forward and digging her heels into his ribs. The horse took off, ears flattened, neck extended, as he galloped over the soggy earth.

A low-hanging sun cast weak rays across the fields, gilding the green grass and streaking the sky in vibrant hues of orange and magenta.

The wind caught in Cassie's hair, tangling it as she leaned closer to the roan's sleek shoulder. Adrenaline pumped through her veins, and the long day at work faded into the background. She'd come home dead tired, found that Ivan was out, and decided to ease the aches from her muscles by riding. Besides, she couldn't help but satisfy her curiosity about Colton and his allegedly stolen horse.

She pulled on the reins, slowing Macbeth at the edge of the woods. As she guided the horse through the undergrowth, she remembered another time she'd ridden this very path—eight years ago—to tell Colton about the baby that hadn't existed.

"It's been a long time," she consoled herself, but she couldn't shake the gloomy feeling as Macbeth picked his way through the shadowy pines.

Before the horse had stepped from the trees, Cassie heard the river rushing wildly. The Sage, engorged with spring rain, slashed a crooked chasm through the wet earth.

The path curved toward the river's banks, and Cassie stared across the wild expanse of water, a physical chasm between the McLean and Aldridge properties. Though the river was the natural dividing line, there was a stretch of grassy bank between the swirling Sage and the McLean fence line, where Colton McLean himself was stringing wire.

Wearing mud-spattered jeans and a work shirt that flapped in the breeze, he winced as he stretched the barbed wire taut between red metal posts. His broad shoulders moved fluidly under his shirt, and his jeans were tight against his hips.

He glanced up when Cassie urged Macbeth forward. A cynical smile twisted beneath his beard. "Here to see the scene of the crime?" he shouted.

"If there was one."

"See for yourself." Straightening, he rubbed his lower back.

She did. Her gaze wandered to the far bank where tire tracks were visible in the soggy ground. The fence had been repaired, but Cassie was convinced that Colton could tell that the wires had been cut. It was just too bad he thought her father was involved.

"So your horse hasn't returned?"

"Not yet. I don't really expect him to."

"Last time he did."

"So I heard." Colton ran the back of his hand across his forehead, and his eyes met hers. "Is Ivan home?"

"He wasn't when I got home."

"Tell him I want to talk to him."

"I have."

"And?"

"He thinks you're out of your mind," she said, tossing her hair from her face. "If anyone took your horse it wasn't Dad."

"I wouldn't be so sure of that."

Goaded, she swung off Macbeth's broad back and walked to the edge of the river. The swift current eddied and rushed over fallen trees and huge flat boulders. The air smelled fresh and damp, and if it hadn't been for Colton and his stupid accusations, she would actually have enjoyed being there.

"So why do you think Dad did it?" she yelled as Colton sauntered to his side of the river. Only forty feet separated them, but it could have been miles. "Why not the Lassiters, the Monroes, Wilkersons or Simpsons?"

"Give me a break!"

"They're all ranchers."

"The wires were cut here, Cass. *Here.* The truck took off from Aldridge land!"

"You think! You're not even sure that Black Magic's been stolen."

A thunderous expression crossed his face. "I'm sure all right."

"Then why not someone else? Someone who knew that you'd automatically think Dad was involved?"

"No one else is *your* father," Colton said through clenched teeth. "No one else has a vendetta against the McLeans."

"A vendetta," she gasped, incredulous. "Come on, Colton, you can't believe—"

"What I can't do is deny that a feud ever existed between your family and mine!"

"But a *vendetta*, for crying out loud! I think you've spent too many years dodging bullets and changing the name on your passports!" If it weren't for the river separating them, she would have gone right up to him and slapped his angular, bearded face. "Either that or you've watched too many old movies!"

"Ha!"

"*If*, and I repeat, *if* your horse really has been stolen, any one of a dozen ranchers could've done it! Black Magic's a bit of a legend around here. Anyone who wanted him could've taken him and made it look like Dad was involved. After all, the feud is common knowledge."

"You're grasping at straws, Cass!"

"And you're condemning my father!" Furious, she twisted Macbeth's reins in her fingers and hopped onto the gelding's broad back. "Get real, Colton, or go to the Middle East or some other war-torn place and leave us alone!"

"I intend to," he said under his breath as he watched her dig her heels into the roan's sleek sides. The horse took off with Cassie, her face flushed and furious, clinging to his back. With a clatter of hoofbeats, horse and rider disappeared into the trees. "And good riddance!" Colton growled, stalking back to the fence and ducking under the restrung wires. He snagged his jacket from the post, hooked it over his finger and swore all the way back to the truck.

Why did he let her get to him? Why couldn't he be immune to the mocking glint in her hazel eyes, the soft curve of her cheek, the sharp bite of her tongue? He'd known a lot of women—many far more sophisticated and glamorous than Cassie—yet none of them had gotten under his skin the way Cassie Aldridge had.

Years ago he'd convinced himself he loved her, that they could make a go of it—and she'd lied to him, tried to trap him into marriage.

And yet he was still attracted to her.

"Fool," he ground out, climbing into the cab of the truck. "Damn stupid fool!"

* * *

"That's right. Two days ago," Colton said, his jaw rock-hard, his fingers clenched around the telephone receiver. "The horse just disappeared."

"And you think he was stolen?" Mark Gowan asked. He was short and stocky with fiery red hair and a keen mind. Colton had known him for years.

"The wires were snipped. No one here did it."

"Have you talked to Ivan Aldridge?"

"Not yet."

"Maybe he was going to replace the section of fence."

Colton's eyes narrowed. "I'll be sure to ask him when I see him."

"What about neighboring ranchers?"

"Vince Monroe, George Lassiter and Matt Wilkerson swear they haven't seen anything suspicious."

"Okay," the deputy said with a sigh. "I'll be out just as soon as I've made a few inquiries."

"Thanks." Colton hung up and strode out of the den. The house was a mess, he thought, surveying the hallway and kitchen. He hoped that Milly Samms would return soon to clean it up—either that or he'd have to don an apron himself.

One side of his mouth curved into a half smile. He'd never admit it, but he had missed the rotund housekeeper with her constant advice and easy smile. *Watch it, McLean*, he warned himself, *you're getting too comfortable here.*

"Never!" he muttered, shoving open the back door.

Outside, the air was clean and fresh. White clouds drifted in a blue Montana sky. Colton walked directly to the stables. Fresh paint gleamed, and new windows sparkled. The building had just been rebuilt; the final touches had been completed this past December.

His teeth ground together. The stables represented all that he detested on the ranch. Eight years before, on the night after Colton had learned of Cassie's lies, his mother and father had been killed in a blaze inadvertently set by Tessa

Kramer's brother, Mitchell. Denver, trying to save his parents and some of the horses, had been burned so badly he'd nearly died. Despite plastic surgery, Denver would wear his scars the rest of his life.

And so, Colton thought wryly, would he. Though his scars were all internal, they were just as deep and painful.

Leaning against the top rail of the fence, he glowered at the building and didn't feel the wind kick up and ruffle his hair.

All the pain and grief had caused him to hate this ranch and everything about it.

He closed his eyes and shuddered. He'd been out riding that evening, trying to push Cassie out of his mind forever, when the gates of hell had literally opened. . . .

The air was hot, the ground dry. Bees flitted near his Stetson, and flies buzzed around his bay gelding's face. "Come on," Colton growled to his horse, unable to shake his black mood. Cassie's deception was turning his gut even as he tried to forget that she ever existed.

He should be glad, he told himself as the bay sauntered slowly across the dry fields to the river. He stared across that silvery slice of water to the woods and beyond. Aldridge property. Cassie's home. He was better off without her.

But the feelings brewing inside him were far from joyful. Even a sense of relief was missing. In its stead was loss and anger, a deep-seated and hateful anger.

So he wasn't going to be a father; he should be walking on air. No responsibilities, no ties, no *wife*!

Damn it all to hell!

More frustrated than he'd been in all his twenty-one years, he climbed off the gelding, kicked at a clod of dust with the toe of his boot and glowered at the Sage. Why had she lied? *Why, why, why?*

The sky turned hazy as diaphanous clouds hid the sun. Colton barely noticed what was happening overhead. His horse snorted a little, then sidestepped nervously.

"Steady," Colton muttered as the first smell of smoke drifted to him. "What's gotten into you?"

Surfacing from his dark thoughts, he froze. A prickle of dread slid like ice down his spine. He noticed for the first time that the day had grown unnaturally dark. The hairs on the back of his neck bristled.

Fire!

He whirled. His heart slammed in his chest.

Black smoke surged upward, billowing menacingly to the sky. "God—oh God, no!" Colton cried, jumping onto his horse and driving the heels of his boots into the gelding's sides.

He rode as if the devil himself were following. Slapping the reins hard against the bay's shoulders, swearing wildly, he stared straight ahead. Fire licked upward, crackling and rising in ugly gold flames through the rafters of the stables.

Red-and-white lights flashed; huge fire trucks rumbled up the lane.

The fence was just ahead. "Come on," Colton urged, racing faster, hoping the horse could clear the top rail. But the gelding, once he understood Colton's intention, skidded to a stop and reared, refusing to take the jump.

Swearing, Colton leaped from his back. "Damn coward," he cried, climbing the fence and spying his uncle's old flatbed parked near a dilapidated sheep shed. He wasn't aware that he was running, just that he had to get to the truck.

Breathing hard, he wrenched open the door, climbed behind the wheel and found the keys in the ignition. Colton twisted his wrist, glancing in the rearview mirror at the horror of the fire. "Come on, come on," he said as the old engine turned over, sputtered, coughed and finally caught.

Colton ground the gears and stomped on the gas. Bald

tires spun, and the truck shuddered before lurching forward.
Colton didn't stop at the gate but drove through, sending
boards splintering in both directions. Within seconds he
brought the truck to a halt near the house. Sirens wailed,
terrified horses screamed and the day had turned to hellish
night.

Heart pumping wildly, eyes smarting from the smoke,
Colton threw open the door and hurled himself out of the
truck, running across the yard toward the flaming stables,
stumbling, gasping for breath.

The fire chief barked orders through a bull horn. Men
were running everywhere. Horses shrieked in pain and fear.

Tessa Kramer and her brother, Mitchell, were bending
over the prone form of her father. Curtis Kramer's hair was
singed, and soot streaked his otherwise white face.

"Give us room," a paramedic ordered as he and another
man tried to revive the old man. The smell of whiskey on
Curtis's breath mingled with the stench of smoke.

"Everybody back off!" the chief ordered.

"What the hell's going on here?" Colton demanded.

The chief ignored him.

Colton stared in horror at the stables. Orange flames shot
out of the roof, and heat rippled in sickening waves from
the inferno.

Curtis coughed loudly and stirred, his red-rimmed eyes
focusing on his daughter. "Tessa, gal?" he murmured, cracking a weary smile.

Colton watched as tears formed in Tessa's eyes. "Thank
God, you're all right!" she whispered, wrapping her arms
around her father's grimy work shirt and burying her head
against his chest. "Did you see Denver—"

"You were with him," Curtis said, and shook his head.
"No one—"

"But Denver's in there! So are his parents," she protested,
her head snapping up.

Colton's knees threatened to buckle. "Oh, sweet Jesus! No! No!" He stumbled backward, and he had to fight to keep back the blackness that was enveloping him. His head felt as if a herd of wild horses were charging through it.

"Hey, you? Are you okay?" a man shouted.

Stumbling blindly forward, Colton started for the stables.

"It's too late!" Mitchell Kramer yelled. "Colt—stop! Damn him!"

"Stay back!" the chief commanded through the horn. "Christ! Somebody stop him—"

A blast ripped through the stables, and the building exploded in a fiery burst. Glass shattered. Timbers groaned and crashed to the ground. Flames crackled and reached to the sky in death-tinged yellow fingers.

The earth shuddered. Colton's feet were thrown out from under him. He was slammed into the ground, hearing the wail of terrified horses and the screams of firemen. *They were all dead!* Denver, Mom, Dad!

Colton's fingers curled in the gravel. Vomit collected in the back of his throat. Sharp rocks dug into his palms. Deep, wracking sobs tore through him. His family, his entire family had been destroyed by the ranch they'd loved. He pounded impotent fists against the sharp gravel until they bled.

"Come on, son," the fire chief said, offering his hand. "There's nothing you can do here."

He struggled to his feet and blinked against tears and smoke.

"Hey—here's another one!"

Two firemen dragged what seemed to be a lifeless body from the blaze.

"Get the oxygen!"

Denver! Colton started forward. The chief's hand curled over his arm. "You'd better wait—"

But Colton didn't listen. He recognized the clothes. But when he was close enough to see Denver's face, he stopped dead in his tracks. His stomach roiled again, and he nearly threw up. Denver's face was blackened by smoke—his hair was singed, and one side of his jaw and cheek had been burned.

"Is—is he—"

"Barely alive! Get out of the way." Dragging Denver, the paramedics headed for the ambulance. "Hold it, Sam!"

Colton started to follow, but the chief reached him again. "There's no room in there!"

Wrenching his arm free, Colton whirled on the older man. His teeth bared, his fists clenched, he growled, "That's my brother, goddamn it, and I don't know how long he's gonna live! Get outta my way!"

"Watch that one—maybe shock," one fireman said to another. "He shouldn't be driving—"

"Frank, Tom, bring that hose over here. . . ."

The chief turned his attention for a second, and Colton jumped into the cab of Uncle John's flatbed, twisted the key and tore out after the ambulance.

"Please, God," Colton whispered in the only prayer he'd ever uttered. "Let him live!"

Miraculously Denver had survived. After several days in a nearby hospital, Denver had been flown to L.A. to face more than one painful session of plastic surgery. And Colton had taken off. His parents were dead; his brother, emotionally crippled, had gone. There was no reason to stay.

Except for Cassie, he thought now as he glowered at the gleaming new stables. In his grief he'd nearly called her. She'd written a note of sympathy, and he, upon reading her kind words, had torn the note into tiny pieces, only to regret it later. He'd reached for the phone, but knew that he was turning to her in grief, not love.

His heart stone-cold, he'd forced himself to push any

loving thoughts of her aside. Though a small part of him still cared, he knew that loving Cassie Aldridge was futile.

Without ever looking back, he had packed his bags and taken off.

And now here he was, he thought grimly. And Cassie was becoming as much of an addiction as she'd been all those years before when he'd met her on the sly, lying to his parents and hers just to have a few stolen moments with her.

"Once a fool, always a fool," he muttered, slamming his hand against the fence. Pain shot through his shoulder, and he winced. As soon as Denver and Tessa returned, he was out of here. This ranch meant nothing to him. Nothing but the smoldering ashes of a past based on lies and sorrow.

Cassie grinned as Beth Lassiter Simpson, nearly seven months pregnant, carried a squirming cocker spaniel puppy into the examination room. Beth's face was framed in soft brown curls. She'd been Cassie's best friend since high school.

"So this is Webster?" Cassie asked, glancing at the pup's chart.

"In the flesh."

"Okay, let's see how he's doing." Cassie took the blond bundle of energy from Beth's hands and settled him onto the stainless steel scales.

Beth's four-year-old daughter, Amy, slid into the room. Her hair was a mass of fiery red curls, the skin over her nose sprinkled with tiny freckles. Amy's huge brown eyes rounded as she stared at Cassie. "You gonna give him a shot?" she asked anxiously.

"A vaccination," Cassie replied with a grin as she took the dog's temperature. "He won't even feel it."

Amy's lower lip protruded. "I *hate* shots."

"So do I," Cassie said, recording the pup's weight and

temperature before slipping her stethoscope into her ears. The poor animal was shaking, his heart pounding like a jackhammer.

Throughout the examination Amy watched Cassie suspiciously. When Cassie pulled the flap of skin behind Webster's neck and slipped the needle beneath the pup's fur, the little dog didn't so much as whimper.

But Amy gasped, her chubby hands flying to her eyes. "I can't look," she whispered to her mother.

"That's it!" Cassie tossed the disposable needle into the trash. "He looks great!" She held the puppy out to Amy, who opened one untrusting eye.

"For real?"

"For real! Take him into the reception area. Sandy, the girl behind the desk, might just have a dog biscuit for Webster and a sucker for you."

"What kind?" Amy asked, already heading for the door.

"Any kind you want."

Grinning from ear to ear, Amy hauled the wiggling cocker pup through the door.

"You have a way with animals—and kids," Beth said.

"I like them both," Cassie admitted. She stuffed her stethoscope into the pocket of her lab coat and leaned against the scales.

Beth grinned. "So do I—most of the time."

"You'd better," Cassie replied, glancing pointedly at Beth's protruding belly.

"Don't tell me! I already know I'm going to have my hands full." She gathered up her purse and glanced at Cassie. "I suppose you've heard that Denver McLean's horse is missing."

Cassie nodded. Beth was the one person other than her father and Colton who knew how much she'd once cared for Colton.

"Colton stopped by yesterday. He was fit to be tied!" Beth declared.

"I know. He seems to think the horse was stolen."

"You've seen him then?"

"Oh, yes," Cassie said with a small smile.

"He's even better-looking now."

"Is he?"

"Didn't you notice?"

Cassie shrugged, though she'd noticed all right. Who wouldn't? Even if the man was a bastard, Cassie understood what Beth was trying to say. Colton was still incredibly male, virile and sexy. Cassie compressed her mouth into a tight line, and drew her brows together.

"Who do you think would have the gall to steal Denver's horse?"

"Who knows?" Cassie replied, thinking again of Colton's angry accusations. At least it seemed that he hadn't spouted off to Josh and Beth about her father. "If you ask me, the horse probably just wandered off."

"Try to convince Colton of that," Beth teased.

"I have. He didn't buy it."

"Well, maybe Black Magic will just turn up like he did last year."

"I hope so," Cassie whispered. If the horse showed up again, it would make things so much easier.

"I'll see you later," Beth called, collecting her spritely daughter and excited pup in the reception area.

"In just about six months," Cassie replied.

Beth shook her head. "Let's not wait that long. We could have a social life that doesn't revolve around rabies vaccinations, you know. I'll have you over for lunch *before* number two is born."

"And I'll hold you to it."

"Good!" Beth grinned, snapping a leash onto Webster's collar.

"Is that it?" Cassie asked Sandy as the door clicked shut.

"Until tomorrow at nine," Sandy replied.

Rotating the kinks from her shoulders, Cassie slipped out of her lab coat, threw it in the laundry basket and washed her hands before walking through the labyrinth of metal cages in the back of the clinic.

At the first cage, Cassie bent on one knee and peered inside. The Monroes' German shepherd was lying listlessly on the floor, recovering from tendon surgery. She slipped her hands into the dog's cage to pat his broad, graying head. He rolled glazed eyes up at her, and his tongue lolled from his mouth. "Hang in there," Cassie whispered with an encouraging smile. "You'll be a new man in the morning."

She passed several other cages, eyeing the Fullmers' Siamese cat and the Wilkersons' pet hamster. Everything was quiet as she turned off the lights.

Outside, lacey clouds gathered over the surrounding hills. An early spring breeze caught in her hair and tossed the bare branches of the old maple near the clinic's parking lot. Cassie climbed into her car and shoved it into gear.

Her thoughts wandered back to Colton and the empty years when he'd been gone. She'd been devastated, of course, but her father had helped her, and she'd thrown herself into her studies at the university, eventually gaining a partial scholarship to veterinary school.

She'd made friends and dated, but never had she ever let anyone close to her again. She just hadn't met anyone who held a candle to Colton. "Idiot," she muttered between clenched teeth.

Why, now? she wondered. Why, after eight years, after enough time had passed that she'd been sure she was over him, did he have to show up?

Chapter Five

Cassie ran the currycomb over Macbeth's shoulder and was rewarded with a snort and kick that barely missed her shin. "Miserable beast," she muttered, slapping his rump playfully. She loved Macbeth and his surly temperament. "Okay, go on!" She unsnapped the lead rope, and Macbeth bolted for the far side of the paddock where he promptly lay down and rolled in the dirt beneath a single spruce tree. "Oh, great," Cassie murmured, seeing her hard work destroyed in an instant.

Long shadows crept across the land, and the sky had turned a dusky blue with the coming of night. "Why do I bother?" Cassie wondered aloud as the horse, his hide dulled by dust and dirt, scrambled to his feet and shook his head.

"You're wretched, you know that, don't you?" Cassie laughed as she washed her hands under a faucet near the barn.

She was just wiping her fingers dry on the back of her jeans when she heard the sound of a vehicle thundering down the lane. She didn't even have to look. She'd been expecting Colton for three days. "Here we go," she muttered under her breath, bracing herself as the engine died and she spied Colton behind the wheel.

Climbing out of the Jeep, Colton hesitated when he saw her. "Is Ivan home?" he asked, closing the door behind him.

"In the house."

"Good. I need to talk to him."

"So you've said."

He cocked one of his roguish brows in amusement. "No arguments from you?"

"Would it change things?"

"No—"

"Then what would be the point?" she countered. "There's no use wasting my breath." Without another word she led him through the back door. Ivan was in the living room, scanning the paper. "We've got company," she announced, trying to ignore the fact that her stomach was twisting in knots. Just being in the same room with her father and Colton brought back unwanted memories.

Ivan glanced up, his gaze clashing with Colton's. With deliberation he laid the paper aside and stood. "I've been expecting you," he said slowly. "Seems as if you've been spreading rumors around town about me."

"I just asked some questions."

Cassie's eyes widened. "You've been telling people in town that you think Dad is behind Black Magic's disappearance?"

"Of course not," Colton said through tight lips as he swung his gaze to her father. "But I did want to find out what you know about it."

"Nothing," Ivan snorted.

"The wires were snipped on the fence between your property and mine."

"Big deal," Ivan muttered, scowling. "If you've come here to accuse me of taking your horse, just do it, get it over with and leave. Or go talk to someone at the sheriff's department."

"I already have."

"And what did he say?"

"Mark Gowan's checking into things."

"Good. Then maybe he can clear up the big mystery. But if you ask me, you and your hands just got careless, McLean, and that damned horse of yours wandered off."

"No way."

"Then ask Kramer. Wasn't it his son who started the fire?" Little beads of sweat dotted Ivan's upper lip, and he was so angry his entire body had begun to shake.

Beneath his beard, Colton blanched. "That's over."

"Oh, right. So now you and the Kramers are one big happy family?"

The younger man's lips thinned. "Careful, Ivan," he warned.

"Look," Cassie interjected, "you came over here to say something to Dad. If you're done accusing, then get down to business, and when you're finished, leave."

Colton's eyes moved from Ivan to Cassie. "All right. Let's talk about the fence."

"Cassie says you claim it was cut."

"It was."

"And you think I did it."

"Or know who did."

"You're barking up the wrong tree, McLean," Ivan growled. Bending near the fireplace, he tossed a mossy log onto the fire in the grate, turned his back on Colton and prodded the log with a poker. "If someone did take your horse, and I'm not saying they did, they must've come onto my property through the north gate that leads to the road—the one we use for the hay baler and combine."

"I know which gate you're talking about."

"Good." Ivan dusted his hands and straightened slowly.

"Why would anyone else go through your land?"

"Ah, motive," Ivan said, rubbing a crick in his back and glowering. "I suppose I've got the best one, don't I? After all, it was my wife your uncle used, my daughter you dallied with—"

"Enough!" Cassie shouted, the old wounds bleeding.

Colton sucked in a swift breath. He clenched his fists, and he took a step forward before getting a grip on himself. "Let's leave Cassie out of this," he said through teeth that barely moved.

"Seems you forget quicker than I do!"

Colton bristled defensively. "What happened between Cassie and me hasn't got anything to do with this."

"Bull!"

Colton's storm-gray eyes darkened with a private agony. Was he still hurting, too? Cassie wondered. But if so, why the witch-hunt?

"You think I would steal your horse, then leave tracks all over my property?" Ivan tossed back. "What do you take me for? I've been burned too many times by the likes of you to take a stupid chance like that!"

"I thought you might like to rub it in."

"Stop it," Cassie cut in. "Everyone's had their say."

Colton slid a glance her way. "So now it's over, eh?"

Deep inside she quaked and her voice shook. "It's been over a long time." She stared straight into his eyes, hoping she didn't look as vulnerable as she felt.

"Go home, McLean," Ivan suggested, seeming suddenly tired and worn, "before I lose my patience altogether."

"I won't let this lie," Colton warned.

"Fine, fine, waste your time and your breath," Ivan suggested. "But don't waste mine."

Colton strode out of the house, and Cassie was right on his heels. Too many buried emotions kept churning to the surface, and she couldn't just watch him leave.

"Your father knows more than he's willing to tell," Colton muttered.

"No way."

"Why not?" He reached the Jeep but didn't climb inside. Instead he faced her, his expression blank, his eyes guarded.

"My father has nothing to hide, Colton. He's just an old

rancher trying to scratch out a living. He doesn't have time for junior high pranks."

"Taking a valuable stallion isn't a prank! It's a crime."

"Go home, Colt."

But he didn't move, and his eyes raked over her. "You've changed, Cass," he observed.

"So have you. What happened to you, Colton? Just what happened to you? For months you've been holed up in the McLean house like some kind of recluse, and now, now when it looks like you're finally getting well, you come over here with accusations that just don't make any sense!"

Colton's jaw slid to one side. "Maybe I've just gotten smarter."

"Smarter or more bitter?"

"Probably a little of both. But then I have learned a few things in the last eight years."

"Such as baiting old men and accusing them of lies?" she lashed out.

He gritted his teeth. "I just wanted to hear what Ivan had to say for himself."

"But you don't believe him."

"I've heard lies before."

The vicious words stung like the bite of a snake. "I never lied to you, Colton, but then you didn't stick around long enough to find out, did you? You believed what you wanted to believe! That way your conscience was clear!"

"*My* conscience?" he repeated incredulously as he reached for the door of his Jeep. "My conscience? I was just along for the ride—remember?"

Cassie wished the tears behind her eyes would go away. "What I remember, McLean, is that you ran—away from me, away from any responsibility, away from any ties. For that, I suppose, I should thank you!"

He whirled, and the hand that had been poised over the handle of the Jeep's door clamped around hers. "I was going to do my duty, Cassie," he growled, his gray eyes flaring dangerously. "But I wasn't about to be conned, just like I'm not going to be conned again."

"I loved you, Colton."

"You didn't know the meaning of the word."

Inside she ached, but she wouldn't give him the satisfaction of knowing how deep her scars ran. Her throat was thick, her eyes moist, but she held back her tears and tossed her hair out of her face to glare furiously at him. "At least I was with you because I wanted to be—not because of some warped sense of 'duty' as you called it!" Her heart was pounding, but she kept her voice cold. "I wanted you and I wanted your child. I cried myself to sleep so many nights, I can't even remember how many there were, but it's over. It's been over a long, long time. So let go of me and go back to your house where you can brood and plot and try to think up paranoid schemes where my father is out to get you!"

He dropped her hand as if it were hot. Some of the color seeped from his face. "That's twisted."

She knew he was right, but didn't let up. She couldn't. Afraid that he might see through her defenses, she said, "Probably. But then, I had a good teacher."

His breath hissed between his teeth, and his jaw slackened. "Did I hurt you that much, Cass?"

Her heart turned over, and for an insane instant she wanted to throw her arms around him. Instead, she bit out, "You only hurt me as much as I let you. That was *my* mistake, not yours." Then, before she said anything that might betray her true feelings, she stepped back and folded her arms over her chest and didn't move until he'd driven down the lane and the sound of the Jeep's engine had faded into the dusky twilight.

Colton sank into the blackest mood he'd been in since he'd awoken in that hospital room in Belfast with tubes attached to his wrist and the pain in his shoulder racking his body. He tried and failed at shoving thoughts of Cassie and her father from his mind. He drank more than he should have, wandered around the empty farmhouse and spent too many hours near the roaring Sage River, staring at the damned Aldridge property beyond.

Gruff with the hands, rude to Curtis, he discovered that almost everyone on the ranch granted him wide berth. Good! He didn't care. All he wanted was to find the bloody horse and for Denver and Tessa to cut their trip short and return.

Two days after his confrontation with Cassie and Ivan, Colton stepped off the back porch and spied Curtis on his way from the stables. But before he reached Colton, Curtis stopped dead in his tracks. "Well, I'll be damned!" he muttered, his old eyes squinting toward the distant hills.

Colton followed the old man's gaze. Morning mist rose from the grassy fields, and the highest peaks of the mountains, snowcapped and craggy, were gilded by a bright Montana sun. In a field near the foothills, a solitary black horse stood, head raised, mane and tail fluttering in the slight breeze. Colton's eyes narrowed. "Is it Black Magic?" he asked, running across the yard.

"Or his twin."

They didn't waste any time. Together Curtis and Colton climbed into a truck and maneuvered through the series of gates to the most westerly field, where the stallion, ears pricked forward, coat gleaming, picked at a few spring blades of grass.

"Where've you been?" Colton asked as Curtis clipped a lead rope on Black Magic's halter.

"And what've you been doin'?" Curtis ran expert hands along the horse's sides and legs, then looked into his eyes. "He looks good," the old man said with a relieved sigh, his gnarled fingers stroking Magic's shoulder. Curtis studied the horse. "Good thing we didn't call Denver. He and Tessa would've worked themselves up over nothin'."

"Right." But Colton was still uneasy. True, the stallion looked none the worse for wear. His charcoal coat was glossy beneath the morning sun, his eyes held the same fire Colton remembered, and he butted Colton playfully. "How the hell did you get back here?"

"Beats me," Curtis said under his breath. "But if I were you, I'd count my blessings."

While Curtis drove the pickup back to the yard, Colton walked the stallion to the stables. Black Magic pulled and tugged at the lead, mincing and sidestepping. "You're full of it, aren't you?" Colton remarked as he closed the final gate and led the horse into the stallion barn.

Curtis was already waiting. The floor of Black Magic's stall was covered with fresh straw. Oats had been spread in the manger. Curtis finished drawing a bucket of fresh water and offered it to the stallion before locking him into the stall. "Okay, now that he's back where he belongs, tell me where you think he was."

"I wish I knew," Colton said with feeling.

Curtis ran a leathery hand around his neck. "I'll still stake a month's wages on Aldridge. You probably scared the bejeezus out of him the other night and he thought he'd better cover his backside. If you ask me, Ivan Aldridge brought our boy, here, back."

Colton's eyes never left the stallion. "Is this exactly what happened last year?"

"About. But he was gone longer."

Puzzled, Colton asked, "Why would Ivan Aldridge have taken the horse last year? If he's got any gripe against the family, it's with me, and I wasn't even around."

"He didn't much like John. It happened before his death." Curtis lifted a shoulder. "He hates the lot of you, you know."

It was a simple enough explanation, but not good enough.

"You just wait. I bet the foals born on the Aldridge spread this year look a lot like this guy." Curtis petted Black Magic's muzzle.

"Then I suppose we'll just have to wait and see, won't we?" Colton's gaze swept the stables before landing on the empty stall next to Black Magic's. "Maybe I'll sleep out here tonight."

Curtis's faded eyes darkened. "You think he'll be taken again?"

"I don't know," Colton replied, unable to shake the restless feeling that things still weren't resolved. Just because the stallion was back didn't mean whoever was behind the theft wouldn't try something else. "But I don't want to take any chances."

Curtis eyed the empty stall. "It won't be very comfortable."

"I've been in worse places."

"And look what it got you."

"I'm *not* losing this horse again."

Curtis forked some hay into Black Magic's manger. "Do whatever you want."

It's not what I want, Colton thought unkindly. But it had to be done. He wasn't about to explain to Denver that he'd lost his prize stallion twice in a few weeks. "Stay with him until I get back."

"Whatever you say."

His mind racing for a possible explanation to Black Magic's disappearance, Colton saddled up Tempest, a sorrel stallion without much personality. Reasoning that the only gate to the field in which Black Magic was found was near the house, Colton decided to check the fence line. Either the stallion had jumped the fence, walked right through the main yard and opened the gate himself, or the fence had been cut again.

"Come on, Tempest, let's figure this out," he muttered as

he swung into the saddle. Pain pierced his shoulder, and the stallion sidestepped gingerly.

Colton held the sorrel to a quick walk, his gaze following the four strands of barbed wire encircling the field in which Black Magic had been grazing.

The fence was intact. Not one strand had been clipped. Nor had any of the sections been replaced. All the barbed wire was the same dull brown that sectioned off the fields surrounding the ranch. "So much for that theory," Colton grumbled.

By the time he unsaddled Tempest, Colton didn't know any more than he had when he'd left. It seemed as if he was all out of options. If he had to sleep in the stables in a sleeping bag, so be it. Just so long as when Denver returned, Black Magic hadn't disappeared again.

"Find anything?" Curtis asked as Colton tossed a worn sleeping bag onto an Army cot he'd positioned in the empty stall next to Black Magic's.

"Nothing." Colton shook his head, baffled.

"If only he could talk." Curtis leaned one arm over the box door and stared at the nervous black stallion.

Colton rubbed his jaw and scowled into the stall that was to be his bedroom for the next couple of weeks.

Was Aldridge behind the horse's disappearance? Or was he just a convenient scapegoat? Could someone else have taken him—Matt Wilkerson or Bill Simpson? Had Denver or John made some enemies that no one knew about? Or, had Black Magic found a hole in the fence and wandered through?

"No way!" Colton decided, slapping the top rail of the box. Black Magic snorted, his ebony coat gleaming in the dim light of the fluorescent bulbs.

Colton knew that the best course of action was just to hold tight until Denver returned. The horse's disappearance, now over, wasn't any of his business. His older brother could deal with it.

And yet, a part of him was still intrigued. Years of unraveling mysteries and living on the edge in some of the most dangerous political hot spots in the world caused his suspicious mind to leap ahead to every available conclusion. He'd find grim satisfaction in exposing the culprit, should there be one.

Thoughtfully he rubbed his chin again, his beard scratchy and rough. And what if that culprit turned out to be Ivan the Terrible? What then? How would he break the news to Cassie? Instead of experiencing triumph and satisfaction, he just might feel guilty as hell.

Angry with the turn of his thoughts, he kicked the wall. A water pail jangled, and several horses snorted and whinnied. Colton barely noticed. His thoughts were too dark. Whether he liked it or not, Ivan Aldridge was Cassie's father and had stood by her when Colton had taken off. Not that she didn't have it coming, he reminded himself, then strode out of the stallion barn to the late morning air.

A small flock of crows cawed loudly and flapped their shiny black wings noisily. "Yeah, yeah, I know," Colton growled, glad to have something at which to vent his frustrations.

He didn't want to think about Cassie or her old man. Too many emotions he'd rather forget kept surfacing. And the fact that she lived just down the road brought temptation much too close. He'd like to see her again; he couldn't even deny it to himself. He'd lain awake more nights than he wanted to admit fantasizing about her. But he'd be damned if he'd get caught in her sweet trap all over again! No, at the soonest opportunity he was making tracks out of this desolate, windswept country, and he was leaving all thoughts of Cassie behind!

* * *

Cassie parked near the garage and frowned when she recognized Vince Monroe's green Chevy. In the past few years Ivan and Vince had become friends—helping each other with odd chores—and though Cassie didn't hold Vince in very high esteem, she kept her thoughts to herself. Her father needed help on the ranch, more help than she could give, and Vince Monroe had broad shoulders and a strong back. The fact that he was Jessica's father shouldn't be held against him, Cassie supposed ungraciously as she hauled two bags of groceries from the car. After all, what had happened between Colton, Jessica and Cassie was long over.

She kicked the car door shut with her foot, then nearly tripped on Erasmus, who had bounded down the steps to greet her.

"You should be careful," she warned the old dog as she backed through the kitchen door and set the ungainly sacks on the kitchen counter. Bending on one knee, she scratched Erasmus behind his ears. The old dog whined in ecstasy, rolling over on his back and exposing his belly. "Glutton," Cassie teased.

"I thought I heard you drive in." Her father, followed by Vince Monroe, walked stiffly into the kitchen. The television was still blaring from the living room, and Cassie made out the sounds of a pre-game talk show. "I was just telling Vince that it was about time for you to show up."

"Glad you missed me," she quipped.

Grinning, Ivan settled into his favorite chair near the wood stove.

As she began unpacking groceries, Cassie silently evaluated the two men. Her father and Vince were as different as night and day. Where her father was lean to the point of being gaunt, Vince was robust and supported a belly that stretched his belt to the last notch. Her father's hair had turned steely and thin, but Vince's sandy hair was thick and vital, his blue eyes still bright and quick. Cassie had the feeling that Vince

Monroe didn't miss much. She'd often wondered if he'd known of her involvement with Colton. As Jessica Monroe's father, he must've realized that his daughter and Cassie had once vied for Colton's affections. Or maybe he didn't. Maybe he wasn't that involved in his daughters' lives.

"I suppose you've heard the news," her father said, grinning widely, his eyes twinkling.

"What news?"

"McLean's Black Magic reappeared. According to Vince, here, Curtis Kramer found him in one of the main pastures."

"But—"

Vince shook his head and chuckled. "The same thing happened last year, you know. The stallion was gone for a few weeks and just showed up again. Old John was fit to be tied!" Vince hooted at the memory, and Ivan chuckled.

"That doesn't make sense," Cassie said, her thoughts tangled in emotions that should have been long dead. "Colton wouldn't make this kind of mistake—he wouldn't have come charging over here like a mad bull, making all sorts of accusations if the horse had just wandered into the wrong field. . . ."

"Boy, I would've loved to have been a fly on the wall when McLean found his horse," Ivan muttered, reaching for the old coffeepot on the stove and pouring himself another cup. "Serves him right. How about a cup?" he asked his friend, but Vince spread his big hands and shook his head.

"How'd you find out about this?" Cassie asked.

Vince set his empty cup in the sink. "I ran into Bill Simpson in town today. He'd been over to the McLean spread and talked to Curtis Kramer. Simpson says McLean and Kramer are still scratching their heads over it."

"You know, everyone at the McLean Ranch is sure he was stolen. Some big conspiracy or somethin'. Only thing they can't explain is why anyone would bother taking the horse just to return him." Vince chuckled deep in his throat. "If you ask me, Colton McLean had one too many shots taken at him. Maybe one grazed his head."

Cassie stiffened, but she didn't jump to Colton's defense. After all, he thought her father was involved. "Where was Black Magic all this time?"

"No one knows—probably with the wild horses," her father said.

Cassie didn't know whether to laugh or cry. She was relieved that Black Magic was safe, but also felt a small triumph. Though she told herself that she had outgrown her need for vengeance, she knew she would feel a warm glow of satisfaction in telling Colton just what she thought of him. She'd love to watch him eat crow! "So the horse was on McLean land the entire time?"

"No one knows for sure."

"What about the snipped fence?"

"Beats me. McLean probably made it up," Vince said as he reached for his hat and rammed it onto his broad head. "Thanks for your help with the tractor," he said to her father. "I owe you." With a wave, he was out the door and down the back steps.

Ivan eyed his daughter. "So what do you think about Colton losing his horse?"

"I don't know," she murmured, watching through the window as Vince's truck lumbered down the lane. "But I bet there's more to it than we know."

"Well, it doesn't matter," Ivan decided, dismissing the subject. "He's got his horse back and he'll leave us alone."

Cassie wasn't so sure. Colton had dragged her into this mess, charged her father with horrid accusations, then stormed out. Surely he wouldn't expect her to ignore the fact that he'd been wrong.

Cassie closed the cupboard and folded the empty sacks. "I think I'll go talk with Colton and see what he has to say for himself," she said, almost to herself. She knew she was playing with proverbial fire, but the idea grew on her. She could almost taste the sweetness of Colton's apology.

"Maybe it would be best to leave well enough alone," Ivan suggested. He wedged off one boot with the toe of the other.

"Like Colton did?" she responded, angry all over again at the gall of Colton McLean. "Maybe you've forgotten, Dad. He came busting over here and practically accused you of being a horse thief!"

"Well, he was wrong, wasn't he? I guess he'll have to live with that." Ivan chuckled.

"And I guess I'm going to give him a piece of my mind!" Cassie relished the idea more and more. "I'll be back later."

"Cass . . ."

She heard her father call her name as the screen door banged behind her, but she didn't care. For the past few days she'd been walking on eggshells with Ivan. He'd been touchy after his meeting with Colton. She'd caught him sitting in the dark, brooding. But now it was over. Now it was time to set the record straight!

After all, she reasoned as she shifted the gears of the old Dodge truck, Colton McLean owed her an explanation. Her fingers curled tight over the steering wheel, and she squinted through the grimy windshield against the final blaze of a dying sun.

She couldn't wait to hear what Colton had to say for himself, but her stomach churned at the thought of facing him again. There was something powerful and potent about Colton—something she could never ignore.

The wheels of the truck ground to a stop as she parked beneath a single oak tree near the front of the McLean house. Pocketing her keys, she swallowed hard, and without taking the time to second-guess herself, marched briskly up the brick path to the front door.

The McLean house was everything the Aldridge home was not. Freshly painted a light gray with slate-colored trim and blue shutters, it stood on a hill in the center of the ranch. A wide veranda flanked the house on three sides, and a sun porch had been built off the back. The yard was kept up and trimmed, even in Tessa McLean's absence.

Cassie didn't waste any time. She climbed the worn steps and knocked loudly on the front door. There she waited, crossing her arms under her breasts and wishing she knew what she was going to say to Colton when she came face to face with him.

Within seconds she heard the scrape of boots.

Her heart began to slam against her ribs.

The door swung open, and Colton himself, stripped bare to the waist, eyed her. His muscles were firm and sleek under skin that was surprisingly dark. Several ugly scars crisscrossed in a purple webbing across his shoulder. A white towel was slung around his neck, and from the dabs of foam near his temple and the fact that his chin was buck naked, she knew he'd been shaving.

Her throat tightened. His skin, recently covered with a dark beard, was now pale but firm. Thin, defined lips curved slightly at the sight of her, though the line of his jaw remained rigid.

"Well, Cassie," he drawled, crossing his arms over his naked chest and leaning the battle-scarred shoulder against the doorjamb. "You're the last person I expected to see. Don't tell me—this isn't a social call. Right?"

Her throat so tight she could barely speak, she stared at him. Without the beard he looked exactly like the young man she'd loved so fervently all those years before. "I—I, uh, heard you found your horse." Dear Lord, why was her voice so soft?

Colton's grin widened. "Good news travels fast."

"And he was right in the middle of your ranch?"

"Approximately," he agreed, amusement plain in his gray eyes.

"So he wasn't stolen after all?"

"Oh, he was stolen, all right. Whoever took him decided to put him back."

"That's crazy!"

Colton tugged thoughtfully on his lower lip. "Maybe they were running scared."

"You *think*."

"I wasn't here, but Curtis is convinced the same thing happened last year."

"Curtis could be wrong."

"I doubt it. Someone 'borrowed' the horse—either for free stud fees or just to get under my skin. Anyway, it won't happen again."

"Why not?"

One side of his mouth lifted, and he snapped the towel from around his neck. "I'll show you. Just give me a minute."

"You don't have to . . ." But he had turned, disappearing into the house.

Cassie waited, listening to the sound of his retreating steps and feeling like a fool. She'd raced over here fully intent on giving Colton a little of his own back. But seeing him stripped to the waist and beardless, she'd been nearly tongue-tied, and the fire that had propelled her over here had been doused by the water of bittersweet memories.

Fingering the rail surrounding the porch, she told herself she should leave, that being alone with him was doing more damage than good, but she didn't want to take the coward's way out. Just as anger had forced her over here, pride kept her from running away.

At the sound of his returning footsteps, she stiffened.

"Okay, let's go," Colton said, striding across the porch. He was stuffing his wounded arm through the rolled sleeves of a loose blue work shirt. He winced at the effort while the tails of the shirt flapped in the breeze.

"Go where?"

"I thought you'd like to see what all the fuss was about." Before she could protest, he took her hand, led her down the porch and around the side of the house.

"Maybe I should just go."

"I don't think so. You came over here to bait me, didn't you?"

"I thought you might apologize."

"Apologize?" he repeated, then laughed. "For what?"

"Let's start with accusing my dad of being a horse thief!"

"The jury's still out on that one."

She yanked hard on her hand, but his fingers only tightened. "You're out of your mind!"

"So you keep saying."

He was walking so fast, she had to half run to keep up with him. Her black denim skirt billowed, the soles of her boots crunched on the gravel. They crossed the yard and headed straight for the stables. Colton shouldered open the door and pulled Cassie into a darkened interior filled with the scent of horses and dust, oil and leather. Stallions snorted and rustled in stalls as they passed, but Colton didn't stop until they came to an end stall.

She recognized Black Magic instantly. Denver's prize quarter horse stallion was the most famous horse in the county—possibly the state. Magic's glossy coat gleamed almost blue beneath the lights, and his only marking, a jagged white blaze, slashed crookedly down his nose.

"This is Black Magic," Colton said grandly, dropping Cassie's hand and eyeing the horse as if he didn't much care for him.

"We've met before." Cassie couldn't keep the sarcasm from her voice.

"Well, take a good hard look at him, Cass. Because no one on the ranch has laid a hand on him since he got back."

"So?"

"So how do you explain that a horse who was supposed

to have been wandering around the ranch in the hills for the better part of a week is in such good shape? Shouldn't he be filthy? It's been raining and yet he hardly has any mud on his coat. And he's obviously not starving. In fact," Colton said, nodding to himself, "I'd say Magic here looks better now than when he was taken."

"Which proves someone took him to use him as a sire," she mocked, blowing a loose strand of hair from her eyes.

"Bingo!"

"But that doesn't wash, Colton. Even if your theory were true—and I'm not saying it is—the thief couldn't claim that your horse was the sire to any of his foals. They wouldn't be any more valuable. So what would be the point?"

"Better offspring. And you're wrong about the value." Colton slid a knowing glance her way. "What's the name of your father's best stud?"

"Devil Dancer."

"And is he a black horse?"

"Yes, but—"

"Just suppose that Devil Dancer's foals turn out to be the best horses you've ever raised. Better than you expected. Better than both the sire and the dam. Not only would the foals be worth more, but Devil Dancer's stud fees would go up."

Cassie almost laughed out loud. The idea was too absurd. "You're really reaching, McLean," she challenged, shaking her head. "Why would anyone, especially Dad, go to all the trouble?" She saw his eyes darken, and she knew. The feud. Of course. Always the feud. "I thought I already told you that what happened in the past is over, Colt," she said, unable to let the subject drop.

"Is it?" His gaze moved from the horse to her, insolently sliding from her crown to her toes. Suddenly the dimly lit barn seemed intimate and sultry, warmer than it had been.

"Of course."

"Then why're you here?" He leaned one of his hips against the stall door, waiting.

"Two reasons," she said, feeling a ridiculous need for honesty. The musty room seemed to close in on her, and she shifted her eyes away from Colton. "First, and I'll admit it, I wanted to gloat."

From the corner of her eye she noticed that one of his dark brows was cocked in interest.

Her pulse leaped crazily. Coming here was a mistake, a serious mistake. She knew that now, but she was trapped, and in all honesty she didn't know if she would run from him if she could. "Believe it or not, Colton, you bring out the worst in me. You came storming over to my house, ranting and raving, parking your backside in the middle of my kitchen, claiming that my father had done you dirt. And I wanted to see how you'd like it if the tables were turned." She clenched her fingers around the top rail of Black Magic's stall. Suddenly self-conscious, she thrust her hands into her skirt.

"And the other reason," he prodded, his voice low.

"The other reason." She licked her lips and plunged on. "It's time everyone forgot there ever was a feud and buried the past." She tilted her face up mutinously and met the questions in his eyes with the cool fury in hers.

"Tell that to your father."

"My father had nothing to do—" she started before his hard brown hand caught her wrist.

"Drop it, Cass," he suggested, gray eyes blazing.

"What's gotten into you?"

He gritted his teeth. He wanted to tell her. Oh, God, how he wanted to tell her that she'd gotten to him again despite all those damned promises to himself. The scent of her hair, the challenge in her eyes, the thrust of her small chin all beckoned him in a primal way he detested. "I don't want any more foul-ups, Cass," he said, his teeth clenched, his fingers curling possessively over her small wrist.

"Meaning?"

"That I don't want to lose Black Magic again!" He cocked his head to the stall next to the black stallion's box, indicating the cot and sleeping bag. "And I intend to make sure it doesn't happen."

A dimple creased her cheek. "Dedicated, aren't you?" she mocked.

"When I have to be."

"Is that right?" she baited, thinking back to a time when she'd needed him and he'd abandoned her. "You couldn't prove it by me!" She yanked her arm free and started out of the barn, away from the intimacy, away from him. She opened the door, but he caught up with her, slammed the door shut with the flat of his hand and grabbed her shoulder, spinning her around. "Let go of me, Colton!" she snapped. Her back was pressed hard against the door.

"Not until you hear me out." His voice had turned softer, the angle of his jaw less harsh. His stubborn gray gaze delved deep into hers. "I didn't mean to insinuate that I didn't care for you."

What she read in his gaze made her sick inside. Pity. He actually *pitied* her! "Don't worry about it."

"But I do, Cass."

"Why?"

"Because we were both young and made mistakes."

"My only mistake was that I loved you, Colton," she said, her voice surprisingly calm. His face was so close she could smell the lingering scent of shaving cream on his skin. "But you taught me how foolish that one emotion can be, didn't you?"

"I never lied to you," he reminded her.

The ache within stretched wide, hurting all over again. "You lied to me every time you held me," she whispered, her heart shattering into a thousand pieces. "Every time you kissed me, every time you pretended to care!"

"I never pretended, Cass," he said, the fingers on her shoulder firm but gentle, the cynicism in his eyes fading in the half light of the barn.

"Liar!" she declared, blinking rapidly, then she stumbled backward, groping for a way to escape. Being here with him, alone in the shadowy barn, was a mistake. Her feelings for him were too deep, the wound of his rejection, though eight years old, still raw and bleeding.

She found the handle and yanked hard, slipping through the narrow opening and taking in deep lungfuls of fresh air.

"This isn't finished, Cass." Colton's voice, barely a whisper, reverberated through her soul.

Forcing herself to walk when her legs wanted to run, she strode to the old truck, climbed inside and turned the key with shaking fingers.

The old engine sparked to life. Cassie cranked the steering wheel and shoved the gears into reverse. She caught a glimpse of Colton standing in the doorway to the barn. Hands planted on his hips, shirttails flapping in the breeze, he glared at her. His face was set once again in a hard, impenetrable mask, his expression cold and distant.

Cassie rammed the truck into first and took off. Gravel sprayed from beneath the tires, and she didn't dare look back in the rearview mirror—afraid that if she did, she might lose her heart all over again to a man who could change from warm to cold as quickly as the winter wind could change directions.

Chapter Six

Colton's shoulder throbbed. After several nights of sleeping on the Army cot, his cramped muscles rebelled and he wondered if standing guard over Black Magic was worth the effort. "This is all your fault, you know," he grumbled to the stallion, throwing wide the outside door.

Black Magic bolted out the door and tore through the rain-sodden fields, kicking and bucking beneath the gray spring skies. His ebony mane caught the wind, his tail unfurled. He seemed more colt than stallion as he raced from one end of the field to the other, whistling sharply to the horses in a nearby pasture.

"Show off," Colton muttered, feeling a grin tug at the corners of his mouth despite his bad mood as he strode to the house.

In the kitchen Colton put on a pot of coffee, then headed upstairs. Stripping away his grimy clothes, he glanced in the mirror, then massaged his strained muscles. He stood for twenty minutes under the steamy hot spray of the shower, and slowly the ache in his shoulder subsided.

By the time he'd shaved and dressed, he felt almost human again. Almost, he thought with a grimace, his thoughts turning as they had of late, to Cassie. "Forget her," he ordered the brooding man in the mirror, and knew it was an impossible task.

Growling to himself, he sauntered downstairs and poured himself a cup of strong coffee. Cassie's accusations hung over him like a pall these past few days. Despite all his arguments with himself, his conscience had begun to bother him. Maybe he had been too hasty in his accusations. Perhaps he'd jumped to the wrong conclusions. Maybe, just maybe, he'd been wrong about Ivan Aldridge.

And maybe he hadn't.

But it didn't help to keep the old rift festering, his guilty conscience prodded. He sipped from his mug, ignored the mess that had accumulated since Denver and Tessa had left for L.A., and slapped a couple of pieces of bread into the toaster. As he waited for his toast, he actually toyed with the idea of driving over to the Aldridge ranch and squaring things with Ivan. He probably owed the old man that much.

Colton didn't believe in making excuses or kidding himself. Deep down, he knew the reason he was considering a visit to the Aldridge spread was Cassie. He wanted to see her again. It was that simple . . . and that complicated.

The phone rang loudly, interrupting his thoughts. He snatched the receiver.

Denver's voice boomed over the wires. "So you are still there," he joked. "Tessa and I had a bet."

"Who won?" Colton asked.

"Tessa. I thought by now you would've gone stir crazy."

"Not quite," Colton drawled, grinning to himself and gazing out the kitchen window to see Black Magic grazing near the fence. "About time I heard from you."

"We've been busy."

"Have you?" Colton couldn't hide his sarcasm.

"Yep. But it won't be long now. We'll be back in less than three weeks."

It sounded like an eternity. Restlessly Colton scraped the nail of his thumb against the wall. "I'll try to hold it together till then."

"Have you had any trouble?"

Colton's eyes narrowed on Black Magic, and he considered telling his brother the truth. But what would be the point? Worrying Denver wouldn't bring him home any quicker. In fact, it would only serve to make his brother angry and nervous. And Denver's temper was as quick to flare as his own. "Nothing I can't handle," he said evasively before hanging up.

He finished his coffee, dashed the dregs down the sink, then strode outside. Clouds rumbled across the sky, and the wind had picked up, whistling through the branches of the oak and pine trees near the barns. He glanced at the Jeep, thought about driving over to see Cassie, and fought like hell to avoid that particular temptation.

Ramming his hands into the back pockets of his jeans, he took off across the yard. The rest of the day he threw himself into his work, repairing broken boards and sagging beams. As his hammer slammed nails into the wood, he tried and failed to shove Cassie Aldridge out of his mind.

"Okay, that's it—the last of today's walking wounded," Sandy said, turning the lock of the front door behind a Border Collie that walked with a pronounced limp from a mending leg.

"Thank goodness!" Cassie quickly cleaned the examination room, then stripped off her lab coat and dropped it into the laundry bin.

In the back room, Craig Fulton the veterinarian she worked with, was closing the final cage on a fat gray tabby. Craig was a short man with thick brown hair, freckles and oversized features in a round face. A bachelor since his divorce three years before, Craig had offered Cassie a job as soon as she'd graduated. His clothes were always a little rumpled, and his thick wire-rimmed glasses tilted slightly to one side.

"It's been a long one, hasn't it?" he said with a tired smile. He'd spent most of the day driving from one ranch to another, examining sheep, cattle and horses.

"Maybe things'll quiet down for the weekend."

"Sure." Craig chuckled. "Just remember, you're on call."

Cassie laughed. Though they took turns answering emergency calls on Saturday and Sunday, invariably they each worked part of every weekend. "I won't forget," she promised as she slung her jacket over her head and shouldered the door open.

Outside, rain poured from a darkening sky. Hunched against the wind, she dashed through the uneven parking lot, skirting the biggest puddles as she hurried to her white pickup. She flung open the door and started to climb inside, then pulled up short. There, slouched insolently against the worn seat on the passenger side, his legs sprawled in front of him, his wet Stetson shoved back on his head, was Colton McLean. "What're you doing here?" she asked.

"Waiting for you."

"Seems you've been doing a lot of that lately."

"Probably too often," he admitted, his sensual lips curved in a self-deprecating grin. "You'd better get in before you get soaked."

She didn't move other than to drop her shoulders. Oblivious to the rain collecting in her hair and sliding down her neck, she glared at him. "*Why* were you waiting for me?"

"The storm broke and I decided I'd rather be dry than wet."

"But you can't just climb into my truck and—"

"You don't lock your pickup any better than you lock the back door," he said. "Come on, get in." He stretched, reaching across with his hand, and his eyes were surprisingly warm. "I won't bite—I promise."

She almost laughed. "I'm not afraid of you, Colton. Bite or not." Ignoring his hand, she climbed into the cab and settled behind the steering wheel. "Don't you have some horse to protect or something?" she needled. "Why, right this very minute someone could be sneaking off with Black Magic to God-only-knows where."

His smile widened. "I guess I deserved that."

"And more."

"I did come on a little strong."

"That's putting it mildly."

Colton shoved his hat further back on his head. A dark swatch of hair fell over his brow. "I didn't come here to argue."

"Good. Now we're getting somewhere," she mocked. "Why are you here?"

"To invite you to dinner."

"You expect me to go to dinner with you?" she asked, stunned. "You're kidding, right?"

"Nope."

"But—"

"Look, Cass, I know I've been a first-class jerk," he admitted. "But I had my reasons."

"And now they've changed?"

"I thought about what you said, that's all. The horse is back, there's no harm done, and I"—his face changed expression and his eyes darkened a bit—"and I'd like to take you to dinner. Think of it as my way of apologizing."

"I didn't know you knew how."

"Maybe I don't. Seems I'm having one helluva time convincing you."

Suddenly the cab felt close. The windows, streaked with rain on the outside, had fogged on the inside, closing Colton and Cassie from the rest of the world. She felt like biting her lip, but didn't. "What would be the point?"

"Believe it or not, we might just have a good time."

Cassie nearly choked.

"And I'd like to spend some time with you," he admitted with a sigh. There was more to it, of course. Colton had argued with himself all day, knowing that being with her again would tangle him up in an emotional rope he wasn't sure he could unknot.

Cassie watched his fingers drum against his knee, saw the dark hair that covered the back of his hand. Her pulse jumped, though she forced herself to ignore it. "I don't know if I can—"

"Is your dad expecting you?"

"No." She shook her head. "He's used to me working late."

"Then why not?" he asked, a small smile teasing his lips again. She caught a glimpse of his sensual mouth, felt her heart flutter, then turned her gaze to the keys in her hand.

"I guess there's no reason," she admitted, jamming the key into the ignition. "Where to?"

"How about Timothy's?"

Her throat tightened. Timothy's was a small, intimate restaurant on the far side of town. She and Colton had been there together years before. "Sure," she said casually. "Why not?" She flicked on the engine, and the old truck roared to life. Her eyes sparkling, she asked, "Need a lift—or would you rather take your Jeep?"

Colton actually chuckled. "I'd rather ride with you."

"Would you?" She couldn't help but smile. "That's a turn around."

"Maybe not, Cassie," he muttered to himself.

Her hands were shaking as she drove out of the parking lot and eased into the gentle flow of early-evening traffic. The wipers swished rain from the windshield, and Cassie squinted against oncoming headlights.

Colton slouched even lower, and she could feel the weight

of his gaze upon her as she drove. She refused to glance in his direction, forcing herself to stare at the shimmering road ahead, concentrating on the traffic.

Timothy's was perched on the banks of the Sage River, near the famous falls for which the town was named. Originally a flour mill, the rambling building was constructed of river rock, mortar and dark cross beams. Near the front door an old waterwheel still creaked and turned, with water splashing over its time-worn planks.

She climbed out of the truck and marched toward the restaurant, all too aware of Colton beside her. He didn't touch her, didn't so much as brush her arm, but she was careful to keep the distance between them wide as they hurried up the slick brick path to wide double doors.

Inside, a huge foyer was lit with flickering sconces and wagon-wheel chandeliers. The stone walls rose three full stories to an arched, beamed ceiling. The floor was smooth stone, and burgundy cloths covered the tables. Kerosene lanterns adorned each table, the quivering flames providing intimate illumination.

"I haven't been here in years," Cassie admitted, following a waiter to the back of the building.

Their table was private, near a huge bank of windows overlooking the swollen Sage River as it tumbled wildly over the falls. Filled with spring rain and the runoff from the mountains, the green water churned in frothy torrents, cascading over steep rocks, crashing some forty feet below to swirl in a swift current. Cassie, aware of Colton, stared through the glass.

"What would you like?"

To run away from here—from you. "Anything." She forced her gaze to his.

When the waiter reappeared, Colton ordered for them both, then settled back in his chair.

Nervous, Cassie sipped from her water glass. Pretending interest in the wine list, she was able to avoid his eyes. Obviously he wasn't going to make this easy.

"So," she ventured, trying to appear calm, though a nervous sweat had dampened her skin. "What changed your mind? It must've been something earth-shattering for you to think you should apologize."

"It was."

The waiter brought their orders—crisp salad, fresh trout, steaming vegetables and a basket of sourdough bread. Once he disappeared again, Colton ignored his food. "You changed my mind, Cassie," he said.

Her eyes flew to his, and he held her gaze, though she could swear his face had turned a darker shade. "Me?"

"All that self-righteous indignation the other day."

"It got to you?" She could barely believe her ears.

He lifted a shoulder. "I guess."

"So you think Dad's innocent?"

Colton frowned. "I wouldn't go that far," he hedged, "but whatever happened with the horse, it's over. As far as I can see, other than that I was made to look like a fool, there was no harm done."

She eyed him thoughtfully. "You expect me to believe you?"

"Believe what you want, Cass," he said with a sigh. "I just thought that instead of working so hard at fighting, we should try to be civil to each other."

Her throat was suddenly dry. "Why?"

"It's long overdue."

Colton picked up his fork and cut into his fish, but Cassie ignored her meal. "So this is your grand gesture to end the feud, is that it?"

He shook his head. "Unfortunately I don't think I can do that," he admitted. "But I'd just like to start over with you."

Start over. Cassie looked away. If only they could roll back the years and erase the pain that kept them apart. She tried to swallow a bite of bread, but it seemed stuck in her throat.

"I think we got off on the wrong foot the other night."

"You think right," she finally replied, trying to remember that she was supposed to detest him. "I'm not crazy about my family's name being dragged through the mud."

"Neither am I," he said, his temper evident in spite of his efforts to remain calm. "And I'm not thrilled about looking like an idiot! Any way you cut it, the horse was stolen while I was in charge."

"*Maybe.*"

Colton had trouble hanging on to his patience. "Anyway, as I said, it's over. Let's forget about Black Magic."

"Amen," Cassie whispered, wishing she could close the door on their past as easily. She toyed with her food, barely tasting it, watching Colton surreptitiously and wishing that all the questions raging in her mind would vanish. "You know," she finally said when the silence stretched long between them, "I didn't think I'd ever see you again."

He shoved his plate aside. "Sometimes things don't go as you plan."

"Would you have come back on your own?"

"You mean, if I hadn't been forced?" he asked, rubbing his shoulder unconsciously. "I don't know. Probably not. There's nothing here now," he said, unwittingly cutting her to the bone. He thought aloud. "Mom and Dad were killed in the fire, and Uncle John died last year. I suppose I might have come back to see Denver once in a while, but I'm not sure about that. In case you don't remember, we haven't always seen eye to eye."

"I remember," she said softly, the memory of Denver intruding upon them at the lake all too vivid. Despite the years that had passed, her cheeks felt hot. "But you own part of the ranch now. John left half of it to you."

Colton's lips curled at the thought of his wayward uncle.

"It was just the old man's way of trying to tie me down. He knew I didn't want anything to do with the ranch, not after the fire. Neither did Denver. But, at least in my brother's case, it looks as if good old Uncle John won. Denver's settled down and become a family man,"

"The ultimate sell-out," Cassie observed, forcing a cool smile she didn't feel.

"Not if it's what he wants."

"And what is it you want, Colton?" she asked, afraid she'd never have the opportunity to question him again. "Danger? Thrills? What?"

"Why do you care?"

"It's something I've always wanted to know," she admitted. "Because all your life it seems that you've either been running from, or racing to, something. I just wondered what it was."

The smile that had touched his eyes faded, and his lips thinned a little. "You never did understand me, Cass."

"Because you never let me."

They were suddenly alone, just the two of them in this crowded room. The quiet conversation and soft clink of silverware dissolved. Cassie heard only the sound of her own breathing and the loud thudding of her heart.

Colton drew in a swift breath, looked as if he was about to say something, but held his tongue.

The long, silent seconds ticked by until the waiter deposited their check on a corner of the table.

As if thankful for the intrusion, Colton snatched up the ticket, reached into his wallet, peeled off some bills and stood in one single motion. "I think it's time to go."

"Past time," she agreed sadly.

They drove back to the parking lot of the clinic where Colton's truck sat beneath the barren branches of a young maple tree. Cassie flicked off the engine and waited. "I guess

I should say thank you," she said, sliding Colton an uneasy glance.

"You don't have to." He reached for the door.

"No"—without thinking, she placed a restraining hand on his shoulder—"I want to. Thanks."

Colton winced, and belatedly she realized she'd gripped his injured muscles. She tried to draw away, but he stopped her with his free hand, enfolding her fingers as his eyes met hers. "It's okay," he assured her. "And as for dinner, you're more than welcome, Cass. Maybe we should consider this the beginning of the end." When she didn't reply, he glanced down at her hand, still resting lightly, teasingly against the soft leather of his jacket. "The end of the feud."

"I think it'll take more than one meal," she said, grinning despite the tension she felt in the small, confined space. She slithered her hand away from his and saw his Adam's apple bob as he swallowed.

"Probably." His eyes locked with hers for an instant, and Cassie's veneer of self-control slipped. She realized in that one sizzling glance that Colton wasn't as immune to her as she'd thought. She recognized the shading of his gray eyes, the slight flare of his nostrils, the restraint in the skin stretched taut across his features. Though they weren't touching, their bodies separated by inches of worn upholstery, Cassie could feel the heat in his stare, noticed the scorch of desire in the twist of his lips.

"I—I'll see you later," she said, willing her voice to remain steady.

"Right. Later." Colton grimaced, and again he reached for the door. This time, however, he swore, and instead of lifting the handle, he twisted back, caught the back of Cassie's head in one hand and pulled her face to his.

Cassie gasped but didn't have time to resist. His lips found hers, and she felt the warm, insistent pressure of his tongue against her teeth. Her mind spun out of control, her pulse began to thunder, and she closed her eyes, allowing herself this one, tiny taste of pleasure. She knew that Colton didn't care for her—no more than he had all those years ago—and yet she couldn't stop herself from tasting him, feeling him, enjoying the bittersweet pressure of his mouth against hers.

His hand became tangled in her hair, and he groaned. When he finally dragged his mouth from hers, he stared at her through passion-glazed eyes. "Some things never change," he whispered raggedly before unlatching the door and sliding outside. "Good night, Cass." Without waiting for a response, he slammed the door shut and turned his collar against the wind. He strode across the parking lot, mentally kicking himself. Why had he kissed her? Why? *That* was a dumb move.

He yanked open the door of his truck, climbed inside and thrust his key into the ignition, swearing under his breath. If he thought kissing Cassie would convince him that it was over between them, he'd been wrong. Dead wrong.

"Fool," he ground out, flicking on the ignition. "God-damned fool!" He glanced in the sideview mirror and watched as Cassie pulled out of the lot.

What would it be like to spend a night with her? A weekend? One kiss had only whetted his appetite for more. Would a weekend in bed satisfy him—fill his need so that he could forget about her? Or would being with her become an addiction—the more time he spent with her, the more he would crave?

"Don't even think about it!" he growled. The woman was trouble. Big trouble. And for once in his life, Colton intended to keep himself out of trouble.

Her father was in the living room watching television when Cassie walked quietly into the house. She could hear the laugh track from a weekly sitcom and Ivan's soft chuckle. She could tell he'd eaten, as she glanced around the kitchen. Though most of the evidence wasn't in sight, as he'd washed his dishes, she noticed the leftover chicken he'd forgotten to wrap and place in the refrigerator.

"'Bout time you showed up," he said when she hung her coat in the hall closet and poked her head into the living room. "Where ya been? Emergency?"

"Not this time."

He glanced up. His reading glasses were perched on the end of his nose, his stocking feet propped on an ottoman. Only one lamp was lit, and the morning newspaper was scattered across an end table with one page folded to a half-finished crossword puzzle.

Cassie decided to come clean. Three Falls was a small town, and it would be better for Ivan to hear the truth from her before someone else spread the news. "I had dinner with Colton."

Her father's bushy brows rose. "Did you now?"

"Uh-huh. He was waiting for me when I got off work, and we drove over to Timothy's."

"Any particular reason?"

Anticipating a battle, Cassie drew in a long breath. "Believe it or not, it was his way of apologizing." She dropped onto the couch beside her father and grabbed the paper with the puzzle.

"McLeans don't apologize."

Cassie grinned. "Well, it was tough. Colton's not very good at it, but he seemed sincere."

"Bah!"

"Prevaricator."

"What?" He twisted his head around, looking at her as if she'd lost her mind.

"Eighteen down—liar. It's prevaricator." She handed the folded newspaper to her father, who scribbled in the answer.

"Just don't go trustin' Colton," Ivan said, glancing up at her before filling in a few more letters.

"Because he's a McLean?"

"That's a good reason."

"Dad," she said gently, "don't you think it's time to end all this nonsense about a feud?"

"Never!"

"But John's dead now."

"That doesn't change what he did," Ivan muttered, his color rising. "And as for Colton, he's very much alive and he's as bad as his uncle. I haven't forgotten how he treated you."

"Neither have I," she admitted, combing her hair back from her face with unsteady fingers. "But I've decided not to dwell on it."

"That's good."

"And I'm not going to act like Denver and Tessa and Colton are a bunch of pariahs."

"I've got nothing against Tessa Kramer," Ivan said quickly. "She's just a fool who lost her heart to a McLean. But Denver and Colton, I've got no use for them. Neither one of 'em would be here if they had their choice. They both made it clear to God and everybody around just what they thought of ranching. Too good for it, you know."

"Denver's back for good."

"Well, who needs him? As for Colton, he's just biding his time until he can leave, and I say the sooner the better." He thrust his jaw out angrily before he looked up, his weathered face softening. "Colton hurt you once, Cassie. But you're a smart girl. You wouldn't let it happen again, would you?"

"Of course not!" she snapped quickly.

"Good." He slapped the newspaper down. "Now, have you had dessert? How about a dish of ice cream?"

"I'm not really hungry."

"Well, I am, so you may as well join me." He straightened, rested a big hand on her shoulder a second, then made his way to the kitchen.

Cassie flung herself back against the cushions of the

couch. Her father was right, of course. Colton McLean had only caused her heartache and grief, while her father had been strong enough to help her pick up the pieces of her life and put them back together. Ivan had done everything he could to help her—borrowed money to help send her to college, encouraged her to go on to veterinary school and had even suggested that it was time she moved out—found an apartment in town. He'd been absolutely wonderful—and he'd been burned twice at the hands of the McLeans. She wouldn't let it happen again.

Cassie thought about her mother—beautiful, raven-haired Vanessa. Without a backward glance Vanessa Shilcoat Aldridge had left after her disastrous affair with John McLean had become common gossip. She'd returned to South Carolina where she'd found herself a wealthy doctor, remarried within a year and subsequently borne three children—Cassie's half brothers and sister, whom she'd never met.

Cassie never saw her mother, nor had she heard from her. Not a card at Christmas, never a call on her birthday. No, Vanessa would never look back. Cassie knew that she and her father had ceased to exist in her mother's mind.

Blinking against tears she'd sworn never to shed, Cassie tried not to think about her mother. Who needed Vanessa anyway? She and Ivan had done all right without her. But the weight in her heart felt like a stone.

"Rocky road or butter brickle?" her father called from the kitchen.

"Really, Dad, I'm not—"

"Oh, hogwash!" He chuckled and returned to the living room, carrying two huge bowls filled with both kinds of ice cream and oozing chocolate syrup.

"I'll get fat," she warned him.

"You?" He glanced down at her lithe body and handed her a dish. "No way! You're built like me. Now, come on, eat up and help me with this damned puzzle." He dropped back to the couch, studied the paper again and asked, "What's an eight-letter word that starts with *b*, ends in *a-l* and means trick? The third letter's a *t*."

"*B*, blank, *t*, blank, blank, blank, *a*, *l*?"

"Right," her father grunted.

Cassie thought for a minute, deliberately scooping up a spoonful of her father's gooey concoction. But she paused midair as the word hit her. "What about betrayal?"

"Betrayal . . . it fits." His lips flattened over his teeth as he scribbled the letters. The only sound was the scratching of his pencil and the barely perceptible chatter of the TV program in progress.

Prevaricator. Liar. Trick. Betrayal. The words rushed through her mind, though her father didn't say anything.

Cassie turned her attention to the television set. She'd thought enough about lying and betrayal and loneliness for one night.

"You know, you're the ugliest beast I've ever slept with," Colton grumbled to Black Magic. He petted Magic's velvet-soft muzzle only to have the horse toss back his head and snort indignantly. "Yeah, well, I don't like it any more than you do."

Colton hung his damp Stetson on a nail pounded into one of the rough-hewn posts supporting the hayloft. Sighing, he sat on the edge of the cot and pushed off one boot with the toe of the other.

He listened to the sounds of the wind whistling in the rafters and the rustle of hay as the horses settled in for the night. There were snorts, chewing noises and a quiet dry cough. Outside, the wind shoved a branch against the build-ing, but Colton didn't hear or see anything out of the ordinary.

Guarding the stallion might well be a waste of time, he thought, as he lay back on the sleeping bag, staring up at the floor of the loft and shifting so that his weight wasn't on his bad shoulder. If that were the case and Magic was safe, there was no reason Colton couldn't sleep in the house in a warm, clean bed instead of camping out here.

"You're just getting soft," he growled to himself, realizing that for the first time in eight years the old ranch house seemed a haven.

It was time to move on, get out of this place before he became complacent and self-satisfied. He considered his life beyond the ranch, remembering foxholes in Afghanistan, the hot, damp jungles of Central America, the blackened rubble of hideouts in war-ravaged Beirut. Why, he wondered, when he'd lived on the edge so long, had it begun to lose its appeal?

Chapter Seven

Beth Lassiter Simpson wasn't one to take no for an answer. And she wasn't taking Cassie's "no" seriously. In Beth's condition every meal was important, and a lunch that could combine friendship, gossip and food was an event. "Come on, you promised," Beth insisted, shifting her ungainly weight from one foot to the other. Planted in the reception area of Three Falls Veterinary Clinic, she crossed her arms over her protruding abdomen and stuck her lower lip out in a childish pout.

Cassie couldn't be tempted, at least not now. "I'm sorry, Beth, I'd love to, you know that. But I can't. Not until Craig gets back from the Wilkerson ranch."

"And when will that be?"

"Probably not more than an hour," Cassie said, glancing at her watch and frowning.

"Good. Then I'll wait," Beth decided. "I have a few errands to run and I'll meet you at The Log Cabin at one-thirty." She must have seen the hesitation in Cassie's eyes. "Come on, Cassie, you've got to eat anyway, and how often is it that I'm in town without Amy? Think about it. In a few more weeks

I'll have another baby and it will be *ages* before we can have lunch together!"

"All right, all right," Cassie agreed, holding her hands up, palms out, in mock surrender while mentally crossing her fingers. "But if I don't show, it's because Craig got held up." Cassie was worried. Craig had left early this morning, driving over to a ranch on the outskirts of town. The rancher suspected one of his horses had come down with equine influenza, which may have developed into pneumonia.

Beth's eyes twinkled. "If you don't show up, I'll come looking for you!" With a giggle, she breezed out of the complex, leaving Cassie to deal with two cases of feline leukemia and a pet rat with a growth on its leg.

Two hours later Cassie was seated at a corner table in the main dining room of The Log Cabin, a house-turned-restaurant that specialized in hearty man-sized meals. Brass lamps hung from the ceiling, and blue-and-white checkered cloths covered the tables.

Beth shoved the remains of her spinach salad aside. "You'll never guess who I saw today!" Her eyes shone with a private secret.

"I couldn't begin to," Cassie admitted.

"Ryan Ferguson! He's back!"

Cassie glanced up sharply and ignored the uneaten half of her sandwich. "But I thought he swore he'd never set foot in Three Falls again."

"Well, he lied. I saw him at the bakery this morning. Amy and I went in to buy some donuts and there he was, big as life, drinking coffee and talking to Jessica Monroe!" She motioned to the waitress, ordered a fattening, sinful dessert, then glanced back at Cassie. "The way I heard it, Denver McLean fired Ryan last winter. Caught him stealing supplies or something."

Cassie remembered the rumors but didn't put much stock in them. After all, she'd been on the unkind side of gossip more than once in her life. "I guess no one knows but Denver."

"And Ryan," Beth pointed out. "You know, I bet he's only daring to show his face because Denver's in L.A.!"

"Ryan has family here."

"Just a sister," Beth said. "And the way I understand it they don't get along."

"That could be just talk. Maybe he's only visiting."

Beth pursed her lips together and shook her head. "Nope. I talked to Jessica about him after he left the bakery. She said he was asking about work."

"You think he's back to stay?" Cassie was surprised. After Denver had accused him of stealing and fired him, Ryan hadn't bothered defending himself and had simply left town.

"Who knows? According to Jessica, Ryan stopped over at her dad's ranch earlier this week, looking for a job." Beth's eyes narrowed. "If you ask me, Ryan could've taken Black Magic—just to get under Denver's skin. It would be like him, too—to wait until Denver was gone!"

"Then why would he stay?"

"Just to see Denver's reaction."

Cassie wasn't convinced. "Seems farfetched to me."

"Maybe," Beth agreed. "Lots of people around here would like to get back at the McLeans. Nobody much liked John." Her lips pursed. "He made more enemies than friends, and even though he's gone, Denver and Colton haven't won any popularity contests around town, either. Both of them turned their backs on Three Falls, then showed up again once John died and they inherited the place. It looks pretty mercenary to some of the ranchers who stuck it out through the bad years."

"Some of the ranchers—meaning Josh?" she asked, mentioning Beth's husband.

Beth shook her head. "No, Josh likes Colton and Denver, but his father Bill, and my dad never had any use for either of the McLean boys."

"Neither does mine," Cassie admitted, wondering just who disliked Denver and Colton enough to risk stealing their horse. This was more than a practical joke—taking a valuable stallion was a criminal offense, and Cassie didn't doubt for a minute that, if given the chance, Colton would press charges.

Beth grinned as the curly-haired waitress deposited a huge wedge of chocolate mousse pie covered with a cloud of whipped cream in the center of the table. "This looks positively decadent," Beth murmured, handing one of the long-handled spoons to Cassie. "Come on, help me out."

Cassie sighed theatrically, but her eyes crinkled at the corners. "First Dad, now you," she murmured, but plunged a spoon into the pie anyway. "I haven't eaten so many calories in an entire month as I've consumed in the last two days."

Beth's lips curved upward. "You could use a few pounds." She took another bite, then said, "I heard you had dinner with Colton last night."

Cassie's brows shot up. "How'd you find out?"

"Josh's brother was there with his wife. They saw you together at Timothy's."

"Colton dropped by after work and twisted my arm," Cassie explained. "Kind of like you did today."

"And so how was Colton? The same as ever? Restless and mysterious?"

"Conciliatory," Cassie said, thinking. "A little on the mellow side."

"That's not the Colton McLean I remember."

"Me, neither," Cassie admitted. "But it was nice."

"So you two ended the feud in one date?"

"It *wasn't* a date."

Beth polished off the last dollop of whipped cream. "If you say so." She leaned back in her chair, linked her hands around her protruding abdomen and sighed happily. "Does he still think someone took his horse?"

"Oh, yes," Cassie replied, nodding. "He's convinced."

"But you don't think so?"

"I don't honestly know. I'm just glad Black Magic is back where he belongs and Colton is off my dad's back."

Colton's watch over Black Magic didn't turn up anything suspicious. In fact, all he got for his efforts was a sore shoulder and a bad disposition from several nights of little sleep.

For years he'd existed on two or three hours' sleep at a stretch, always wary, always concerned that he might wake up with a knife against his throat or the muzzle of a gun in his back. And yet, since he'd been back in Montana, the hours of physical labor on the ranch made demands on his body that five hours of sleep each night couldn't replenish.

"It'll get better," he told himself, but secretly wondered if the reason he was tired all the time was that his nights were filled with wild dreams of Cassie—startling, vivid images that he couldn't erase from his mind. He'd wake up burning for her, wishing there were some way to douse the fire searing through his mind and body.

Short of finding a woman, he had no cure. As he saw it, he had two options. Chase her down and start rebuilding a relationship or find someone else.

"Fat chance of that," he told himself, knowing that as long as Cassie was nearby, no other woman would do. He jammed his pitchfork into a bale of hay, then made his way outside. It had been two days since he'd seen Cassie, and it seemed a lifetime.

Glancing around the sun-dappled fields, he felt a kinship with this land he hadn't experienced in years. Swollen-bodied mares grazed, picking at grass. Red Wing and Ebony, Tessa's favorites—the pride of her small herd—moved slowly with the rest of the mares. Colton hoped they wouldn't foal until Tessa and Denver returned, as Tessa had been anticipating the birth of her prize stallion, Brigadier's offspring, for months.

In another field, yearlings cavorted, kicking up their heels and playfully nipping one another's necks.

No, this place wasn't so bad if you could stand the lack of excitement, he decided as he strode to the Jeep. It was fine for Denver. His older brother had changed over the years. But Colton hadn't, and if it weren't for Cassie there wouldn't be anything for him here.

The turn of his thoughts worried him. Admitting that Cassie was more than a passing attraction bothered him. But there it was. Colton believed in "calling 'em as he saw 'em," and unfortunately he was forced to recognize the simple and annoying fact that Cassie Aldridge had gotten to him all over again. A restlessness overcame him—the same restlessness he'd experienced every night since that evening when he'd first seen her again.

"Idiot," he muttered, striding across the yard and up the steps of the back porch. He flung open the back door and stopped dead in his tracks.

In the kitchen, an old apron tied around her thick waist, Milly Samms was polishing the stove. Her steel-gray hair had been freshly permed, and she bit her lower lip as she worked furiously. She glanced toward Colton, then stopped, her mouth dropping open. "Well, look at you," she said, a wide smile cracking her round face. "I barely recognized you without your beard!"

"I got tired of it," he said, eyeing her as she continued her work at a fever pitch. "I thought you weren't due back for another week."

The housekeeper nodded. If she noticed his impatience, she didn't comment. "I wasn't. But I heard about Black Magic and decided to cut my vacation short."

"He's been found."

"That's what Curtis said, but I didn't want to let Denver and Tessa down."

Colton grinned in amusement as he hung his hat near the back door. "We were surviving."

With a frown, Milly motioned to the cluttered counters and spotted wood floor. "Looks like you could use a little help—a woman's help. Tessa spent all last fall remodeling this house, the least you could do is keep it up while she's gone."

"I'll remember that," Colton replied, noting the freshly painted cupboards, tile counters and polished oak parquet floor. Between his sister-in-law's hard work and Denver's financial help, the old farmhouse had taken on a fresh luster.

"Do!" Milly said with mock severity as she placed a cup of coffee on the counter near Colton. "So tell me all about Black Magic. The way I heard it from Madeline Simpson, you think he was stolen again."

"That's right," Colton allowed, blowing across his cup before explaining the events of the past three weeks. Milly didn't stop scrubbing and shining every pot and pan in the house as well as the countertops, refrigerator and light fixtures. She listened to him, interjected her own two cents when appropriate and never once sat down.

"Well, all's well that ends well," Milly finally said when Colton had finished. She washed her hands for what had to be the tenth time, then wiped them on her apron.

"If it's ended."

"You don't think it'll happen again!"

"I hope not, but we don't know for sure, do we?" he replied, his eyes narrowing.

"I suppose not," Milly said absently. She stood in the middle of the kitchen, surveying her work. The appliances and brass-bottomed pots gleamed. "But I wouldn't be thinking Ivan Aldridge was behind it, you know."

Colton raised a skeptical brow.

"It could've been anyone around here. There's a lot of good will and friendliness in ranching," she said thoughtfully as she poured herself a well-deserved cup of coffee and added a spoonful of sugar. "But there's a lot of jealousy and envy, too. All the ranchers in these parts lost money a few years back. Winters were bad, crops ruined and some of the stock froze to death. But this place"—she gestured grandly to the house and beyond, through the fields—"managed to get by. Barely, mind you. When Denver returned, he was fit to be tied—claimed Tessa and Curtis had run the ranch into the ground. But he soon found out that she'd turned the corner, forced McLean Ranch into the black when some of the other ranchers, Bill Simpson, Matt Wilkerson, Vince Monroe and the like, were having trouble keeping the banks from foreclosing."

"Seems as if they all made it," Colton observed.

Milly frowned. "By goin' further in debt."

"Including Aldridge?"

She shrugged her big shoulders. "Don't know, but it wouldn't surprise me. Cassie got herself through college and veterinary school somehow, and that's not cheap!"

"Curtis seems to think Aldridge is the most likely suspect."

Milly's steely brows quirked. "So now you're listening to a Kramer!"

"He's family."

"You didn't always think that way."

"I was wrong," Colton admitted, thrusting his jaw out a bit.

"Yes you were, and you might be again. Just because there was a feud between the families, doesn't mean that Ivan's going to do something about it. Leastwise not anymore. And as far as what Curtis thinks . . ." She snorted. "He's as stubborn as a bull moose." Colton thought she was so agitated that she might spill her coffee as she raised it to her lips and took a sip. "Well," she finally conceded, "I suppose we're all entitled to our opinion."

"Even me?" Colton asked, his eyes glinting with amusement.

"No, you're the one person on this ranch that doesn't count," she teased, then chuckled to herself. "By the way, I found something earlier—now where'd it go?" She reached into the closet and pulled out a shoulder bag containing his 35-mm camera with a wide-angle lens. "This yours?"

Colton nodded, accepting the bag.

"It was in the den beneath a stack of newspapers a mile high! Thought you might be lookin' for it."

"Haven't had much use for it here."

"Why not? Seems to me you can take pictures of anything." Her old eyes twinkled. "You don't have to limit yourself to war and political scandals and all the rest of that nonsense."

"Nonsense, is it?"

"If you ask me."

He slung the strap of the bag over his shoulder. "I guess I'm just not into pastoral scenes."

"Maybe it's time you changed. Slowed down a bit. Before the next bullet does more damage than the last one."

"It won't," he assured her, setting his empty cup in the sink. "Thanks for the coffee."

"Anytime."

With the same restless feeling that had followed him in, Colton shouldered his way through the door and walked outside. He considered Milly's advice, discarded most of it, but couldn't help wondering if she were right about Ivan. How much simpler things would be if Aldridge weren't behind Black Magic's disappearance. How much easier his relationship with Cassie would be.

Loading his camera without thinking, Colton lifted it, staring through the lens and clicking off a few quick shots— Len, tall and rawboned, the epitome of the twentieth-century cowboy, working with a mulish buckskin colt; Curtis leaning against the top rail of the fence, smoking and eyeing the surrounding land; the sun squeezing through thin white clouds. Snap. Snap. Snap.

And yet his mind wasn't focused on the image in the lens; his thoughts kept wandering to Cassie. He forced himself to concentrate. Snap. He caught Curtis leading Black Magic outside. Snap. A shot of the horse yanking on the lead rope and rearing against a backdrop of late afternoon sky.

The clicking of the shutter sounded right. The view through the lens looked right, and yet, something was missing— something vital—that surge of adrenaline he'd experienced so often when he'd stared through the eye of the camera.

"Hell with it," he muttered, savagely twisting on the lens cap and shoving the camera into its case. Without considering the consequences of what he was doing, he shouted to Curtis that he'd be gone for part of the evening, advising the older man to lock Black Magic in his stall. Then he strode angrily across the yard to his Jeep. He jammed his key into the ignition and growled an oath at himself. Tonight, come hell or high water, he was going to see Cassie again.

She saw him coming. Pale sunlight glinted against chrome and steel. Tearing down the narrow lane, the motorcyclist bore down on her. Yanking hard on the steering wheel, Cassie felt the old truck shimmy, its wheels bouncing on the uneven ground as she made room. The motorcycle sped past. The driver, dressed in black from helmet to boots and huddled over the handlebars, didn't glance her way as he drove recklessly on the narrow lane leading from the Aldridge house.

"Damned fool!" Cassie muttered, her heart pounding as she stared into the rearview mirror and watched as the motorcycle disappeared around the bend.

She eased the truck back into the twin ruts of gravel that comprised the lane and drove the final quarter-mile to the house. Her heart was still thundering wildly when she parked her pickup near the garage. "Who was that?" she demanded, hopping out of the cab and spying her father in the door to the barn. Erasmus yelped at the sight of her and bounded over, whining and wiggling at her feet.

"Ferguson," Ivan replied.

"Ryan Ferguson? What was he doing here?" Bending down, Cassie scratched the old dog behind his ears. "He drives like a maniac!"

"He was looking for work." Her father wiped his forehead with a handkerchief and stuffed it back into the pocket of his overalls. "I hired him."

"You did *what*?" she fumed, still shaking from the close call. "He nearly ran me off the road!"

Ivan's eyes filled with concern. "Did he?"

"Didn't you see it!"

"I was in the barn." He placed a hand on her shoulder. "Are you okay?"

"No thanks to him!" she snapped angrily.

"I'll have a talk with him," Ivan said, frowning and staring at the lane. "He starts work tomorrow."

"Tomorrow?" she repeated, stunned. "Why?"

"'Cause I need help, that's why," Ivan replied. "The mares will start foaling next week, and I'll be planting grain soon, not to mention the regular chores."

"But why Ryan Ferguson? Denver McLean fired him because—"

"I know why Denver claims he fired him, but Ryan swears he was innocent. No charges were ever filed, you know."

"Then why did Ryan leave town?"

"He says he quit, that he just needed some time away. Can't say as I blame him. Workin' for the McLeans must be hell."

"Oh, Dad, that's crazy. John McLean stood by Curtis Kramer when everyone else in town blamed him for the fire on the McLean Ranch. And some of those hands at the McLean place have been there for years. They love it."

Ivan clenched his teeth. "Don't mention John McLean to me!" he ordered, starting for the back porch at a furious pace.

"But he did."

"So now he's a saint, right? And I give another wrongly accused man a job and I'm not right in the head," he called over his shoulder.

"I didn't say—"

Her father reached the porch and whirled, his eyes bright. "John McLean is the single reason Vanessa left me and you grew up without a mother!" he reminded her, his words slicing open an old, painful wound. The back of Ivan's neck was flushed scarlet. "You know how I feel about the McLeans, so let's drop it!"

Cassie heard the rumble of an engine and glanced toward the drive. "I, uh, don't think that's possible."

"And just why the hell not?"

Cassie's heart felt like it had dropped to the ground. "Because it looks like Colton is on his way."

"What?" Ivan turned his gaze to the front drive. "Blast that man! What's he doin' here?"

"I guess we'll just have to wait and find out," she said, but she wished Colton's timing were better. Right now her father would like to tear anyone with the name of McLean limb from limb.

"He's not welcome here!" Ivan snapped.

"He knows that. So why don't you listen to what he has to say? It must be important," she said, trying to calm him down before another confrontation between her father and Colton exploded.

Ivan's eyes narrowed. "I've heard enough McLean lies to last me a lifetime, and I would have thought the same goes for you!"

"Colton never lied to me," she said, her back stiffening.

"No," Ivan allowed, "but what he did was worse! He accused you of lying, using him, trying to trick him into a marriage he didn't want." The flush on his neck spread upward, and his eyes flared. "Don't ever forget, Cassie, Colton McLean tried to destroy you!"

"I can handle myself!"

"Can you?" her father tossed back, the lines of strain near his eyes becoming less harsh. "I hope so." With that, he stormed into the house, Erasmus on his heels.

The screen door banged shut, and Cassie flinched. Her father was right, of course. Colton had wounded her so deeply, she thought she'd never be the same. And she wasn't. Colton had single-handedly devastated the young naive girl she'd once been. It wouldn't happen again. Now she was older and, she hoped, much wiser. That young girl could never be hurt again, and she would try her best to make sure the woman she'd become wouldn't suffer at any man's hands, including those of Colton McLean.

Watching as Colton parked his Jeep near her truck, she waited by the steps. As he got out of the truck, his gaze met hers, and one side of his mouth lifted in that same irreverent smile she'd always found so fascinating.

"I just couldn't stay away," he said, as if answering the questions in her eyes.

"Seems you didn't have much trouble for eight years," she pointed out.

"Ouch." He shoved his hat back on his head and studied her thoughtfully. "Am I back on the bad list?"

"You were never off," she said, trying to remain firm, but she couldn't keep the twinkle out of her eyes. "Face it, McLean, you're bad news."

"You've been talking to your father again."

"Maybe he's just been setting me straight."

Colton chuckled. "You know, Cass, you can be positively mean when you want to be."

"And you deserve it."

Without warning, he grabbed her arm and spun her around so quickly, she slammed into him.

"Hey—"

"Let's start over," he suggested, his gaze warm, the scent of him as fresh as a sun-drenched Montana morning. His breath touched her face in a gentle caress.

"Too late," she said, trying to keep her voice light, attempting not to notice that her breasts were crushed against his chest, her thighs pressed against the hard length of his, her body responding to the closeness of his.

Strong arms held her prisoner. "I thought we'd gotten past all that."

"Past the fact that you accused my father of horse thievery? Or past the feud? Or past the night you accused me of lying to you before you walked out the door?" she asked, the words tumbling out in a rush.

He tensed, every muscle suddenly rigid. "I think we'd better leave well enough alone."

"But nothing was ever 'well enough,' was it?"

"What do you want from me?"

"The chance to explain why I couldn't tell you that I wasn't pregnant eight years ago," she shot back, her insides quaking. Standing so close to him stirred up all her old insecurities, but this time she wasn't going to back down.

Something flashed in his eyes. Pain? Or pity? "Does it matter?"

She gasped. Of course it mattered! More than anything had ever mattered. "Eight years ago it was all that mattered."

"Eight years is a long time," he said, his eyes focused on her lips.

"It seems like yesterday."

Colton just stared at her. "Clichés, Cass?" he drawled, suppressing a laugh, his mouth curving into an amused smile.

Instantly infuriated, she sputtered, "You are, without

question, the most insufferable, egotistical, bloody bastard that ever walked this earth!"

Colton laughed, a deep rumbling sound that erupted into the evening air.

"You think that's funny?" she said, jerking away, her black hair flying in front of her eyes, her fingers curling into fists of frustration.

"No, I think it's probably the truth," he admitted with an exasperating, devilish grin. Quick as a cat, he tugged on her arm, yanking her back against him. "What is it about you?" he wondered aloud. "One minute I think you're the most intriguing woman I've ever met, the next I realize you're a pain in the backside."

"Like you."

"Exactly," he said, his eyes growing dark as they focused on her lips.

Cassie's throat closed.

Slowly, with painstaking deliberation, he lowered his head and brushed his lips over hers.

Cassie had to bite back a moan.

His lips molded over hers, and her knees nearly buckled. Her conscience told her to stop this madness, and she tried. Though she attempted to push him away, he wouldn't relent, holding on to her with a fierceness bordering on desperation.

Her palms against a solid, denim-clad chest, she struggled a little as his tongue touched the inner recesses of her mouth.

A seeping warmth flooded her limbs, and though she thought perversely that she should bite him, she didn't. Instead, she closed her eyes and sighed. What was the point of fighting when she'd been waiting for eight years for him to take her into his arms?

When he dragged his lips away, she whispered, "You're positively annoying!"

"And you love it."

"Don't flatter yourself!"

"Come on, Cass," he whispered suggestively, "admit it. It keeps you interested."

She slid a glance at him from beneath the fringe of her dark lashes. "I'm *not* interested."

"Bull!" He touched his forehead to hers. "Let's not argue."

"Seems inevitable."

"Nothing's inevitable," he whispered, and her heart turned over. "Now, tell me, is Ivan the Terrible around?"

"*Dad* is in the house. And he's not in a great mood. I wouldn't be calling him any names."

"I won't," Colton said, releasing her and starting up the back steps. "As a matter of fact, I'm here to apologize."

Cassie's brows lifted. "You're just full of surprises, aren't you?"

"It keeps you on your toes."

"Don't bother."

He grinned despite her sarcasm. "I decided that the other night when I told you that I was wrong wasn't enough; that I should tell Ivan he's off the hook."

"I don't think he really cared one way or the other," Cassie said. She tried to sound calm, but her spirits were soaring. Colton was taking the first step; maybe Ivan could find it in his heart to forgive him. And perhaps she could forgive him as well.

"At least I'll have tried."

Cassie smothered a smile. "Enter, Daniel, into the lion's den."

Colton laughed as Cassie opened the back door. Erasmus bolted through, nearly knocking her over as he ran, pell-mell, down the stairs and streaked across the backyard, startling a flock of blackbirds in the leafless apple tree. "You know, you're not on his top-ten list of favorite people right now."

"I figured that."

Together they walked into the kitchen. Ivan was seated

at the table, a mug of coffee in one hand. "McLean," he said without preamble.

Colton stopped just inside the door and swept his Stetson from his head. "Thought you'd want to know Black Magic's been found."

"I heard." Ivan's gaze bored into the younger man's eyes, but Colton didn't flinch. "Rumor has it he just wandered off and decided to come back on his own."

Colton's lips thinned. "I doubt it. But I've decided that I judged you too quickly."

"Probably just force of habit."

Colton's jaw worked. "Look, I just stopped by to say I'm sorry I came down on you so hard."

Ivan shifted his gaze away. "A little late for apologies, isn't it?"

"It's probably too late for a lot of things," Colton admitted with a grim smile, flicking a glance at Cassie. "But that doesn't mean we can't bury the hatchet."

"Just like that?"

Leaning a hip against the counter, Colton shook his head. "I suppose it'll take a little effort."

"And a lot of forgetting." Ivan scowled into his coffee cup, then took a long, last swallow. Dropping his feet onto the cracked linoleum, he shoved himself upright, straightening slowly. "There's been too much bad blood between our families to pretend it didn't exist," he said deliberately, rubbing his stubbled jaw. "I don't think we can even begin to bury it all."

"Dad . . ." Cassie protested.

"Look, McLean, you've said your piece and I've listened. In all honesty, I'm glad the horse is back. As for the rest"—his brows drew together and he lifted one shoulder—"I see no reason to change things. As far as I'm concerned, you're still not welcome here."

Cassie's spirits crashed. "Please, Dad, think about this—"

"Think about it?" Ivan retorted, his lips thinning. "I've thought too long about the McLeans. You might be falling for his line, but I'm not!" he growled.

"I just think it's time we settled some things."

"Tell that to your mother, why don't you?" His old eyes gleaming, he stood. The cords in his neck had stretched taut as he warned, "Be careful, Cassie. You're twenty-five now—old enough to make your own decisions—and I can't tell you what to do. But just be damned careful."

"Dad, wait—I think we should talk about this. . . ." Cassie followed him out of the room, but Ivan shook his head sadly, ran a shaking hand over his forehead and climbed the stairs.

"Get rid of him. Then we'll talk."

Cassie felt pulled and pushed. On one hand she wanted to shove aside all the pain of the past, get on with her life. On the other, she knew her father was right. One apology didn't erase years of agony and mistrust.

Her stomach in knots, she walked back to the kitchen where Colton, twirling the brim of his hat in his fingers, stared out the window. "Charming fellow, your father," he muttered.

"He can be."

"You couldn't prove it to me."

"That works two ways."

Colton frowned, his brows drawing together in a single, stubborn line. "Let's get out of here."

"I just got home!"

"I know, but I'd rather go someplace where I'm welcome. And I'd like you to come with me."

Cassie hesitated. Tempted not to ask any questions and just take off and follow him, she had to force herself to slow down. "Why?"

"Because I want to spend some time with you," he said simply, his expression still perturbed.

Her pulse jumped. "Do you think that's smart?"

"I *know* it isn't, but what could it hurt?" He flashed her an uncertain grin, and Cassie's heart lurched. Seeing a vulnerable side to Colton, a part he tried so hard to keep hidden, touched her as nothing else could.

"I'd hate to think—"

"Then don't think. Just come with me."

She attempted to swallow all her doubts. "Okay." Wondering if she were making the second-worst mistake of her life, she breezed past him and walked outside. Afternoon shadows had lengthened, the sunlight was weak, the air cool. Shivering, she stuffed her hands into the pockets of her down jacket and crossed the yard.

Colton opened the door of the Jeep and helped her inside.

As he slid behind the steering wheel, Cassie glanced at the house. "I hope you know I feel like Benedict Arnold."

"Your father'll get over it."

"I don't know," she thought aloud as the Jeep lurched backward and cut a wide circle near the barn.

"You're twenty-five—Ivan himself pointed out that fact."

"Oh, so now I'm old enough, is that it?" she said, a sad smile toying with her lips.

"Old enough?"

"Don't you remember? That was your big argument against 'us' way back when. You thought I was just a kid."

"You were," he said, grinding the Jeep's gears and taking off down the twin ruts of the lane.

At the highway he didn't turn toward Three Falls, but guided the old rig in the opposite direction.

"Where're you taking me?" she asked.

He cast a seductive glance in her direction. "If I told you, I'd spoil the surprise."

"What surprise?" she demanded, a ripple of delight darting up her spine. Unpredictable, mysterious and secretive, Colton was never dull. "You know, this is starting to look like a kidnapping."

"I thought we'd already established the fact that you're not a kid anymore. Besides, you came willingly."

"I guess I can't argue with that," she thought aloud, her nerve endings tingling in anticipation as she leaned back in the seat and squinted through the windshield.

They were headed west, and cathedral-spired mountains, their craggy slopes snow-laden and sheer, pierced the dusky sky.

Cassie gnawed nervously on the inside of her lip. Where was Colton taking her? she wondered, and more important, *why*?

Chapter Eight

Colton drove through a neighboring town and into the mountains. "We're going to Garner's Ridge?" she asked, surprised. "A ghost town?"

Colton laughed, and the rich sound filled the interior of the Jeep. The road twisted upward, turning to gravel as it wound through the pines and brush. The Jeep bounced and shimmied. Eventually the gravel turned to dirt. A sheer granite wall rose on one side of the deserted road, while forested cliffs fell away on the other.

When Colton shifted, his fingers nearly brushed her knee. As the Jeep rocked, their shoulders touched fleetingly.

The road narrowed around a final bend, and he slowed the Jeep to a stop at the end of what once had been the main street. A row of dilapidated buildings with sagging roofs and listing walls lined the narrow alley.

"Not much, is it?"

Together they walked through the old mining town where, nearly a hundred years before, gold had been discovered. In the beginning miners had flooded the area but later moved on because the mother lode had never been found. The few settlers who had arrived had left within twenty years.

Colton stepped onto the ramshackle boardwalk and shouldered open a door, which groaned as the rusted hinges gave way. Mice scurried across ancient floorboards, and a huge hole in the roof allowed a view of the darkening sky.

"Why did you bring me here?" Cassie asked, cautiously peeking through what little glass remained in the broken windows.

"I thought we needed a chance to be alone."

"You, me and the ghosts?"

Colton chuckled and grabbed her hand. "I thought we needed to put everything into perspective," he admitted. "Sometimes too many other people and things get in the way."

"Meaning Dad?"

"For one. Uncle John for another."

"Not to mention Black Magic."

"Right," he said quietly, walking back through the front door of the old general store and down the uneven steps. Outside, he propped one shoulder against the rough bark of a huge pine tree.

Mist rose eerily from the forest floor, forming pale clouds near the buildings and giving the shadowy old town an aura of mystery. "You could almost believe real ghosts live in this town," Colton murmured.

"And do you see any spirits?" Cassie stood next to him, her gaze following his. "Any ghosts from your past?"

"The only ghost I've had to deal with is you," he admitted.

"Me?"

"That's right." Touching her lightly under the chin, he tipped her face up to his, staring into near-perfect features that were already indelibly etched in his mind. Her cheeks were rosy, her hazel eyes wide as they searched his, her ebony hair curling softly around her face. "I've been trying to exorcise you for eight years."

"And were you successful?"

His mouth tightening at the corners, he said, "Doesn't look like it, does it?"

"It did for eight years."

His eyelids lowered to half-mast. "Not really."

Cassie's heart pounded. If only she could believe him. "And now?"

"Now is difficult, Cass," he admitted. "A real problem. Every time I shove you out of my mind, you find a way to push yourself right back in."

"Not true. I haven't bothered you once."

"Ah, Cassie," he said with a world-weary sigh, his defenses slipping. "You didn't have to try. You were always there—even when I thought I'd forgotten you, something would trigger a memory, and there you'd be."

"If you expect me to believe that you've been pining for the past eight years—"

"I don't pine."

"I didn't think so."

"But I was bothered."

"Not enough to call, or write, or stop by," she pointed out, trying to remember just how much pain he'd caused. But here in the half-light, alone with him, those agonizing memories seemed to slip away.

"I wasn't around."

"Your choice," she reminded him, aware of his fingers, hard and warm, against her chilled skin, and angry with herself for even listening to him.

"I didn't *want* to be bothered," he said tightly, slowly caressing the column of her throat, his gaze delving even deeper into hers.

Darkness settled between the decrepit facades of the time-worn buildings, and Cassie wished she had the willpower to draw away, to demand to be taken home, to tell him she never wanted to see him again as long as she lived. But she didn't.

Mesmerized by his silvery eyes, she asked, "What made you change your mind?"

"You."

She laughed, and the sound echoed through the trees.

"I'm serious," he said softly. "As long as I was in another city, or state or country, I could keep away from you. But once I was back here—"

"You've been here for months," she cut in, forcing herself not to fall under his spell. "You didn't come see me until Black Magic disappeared."

A crooked smile twisted his lips. "Part of the time I was laid up," he replied, bending to push his face closer to hers.

"And the rest?"

"Willpower."

"So much for my powers of seduction," she mocked.

"Oh, you've got them," Colton whispered, his breath fanning her face, "and I'm not immune. But I had everything under control. Until I saw you again."

"What's this all about, Colton?" she asked, her voice sounding more ragged than she'd hoped. She wanted to appear in control when all of her senses were reeling; her nerve endings tingled from his touch, her nostrils were filled with his scent, her eyes were riveted to the sensual line of his lips.

"I just wanted to be alone with you," he admitted, his voice as rough as her own.

"In a ghost town?"

"Anywhere." Suddenly his mouth crashed down on hers, his fingers winding in her hair. The sounds of the night disappeared, and all Cassie heard was the wild cadence of her heart and the answering drum of Colton's. All she felt was the strength of his arms surrounding her and the force of desire raging between them, a desire so strong it destroyed all rational thought, a desire so potent it heated more quickly than it had eight years before.

"This—this is a big mistake," she murmured, dragging

her mouth from his and searching for some shred of her sanity. *What am I doing?* she wondered, her breath short and shallow.

"Not our first." He kissed her again, thrusting his tongue wondrously between her teeth. With one set of fingers tangled in her hair, he pressed his other hand insistently against the small of her back.

Through her clothes she could feel the sheer force of his body, the strength of his muscles, the passion racing through his blood.

Think, Cassie! But she couldn't, and as the weight of his body dragged her down to a bed of pine needles and soft boughs, she sighed and wound her arms around his neck. *I love you*, she realized with a sinking heart. *I always have.*

His mouth covered hers, and she didn't fight the warmth invading her. A familiar heat rushed through her blood like quicksilver, pounding in her eardrums as she lay with him.

He slipped his fingers beneath her sweater, reaching up, touching the silky lace of her bra, causing her skin to tingle. Her nipple grew hard with anticipation, and when the tips of his fingers brushed lightly against her burgeoning breast, she shuddered.

"I've missed you, Cass," he admitted, kissing her lips gently as his hand surrounded her breast.

Her heart clamored crazily as he stroked. Her concentration scattered in the wind. "I—It was hard to tell."

"Because I didn't want to admit it," he conceded, his teeth tugging gently on her lower lip, his hands moving erotically beneath her sweater, kneading her warm, soft flesh, causing a maelstrom of emotions to roil within her.

With her own fingers she found the buttons of his shirt, slipped under the coarse fabric, and touched skin stretched taut over a washboard of corded muscles.

He sucked in a swift breath, his eyes fluttering closed. "You're a witch," he whispered.

"First I'm a ghost, now a witch," she murmured. "No wonder I'm crazy about you."

"Are you, Cass?" he asked, his eyes suddenly flying open.

"I must be—crazy, that is. Creeping around a ghost town, falling into the arms of a man who swore vengeance on my family. Honestly, Colton," she said, her good humor surfacing, "this is something out of a bad horror movie."

His grin was a slash of white in the darkness. "Don't worry, I'll protect you. Trust me."

The last words spilled over her like a bucket of ice water. "Trust *you*?" she said, all warmth instantly seeping from her body. "After everything that's happened between us?" Though Colton's grip on her tightened, she pushed him away. She needed to be free to think. "What about you, huh? Trust is a two-way street, Colton, and last time I looked, you didn't trust me or my dad!"

He reached for her, but she withered at his touch, straightening her sweater and drawing her jacket around her. Pine needles scratched against her back.

What was she doing here with him? What had she been thinking? "I think we'd better go!" she said, her teeth chattering as she scrambled to her feet.

Colton was on his feet in an instant, pinning her against the prickly bark of the pine tree. "What is it, Cassie?" he demanded, his square chin thrust forward, his gray eyes slits. "What's on your mind?"

"Trust isn't something given, it's earned," she said, her own chin inching upward mutinously. "And you can never expect me to trust a man who, without waiting for a word of explanation, walked out on me."

"There was nothing to explain!"

"There was plenty!" she nearly screamed, the words that had burned so bright in her mind leaping to her tongue. "I thought I was pregnant, Colton, and I was scared. Scared to death that you'd reject me."

"Bah!"

"I had all the symptoms. I threw up at least once a day, my period was late and I'd been sleeping with you without a thought for birth control!"

Under the shifting moonlight she witnessed the blanching of his face.

"But it didn't matter, you see. You were right. I was too young to care, to understand what a burden a child would be. I could only see the good side, the thrill and joy of sharing everything with you, of bearing your son or daughter—"

"Cassie, don't," he warned, his skin stretching tight across his rugged features.

But she couldn't stop. As if a dam had suddenly given way, Cassie's words tumbled out in a rush. "I trusted you once, Colton. And I loved you. Good Lord, how I loved you. But you took that love and trust and turned it against me, believing what you wanted to believe so that you could leave Montana and not look back! You told me over and over again that you didn't want a wife, that we were too young, that we had dreams we had to chase, and the first chance you got, you turned your back on me and took off! So don't talk to me about trust!"

Colton's jaw had become rigid, and the hands imprisoning her against the tree had curled into fists. Under the wrath of Cassie's fury, Colton didn't notice the splinters in his palms nor the pain. "Are you finished?"

"There isn't any more to say." She tried to duck under his arm, but he captured her wrist, spinning her back.

"There's a helluva lot."

"You have *reasons* for the way you behaved? *Excuses?*"

"Just the truth. You were pushing too hard, Cassie. You'd been hinting at marriage for a long time. The baby seemed convenient, especially when it never existed."

"Maybe I was just hoping."

"And maybe I didn't like being played for a fool!"

"Only one person can make a person look like a fool, Colton," she snapped. "And that's the person himself." Wrenching her arm free of his grasp, she started for the Jeep. But in three swift strides he was walking with her, matching her furious steps with those of his own. "Would it help if I said I'm sorry?"

"No!"

"Why not?"

"Because you don't *believe* me, Colt. And that's what this is all about!" She couldn't stop the hot tears that burned in her eyes. At the Jeep she spun to face him. "You were right, you know. We were too young. But I would've waited if only I'd felt you cared."

Leveling an oath at himself, Colt swore, his emotions battling deep inside. He brushed his finger over the slope of her cheek, sweeping aside a tear. "I cared," he said, his voice raw with emotion. "God, I cared. And it scared the hell out of me." He drew her into the circle of his arms and kissed her forehead. "I'm sorry," he whispered, sighing heavily. "I never meant to hurt you. If you don't believe anything else, please believe that I never intended to cause you any kind of pain. I should've told you all this a long time ago, but I couldn't. I didn't understand it myself for a long time, and when I finally did, my pride stood in my way."

She felt a shudder rip through him and heard the catch in his voice. After eight long years, she believed him. Deep, racking sobs tore through her soul. She cupped his face between her hands, feeling his warm skin beneath her fingers, knowing in her heart that he was finally baring his soul.

He turned his face in her hands, kissing her palms. "If there were a way to erase all our mistakes, I'd do it, Cass," he said. "And if I knew how to prove that I cared then and I care now, I'd do it." He kissed her forehead and held her close.

She buried her face against his leather jacket and took in long, calming breaths.

Time passed, the silence a balm to old wounds. Cassie felt suddenly freed, unburdened from a weight so old it had become a part of her.

"Come on," he cajoled. "I'll take you to dinner. Anywhere you want!"

"Paris?" she replied, blinking and smiling through unshed tears. He chuckled, though his gaze, staring deep into her eyes, remained sober. "If that's what you want."

"I guess it doesn't really matter." She sniffed to keep from crying and made a valiant attempt to disguise the depth of her emotions.

"How about if we take a rain check on Paris and try something closer?"

"I'll hold you to it, you know. I won't forget."

"Oh, yeah. I know, Cass," he said, opening the passenger door of the Jeep and helping her inside. "I know."

The minute they stepped through the door of the Pinewood Café, Cassie knew they'd made an irreversible mistake. Every eye in the small restaurant seemed to have turned curiously in their direction.

Most of the booths, upholstered in a forest-green Naugahyde, were filled. Smoke curled lazily to the ceiling, where a wheezing air-conditioning unit was fighting a losing battle to clean the air. Voices buzzed in low tones, glasses clinked and waitresses bustled from one table to the next.

As Colton touched Cassie's elbow and guided her to a booth near the back, she recognized Matt Wilkerson and Bill Simpson at one table, Nate and Paula Edwards at another, and Vince Monroe with his wife, Nadine, and daughter, Jessica, just being seated. Half the town seemed to have decided to have dinner at the Pinewood.

Cassie nodded to a few people who waved to her, smiling at those who didn't. She wondered if her lips still looked swollen, or if mascara darkened her cheeks. She'd swiped at her eyes in the Jeep and run her fingers through her loose, bedraggled curls, but she knew she must look like something the cat had dragged in, only to toss out again.

Most people in Three Falls knew her since she'd grown up in this small town and become one of two veterinarians who helped the neighboring ranchers with their stock and the townspeople with their pets. Managing a bright smile, she tried to act as if dining with Colton McLean were the most natural thing in the world.

"Popular spot," Colton observed, glancing around the room as he hung both their jackets on a post separating their booth from the next.

"Maybe everyone knew we were coming," she quipped, sliding into the bench across from him.

Colton laughed, and Cassie felt most of the interested gazes turn back to their meals, though she was sure that Jessica as well as her father cast more than one sidelong glance in their direction.

A slow smile spread across Colton's face, and he leaned back casually, his dark hair falling over his forehead, his face a mask of ease.

A tiny waitress with a brunette ponytail swinging behind her and a uniform that matched the upholstery hurried toward their table. "Hi, I'm Penny," she said a trifle breathlessly as she handed them each a plastic-covered menu. "The specials tonight are stuffed trout and prime rib. I'll give you a few minutes to look over the menu, then I'll be back for your order." With a quick smile she scurried to the next table. She seemed nervous and flustered, as if this were her first night on the job.

Cassie quickly scanned the menu, which she knew by heart. After Vanessa had left, her father had brought her to the Pinewood every Thursday night. Though the restaurant had changed hands and decor several times, the menu hadn't varied much.

"I'll have the game hen," she decided when Penny appeared again. Colton ordered a steak and fries. Penny scribbled furiously, biting on her lower lip as she concentrated.

"Dessert?"

"Not for me," Cassie replied.

"I'll wait until after my meal," Colton put in.

"It'll just be a few minutes." Penny walked quickly to the counter, filled their drink orders and returned to set a glass of iced tea in front of Cassie and a chilled glass and bottle of beer on Colton's side of the table.

"If you need anything else, just let me know," she said, eager to please. As she dashed through swinging doors leading to the kitchen, Cassie sipped her tea and Colton nursed his beer. The front door swung open again, and a rush of cool night air followed a young man into the pine-paneled room.

Cassie looked casually toward the door, and her fingers tightened over her glass. Ryan Ferguson, his helmet tucked under one arm, strode to a booth near the front window, where a pulsating green-and-yellow neon sign promoted a local brand of beer.

Colton saw her lips part in surprise. "See a ghost?"

"We're not in the ghost town anymore," she replied, turning back to him.

But Colton's eyes narrowed on the man Cassie had watched entering the room. Tall and fit, with unkempt dusty blond hair and small brown eyes, he carried himself with a cocky aloofness that was emphasized by his black leather jacket and pants. Colton guessed his age around twenty-five, give or take a couple of years.

With obvious disdain, the man tossed his motorcycle helmet onto the seat next to him, unzipped his jacket and searched in a pocket for a pack of cigarettes. He didn't glance around the room at all and seemed in a world of his own as he lit up and blew a stream of smoke toward the ceiling.

"You know him?" Colton asked, wondering if the man had been Cassie's lover, then immediately discarded the idea. Cassie may have had her share of half-baked love affairs in the past years, but instinctively Colton guessed this guy wasn't her type.

"Don't you?"

Colton shook his head. "Should I?"

"He grew up around here. Worked for Denver. And now I guess he's going to work for Dad. His name is Ryan Ferguson."

The name sent off warning bells clanging through the back of Colton's mind. "Isn't he the guy you thought might have been out to get Denver because Denver fired him a while back?"

"One and the same. He's back in town."

"As of when?" Colton's mind raced to new conclusions. Was Ryan Ferguson the key to the puzzle of Black Magic's disappearance? Colton's gaze shifted quickly around the room. Several people had noticed Ryan's entrance. Bill Simpson's gray brows rose, then he turned back to his wife. Vince Monroe's eyes narrowed on the younger man. Colton swung his gaze back to Cassie. He asked again, "When did Ferguson blow back into town?"

Lifting a shoulder, Cassie swirled her straw in her tea. A lemon wedge shifted between the ice cubes. "I don't really know—a little while."

"And he's been working for your dad?"

"No. Dad just hired him this afternoon."

Colton's thoughts turned a new corner. Was it possible that Ryan Ferguson and Ivan Aldridge had been in on the horse-napping together? He didn't want to think so. "He doesn't look like the type your father would want hanging around."

"Dad needs help." She offered a feeble smile. "Because

of my job, I'm gone a lot—a lot more than either Dad or I imagined. And I'll be moving out soon."

Colton's head snapped up. This was news. Cassie was actually going to cut the strings that bound her to Ivan? "Where to? When?"

"Probably an apartment here in town, sometime this summer."

Colton's concerns about Ryan Ferguson were shoved to the back of his mind. "Why?"

"It's time, don't you think? I just moved back home until some of my college debt was paid off and to lend Dad a hand. But as I said, I'm not around enough to help much, and now that I'm out of school, he can afford to pay someone."

"So why did he choose Ferguson?"

I wish I knew, Cassie thought. "Ryan needed a job, I guess."

Colton settled back in his booth and watched Ferguson throughout the meal. The man, though dressed in basic *Road Warrior* attire, seemed harmless enough. But, as Colton had learned from years of dealing with some of the most deadly terrorists in the world, looks could be deceiving. Ryan Ferguson was worth checking out.

Vince Monroe scraped back his chair. Colton glanced his way and caught the older man staring at him—hard—and the warning hairs on the back of his neck rose. Though Vince's big face remained bland, his eyes gave him away. Colton recognized cold, hard hatred in Vince's stare.

Jessica turned her head in Colton's direction, offered a wobbly smile, which Colton returned with a friendly grin, then walked out on her father's arm without a word.

"I get the impression the Monroes aren't crazy about me," Colton thought aloud, wondering just how many of the local ranchers felt alienated from the McLeans.

"Vince has had some bad luck."

"That's my fault?"

"No," Cassie admitted, rolling her napkin nervously. "But there is Jessica."

"I told you, there was never anything between Jessica and me."

"Does she know that? You know, it's just possible you hurt her, Colton, and if you did, her father wouldn't count you on his list of ten favorites."

Colton rubbed his jaw pensively. The hate sizzling in Monroe's glance couldn't be explained by the fact that Colton had gone out with Jessica a couple of times, then left town. "I don't think this has anything to do with Jessica. There's got to be more. What happened between the Monroes and the McLeans while I was gone?"

"I don't know, except that Vince was forced to sell some of his stock to Denver last year."

"I'd think he'd be pleased that Denver would bail him out," Colton said, his gaze following the stiff set of Vince's shoulders as the big man shoved the door open.

"I doubt it," she said, her appetite disappearing. "The same thing happened to Dad a few years ago. He had to sell a horse to Tessa before she married your brother. It never set well with him."

"Anything remotely associated with the McLeans doesn't set well with Ivan."

"He has his reasons," she added. "You know, Dad can be a wonderful, caring man. He's done nothing but take care of me all of my life. You just have to give him a chance."

To her surprise, he reached across the table and placed his hand over hers. "I'm trying, Cass. Believe me, I'm trying." His work-roughened fingers smoothed the skin across the back of her hand, and a ripple of pleasure ran up her arm. "Come on, I'd better get you home," he said with a cynical grin. "I wouldn't want to get on the bad side of your father."

"Right," she retorted, but grinned as he helped her into her coat.

Outside, the night was cool and still. Together they walked to the Jeep beneath a night-black sky. Cassie's lips felt cold, her skin chilled, and yet being with Colton created an inner warmth that radiated to her fingers.

As he opened the door for her, he grabbed her hand, gently pulling her against him and kissing her with all the passion of eight lost years. "Thanks for coming with me tonight," he whispered.

"Thanks for asking."

They drove back to the Aldridge ranch in silence, but Colton remembered the people in the café and the hostility he'd sensed, the crackle of unspoken anger. Not from everyone, of course, but the Monroes and the Wilkersons had been far from friendly—and then there was Ferguson. Ivan's hiring Ryan bothered him a great deal without his really knowing why.

Cassie touched his shoulder. "You look like you're a million miles away," she said, tucking her arm through his.

One corner of his lip lifted. "Not that far."

"Where?"

"Back at the restaurant." He shifted down and turned into the lane. The windshield wipers slapped the raindrops aside. "Has your father known Ferguson long?"

"All his life. As I mentioned, Ryan grew up around here, too," she said. "Why?"

He drove into the yard. "Just curious."

"Or suspicious," she challenged.

"I guess I'm a little of both."

"Oh, Colton, I thought this was over," she said with a sigh. "I thought that since Black Magic was back, you'd be satisfied."

"Relieved. Not satisfied."

"Good night, Colton," she whispered, refusing to get into another argument. She grabbed the door handle, but Colton reached out and trapped her next to him.

"Don't go," he whispered against her ear. "Not yet."

"You could come inside."

Colton chuckled. "Ivan wouldn't like that much."

"He'd get over it." She smiled almost shyly and traced the hard line of his jaw with one finger. "Despite what you may think, he's not an ogre. He's been very good to me."

"And you've been good to him."

Blushing a little, she said, "Except where you're concerned."

Colton's teeth gleamed in the dark interior. "I haven't completely corrupted you yet," he murmured, his lips moving gently over her hair, causing goose bumps to rise on her skin. "But just give me time."

"I can't wait," she teased back, then caught her breath as he lowered his mouth over hers. Her heart began to beat wildly.

"Oh, Cass," he murmured thickly as he lifted his lips from hers. His eyes were glazed; his hands trembled as he touched her cheek. "What am I going to do with you?"

"I was just wondering the same about you," she admitted, her voice so husky she barely recognized it as her own.

"I'll call," he promised.

"And I'll hold you to it." She kissed him on the cheek, then scrambled out of his rig, waving as he shoved the Jeep into gear and took off in a spray of gravel. She stood in the yard, oblivious to the quiet, moonless night, as his taillights disappeared in the distance.

Lighthearted, she gathered her skirt in her fists and ran quickly along the path to the back porch.

She was still smiling to herself when she let herself into the house and found her father in the living room, his reading glasses poised on the tip of his nose as he worked on another crossword puzzle. Only one lamp burned, and the television, turned down so low she could barely hear a sound, gave off a pale gray glow.

"Have a good time?" Ivan asked. His voice was flat. He didn't bother looking up.

"The best!" She wasn't going to let her father's disapproval destroy her good mood. Not tonight.

Frowning, he slipped his glasses from his nose, then polished the lenses with the tail of his shirt. "I wish I knew what it was about Colton McLean that mixes you up."

"I'm *not* mixed up," she said, plopping down on a tired-looking ottoman and noticing the lines of strain that had deepened near the corners of her father's eyes.

"So now Colton McLean is a god again?"

"Not a god."

"Then a hero."

"No—but not a villain, either. He's just a man."

He snorted, tossing his folded newspaper aside. "You've gone out with a lot of men," he said quietly, "and not one of them has even made you smile."

"Not true, Dad."

"You never gave them a chance."

Cassie frowned. "What're you getting at?"

"Four years of college—then veterinary school. All that time and you didn't let one man get close to you—not really. And now Colton McLean blows back into town, sticking around only long enough for the bullet wound to heal, and you're acting like a schoolgirl with a fresh case of puppy love." He sighed heavily. "It's beyond me why you'd give a man who's only caused you heartache a chance to hurt you again."

Cassie didn't want her father to deflate her soaring spirits, so she said, "Look, we've been over this." Bending down, she placed a kiss on his forehead. "I'm okay."

"I hope so," she heard him whisper over the rustle of newspapers as she dashed up the stairs to her bedroom. In a way, her father was right, she supposed as she stared at her room with new eyes. It was a young girl's room. Though the movie posters and ruffles had been replaced years ago and her canopied bed was long gone, the evidence of her childhood remained. Everywhere, from the neglected records stacked in the closet to blue ribbons she'd won at a local fair, there were reminders of her youth, a girlhood devoid of a mother and an adolescence dominated by one single obsession: Colton McLean.

She swallowed hard as her father's advice rang in her ears. She was falling in love with Colton again, and there wasn't much she could or would do about it. But this time she was older, a grown professional woman with an education, a fledgling veterinary practice and a purpose in life. Colton McLean could never change that, nor could he determine her happiness as he once had. Or could he?

With a frustrated scowl, she dropped onto the eiderdown quilt of her brass bed and stared at the ceiling. Unconsciously she hugged a pillow to her chest and shoved aside any lingering doubts about her own future. She was her own woman, and nothing, not even Colton, could change that.

Chapter Nine

The next afternoon, while she was handing a recuperating Himalayan kitten to its owner, Colton burst through the waiting room door. His gaze collided with Cassie's. "I need you," he said the minute Mrs. Anderson walked outside.

The look on his face was desperate. His jaw sported a day's growth of beard, his eyes seemed sunken and his knuckles were white as he rammed his fingers through his hair.

Cassie swallowed hard. How many years had she waited to hear those three words. But uttered in the middle of the waiting room, they didn't ring with the desperation and love she'd hoped to hear. "What's wrong?"

"It's Black Magic."

Of course. Cassie clamped her jaw together. *Always Black Magic.* "What about him?"

"Oh, hell, I don't know. But he's not right. He's not eating— and he seems weak. His temperature is over 103 degrees."

Cassie felt a stab of instant remorse for her selfish thoughts. "Is he coughing?"

"No."

"Nasal discharge?"

Colton rubbed his jaw pensively. "Not that I noticed. But he was restless last night."

"What about his vaccinations?" Cassie asked, considering the symptoms. "Are they up to date?"

"I assume so—Tessa and her old man are pretty sticky about that. They don't fool around when it comes to the animals and their health."

Cassie lifted an eyebrow. So Curtis Kramer had managed to change Colton's opinion about him. Maybe there was hope for the Aldridge team. "Let me check our records." Quickly Cassie flipped through the files, pulled up the chart for the McLean Ranch and scanned Black Magic's immunization record. "It looks current," she murmured, mentally checking off the most common problems as she read Black Magic's history. "Any other symptoms?"

Colton, his lips compressed, shook his head. "All I know is that this came on like that!" He snapped his fingers for emphasis. "I showed him to you just the other day. He was fine."

Nodding, Cassie remembered the sleek black stallion, the health that fairly oozed from his mischievous eyes and glossy ebony coat.

No wonder Colton was worried. "I'll come out and have a look," she said, managing a practiced, professional smile, which belied the fact she was concerned. "Maybe he's just having a bad couple of days." But she didn't believe it for a minute. Black Magic was healthy and young; there was no reason for him to be listless or out of sorts. "Craig should be back any minute," she said, checking her watch and the appointment book. Fortunately she'd seen her last scheduled case of the day.

Shrugging out of her lab coat, she said to Sandy, "If we get an emergency call or someone comes in before Craig gets back, telephone me at the McLean Ranch. Someone will be near a phone." She glanced at Colton for confirmation.

He nodded. "Milly's back at the house, and we have extensions in the barns."

"Good." With a few last-minute instructions to Sandy, she grabbed her veterinary bag and followed Colton outside.

"I'll give you a ride," he suggested, but Cassie shook her head. As much as she'd have liked to have a few minutes alone with him, she didn't want to end up stuck at the McLean Ranch depending upon him to take her home to her father's house.

"I'd better take my own truck. I'll meet you there."

Colton gave her a quick nod and hopped into his rig. Less than a minute later he'd headed out of town.

Cassie followed at a safe distance behind, wondering what could be wrong with Denver's prize stallion. Worries plagued her. Fever. Fever from what? Infection? Virus? She gnawed on her lower lip as she drove. The McLean Ranch was known for the high-quality care given its stock. Petty jealousies aside, most of the ranchers in the area respected Tessa Kramer McLean's handling of the horses and cattle. And Denver, since he'd returned, had proved himself a capable, caring rancher.

But both Tessa and Denver were gone—and had been for several weeks. What kind of a rancher was Colton? Hadn't he sworn to hate everything to do with the ranch? Wasn't he here only to recuperate?

"Stop it!" she muttered angrily to herself as she flipped on the radio. Obviously Colton cared about the ranch or he wouldn't have raced to the clinic, looking haggard and worn. Nor would he have assumed the responsibility for the ranch and stock if he hadn't been prepared to give it his all.

He was already out of his Jeep and talking to Curtis by the time she drove into the yard, which separated the main house from the stables and barns. His arms crossed over his chest, his face drawn, he listened as Curtis talked.

". . . Afraid so," Curtis was saying as he puffed on the cigarette dangling from his lips and squinted through the smoke. "Whatever it is must be contagious." Casting a skeptical glance at Cassie, he added, "I hope you know your stuff." He tossed his cigarette to the gravel and ground it out with the toe of his boot.

"Contagious?" Her heart sank. "Another horse has symptoms?"

"See for yourself." Without another word, the wiry ranch foreman led Cassie and Colton into the stallion barn.

The minute she saw Black Magic, Cassie knew Colton's fears were well-founded. Something was wrong—very wrong.

Gone was the handsome, vital stallion she'd seen only days before. Now Black Magic held his head stiffly; his eyes, once bright, were dull. "Poor baby," Cassie murmured as she examined him carefully, running her fingers over his body, checking nose, mouth, ears and eyes. His temperature had climbed to 104 degrees, his pulse had elevated significantly, and there was some nasal discharge.

"Well?" Colton asked, frowning as she carefully touched the stallion's jaw. Her fingers encountered hot swelling over his lymph nodes, and Black Magic tossed back his head, knocking Cassie's hand away from the abscess.

"It looks like strangles," she said.

"Strangles? What the hell is that?"

Curtis swore roundly and shook his head. "Distemper."

"Damn!" Colton pressed his lips together in mute frustration. "He's got to be isolated immediately."

"Might already be too late," Curtis muttered.

"Too late for what?" Colton demanded.

"To protect the other animals. This stuff runs through a stable like wildfire," Cassie said. "Anything he's come in contact with could be contaminated. All his feeding and grooming utensils should be disinfected daily in an antiseptic solution. All the straw in his box will have to be burned." She flipped her bag open, located a hypodermic and bottle of penicillin. "His throat's sore, so I want him fed warm mashes. And don't feed him on the ground—use a sterile bucket. Keep him inside for the next couple of days, but make sure he gets plenty of fresh air." Quickly she injected Black Magic, then reached into her bag again and handed Colton a tube of medication. "Apply this liniment over his abscess so it will mature faster and can be drained."

Colton stared at the sick stallion. "Isn't there some vaccine against this sort of thing?"

Cassie nodded thoughtfully. "There is, but it's controversial. I don't even use it on our stock. Too many side effects. The best prevention is to avoid exposure." She glanced down the row of stalls in the stallion barn. "What's he been in contact with? Any other horses?"

"That's the million-dollar question, isn't it?" Colton tossed back at her, his eyes narrowing. "No one here knows."

"But—" she started to argue, then understood.

"Obviously he caught something while he was gone," he surmised sardonically. "Son of a—"

"You don't know when he contracted the disease," she cut in.

"It's a pretty damned good guess!"

Curtis stepped in before Cassie could answer. "Let's just calm down," he suggested, eyeing both Cassie and Colton. "Is this going around?"

Stung by Colton's hot retort, she said, "Not that I know of, but Craig was called over to the Monroe ranch this morning and he's been at Matt Wilkerson's this afternoon."

"What for?"

"I'm not sure," she said worriedly. "But some of their horses weren't feeling well."

Colton clamped his jaw tight. "Looks like there might be an epidemic, although this stallion"—he hooked a thumb at Black Magic—"hasn't been in contact with any horse other than those on this ranch and those he met while he was gone!" He glared at Cassie for a second before his face slackened as if he'd realized arguing wouldn't help. He swung his gaze to Curtis. "You said there was another horse with symptoms?"

"Tempest."

Colton sucked in a swift breath. Tempest wasn't one of the finest horses on the ranch. In fact he was pretty much mean-tempered and nondescript. For those very reasons he appealed to Colton. In the past few months Tempest had become Colton's favorite mount. "Great," he murmured sarcastically. "Let's check him out."

Cassie had to run to keep up with Colton's long strides. His boots sounded on the concrete, and inquisitive dark heads poked from the stalls as Cassie walked quickly to the far end of the stables.

Colton stopped at one box, and Cassie nearly ran into him. She looked into the stall and sighed inwardly. Tempest was sick all right. The sorrel stallion looked listless and weak. His water and feed hadn't been touched. Cassie guessed his temperature was high, his pulse elevated. She washed her hands, snapped on a new pair of gloves and examined him as she had Black Magic.

"Has he got it, too?" Colton asked.

"Yes." Wearily Cassie blew a strand of hair from her eyes. These two horses were just the first in the McLean stable to come down with the disease. She found a new needle and a dose of antibiotic, which she gave to Tempest before patting the stallion's shoulder.

She slipped out of the stall, stripped out of her gloves and reached again into her veterinary bag. Handing a large bottle of antibiotic tablets to Colton, she instructed, "I want Tempest and Black Magic quarantined."

"How serious is this?" Colton asked.

Cassie didn't mince words. "It's serious, but unless either horse develops complications, they should survive."

"What kind of complications?"

"Pneumonia for starters."

Colton exhaled heavily. "Pneumonia, huh? Great. Just goddamn great."

Wishing she could offer him some consolation, she said, "Pneumonia's just one of the complications, but let's not worry about that now. Both your stallions are young and strong. The antibiotics usually work. Tempest and Black Magic should make it, but the next few weeks are going to be rough."

"As long as they pull through."

"They should—really." Without thinking, she touched his arm, and the muscles beneath his sleeve flexed. Cassie turned to the foreman. "Are there any other horses with symptoms?"

"Not so far. Len checked the entire herd."

"Including Tessa's animals?" she asked, knowing how dear Tessa's horses were to Colton's sister-in-law.

Curtis nodded stiffly. "They looked fine."

"What about any neighboring mares the stallions may have serviced?"

"The first mares were due to arrive next week." His lips pursed together as if pulled on a drawstring. "I suppose that's out, right?"

"Absolutely. You have no choice but to cancel."

Curtis's old shoulders drooped.

"Now wait a minute," Colton cut in. "We can't—"

"You don't have a choice! You're lucky only two of your horses are infected!"

"She's right," Curtis said, frowning so deeply his face became a mass of lines.

"I'll have Len clean out their stalls and disinfect everything," Curtis said as he snapped a lead rope on Tempest. "We'll stable them in the old foaling shed. Come along." Curtis clucked his tongue and gently pulled on the lead. Tempest, his head extended rigidly, followed docilely behind.

Colton, leading an equally sluggish Black Magic, opened the door, trailing Curtis toward a weathered older building that was now used only for storage.

Slowly the unhappy caravan made its way across the yard

and through two paddock gates to the small building. Inside, the shed was clean and light. While Cassie held the horses, Curtis and Colton swabbed the floor with antiseptic, then quickly spread straw and carried feed and water to the horses. Neither stallion took any notice.

Cassie's heart went out to the sick animals. Though, if lucky, they would both survive, the disease could disable and scar them. Once the stallions were settled, she said, "I think I'd better look over the rest of your herd." Mentally crossing her fingers, she silently prayed she'd find no other horse with symptoms.

"You think it's spread?" Colton's voice was grim, as if he was steeling himself for the worst.

"I hope not," she whispered, stuffing her hands into the pockets of her skirt. For the next three hours she examined every horse on the McLean Ranch, including the swollen-bellied mares ready to foal.

Colton never left her side, studying each animal as she did, waiting, his face gaunt, to hear that yet another horse was stricken.

"So far, so good," Cassie said as she examined the last of the horses, a chestnut with a crooked white blaze—Tessa's favorite stallion, Brigadier.

Impatient at being examined, Brigadier minced this way and that in his stall, shifting his sleek rump and hindquarters away from Cassie's expert hands or jerking his head away when she attempted to look into his eyes and nostrils. "Feisty one, aren't you?" Cassie murmured, relieved she hadn't found any more cases of strangles than the first two.

Brigadier snorted haughtily, and Cassie gave him a playful slap on the rump. "This one's healthy!" Encouraged slightly, she squeezed through the stall gate and walked outside with Colton.

"For how long?" Colton asked.

"I wish I knew. It depends. Has he been in contact with the infected horses?"

Colton shook his head. "Tessa's always kept her horses separate, even after she and Denver married."

"And the rest of the herd?"

"You've seen it. The mares and foals are in one field, the yearlings in another, the stallions and geldings even more isolated. In fact, since Black Magic's been back, he hasn't been around any of the other horses—including Tempest."

"Then maybe you're safe," she said as she scanned the maze of pastures and paddocks comprising the ranch. The evening air was moist, but warm. The last streaks of sunlight blazed across the mountains, gilding the highest peaks and streaking the sky with swatches of lavender and magenta. Playful fillies and colts scampered through the lush grass, kicking and bucking, galloping in uneven strides through the fields.

"Aside from another animal, how does a horse get it?"

"Contaminated surroundings, water or food. Sometimes from droppings or from contaminated utensils."

"What's the incubation period?"

"Two days to a couple of weeks."

He raked stiff fingers through his hair, shoving a wayward clump that hung over his forehead back. "So any horse that's come in contact with Black Magic could be infected?"

"Yes." She could tell by Colton's grim expression that he understood the size of the epidemic he might have on his hands.

Guilt weighting his shoulders, Colton felt as if he hadn't slept in days. "I guess I'd better call Denver." Absently rubbing his wounded shoulder, he grimaced. He'd kept Black Magic's disappearance from Denver to save him any worry, and it had blown up in his face. Denver would be furious!

"Do you want me to talk to him?" Cassie asked.

"This is my problem," he snapped. Then, hearing the bite

in his words, Colton forced a thin smile. "I mean, I'll handle it. But why don't you come with me—as my backup. Just in case Denver wants a more professional opinion."

"Fair enough."

Gritting his teeth, Colton strode into the house, marched into the den, picked up the phone and dialed.

As he waited for the connection, he sat on a corner of the desk and drummed his fingers on the scarred wood. Explaining this would be hell. The phone rang four times before a recording answered. "Great," Colton muttered. He wasn't about to tell a recording machine what was going on. Instead, he just asked Denver to call him as soon as possible.

"No luck?" Cassie asked.

Colton laughed bitterly. "I think I ran out of luck about six months ago."

"Things'll get better."

"Will they?" he asked, squinting through the window to the yard beyond. He watched as Len and Curtis, their backs bowed with feed sacks, trudged into the broodmare barn. "Is that your *professional* opinion?"

"No."

"I didn't think so." He rubbed the tight knot forming in the muscles between his shoulders. God, he was tired. He'd been awake most of the night, tossing and turning on that damned cot, his mind filled with images of Cassie and the ranch and a future that was far away. A future spent looking through the lens of a camera in some godforsaken land. Alone. Without Cassie.

She had dropped onto the arm of a worn couch and was staring at him with those wide, soul-searching eyes. The kindness and concern in her gaze bothered him. "Are you okay?" she asked.

"Do I look okay?"

Cassie smiled faintly. "The truth?"

"Don't hold back."

"You look like hell," she said.

"Thanks for the compliment." He forced one corner of his mouth up. "That's better than I feel."

"It's not your fault."

"Isn't it? I lost the horse, didn't I? It happened while I was in charge!"

"Wait a minute, Colt! Before you go on an extended guilt trip, let's look at the facts, okay?" She pushed herself to her feet, and her cheeks flushed. "We're not certain Black Magic caught this while he was 'lost.' And as far as you being responsible, I don't think you should be beating yourself up over it. The same thing happened last year and you weren't even here!"

"Last year Black Magic survived."

"And he just might this year," she said, crossing the room to stand only bare inches from him, "unless we all give up on him! Have some faith."

"Do you?"

"I told you, usually the disease isn't deadly."

She was so close that Colton could see the ribbons of green in her hazel eyes, smell the scent of her. Her black hair gleamed in soft, tangled curls that rested against her cheeks and fell past her shoulders. "And what else do you have faith in Cass?" he asked, reaching forward, curling his fingers around her arms.

Cassie didn't breathe. Her gaze flickered downward to where his long legs swung from the corner of the desk, brushing intimately against her skirt.

"That . . ." She swallowed hard. "That depends."

"On?" Colton's blood began to surge through his body. She was, without a doubt, the most bewitching woman he'd ever met.

"On you, Mr. McLean," she said, her lips parting, the pulse at the hollow of her throat leaping out of control. "I'd like to have faith in you."

His insides turned molten.

"Maybe you should."

She tilted her chin. "Should I? Why?" she asked, her warm breath fanning his face.

"Colton? You in there?" Milly Samms's voice drifted through the door. A loud rap echoed through the room.

Cassie froze in his arms for just a second. Blushing like a teenager, she quickly stepped back.

Colton, slightly amused, cleared his throat, but his voice was still raspy. "Come in."

"It's time for din—" Milly stopped in midsentence as she stepped into the room. "Oh, Cassie! I didn't realize you were still here."

Cassie stuffed her hands into the pockets of her skirt. "I thought I'd stay awhile, until we were sure none of the horses came down with the virus."

"Virus?" Milly asked.

Colton explained about Black Magic and Tempest, and told the housekeeper about the possibility of an epidemic. "I tried to get hold of Denver, but he was out. If he calls back, I want to talk to him. Immediately."

Milly's round face had turned ashen. "What about the foals?"

"So far, so good," Cassie said, "but I think I'd better stick around for a while."

"Then come on in to dinner," Milly insisted.

Cassie held up a hand. "No, I couldn't—"

"Nonsense. I always make enough to feed the entire Third Battalion, so you just come along." Before Cassie could protest any further, Milly swept out the door and hurried off toward the kitchen.

"I really can't," Cassie said to Colton once the housekeeper's footsteps had faded.

"Why not?"

"Because. I don't want to intrude—"

"You won't. Besides, I want you to stay." He touched her lightly under the chin, forcing her gaze to his, and for the first time that day Cassie saw tenderness tempering the passion in his eyes.

She swallowed nervously. Staying with Colton seemed natural and right, and she might be able to help if any of the rest of the stock came down with the virus.

"Don't tell me," Colton joked, "you've got a better offer."

"Millions of them."

"I thought so."

Cassie's lips turned up at the corners. "Actually I'm on my own tonight. Dad's playing cards with some friends."

"Then I insist."

"And I accept," she said, burying any lingering doubts. Tonight Colton needed her, and, unfortunately, she needed him.

Milly Samms proved an excellent cook. By the time the pork chops, potatoes, gravy, fresh asparagus and cherry pie had been served and devoured, Cassie was stuffed.

Curtis and Len had already left. Only she, Milly and Colton lingered over half-full cups of coffee at the McLeans' large dining room table. "I'll help with the dishes," she offered, but Milly wouldn't hear of it.

"You go tend to the horses, and I'll handle this."

"But—"

Colton reached over and squeezed her hand. "Don't argue," he said. "The kitchen is Milly's turf. She kicked me out just the other day."

"And a lucky thing, too," Milly said, picking up a few of the platters of leftover meat and potatoes. "This place was fallin' down around your ears and you didn't even know it."

"It was just a little messy."

"A little? A little, he says," she muttered under her breath, chuckling to herself.

Cassie reached for the butter dish. "At least let me clear—"

"No way. You're the guest, remember? Now put that down." Casting Cassie a look that dared her to defy her authority, Milly carried a stack of dishes through the swinging doors to the kitchen.

Cassie felt a bitter pang of disbelief. Milly had referred to her as a guest. In the McLean house. Never in all of her twenty-five years had she entered the house as a guest; not even when, years before, she'd thought she would marry Colton. She was an Aldridge—not a friend.

"I'm the veterinarian," she corrected, shoving her chair back. "And I'd better go check on Black Magic."

The phone rang, and Colton jumped. "Denver," he said just as Milly called, "Colt—Denver wants to talk to you."

"Here goes nothing," he mumbled under his breath, but said more loudly, "I'll get it in the den." Cassie shoved back her chair and started for the door, but Colton added, "Don't leave until I'm done talking with my brother."

She glanced over her shoulder. "I wasn't planning on it."

"Good." Colton walked into the den and snatched up the telephone receiver. "I'm glad you called," he said, stretching the truth a little. "We've got a problem." Blow by blow, he explained about Black Magic's disappearance, return and subsequent poor health.

Denver didn't say a word—not one comment as Colton continued. But the tension stretching over the telephone wires was nearly palpable.

". . . So hopefully, none of the other horses are infected," Colton finished.

"Hopefully? *Hopefully?*"

"It's still too early to tell."

"Damn!" Denver swore long and loud. When he was through ranting and raving, he growled, "And you're sure Tessa's horses are okay?"

"I can't be sure of anything," Colton admitted, running a

hand over his scratchy jaw. "But they're the least likely as they haven't been near Magic or Tempest."

"I guess I should be thankful for small favors."

"I suppose," Colton said, feeling defensive. Was this really his fault? Or should someone have clued him in that Magic was lost last year? He leaned a hip against the desk. There was no reason to start pointing fingers anyway. It wouldn't change a thing.

"Son of a bitch!" Denver was still showing off his rather limited vocabulary.

"Exactly."

"We can't leave tonight—but we can cut the trip short by a week."

"I don't see why. There's nothing more you can do."

"Except wring the neck of the bastard who stole Black Magic in the first place! Obviously Magic caught the virus while he was gone."

"Looks that way." Colton heard Denver's swift intake of breath.

"Do you think it was deliberate?"

"Deliberate?" Colton repeated, his gaze shifting around the room.

"Yeah. Isn't it possible that whoever's behind all this is more deadly than you think? Maybe stealing Black Magic was more than just an irritating prank."

Colton didn't like Denver's line of reasoning. "You honestly think someone would infect Black Magic on purpose?"

"Hell, I don't know!" Denver thundered. "But you have to admit it's a distinct possibility. In fact, it's downright plausible!"

"That's a little farfetched," Colton said, wondering if his brother were even more jaded than he.

"Is it? No more farfetched than someone stealing the horse just to cause a little trouble! Think about it, for God's sake! Strangles could cripple the ranch. Not only could we lose livestock and rack up a fortune in vet bills, but the stallions will be out of commission during the breeding season. No one in his right mind would send a mare to a ranch with that virus floating around. This was no accident!"

"No way—"

"It's happening, damn it!" Denver nearly shouted.

Colton suddenly felt tired. What if Denver was right? He closed his eyes and listened to his brother's rapid, angry breathing. "Look, I'll warn Curtis and tell him what you think. I'm not saying you're right, but I suppose there's the chance someone's that vindictive."

"Someone like Ivan Aldridge."

Colton didn't comment. Even he didn't think Ivan was capable of anything so treacherous. "It's not Aldridge."

"How do you know? Has anyone talked to him?"

"I have. He and Cassie swear he's not involved."

"He and *Cassie*? What's she got to do with it?"

"She's here now. She's the one who diagnosed Black Magic."

Denver's breath hissed between his teeth. "Why not Fulton?"

Colton's back stiffened. "He was busy," he snapped.

For a minute Denver didn't say anything, but Colton could feel the anger, the unspoken accusations crackling over the thin telephone wires. "Keep me posted," he finally ordered.

"Will do." Colton hung up feeling oddly protective of Cassie and her father. Though there was no love lost between Ivan and himself, Colton couldn't imagine the man intentionally hurting any animal—even an animal belonging to the McLeans. Nor did he think anyone around here would. Ranching stock was looked upon with a reverence that couldn't be compromised.

He walked through the kitchen and found Milly putting the last of the dishes in the dishwasher. "How did Denver take the news?" she asked as Colton reached for his hat and jacket near the door.

"About as well as I expected."

"That bad?" she quipped, but the joke fell flat.

"Worse," he muttered, glancing around the kitchen. Nearly everything was put away. "Why don't you take off?"

"In a few minutes." She polished the bottom of a gleaming copper pot and looked up to offer an encouraging smile.

Colton kicked open the door and strode quickly down the back steps. Outside, the sky was dark. A few pale clouds drifted across a half moon, and the breeze brushing his cheeks held the lingering chill of winter.

His boots crunched on the gravel as he strode across the yard. Was it possible? Would someone intentionally try to destroy the McLeans—and use the livestock to do it? The ugly thought soured his stomach as he yanked open the door to the old foaling shed.

There he found Cassie with Black Magic. She was talking quietly to the horse, her voice soothing, her hands gentle as they ran along his neck and shoulders. Glancing up at Colton, she forced a thin smile. "His fever hasn't gone up."

"Is that good?"

"I think so—but it's still too early to tell."

"And Tempest?"

"No change. Neither one has eaten anything." She slipped out of the stall and washed her hands while Colton observed both stallions. Listless and dull, Tempest barely flicked his ears when Colton walked to his stall. His head was still painfully extended, and his eyes held no spark.

"Hang in there," Colton whispered, wondering if the once-ornery stallion would take a turn for the worse.

"What did Denver have to say?"

"Nothing good," Colton evaded. There wasn't any reason to confide in Cassie—not yet. Denver's theory was just angry words. When he calmed down a little, he would probably change his mind. Or would he? Uncomfortable, Colton glanced from Cassie back to Black Magic, wondering who was responsible for this mess and coming up with only his own name.

"I want to check the other horses again before I leave," Cassie said. "Just in case."

"Right." Colton led the way through the various buildings. Fortunately all the horses, though disturbed slightly at the unusual intrusion, looked fine. Colton waited for Cassie at the door and snapped out the lights as she walked outside.

Aside from her truck and Colton's Jeep, the parking lot was empty. Milly and the hands had already left. With Colton at her side, Cassie started for her car, but he grabbed her hand, turning her to face him. He didn't want her to leave, not just yet. Having her here was comforting. She looked up at him expectantly, and his insides quivered. "If I didn't say it before, thanks for dropping everything and coming over."

"All part of my job," she replied.

He didn't let go of her hand. "But you stayed. That was above and beyond the call of duty."

"Not really." Somewhere in the distance a night bird called plaintively, and a mild breeze caught in her hair and murmured through the trees. Cassie's eyes were luminous in the pale moonlight. Withdrawing her hand, she wrapped her arms around herself, as if she were chilled to the bone.

"Cold?"

"I'll survive."

"Come here." Before he really knew what he was doing, he reached forward and drew her into the circle of his arms, pulled her close against him, her legs inside his.

Closing his eyes, he blocked out his worries about the ranch, his doubts about his occupation, and even the past. He only thought about the here and now. His heart slammed out of control as he lowered his head and brushed his lips over hers.

"Colton . . ." she whispered in protest. "Maybe we should think about this—"

"Too late," he murmured into her mouth, and any other arguments were stilled as he pressed his tongue insistently against her teeth. With a soft moan, she parted her lips.

Colton's pulse pounded in his brain. Desire became an obsession, fortifying his blood, numbing his mind to anything but this one, gorgeous woman. She didn't resist any longer. Her body was soft and pliant as he spread his hands across her back. Her mouth opened willingly, deliciously. He touched her tongue, and it danced with his.

She wound her arms around his chest, her fingers pressed against his back.

He couldn't stop himself. He groaned, kissing her harder, his lips demanding, hers yielding. His mind forgot everything but Cassie—sweet, beautiful Cassie.

Unbuttoning her blouse, he let the fabric fall open, exposing the swell of her breast, her creamy white skin mounding gently over the white lace of her bra. Beneath the sculpted lace, her nipple was dusky and taut, poking out enticingly.

The fire in Colton's loins burned hotter, and without a thought to time or space, he slid a silky strap from her shoulder with one hand, while pressing against the small of her back with the other. Her breast spilled over the lace, full and ripe, her tiny veins visible beneath the creamy skin.

Colton wound his legs around hers as he took her nipple in his mouth and pulled gently with tongue and teeth.

"Oh, Lord," she murmured as he suckled and nuzzled, her sweet, sure femininity enveloping him in a seductive cloud of passion and promise.

His hands shook as he lifted the gentle white swell and licked the dark button to hardness. Cassie's head lolled back, her throat arched, her hips fit snug against his.

Colton could barely stand as he turned his attention to the other lace-ensnared nipple, and he fanned his breath across the flimsy fabric. Her fingers twined in his hair, Cassie guided his mouth to the sweet, dark bud, and he took her breast, lace and all, into his mouth, leaving the other to be cooled by the chill spring breeze.

He could no longer stand on unsteady legs, and he dragged Cassie to the ground. Oblivious to the grass, he caressed her body, found her lips again and kissed her with an intensity that numbed his brain. "Stay with me," he whispered against her ear, feeling her tremble beneath him.

"I-I can't."

"Sure you can."

"Oh, Colton . . ." Knowing she was courting disaster, Cassie felt herself giving in. She'd simply have to find some way to explain her absence to her father . . . and she was old enough to make her own decisions.

Colton moved his hands seductively against her skin, and her mind spun in crazy, delicious circles. A liquid warmth deep in her center swept through her blood, carrying her away on a moon-kissed cloud of passion.

The cool night air touched her bare breast, then Colton's hot lips followed, dipping lower to her abdomen, his fingers finding the waistband of her skirt.

"Make love to me, Cassie," he rasped, his voice sounding far away. "Make love to me and never stop. Don't stop."

Where had she heard those words before? she wondered vaguely. Then, with searing clarity she remembered that it had been she who had pleaded with him to make love to her, to take away her virginity, to *love* her.

She froze, and the desire burning so bright only moments before cooled. "I—I think I'd better leave," she said, squirming under his insistent caress.

Colton lifted his head, and her heart constricted. His features, washed in the pale moon glow, seemed more clearly defined and angular than usual. His eyes, as silver as the moon-washed land, burned with passion. "Why?" he asked, his voice so low she could barely hear it.

"I'm not ready to make the same mistake twice."

"This is *not* a mistake."

"Then it'll wait," she said, swallowing back the urge to tell him she loved him. She sat up then to adjust her bra and, afterward, forced her hands to her sides when all she wanted was to place her palms against his cheeks and kiss him.

"What happened, Cass?"

"A severe case of déjà vu." Straightening her blouse, she was glad for the shadows in the night, thankful he couldn't see the blush burning her neck and staining her cheeks.

Colton pulled himself into a sitting position and jammed his fingers through his hair. "We're not kids anymore."

"Then maybe we'd better stop acting like them!"

His eyes blazed. "All right. Let's start again—more mature this time. I want you to stay with me, Cassie," he said, his gaze piercing hers with an intensity so powerful, she couldn't look away. "Stay here. In my bed. Spend the night with me."

Oh, God. The temptation was almost too much. *Alone with Colton—for an entire night!* "Sorry," she replied, hoping to sound sophisticated, though her voice was strangled. "I'm not into one-night stands . . . Ooh!"

As quickly as a cat, Colton shoved her back onto the ground, pinning her shoulders against the earth. "I wouldn't call eight years a one-night stand."

"Eight years?" she repeated. "Eight years? When were we together in the past eight years? And where were you? Who were you with?"

Some of the anger disappeared from his eyes. "There weren't many, Cass," he admitted with a sigh. "And none of them held a candle to you."

Her throat burned, and she wanted to believe him. Oh, God, how she wanted to believe him.

The fingers forcing her down became gentler. "What about you?" he asked quietly.

"You want to know about my lovers? All of them?" she asked, and was surprised at the pain in his eyes.

"No—that's your business, I suppose."

"Well, there were none. Not in college and not here," she admitted, suddenly wanting him to know, to understand just how important he'd been.

"None?" he hurled back at her, disbelieving.

"*Nada*."

"Oh, Cass," he whispered, releasing her. "No wonder your father hates me."

"He doesn't—"

"Of course he does." Standing, he dusted off his hands, then offered one to her.

She took his hand, and he pulled her up but didn't let go of her fingers. "You know," he admitted. "I've always cared about you. Always."

The lump in her throat swelled, and she could barely get out her reply. "S-so you said."

He kissed her forehead so tenderly she nearly broke apart inside. "Please," he whispered, "stay."

"Not tonight." Pulling her hand away, she shook her head. "Not yet. Before I sleep with you, Colton, I want to think things through."

"That sounds a little cold and calculating."

"No. It sounds smart." Placing her hands on his shoulders, she lifted herself to her toes and kissed him on his forehead. "Last time I thought with my heart, this time I'll use my head."

Before she could draw away, his arms circled her waist. "Tell me," he asked, "just how much does your father hate me and Denver?"

"Denver I'm not sure about, but he detests you."

Colton was silent, his expression unreadable.

"That isn't a surprise, is it?"

"No." He lifted a shoulder as if he didn't care, but Cassie

felt there was something he was holding back—something he wasn't telling her as he released her.

He walked her back to her pickup, but he didn't say another word. And as she drove away, she saw him standing in the moonlight, his shoulders rigid, his back ramrod straight, his fists planted on his hips.

Chapter Ten

"**C**onfounded things!" Ivan yanked on his boots, grimacing until his foot slid inside. Seated near the wood stove, he glared up at Cassie. "You got in late last night."

Cassie nodded. "I was at the McLean place. Two of their horses have come down with strangles."

"Strangles?" His booted foot clattered to the floor. "Around here?"

"Looks that way to me."

"Which horses?"

"Black Magic and another stallion—a sorrel named Tempest."

Glancing at his watch, Ivan straightened and massaged a kink from his back. He crossed the kitchen and filled a blue enamel cup with the coffee warming on the stove. Was it her imagination, or had he paled slightly? "The rest of the herd okay?" He offered her the mug.

"As far as I can tell. But I was going to stop by on my way into town." She took a sip of the bitter coffee and made a face. "Why can't you learn to make a decent cup of coffee?"

"It's fine," he grumbled, "you're just picky. I sent you off to college, and what did you come home with?"

"A degree," she teased.

"That and some 'refined' tastes," he kidded back, but the familiar spark in his eyes didn't appear. "You gonna be late again?"

"I don't know," she said, thinking of Colton and Denver McLean's ailing horses.

Ivan dashed his coffee into the sink, then grabbed his jacket. "I'll see you later," he said. "I've got to feed the stock, then run into town to order some parts for the John Deere." Whistling to Erasmus, he sauntered outside.

Through the window, Cassie watched him cross the yard. He stopped to pet a few of the mares' muzzles and laughed out loud at a skittish colt's antics before he disappeared into the barn. He'd been good to her, she thought as she slung the strap of her purse over her shoulder and pushed open the screen door. She was greeted by the dewy scent of morning and the obtrusive whine of a motorcycle engine shattering the crisp air.

Ryan Ferguson was on his way to work. His employment shouldn't bother her, she told herself as she tossed her purse into the cab of her truck, but it did. She waited until he'd brought the cycle to a stop, switched off the engine, yanked off his helmet and swung off the bike. His hair stuck out in uneven blond tufts, and he smoothed it with the flat of his hand.

"You nearly ran me off the road the other day," she said as he lifted interested brown eyes to hers.

"Didn't mean to."

"You should look where you're going."

"I do." One side of his thin mouth lifted cynically. "You shouldn't hog the entire lane. There was room enough. Besides, Ivan gave me enough of a lecture." He glanced around the yard. "Is he here?"

"In the barn."

"Don't bother showing me in," he mocked. "I'll find my

way." He left his helmet on the seat of his motorcycle and without a backward glance turned toward the barn. Erasmus, startled as he'd been lying under his favorite juniper bush, growled a little. "Ah, shut up," Ryan muttered, pushing hard on the barn's creaking door.

"Wonderful man," Cassie told herself, wishing her father hadn't hired him as she climbed into the cab. Ryan Ferguson had never done anything wrong—at least nothing that had been proven—and yet she didn't like him. Nor did she trust him.

She sent a scathing glance toward the gleaming black motorcycle before shoving the old truck into gear. She clenched her fingers over the wheel, and her thoughts turned to Colton and how close she'd come to staying with him.

As she'd driven home, she'd argued with herself and been glad that her father had already turned in for the night. She, too, had been bone-tired, and even though she'd thought about Colton McLean, even fantasized about him a bit, she'd fallen asleep quickly. So she hadn't had too much time to consider the subtle change in their relationship.

"Don't kid yourself," she said, shooting a glance at her reflection in the rearview mirror, "nothing about your relationship is subtle. Nothing about Colton is subtle. That's the problem."

Shifting down, she turned into the lane leading up to the small rise on which the McLean house stood so grandly. The two-storied farmhouse gleamed in the morning sunlight, though for years it had been allowed to run down until Denver had returned. Denver had brought with him the cash for a fresh coat of paint, new shingles and repairs.

Spying Colton's Jeep, she caught her lower lip between her teeth and tried not to notice that her pulse had quickened. *This is business*, she told herself as she parked near the garage, grabbed her veterinary bag and hurried to the front door, where she pounded on the thick, painted panels. Within seconds she heard a scurrying of feet.

The door swung open, and Milly, wiping her hands on her ever-present apron, forced a tired smile. "Thank goodness you're here. The men are up at the old foaling shed."

Cassie's heart sank. She knew instantly from the deep lines between Milly's eyebrows that one or both of the horses had taken a turn for the worse.

"It's Tempest. He was down this morning," Milly said.

"Why didn't Colton call me?" Cassie asked.

"He did. Just a little while ago. Your father said you were on your way."

Cassie didn't wait for any further explanation. She raced down the steps, rounded the house and ran through long grass to the smallest of the outbuildings.

She shoved against the door, and it creaked open. Inside, the scents of horses, leather and dust mingled together. Dust motes swirled in front of the windows as she breezed down the short corridor to the end stall.

Colton and Curtis, their shoulders drooped, were already inside the stall. "How is he?"

"Not good," Curtis bit out.

The foreman was right. Tempest seemed weak. His head hung at an alarming angle.

Cassie didn't waste any time. She slipped into the stall and examined him quickly. His temperature was soaring, and his pulse was much too rapid. "Come on, boy," she whispered, wishing there were something she could do and feeling absolutely helpless. What good were degrees and all her training when she couldn't save this horse? "Just hang in there." She patted his shoulder, then checked his food and water. "Has he eaten anything?"

"Isn't interested." Curtis shoved his hair beneath his hat. "We forced the antibiotics down him, but that's about it."

"Water?"

"A little."

"I don't want him to dehydrate," she snapped.

Curtis shoved his hat back on his head. "Neither do we."

Feeling helpless, she patted Tempest's soft muzzle, then walked back to Black Magic's stall. "This one looks better," she said, a little relieved. A cantankerous spark flared in Black Magic's gaze.

Colton's lips thinned. "But for how long?"

"I don't know," she admitted. "Has anyone checked on the other horses?"

"Yep." Curtis dug in his breast pocket, reaching for a crumpled pack of cigarettes. "Len and I looked 'em all over this morning. Everything looks okay."

"That's the good news," Colton said thoughtfully as they walked outside and he shut the door securely behind him. "What little of it there is."

Curtis lit up and blew a stream of smoke toward the blue Montana sky. "I'll see about cleaning all the tack—makin' sure that Black Magic's and Tempest's things are gone over. And we'll clean out the stalls and wash all the equipment again." He ambled toward the tack room, leaving Colton and Cassie alone.

Colton rammed his hands into the back pockets of his jeans. His expression pensive, he scoured the valley floor with his gaze, as if he could find some clue to an unsolved puzzle. "When I got through to Denver last night, I told him everything that had been going on in the past few weeks—including the fact that Black Magic was missing for a while."

Cassie's stomach knotted. She could tell just by looking at him that something important was to follow, and she guessed what it was. "He thinks the horse was stolen and that Dad did it," she said without any emotion.

"He's *convinced* the horse was stolen. What he's not sure about is if the horse contracted the disease by accident or if it was done on purpose."

"On purpose?" she repeated, her mouth dropping open. "What do you mean?" But the ugly realization was beginning to dawn on her. "Oh, Colton, no! He couldn't think someone would intentionally hurt one of your horses!" she said, horrified at the implications. "That's—that's tantamount to germ warfare!"

Colton nodded, shoving the brim of his hat away from his eyes. "I'm just telling you what his gut reaction was."

"Then his gut reaction was wrong!"

"He didn't seem to think so."

"And you? What about you?" She grabbed at the smooth leather sleeve of his jacket. "Tell me you think he's wrong," she demanded, her eyes boring into his, her fingers clenched anxiously. He couldn't think Ivan was involved in anything so sinister.

"I hope he's wrong."

"*Hope?*" she repeated, nearly shrieking. "Don't you know? Oh, Colton—"

"Look, Cass, I'm just telling you, that's all," he said sharply.

She dropped his arm as if it were a red-hot coal. "This time Denver's gone off the deep end," she said angrily. "But then he has a history of that, doesn't he?"

"So does your father."

The wound cut deep—like the slice of a razor. Whirling, she poked a single finger at his chest. "My father has his reasons for not trusting you and for hating your uncle. But I thought we were going to bury the hatchet and try to forget all that. I even thought we were going to try to 'start over,' isn't that what you said? Well, someone better clue Denver in!"

"I will. When he gets back."

"And when will that be?"

"As soon as he can."

"Great! I can't wait to give him a piece of my mind," she declared, turning on her heel and starting for her pickup. Of all the insane, horrid notions! If Denver McLean were here right now, Cassie would personally throttle him!

Righteous indignation staining her cheeks the color of the dawn, she threw open the door of the truck and climbed inside. But before she could slam it closed, Colton had wedged himself between the door and seat. "Now who's jumping off the deep end?" he demanded.

"Excuse me, but I think my reputation and my father's were just assassinated." She jammed the key into the ignition. The old engine caught. "I'd just like to know, Colton," she said, looking down at him from her perch in the truck's cab, "what happened between last night and this morning! Remember last night—out here in this very yard? Weren't you the guy trying to get me to stay with you? Sleep with you? Make love to you?"

His fingers flexed, the knuckles white.

"Well, I'm not interested," she said. "Not until you and I have some *mutual* trust!" With a toss of her head, she slammed the truck into gear.

By the time she reached the clinic, Cassie had cooled off. Her anger had given way to incredulity, disappointment and indignation.

"Any messages?" she asked, letting herself in through the back door and catching Sandy feeding the few patients housed in the cages of the back room.

"No—and your first appointment isn't until nine." She poured feed pellets into a small dish and placed them inside the hutch of an ailing white rabbit. "Coffee's on if you want some."

"Thanks. I could use a cup. I just hope it's *not* decaf."

"Ouch. Bad morning?" Sandy asked.

"You could say that." Cassie checked on the Edwards's poodle and the three puppies that had been brought into the world via Cesarean section. "How're you?" she whispered, petting the dog's soft gray head as the tiny puppies squirmed and squeaked, shifting into position against their mother's shaved belly. Cassie eyed the neat row of stitches and the ochre color of disinfectant staining the bitch's underside.

"Puppies are doing fine—Mom feels a little ragged," Sandy said.

"I don't blame her," Cassie murmured to the dog, and was rewarded with a sloppy tongue against her palm. "You are feeling better, aren't you?" she said, grinning as she stood and gratefully accepted a steaming cup of coffee from Sandy.

"Craig wanted me to remind you about the Edwards's party Friday."

Cassie made a face. She'd completely forgotten about the annual event. As this was her first full year working with Craig, and Nate Edwards brought a lot of business into the clinic, Craig was adamant she attend. "I don't suppose you know of a way to get out of it?"

"Why would you want to?"

"I hate those things!" Cassie replied.

"Oh, but it's great! No one can throw a party like Paula Edwards!"

"No one would want to." After examining the animals housed in the cages, she asked, "Has anyone called in about sick horses? Horses with an elevated temperature or pulse?"

"Only Colton McLean yesterday and Vince Monroe a few days ago. Craig went out to see the mare."

Vince Monroe! One of her father's best friends. Her palms began to sweat. "Do we have that file?"

"Unless Craig has it with him." Sandy walked through a connecting door to a small file room, ran one finger across the color-coded tabs and pulled out a thick folder for the Monroe ranch. "Here it is," she said, handing the bound sheaf of papers to Cassie.

The most recent entries were in the top pages. Cassie saw where Craig examined a foal with a bowed leg and a mare with a slight fever. But there was no hint of strangles. She felt immediate relief.

"Craig hasn't mentioned anything more serious—like strangles, has he?"

Sandy frowned as the back door opened, letting in a breath of cool morning air. "Nope—at least not to me."

"Did I hear someone talking about me?" Craig asked as he stepped into the back room.

"That's right, and we've been saying hideous and vile things about you," Cassie teased, her black mood lifting at the sight of Craig's frizzy hair and flushed cheeks.

"I thought so." He hung his jacket on a hook near the door, then slid his arms through the sleeves of a starched green lab coat. "What's up?"

"There's an outbreak of strangles at the McLean Ranch."

"Strangles?" Craig let out a low whistle. "Which horse?"

"Black Magic and Tempest. Both stallions." While Craig walked into the tiny kitchen area and poured himself a cup of coffee, Cassie told him everything that had happened.

"And Colton thinks Black Magic picked it up while he was missing?" he asked thoughtfully, stirring sweetener into his cup.

"That's the way he figures it."

Craig's lower lip protruded thoughtfully. "Makes sense, I suppose. And the timing's right. There are some wild horses that live up in the mountains. McLean's stallion could've gotten mixed up with them."

Cassie shook her head. "I don't think so. The way Colton and Curtis Kramer tell it, Black Magic looked as good when he returned as when he left. He was groomed and cared for. I saw him soon after, and I'd say he hadn't spent any time in the wild."

Craig frowned. "So Colton still thinks he was stolen."

"Yes." *And more, much more.* Cassie placed her empty cup into the small sink. "If he's right, and some rancher 'borrowed' the stallion, we've got at least one more case of strangles. Probably more."

"More like an epidemic." Craig scowled into his coffee as he swirled a spoon in his cup. "I haven't heard of any other cases, but I'll call around to the other clinics in the county."

The front bell tinkled, signaling the arrival of the first appointment.

"Oh-oh, duty calls. That's probably Mrs. Silvan for her rabbit. She'll want to talk to you," Sandy said to Craig.

Craig took one gulp from his cup, then set it aside. "I'll bring Herman into room two."

"Great." Sandy hurried to her desk in the reception area, which was located on the other side of the file room and separated the waiting area from the examining rooms.

Craig motioned to the half-empty kennels and said to Cassie, "Look, if you want to take off early this afternoon and check on the McLean horses, feel free. Unless we get swamped with emergencies, I can handle things here. The same goes for tomorrow. I don't have any surgeries scheduled, so I'll hold down the fort."

"You're sure?"

"I think you're due for a day off," he said, then grimaced. "But dealing with strangles won't be any picnic."

"Don't I know," Cassie agreed as the front bell chimed again, and Craig lifted the fat white rabbit from its cage.

Inside the broodmare barn Colton studied the swollen-bodied bay with a jaundiced eye. Red Wing was anxious, her eyes rolling backward, her ears flattening as Curtis tried to examine her for signs indicating she was about to foal.

"Yep. She's ready," Curtis said, patting the mare fondly.

Colton wanted to swear. The last thing he needed was new, fragile horses being exposed to God-only-knew-what. "You're sure about this?"

"Sure as I can be. My money says she'll foal tonight— tomorrow night at the latest."

"Great." Colton grumbled.

"Too bad Tessa won't be here to see it," Curtis said wistfully as he slipped out of the mare's stall. "She's waited a long time for this."

Colton didn't answer. In a mood as dark as Black Magic's hide, he strode outside, barely noticing that the wind had turned, kicking up from the west.

Though it was barely four o'clock, Milly had already snapped on the kitchen lights. The windows glowed from within. Colton climbed up the back steps, kicked off his boots and hung his jacket and hat on pegs in the porch, then shouldered his way into the house.

It was filled with the scents of nutmeg, strong coffee and pot roast. Milly was sweeping what appeared to be a spotless kitchen floor. She glanced up when he appeared. "You got a call this afternoon. Some guy from a magazine. Grover, he said his name was."

Colton didn't really care. "What'd he want?"

"To talk to you." Milly leaned on her broom, looking miffed. "Wouldn't tell me any more than that. I left his number in the den."

Colton couldn't help but smile. He'd gotten used to Milly and her bossing, Curtis and his cantankerous ways, and Cassie—Lord, how she'd gotten under his skin. He knew what Steve Grover wanted, and for the first time in his life, he wasn't interested.

In the den, he glanced at the number, dialed and worked his way past a receptionist and a secretary before being connected with Steve.

"McLean!" Steve nearly shouted. "I'd about given up on you. Thought you might have dropped off the face of the earth."

"Not yet," Colton said, a slow smile spreading over his

face as he pictured Steve Grover, a man of about five foot
eight, whip-thin and charged with energy. He would give
odds that even now Grover was pacing in his office, stretching the phone cord taut.

"Ready for a new assignment?"

"I could be," Colton evaded, propping one hip against the
desk and staring out the window to the ranch beyond. Playful
colts cavorted in one field while red-and-white Hereford
cattle lumbered in the next. "Where?"

"South Korea."

"When?"

"Yesterday."

Colton laughed. "I guess you should've called sooner."

"You're right." Grover let out a long breath. "All kidding
aside, the plane leaves Sunday night from Seattle."

"Seattle," Colton repeated, watching Cassie's white truck
pull into the side yard.

"Right. Direct to Seoul. We're sending a team. Knox,
Winston, Overgaard and you, if you'll go."

Colton watched as Cassie slid out of the cab, tugged on
her jean jacket, then hurried up the front walk. His heart
lurched, and he couldn't help but smile. "Sorry, I can't make
it," he said without even thinking.

"What?"

"Can't do it," he said again. "I've got some problems here
to tend to."

"But this might be the biggest story of the year. The stu-
dents are rioting, the militia's been called in and there's talk
of a North Korean offensive."

"Send someone else."

"But—"

"Talk to you later." Colton dropped the receiver, severing
the connection. His blood pumping, he strode straight to the
front door, opening it just as Cassie pushed the doorbell.

Folding his arms over his chest and leaning one shoulder

against the doorjamb, he drawled, "I didn't expect to see you again so soon."

Cassie tossed her hair away from her face. "I'm on my way home; I thought I'd see if Tempest was any better."

"About the same."

"And Black Magic?"

"He's a little improved," Colton said, taking her chilled fingers in his large hands. "Come on, you can take a look for yourself." He pulled her through the door, kicked it closed and walked along the hall toward the back of the house.

"Cassie!" Milly chimed as Colton led her through the kitchen. "You're just in time for dinner!"

"Not tonight—really," she said when she read the disappointment in Milly's eyes. "Another time."

"I'll hold you to it."

"Other plans?" Colton asked, one dark brow rising.

She didn't respond.

"Seriously, why not stay?" Colton asked. He had let go of her hand long enough to open the back door to the porch and start yanking on his boots.

Cassie's eyes narrowed. "Unfinished business."

Looking at Milly, Colton cocked his head in Cassie's direction and explained, "I insulted Cassie this morning."

"Did you?" Milly smothered a smile as she glanced from Colton to Cassie and back again. "Then I guess you'd better apologize and ask her to dinner."

A lazy smile tacked to his face, he drawled, "I just might."

Cassie's blood began to boil. How ingratiating! How absolutely conceited!

Milly lifted the lid of a pot on the stove. Spicy-scented steam filled the room. "Did you get hold of that Grover fella?"

Colton grunted as he pulled on his other boot. "I did."

"And?"

"And I told him I was too busy to hop the next jet to South Korea."

Cassie glanced up at him sharply. Was he serious? His responsibilities here superseded his need to live life on the edge? *That* would be a first.

"Come on," he insisted, reaching for her hand again. He held open the door as she slipped through. "There's another reason I decided to stay."

"Oh? And what was that?"

"A beautiful woman."

He heard her swift intake of breath, saw a glimmer of hope spark in her gray-green eyes. "I saw you getting out of the truck and I . . ." He let his voice trail off. Colton had never been good at making promises he wasn't sure he could keep. Nor did he believe in painting a rosy picture that might some-day dim.

Cassie angled her face up at him, her cheeks flushed from the cold, her expression serious. His hands felt so warm.

"Well, I guess you were right," he admitted. "There is some unfinished business between us. Lots of it."

"And you want to finish it?" she asked, doubting him, pulling away so she could think.

His eyelids lowered a fraction. "I don't think we can leave it as it is."

"Don't try to snow me, McLean," she said, remembering all too vividly the accusations that hung between them. Marching stiffly along the trail leading through the grass to the stable yard, she said, "I'm not as easily conned as I was when I was seventeen. Dad was right, you know. You McLeans are all cut from the same cloth!"

"I never conned you."

"Seemed that way." She reached the old foaling shed and grabbed for the door, but as she pulled on the latch, the flat of Colton's hand slammed the door back against its casing. Looking up so that her gaze collided with his, she thrust out her chin mutinously.

"Let's not get into all that, Cassie. What we're talking

about is the here and now. The reasons these horses are sick. That's all."

"And that includes insinuating that my father would intentionally cause an animal suffering and pain!" Her face burned with a simmering anger.

Colton's frustration was plain in his expression. "If it's any consolation, I don't think Ivan would hurt the animals."

"Not even to get back at you?" she taunted, unable to resist baiting him.

"Not even then."

"Good. Now all you've got to do is convince Denver."

And that won't be easy, Colton thought as he slid the latch away from the door and held it open.

Cassie stepped inside and was greeted by a soft nicker. "Look at you," she whispered, walking up to Black Magic and patting his nose. Turning her head, she grinned at Colton. "He's already better." But when she touched the swelling under his jaw, the horse flinched, snorting impatiently and tossing back his head. "Steady, boy, I didn't mean to hurt you."·

The shed was warm and dry. Fresh, sweet-smelling straw had been scattered over the floor, and Magic's box was filled with oats.

Tempest, however, hadn't improved. In fact, he looked worse. Whereas Black Magic's temperature was slowly falling, Tempest's continued to rise, and his nasal discharge was constant and opaque. "Has he eaten anything yet?" Cassie asked, already guessing the answer.

Colton shook his head. "Curtis has tried to get him to eat. So has Len. But it's a major battle just to force the antibiotics down his throat."

"Come on, boy," Cassie whispered, frowning a little. "You can do it."

The big sorrel didn't move, didn't so much as flick an ear in her direction. Patting his strong shoulder, she sent up a silent prayer for this horse and the rest of the McLean stock.

Together, she and Colton made the rounds again. One of the yearlings had started to cough, and Cassie ordered him isolated immediately. "It might be nothing more than a cold," she said, crossing her fingers as Curtis led the horse to a stall far from the others, "but we can't take any chances."

Curtis, Len and Daniel started the task of cleaning out the yearling's old stall, and Colton, more charming than usual, convinced Cassie to stay for dinner.

Later, he and Cassie walked to the broodmare barn and found Red Wing shifting anxiously, pawing at the straw.

"She's ready," Cassie said, keeping a watchful eye on Tessa's little mare. She leaned her elbows on the top rail of the stall and bent forward to get a closer look.

Colton stood behind her, so close she could feel the body heat radiating from him. "Maybe you should stick around," he suggested, his breath on her nape. "She might need you." He slipped his arms familiarly around Cassie's waist, linking them at her abdomen, pressing gently so that her hips rested against the firm saddle of his thighs.

Think, Cassie, she told herself, wishing she had the willpower to squirm away from him. But she didn't, and the tips of his thumbs gently pressing against the underside of her breasts caused a stirring deep inside her.

"I—I should go home."

"You told me your father never expects you."

"I do work odd hours, but—"

"But nothing. Stay here. The horses need you. And so do I."

She closed her eyes and swallowed against the huge, burning lump that suddenly filled her throat. "Colton, don't—"

"You said we had unfinished business."

"I didn't mean *this*!"

"But I did." How could she concentrate when his lips were hovering over her crown, his fingers splaying possessively across her abdomen, his warmth seeping through her clothes to caress her skin?

Gathering all her strength, she turned to face him. "So now you want me. Is that it?"

"Yes."

Her stomach fluttered and her heart pumped faster as she noticed the sexy slant of his mouth, the cocksure lift of his brows. *Cassie, use your head!* She forced her chin up, challenging him with her piercing gaze. "After all these years, all the heartache, all the misunderstandings and even this— this accusation of Denver's that my father was part of some insidious plot to destroy your livestock and your ranch—you want me?"

"Don't confuse me with my brother," he warned.

"And don't blame me *or my father* for something we didn't do!"

The corners of his mouth moved slightly, and she couldn't help but drop her gaze to the thin, sensual line of his lips that hid all-too-perfect teeth. Her heartbeat went wild; her breath fairly burst in her lungs as he tightened his arms around her, crushed her breasts against his chest and kissed her long and hard and lazily, as if they had all the time in the world.

Cassie closed her eyes, holding on to this one breathless instant and telling herself what had gone before didn't matter. His tongue slid between her teeth, and she welcomed its touch. All thoughts of denying him vanished.

Colton groaned, a deep primal sound that caused an answering moan from her. His hands moved up slowly, lifting, surrounding her breasts with a sweet, tortured reverence that nearly moved Cassie to tears. His thumbs stroked gently across her blouse. Her nipples hardened, the skin stretching tight, an ache forming deep in her center. "Stay, Cass," he whispered. "At least for a little while."

She wanted to say no. Deep in her heart she knew she

was making an irreversible mistake. "For a while," she agreed, and his lips moved hungrily over hers.

He lifted her from her feet and carried her to the far end of the barn. Still holding her, he switched off the lights and kicked open the gate to an empty stall. Fresh, sweet-smelling straw covered the floor.

Colton grabbed a clean blanket with one hand, dropped it over the straw and gently laid Cassie on the makeshift bed. "What if someone comes here?" she said, though her mind was fuzzy.

"No one will."

"But—"

"Shh. Milly's busy, and Curtis and the rest of the hands are in the fields. It's just you and me." Covering her mouth with his, he lay with her, his legs entwined with hers, his arms holding her tight against him.

Outside, the wind whispered through the trees. Cattle lowed, and a night bird called softly. The inside of the barn was warm; horses shifted and sighed, and Colton carefully lifted her sweater over her head.

In the half-light, Cassie stared up at him. No longer a naive girl of seventeen, she curled her hand around his neck and bent his head so that their lips could mesh. She sighed when he pushed the strap of her camisole off her shoulder.

His lips nibbled at the sculpted lace, and his tongue traced a sensual pattern against her skin. She shivered, but not from the cold. Anticipation caused tiny bumps to rise on her flesh. He warmed them with the caress of his tongue.

"Colton," she whispered, arching closer.

"I'm right here, love." He lifted his head and stared at her, and for an instant Cassie forgot about the pain of the past, forgot how he'd abandoned her, forgot that he'd sworn never to trust her again. "God, you're beautiful," he murmured, tucking his palms under her breasts and tenderly lifting them upward until both nipples peeked over the lace.

With a moan he took one little bud in his mouth and laved it with his tongue, lashing and flicking, causing Cassie's mind to spin, her breath to come in short gasps.

She wound her fingers in his hair, holding him close as he moved from one breast to the other, letting the night air cool the wet trail against her skin while he stoked a fire already raging through her blood.

Her hands moved of their own accord, tugging on his jacket and shoving it impatiently over his shoulders. Colton struggled out of it and flung it into a corner of the stall. It was quickly followed by his shirt, and she ran her fingers intimately over the hard, corded muscles of his chest and back. He kissed her again, his mouth molding over hers.

Strong and lean and sinewy, his hard body fit against her softer flesh. The mat of dark hair on his chest brushed and tickled her breasts. His dark, stubbled jaw prickled her cheeks.

His hands moved swiftly and without hesitation. Easily he unbuttoned her skirt and slid it, along with her pantyhose and panties down her legs, stripping her bare. Then, once she was lying naked in the straw, her breasts rising and falling as rapidly as her breath, he knelt above her, unbuckled his belt, slid the leather strap through the loops and let it drop.

Her throat was suddenly desert-dry, and their gazes touched, locked, ignited. With one deft movement he slid his jeans over his own hips and thighs.

Cassie had trouble swallowing. For years she'd dreamed of just this moment. Unashamed, she stared at him, his raw nakedness, the downy hair on his legs, the shadowy apex of his legs.

Teeth sinking into her lip, she watched as he lazily lay over her, his weight settling comfortably against her, his skin fusing with hers.

"This is the time to say no," he said, swallowing, his voice deep and husky, one hand slowly running from her rib cage to her ankle and back again. "Stop me before it's too late."

"I . . . I don't want to," she admitted.

His gaze shifted to her face, then to the darkened corners of the huge room. "Oh, Cass," he murmured, his hands twining in her cloud of dark curls, his face twisted into a tortured expression. "Why couldn't I ever forget you?"

"Probably for the same reason I couldn't forget you."

His lips crashed down on hers, and there was no turning back. Their tongues met and danced while they explored, caressed and teased with their hands. She traced the scars on his shoulder; he trailed his fingers along the curve of her spine, and a dewy sheen of sweat melded his body to hers.

The ache within her stretched wide as his manhood brushed against her abdomen and thighs, teasing, titillating, driving any last-minute doubts from her mind.

Balanced on his elbows, he held her face between his hands and stared down at her flushed, sweat-dampened face. "I love you, Cass," he admitted, his eyes burning bright with passion. "I always have."

Tears sprang to her eyes. His buttocks flexed, and he entered her, thrusting long and hard into the aching emptiness only he could ever fill.

Cassie's breath escaped in a rush. As he moved, she moved, too, her body responding to his rhythm, her mind void of all but this one, virile man.

"Cassie, oh, love," he whispered over and over as his tempo quickened, his thrusts driving deeper.

Blood thundered through her head, and brilliant sparks of gold and red flashed in her eyes. She convulsed, her nails biting into his back.

"I can't—hold back . . ." And he didn't. In a powerful explosion that was answered only by her own, he fell on her, his muscles straining, his voice crying out her name lustily.

Collapsing on her, his heart thudding as wildly as her own, Colton held her close. The edge of his hairline was damp, his breathing hard and fast.

Cassie wound her arms and legs around him, wishing she never had to let him go—and knowing that she would. Colton McLean wasn't a man to be tied down, and she wasn't fool enough to think she would change him. She fought a losing battle with tears and kissed him over and over again— afraid she'd never get another chance.

Chapter Eleven

Cassie had nearly fallen asleep when she felt Colton's muscles tense. Instinctively she clung to him. "Mmm. What's wrong?" she murmured, then stretched languidly.

"Nothing," he whispered, kissing her crown and levering up on one elbow. The barn was dark, but even so, she knew he was squinting, listening.

She heard it, too. A horse's low painful moan. *Tessa's mare! Red Wing!* Instantly awake, she scrambled into her clothes, shook the straw from her hair and fumbled for the light switch. Colton found it first, snapping it on. Harsh illumination flooded the huge room, accompanied by the nickers, snorts and whinnies of the other horses.

Tucking her sweater into the band of her skirt, Cassie hurried to Red Wing's stall. Inside, the mare was laboring, her breathing rapid, her eyes wide. Cassie reached for the latch of the stall gate.

Red Wing's water broke in a gush, filling the air with the scent of birthing.

Here we go, Cassie thought, her hands on the gate. If Red Wing could deliver alone, Cassie wouldn't offer any help. "Calm down, girl."

But Red Wing, her ears flicking nervously, eyes bulging and sweat darkening her coat, moved nervously. Veins stood out beneath her glossy hide. She shuddered with the next contraction.

"Come on, Red Wing, easy now," Cassie coaxed. Still, Red Wing paced restlessly. Cassie felt Colton beside her. "I'll need clean towels, water and iodine," she said softly as Red Wing moaned again. Cassie opened the gate and slipped into the stall. Gently, careful of Red Wing's shifting hindquarters, Cassie examined her. "Steady, girl." Part of the amniotic sac was visible, and gently, Cassie probed at the big white balloon. She found the foal's nose and one foot. Only one. Not good.

"Here you go," Colton said softly, hauling the towels and water bucket into the stall.

"I'll need your help."

"Problems?"

"One foot is twisted back on itself," she said, trying to keep the worry from her voice. "This way it won't fit through the birth canal. We'll have to push the foal back in, straighten the leg and then help it out."

Colton rolled up his sleeves. "Just tell me what to do."

Gently, so as not to break the umbilical cord or the sac, Cassie nudged the foal backward, then eased the bent foot forward. The entire procedure took only a few minutes, but it felt like a lifetime. Fortunately Red Wing didn't lash out with teeth or hooves.

"Okay, now . . ." She guided Colton's hand. "Now, when the mare contracts again, pull down, gently of course, to help the foal out."

He glanced her way. "Got it." The next contraction ripped through the mare a second later, and both Cassie and Colton tugged on the tiny legs until the feet and head were free. An instant later Red Wing moaned painfully, and another contraction pushed the foal's shoulders through. Once the shoulders were out, the rest of the foal slid to the floor in a rush of birthing fluid.

The umbilical cord broke. Cassie quickly ripped open the sac and cleaned out the colt's nose. "Come on, breathe," she whispered, trying to infuse life into the tiny horse.

As Red Wing hadn't yet claimed her foal by licking it, Colton grabbed a towel and began rubbing its wet sides. The little horse's eyelids and lips were blue. "Come on, come on," Cassie begged, waiting for the colt to breathe as she slipped her hand beneath its nose and felt the first warm rush of breath from its lungs. The foal's small ribs expanded, its huge eyes blinked open curiously, and Cassie wanted to shout with joy. "Isn't he beautiful?" she cried, reaching for the iodine and dousing the colt's umbilical stump.

Red Wing snorted, eyeing the dark, straw-flecked, spindly legged bundle.

"Watch out," Cassie warned. Colton jumped before Red Wing's teeth found his back. "I think Mama wants to take over."

He flashed her a quick grin. "Good. Let her. I don't think I'm much of a midwife." He moved out of the mare's range.

"Oh, I don't know, McLean," she teased, unable to stop smiling over the lump swelling in her throat. "For a man who swears he hates anything to do with ranching, you did a fair job."

"I'll take that as a compliment."

"It was meant as one." She glimpsed at him from the corner of her eye. His shirt still open, Colton fastened his gaze on mare and foal. Virile and tough, yet tender and caring—no wonder she'd never stopped loving him. Quickly Cassie worked on the mare, making sure that eventually all the afterbirth would fall from the mare naturally.

Ignoring Cassie, Red Wing washed her new charge with her tongue, stimulating the colt's circulation and cleaning him. She nudged him with her huge head, nickering softly, urging him up on spindly legs that refused to hold him.

He would struggle upright only to fall in a cross-legged heap or to land on his head.

"He could use a few ballet lessons," Colton said.

"Maybe you should name him Misha."

They stepped out of the stall and washed as best they could. Colton chuckled. "I'll tell Tessa when she gets back."

"Do." She didn't pull away when Colton's arm surrounded her, and yet she felt suddenly awkward. There were still tremendous hurdles between them. Denver's accusations for starters. Did Denver really think her father could be a part of such a heinous crime as deliberately infecting Black Magic with a virus? Once that was cleared up, which she was sure would happen soon, then there was still Colton's need for danger and thirst for faraway places, while she belonged here. And the past—there was always that black cloud threatening to spill over them. Had Colton really put it to rest?

The little colt nuzzled his mother's flank and finally found his first meal. A huge smile spread across Colton's square jaw, and he hugged Cassie even tighter. "Finally!" he muttered.

"Tessa will be proud."

"She should be." He glanced down at her, and the kindness shining in his flinty eyes received an answering grin. "You, Ms. Aldridge, are a first-class mess."

"I am?"

To prove his point, he plucked a piece of straw from her hair. Cassie stared down at her clothes, ruined with blood and amniotic fluid. "I guess you're right."

"How about a shower?" he suggested, his eyelashes lowering seductively.

"Not a chance." But she laughed, imagining a rush of water tumbling over Colton's bare skin and thick, dark hair.

"Why not?"

"Oh, I can think of about a dozen reasons. Let's start with Curtis, Len, Daniel, Milly—"

"I already told you the hands are busy, and we could have Milly run an errand to town."

"No way." But she giggled.

"It could be fun."

His gaze delved into hers, and she suddenly felt as if a tight leather strap had been placed around her chest, making it impossible to breathe. Her stomach trembled. "You're positively wicked, Colton McLean."

"One of my most endearing qualities."

As the foal suckled and a few of the other horses nickered softly, Cassie was caught in the magnetism of Colton's eyes. "I, uh, think we'd better find Curtis," she said. "He'll want to see Red Wing's new foal. And then I think I'd better go home."

Colton leaned a shoulder against the rough boards of the wall. His jaw slid to the side. "Afraid?" he asked.

"Of what?"

"Of me?"

"No!"

"Of us?"

"There is no 'us.' There never was. Remember?" Her heart pounded crazily, and the atmosphere in the barn became even more intimate.

"No us—then what was that a little while ago?"

"Passion."

"So you're afraid of passion."

"No!"

"Then why not stay?"

She gulped, her mind spinning. All these years she'd wanted to be with him, and now her emotions were stretched taut. Their relationship had gathered the steam of a freight train running out of control. "You're the one who so graciously pointed out what a mess I am," she said, not ready to tackle the more serious issues.

"You could change here. Wear something of Tessa's. Or"—his voice lowered—"something of mine." He slid a sizzling glance her way.

"I'd look pretty silly in a Stetson, leather jacket and Levi's." Shaking her head, she said, "Thanks for the offer, but I don't think so. I've—I've got to get home."

"Why? Ivan's not expecting you."

Ramming his hands into the back pockets of his jeans, he focused an intense gaze on her and crossed the small space separating them. "Things have changed between us, Cass."

"Have they?" She thought about making wonderful love to him in the straw, and blushed like a schoolgirl. "Yes, I suppose they have." She began to twist her fingers in the folds of her skirt, and she mentally shook herself, kept her hands steady and tilted her face to his. "So where do we go from here?"

"I wish I knew." As if unable to help himself, he cupped her determined chin. Her skin quivered, and she knew that if she didn't leave now, she wouldn't be able to.

"So do I," she admitted, stepping away, needing time and space to think. Years ago she'd rushed things, chased him with all the foolishness of a teenage girl in the throes of puppy love, and she wasn't about to play the fool again—not even for Colton.

"Are you going to the Edwards's party?" he asked as she reached the door.

"I have to. Command performance."

He smiled at her irreverence. "Would you go with me?"

"I'd like it very much," she admitted.

"Then I'll pick you up at seven."

Nodding, she pushed open the door and called over her shoulder, "I'll see you later."

"You can count on it."

She climbed into her pickup and glanced at her reflection

in the rearview mirror. Twinkling hazel eyes returned her stare, and her heart pounded crazily in her chest. Time and distance wouldn't matter much, she realized, because, like it or not, she was in love.

She didn't see Colton for two days. Though she dropped by the ranch several times to check on Black Magic and Tempest, she never caught a glimpse of Denver McLean's younger brother. Milly explained that he had "business in town," Curtis was evasive but polite, and Cassie couldn't help thinking that Colton might be trying to give her a hint. Had the love they'd shared been a mistake—just like before?

Though wounded, she hid her feelings and went about her job. Black Magic was recovering well. His temperature had dropped to normal and his abscess had matured. Cassie drained the abscess, then cleaned the cavity with a mild antiseptic solution. Black Magic didn't like her ministrations much and tried to nip her.

Tempest seemed to have turned the corner, but his recovery was much slower than Black Magic's, and the yearling was following the path of Tempest. Cassie was worried about those two horses because of the threat of complications such as pneumonia or, more rarely, abscesses in the internal organs. She crossed her fingers as she left the old foaling shed and started for her pickup. Unwittingly she scanned the near-empty yard for Colton's Jeep.

Was he avoiding her? He hadn't called, nor stopped by. Maybe he regretted making love to her. And perhaps his change of heart was for the best.

Frowning, she drove home and parked near the garage, wedging her truck into the small space left between Vince Monroe's pickup and Ryan Ferguson's motorcycle.

She wasn't in the mood to face either of the two men, but

she had no choice, she supposed, as she climbed out of the cab. Erasmus streaked out of the kitchen, yipping at the sight of her and bounding across the yard. He jumped up, placed huge muddy paws against her skirt and barked.

"It's good to see you, too," Cassie said, eyeing the dirty streaks on her skirt. "Come on, let's see what's going on."

With Erasmus bounding at her heels, Cassie climbed the back steps and shoved open the door. Inside, the men had gathered around the kitchen table. Newspapers, coffee cups and ashtrays covered the scarred surface. Smoke drifted to the ceiling, and all conversation stopped abruptly. Three sets of eyes turned toward her, and she felt as if she, in the very house where she'd grown up, was an intruder.

"Am I interrupting?" she asked, and her father waved her question aside.

"'Course not."

Vince Monroe cast her a cursory glance. "Evening, Cassie," he drawled, scraping back his chair and standing.

Always the gentleman, Cassie thought uneasily, noticing that Ryan hadn't bothered getting to his feet. Not that she cared. His eyes followed her, and he inclined his head, though he didn't move the one booted foot propped against her favorite chair. A cigarette dangled from the corner of his mouth, and smoke curled lazily over his head. His helmet sat on the floor next to him, and an insolent smile curved his lips.

A tense undercurrent charged the room. Cassie forced a playful grin in an effort to lighten the mood. "What is this?" she asked. "An old hens' meeting?"

Ivan laughed, Vince guffawed, and Ryan's dark eyes glinted.

"Yeah, that's what it is." Ryan finally lifted his foot and kicked the chair toward her. "Except that it's an old roosters' meeting. We could use a hen or two. Join us," he invited.

Ivan's smile fell from his face, and he sent Ferguson a warning glare.

"I can't," she said, glancing toward her father. "I've got to get ready. You, too."

"For?"

"Nate and Paula's party."

"Oh, that." Ivan shook his head and glowered at the thought of the Edwards's annual event. "I'm not going."

"Why not? Nate's one of your friends."

"I know, I know. But I got things to do," her father said gruffly. "I think Sylvia's going to foal tonight." Sylvia was her father's favorite mare—the best on the ranch. "But you go along. McLean called. Said he'd take you."

Cassie's heart somersaulted joyously. So he hadn't been avoiding her! But still, that didn't explain her father's change of heart. Or did it?

Vince drained his coffee cup. "It's time I was rollin' along," he remarked, stretching his big arms. "Otherwise the wife'll be callin'." He snatched his huge, gray Stetson and stuffed it onto his head, walked to the door, then paused, as if he'd had a sudden thought. His eyes found Cassie's, and the pale blue orbs glittered a bit. "So how're things at the McLean Ranch—those horses of his getting any better?"

"Much," Cassie replied, experiencing a sudden chill. Vince Monroe had always made her uncomfortable, but this evening the feeling was even stronger. "Black Magic should be good as new in a few weeks, and the others—well, they're coming along."

"Good," Monroe said gruffly. "Helluva thing that strangles. McLean's lucky no more than a few horses got it."

"I don't think he's feeling very lucky about it," Cassie said, eyeing the older man warily.

"All a part of ranching. The bad part. Good night, Aldridge."

He squared his hat, exchanged glances with the other men and strode outside.

Ryan took a final drag on his cigarette and snatched up his helmet. "I've got to be shovin' off, too." His sultry gaze touched Cassie's before he stubbed out the butt and glanced at Ivan. "I'll see you in the morning."

Ivan nodded. "If I'm not here, I'll probably be with the mares. My guess is that Sylvia won't wait too long."

"I thought she wasn't due for a couple of weeks," Cassie said.

"She isn't, but you try and tell her that," her father joked, though his eyes didn't sparkle as they usually did.

"Later," Ryan called over his shoulder as the door banged shut behind him.

"Do you want me to stay?" she asked.

"Nope. Go along. I'll handle things here." Glancing down at his hands, he scratched one finger nervously across his thumb.

"I thought you were going to Nate's party."

Ivan scowled, his forehead creasing. "You know how I feel about gettin' all dressed up."

"It can be fun," she said, remembering Sandy's words and feeling like a hypocrite. Before Colton's invitation, Cassie hadn't been looking forward to the party, either.

"It's a pain in the butt."

"Since when?" she asked, knowing how her father loved a few drinks, a dance or two and a chance to see all his friends gathered together.

"Since that mule-headed mare decided to deliver."

"Or since I decided to go with Colton," she prodded, feeling there was more to it than he was admitting.

Ivan made a face. "As you're so fond of tellin' me, it's your life. It goes without sayin' how I feel about you going anywhere with Colton McLean. It was all I could do not to hang up on the bastard today—but I didn't. Because of you."

"Thanks."

He bit the corner of his mouth. "I don't suppose I can change your mind?"

"Not a chance."

He sighed and turned his gaze to the table. He clamped his jaw hard, and a muscle worked furiously at the side of his neck. "I can't give you any more advice, Cassie. Even if I did, you're too stubborn to listen. But just"—at a sudden loss for words, he shook his head—"don't rush into anything you can't get out of."

"I won't," she promised, wondering if being careful where Colton was concerned was possible and knowing in her heart that it didn't matter.

Glaring at his reflection in the hallway mirror, wondering if he'd had one sane thought since making love to Cassie, Colton tugged at the impossible knot of his tie.

He hadn't talked to her in two days, and it hadn't been his choice. He'd known she wanted breathing room and, because he'd felt the same way years before, he'd given it to her.

He twisted his head, loosening the knot. His fingers were sweaty as he thought about the evening stretching out before him. Tonight Colton planned to enjoy every second of Cassie's company. He'd even managed to talk to her father on the phone and keep his temper in check. Hurdle number one. There was just one more: Denver.

Colton heard the old truck rattle up the drive, and he braced himself. Denver had called last night with the news that he and Tessa would be arriving today. Curtis had left several hours earlier to pick them up at the airport. And now they were back.

Colton wasn't looking forward to confronting Denver, but

he didn't have much choice. With a last scowl at the tie, he ripped it from around his neck and hurried downstairs and through the back door.

Before Curtis could crank on the emergency brake, Denver sprang from the cab and helped Tessa, her pregnancy in full bloom, from the truck.

They made a striking couple, Colton decided. Denver, tall and broad-shouldered with raven-black hair and piercing blue eyes, and Tessa, her hair a vibrant red-gold, billowing behind her, her skin tanned, the bridge of her nose dusted with a smattering of freckles. Together, fingers linked, they dashed up the path.

Colton tensed. His relationship with his older brother had always been volatile. Though they respected each other, and probably would defend each other to the death, there was always a keen sense of competition between them—a love-hate relationship that had mellowed only slightly over the years. Their pride and hot tempers often got in the way of their common sense.

Tessa dashed up to her brother-in-law and gave him a fierce hug. "Dad said Red Wing foaled the other night!" she cried, her hazel eyes bright. "A colt! Brigadier's first! I can't wait to see him!" She turned her eager face up to her husband's. "Come on."

Denver looked about to argue, but the delight so evident on her face must have changed his mind. "Can't it wait?"

"No! Denver, come on! You know how important this is!"

"Yeah, I know," Denver said with a half smile. "Let's check him out."

Tessa was already heading toward the brood mare barn, striding ahead of her father and the two McLean brothers. Inside, in a large, straw-covered stall, Red Wing guarded the gangly bay colt. His eyes were round and wide, his nostrils flared, his ears twitching nervously.

Red Wing, usually calm and friendly, placed her body squarely between the intruders and her foal. Her ears flattened to her head, and she eyed everyone, including Tessa, suspiciously.

"Look at him," Tessa cried, fairly glowing. "'He's gorgeous."

Curtis laughed. "You wouldn't have thought so if you'd been here when he was born."

Colton's guts twisted at the memory, and his vivid recollection of that night, lying in the straw, filled with the scent and feel of Cassie . . .

"Good thing Cassie was here," Curtis rambled on, and Denver shot his brother a killing glance. "This little guy was all twisted up, one foot caught back. Cassie had to help Red Wing out."

"I should've been here," Tessa said, staring guiltily at the inquisitive colt. Peeking from behind his mother's rump, he stretched his long neck and blinked. "He's perfect!"

Her father hugged her shoulders. "That he is, gal."

"It worked out," Colton replied. He glanced to the far wall and the box stall where he'd spent nearly an hour in the delicious rapture of Cassie Aldridge. His insides melted. Just at the thought of their lovemaking, he felt his passion surge.

Jamming a fist into his pocket, he shifted, ignoring the lofty lift of one of Denver's dark brows.

Denver pinned Curtis with a cool glance. "So now you're a fan of Cassie Aldridge?"

"The girl knows her stuff," Curtis said.

"And her father?"

He snorted. "Him I could live without."

"Enough," Tessa insisted. "Let's not spoil all this." She slipped into the box.

"I don't know if this is such a good idea," Denver said, turning his attention on his wife, but, as usual, when it came to horses, she ignored him and stroked Red Wing's soft muzzle.

"It's okay," Tessa said, either to Denver or to the horse. Colton couldn't tell which.

Denver's gaze slid to his brother, and he eyed Colton's suit. "Going somewhere?"

"To Nate and Paula Edwards's party. You're invited, too."

Tessa gasped. "I'd forgotten all about it!"

Denver frowned at his pregnant wife. "It's been a long day—"

"Don't you try to weasel out of it," she warned, eyeing him over her shoulder. "I promised Paula months ago!"

Denver's scowl deepened. "I thought pregnant women were supposed to slow down."

She laughed gaily. "Well, I guess you thought wrong. Paula's pregnant, too, you know."

Colton couldn't swallow the smile that pulled on the corners of his mouth. He loved watching Tessa bully Denver. No one else had ever been able to tell his mule-headed brother anything, but Tessa, half his size and as clever as a fox, had managed to wrap Denver McLean around her little finger.

Denver, disconcerted, sighed. "Maybe we should look at the other animals. How's Black Magic?"

"Better. But Tempest's just not snapping out of it as quickly," Curtis muttered, running a leathery hand around his neck and squinting thoughtfully. "Why don't you two get changed, have a cup of Milly's coffee, then we'll take a look?"

"Let's just do it now," Denver said impatiently.

Tessa could barely tear herself away from Red Wing and the new foal, but Denver convinced her.

Inside the old foaling shed, Denver studied Black Magic, Tempest and the buckskin yearling, who was improving, though slowly.

Tessa's face fell, her expression becoming dark. "Denver thinks this happened when Black Magic was stolen," she said, her fingers gripping the top rail of the stall so tightly her knuckles blanched white.

Colton whispered, "So do I."

She glanced up at him, then to Denver, who was talking with Curtis at the far end of the shed, near Tempest's stall. "But he thinks someone did it on purpose."

"You don't?"

"I can't imagine it. Hurting innocent animals to get back at us?" She shook her head, and her hair shone pure gold under the artificial lights. "No way. No one around here is that mean."

"I hope you're right," Colton said, glancing to where Denver stood staring in frustration at Tempest. Grim lines creased Denver's forehead, and his fists had curled angrily. "I hope to God you're right."

Chapter Twelve

By the time Colton knocked on the front door, Cassie had already been waiting fifteen minutes. She flew down the stairs, the skirt of her silk dress billowing behind her like a trailing scarlet cloud.

At the door she paused, took in a long, steadying breath, then turned the knob.

Colton stood under the porch light. His dark hair gleamed, and he looked totally uncomfortable in a dark gray suit, starched white shirt and crimson tie. If not for the jaded glint in his eyes and the cynical twist of his lips, she might not have believed this dashing man to be the irreverent rogue of her dreams.

"Are you ready for this?" he asked, crossing his arms over his chest as he surveyed her from head to toe.

"As ready as I'll ever be," she quipped, though a nervous knot tightened in her stomach as she reached in the closet for her long black coat. She felt self-conscious with her hair twined away from her face in delicate French braids, her silk dress much more sophisticated than any she'd ever owned, her impractical high-heeled shoes.

Outside, the spring night was warm. A warm wind stole

through the shadows, rushing around the corners of the buildings and soughing through the trees. Stars winked brightly, and beams from a half-moon washed the earth in blue-gray incandescence.

"Don't you have to say goodbye to your father?" Colton asked.

She shook her head. "Already did."

"He's not going? I thought every rancher in a four-county area was invited."

Cassie settled one shoulder against the passenger door. "He's staying with Sylvia, who's due to drop her foal anytime."

Colton didn't respond as he drove onto the main highway and turned west. They rode in silence until the Edwards's ranch came into view. One of the largest spreads in the state, Nate Edwards's ranch sprawled as far as the eye could see. The house, a plantation-style home that looked as if it belonged in Virginia, stood in stark relief against the black night. With white siding, brick facing, bow windows and blue shutters, the Edwards's home rose three full stories and was ablaze with lights. Cars, pickups and four-wheel drive rigs lined the circular drive.

"I guess I'd better warn you," Colton said as he parked, "Denver and Tessa got home today. They'll be here."

Though she felt a nervous jolt at the thought of meeting Colton's judgmental older brother, she tossed her head. "Why the warning?"

"Denver can be—"

"I know how Denver can be," she shot back. "A lot like you." With a sweet smile, she opened her side of his Jeep and stepped outside. She heard Colton's chuckle and pretended that her nerves weren't stretched tight.

Colton caught up with her on the brick steps just as she rang the bell. Laughter and conversation sifted through the closed windows.

Colton tucked his arm around her waist. "You know," she said, hearing footsteps approaching, "I thought you were avoiding me."

"Never." He squeezed her, and she couldn't help but grin.

"You haven't been around the ranch lately."

"Because of Denver. I had to talk to his attorney in Helena and get a few things ready . . . besides," he glanced down at her, and the hand against the small of her back felt suddenly warm, "I thought you wanted a little time to think things through."

"I did—"

The door flew open, and Paula Edwards, her red hair piled high on her head, abdomen protruding roundly, waved them inside. "Colton and Cassie! Come in, come in. Here, Nate, take Cassie's coat."

A burly, muscular man whose dark hair was shot with gray, Nate Edwards was fifteen years older than his young wife. He sported a gold-capped tooth and a recently added mustache. Wearing a western-cut suit and string tie, he reached for Cassie's coat and hung it in the closet. "How're things going?" he asked Colton.

"Better. Denver got back today."

"So now you can take off again, eh?" Nate asked, clapping Colton on the back. "You never were one to sit around much."

Colton slid a heart-stopping glance to Cassie. "Maybe I've changed."

"Sure you have," Nate agreed with a throaty chuckle. "I'll believe that when palm trees sprout in the Rockies. Come on in and let me buy you a drink." He led them into a huge living room where other guests mingled and sipped from tulip-shaped glasses. Quiet conversation was muted by the sound of music drifting from an adjoining room.

"Champagne or Scotch?"

Colton glanced sideways at his host.

"Scotch," Nate decided, taking his place as bartender at a

mirrored bar and pouring Cassie a glass of champagne. He handed them their respective drinks, then tugged at the strings surrounding his throat. "Damned things. I don't know why Paula insists we dress up."

"It's just her way of keeping you in line," Cassie teased, sipping from her glass.

"I s'pose. Sure is a bother, though." Nate poured himself a stiff shot and took a swallow. "Sorry to hear about all your trouble with Black Magic. A damned shame, that's what it is. Lost twice in two years and now strangles. Sometimes ranchin' can be a real bitch." He shook his head and smoothed his hair.

Cassie stiffened, expecting Colton to argue about the horse being stolen, instead he just nodded affably, though his jaw was clamped tight.

The doorbell pealed, and Nate, catching Paula's eye, finished his drink quickly. "Duty calls," he muttered, sauntering toward the foyer and leaving Colton and Cassie in a room crowded with neighboring ranchers and townspeople.

Cassie knew almost everyone. She smiled and waved, made small talk and mingled. Colton didn't leave her for a minute. More than a few people glanced their way, and some of the ranchers' smiles seemed forced. She felt hateful undercurrents in the air.

Matt Wilkerson's lips had flattened at the sight of Colton, and Vince Monroe's smile had fallen from his face.

Then Cassie saw Jessica Monroe sliding Colton secretive glances.

Jessica's blond hair spilled over her shoulders in luxurious waves, and her white satin-and-lace dress seemed almost bridal. She sipped champagne, giggled and kept her arm looped through Ryan Ferguson's, though her gaze wandered over the crowd and lingered on Colton. Colton didn't seem to notice.

"Cassie!" Beth Simpson waved from the far side of the

room. She'd already kicked off her shoes and was seated in an apricot-colored velvet chair. Her dress, a billowing amber-and-yellow print, spilled over her distended belly.

Glad to see a friendly face, Cassie waved back and wound her way through the knots of people to her friend. "I thought you were supposed to be in the hospital," she said, remembering the gossip she'd heard in town. "What're you doing here?"

"Waiting for my water to break," Beth grumbled. "I did go into County General, but it was false labor. I felt like a fool, too, since this"—she tapped her abdomen—"isn't my first."

"Well, you fit right in," Cassie observed just as Denver and Tessa walked into the room. Tessa looked absolutely radiant. Her face was glowing; her strawberry-blond hair shimmered under the dimmed lights. "It looks like we've got an epidemic of pregnant ladies," she joked.

Beth laughed, but Cassie's eyes were drawn to Colton's older brother. Denver was as handsome as ever. Even though he'd suffered several plastic surgeries after the fire, he was as ruggedly good-looking as Colton. He never left Tessa's side as they wended through the crowd.

A few faces turned his way, and a few people exchanged meaningful glances. Ryan Ferguson noticed him and stopped dancing with Jessica. Hatred seemed to radiate from his body, and he took a step forward, but Jessica's hand restrained him.

Denver didn't seem to notice.

Tessa spied Colton and Cassie and, dragging her recalcitrant husband behind her, made a beeline across the room. Colton shifted closer to Cassie, keeping one arm around her waist as Tessa joined them. "I can't thank you enough," she said breathlessly, her hazel eyes shining on Cassie. "Dad says you single-handedly delivered Red Wing's colt."

"Not so single-handedly. Red Wing did all the work, and Colton helped."

"Did you?" Tessa arched one fine brow at her brother-in-law.

"I just took orders," Colton clarified.

"That I'd like to see!" Tessa said, giggling as Denver, standing behind her, wrapped possessive arms around her thick waist.

"I guess I owe you, too," Denver conceded, though he didn't smile and his blue eyes were dead serious. "You managed to save Black Magic and a couple of others."

"We all did." Cassie started to relax, but she felt Colton's muscles stiffen. "Hopefully you won't have any other cases."

Denver's eyes narrowed. "What about the other ranchers in the valley. Has anyone else had a problem?"

Cassie bristled, taking the hint. "None that I know of." When Denver didn't seem convinced, she added, "Craig and I talked about it—since strangles is so contagious. He's afraid that Black Magic linked up with some wild horses who have the disease."

"Just let me know if you hear of any other cases," Denver said before Tessa sent him a killing look.

"You, husband dear, have a one-track mind. Cassie didn't come here to discuss her work and, except to thank her for helping out at our ranch, neither did I. Let's dance."

"Good idea," Colton added as Tessa linked her fingers with her husband's. She led Denver toward an adjoining room that had been cleared of furniture. The oak floor had been polished to a golden shine, and a few couples were gliding over the gleaming parquet.

"No dancing for me," Beth said as Colton cupped Cassie's elbow.

Cassie chuckled despite Denver's pointed remarks. "Maybe

it's just what you need to convince that baby to come into the world."

"The baby's not the problem," Beth replied as her husband, balancing two platters of food joined them, "my feet are!"

"Come on," Colton whispered into Cassie's ear. He tugged on her arm and guided her through a wide arch. Folding her expertly into his arms, he held her close, moving to the soft strains of a slow tune. Other couples swirled around them, but Colton didn't seem to notice. "If I haven't said it before, you look sensational."

"Thanks." She colored under his compliment and felt the warm whisper of his breath against her bare nape. "I feel ridiculous."

"Why?"

"This"—she looked down at her dress—"is out of character for me."

"You can't run around in jeans and lab coats all the time."

"Oh, and you're comfortable?" She arched her black brows, daring him to lie.

"As long as you're in my arms," he shot back, his steely eyes glinting wickedly.

"Where'd you read that?"

"I didn't. I saw it in some movie."

"Figures." She laughed, and they danced together, oblivious of the crowd or anything but each other. Colton swirled her and held her, and she forgot the hostility she'd felt when they'd first joined the party.

Laughing, she danced with him, held him, felt his lips press kisses against her hair until she thought she would drop. "I think we could use a break," he murmured against her ear.

"Amen."

"Would you like something to drink?"

She nodded and started to follow him to the bar, when she spied Craig talking with a tall, slender man she didn't recognize. Craig had one hand tucked in the pockets of his slacks, the other wrapped around a half-filled old fashioned glass. He caught her eye and waved her over.

Without waiting for Colton, she skirted the dancing couples and joined the two men. "Wonderful party," she said, smiling. "I'm glad you talked me into coming."

Craig chuckled. "Maybe next time I won't have to put a gun to your head."

Rolling her eyes, Cassie conceded, "Okay, okay. I was wrong."

"Now that that's settled, I'd like you to meet a friend of mine." He indicated the tall, slender man next to him. "This is Frank Belmont—Dr. Frank Belmont. We went to school together. Frank's got a clinic downstate. Cassie works with me— I think she plans to buy me out in the next couple of years."

Cassie smiled. "Maybe around 2030 when you're ready to retire."

"I'll keep you to it." He swirled his drink and sobered. "Frank saw another case of strangles a few weeks ago," he said.

Cassie's eyes flew to the other man. "Where?"

The two men exchanged glances. "Around here," Craig explained. "One of Vince Monroe's mares. She was quarantined."

"But why didn't he call us . . ." she asked, already knowing the answer. Then they would have known that Vince had been involved in Black Magic's disappearance. An odd mixture of relief and fear coursed through her. Relief that Vince Monroe was most likely the culprit and fear that her father was involved. He and Vince had become thick as thieves lately. Her stomach turned over.

"I asked Vince about it earlier," Craig said, frowning into his drink.

"And?"

"He said he'd called, couldn't get through and stopped by but we were closed. He knew Frank and called him."

"We have an emergency number," Cassie pointed out.

"I know."

Cassie searched the room, but the towering form of Vince Monroe wasn't in sight. "Where is he?"

Craig lifted a shoulder. "Maybe he already left. It is getting late."

"Speaking of which, I'd better get going," Frank said. "It's a long drive home."

Cassie spied Colton leaning against the bar, his tie loose, his eyes filled with amusement as he stared at her. He hooked a finger in her direction and held up a tall glass of champagne.

Her heart turned over as she moved through the groups of people, and she wanted nothing more than to tell him about Vince Monroe, but she couldn't, not until she had more substantial proof. She wasn't going to accuse anyone before her facts were straight. If Colton had taught her anything eight years ago, it was to listen to all sides before hurling accusations.

"Talking shop?" he asked once she was close enough to hear.

"Umm." She accepted the glass from his hand and didn't protest when he wrapped one arm around her.

"Well, enough of that," he whispered in her ear, sending delicious tingling sensations down her spine. "We have more important things to do."

"Such as?"

"You'll see," he said mysteriously, and Cassie silently agreed. She had lots to do. As Colton took her hand and pulled her toward the dance floor, she spied Jessica Monroe leaving with Ryan Ferguson, and she wondered if Jessica or Ryan or both were involved with Vince. Or—worse yet— her father.

Hours later, when the guests began to leave, Cassie found Paula and thanked her, while Colton located her coat and slipped it over her shoulders. The tips of his fingers grazed her bare arms, and she shivered a little.

Outside, the night was surprisingly warm. Only a few clouds dared creep across the moon. A mild breeze caught in Cassie's hair and snatched at her skirt as she hurried to the Jeep.

She'd barely settled into the passenger seat when Colton started the rig. "It's too early to take you home," he announced.

"It's nearly midnight."

"Like I said—too early." Flashing a devilish grin, he cranked the wheel and the Jeep roared toward the main highway.

"Don't tell me, you're kidnapping me again."

"Nope."

"Then where are we going?"

"Somewhere we should've gone a long time ago," he replied. His voice had grown deep, his gaze thoughtful.

"And where's that?"

"The lake."

Her heart nearly stopped beating. Vivid memories haunted her—memories of making love with Colton, of cold water and a brilliant summer day, of the scent of pine mingled with the musky odor of sweat and of their sweet, precious day being ruined by Denver McLean astride a rangy bay gelding. "There's no road to the lake."

"Then we'll ride."

"Ride? You mean ride *horses*—like this?" she cried, glancing down at her dress, but couldn't help giggling at his wonderful sense of the ridiculous. She considered telling him about Vince Monroe's horse, but didn't—there was time later. For a while she didn't want anything to come between them. And until she had her facts straight, there wasn't much she could do.

"Why not?" he asked.

"If you don't know, I couldn't begin to tell you."

Colton laughed and yanked off his tie as the Jeep tore down the highway toward the McLean Ranch.

"You're out of your mind!"

"So you've told me." He guided the car up the lane leading to the house, parked in the yard and grabbed Cassie's hand, pulling her to the stables where the geldings were housed.

Inside, while Cassie blinked against the bright lights and her nostrils filled with the scent of horses, leather and musty hay, Colton saddled two geldings, a short gray creature named Lamont and a lanky buckskin called Joshua.

"I don't suppose you have a sidesaddle," she said as he tightened the cinch around Lamont's belly.

Colton shook his head and glanced at her from the corner of his eye. "You'll just have to hike up your skirts."

The joke had gone on long enough. "Colton, you're not serious . . ." she said when he slapped Lamont's reins into her hand and opened the stable door. The gray pricked his ears and lifted his head.

"Where's your sense of adventure?"

"I think I left it in the drawer with my common sense," she said, taking off her coat and tossing it over one of the stall gates before following him and Joshua through the door. "This is madness—sheer, unadulterated madness!"

Colton swung into the saddle, and Cassie, caught in the excitement of it all, followed suit. Her skirt bunched around her thighs as she prodded Lamont with her knees. The eager little horse took off, swinging into a gentle gallop and keeping up with the buckskin's longer strides.

The wind rushed at Cassie's face, yanking the pins from her hair, stealing the breath from her lungs and snapping her skirt like a long, scarlet banner. She leaned forward over the horse's shoulders, adrenaline pumping through her system, her spirits soaring as the gelding's hooves thundered against the thick spring grass.

Ahead, washed in the moon's silvery light, the pine forest loomed before them, and through the trees the reflection of the clear water appeared jewellike against the black tree trunks.

She felt her mount take the bit in his mouth and leap forward, his ears flattening back against his head as he challenged the bay. Colton's horse responded, and soon the animals were charging across the field, hoofbeats thundering, nostrils wide, eyes sparking with defiant fire.

Cassie leaned lower, urging the little horse on, whispering words of encouragement. Racing across the moon-washed fields beneath a spray of glittering stars, Cassie rode hard, tears smarting in her eyes.

Colton's laughter rang through the night, and her heart skipped a beat. How long had it been since she'd felt so carefree, so young?

At Colton's whoop, the bay leaped forward. Though Lamont labored, he couldn't catch the longer-legged horse.

Near the edge of the forest Colton reined his horse to a slow walk. Lamont, dancing and snorting, caught up with him and tried to take a nip out of Joshua's backside.

"Sore loser," Colton teased, guiding his horse along the overgrown path through the pines. Cassie followed a few steps behind. The sounds and smell of the forest closed in on her: the deep-throated hoot of an owl, the crackle of twigs and rustle of leaves and the fresh fragrance of pine and soil.

The trees gave way to the banks of the lake. Pale rocks rimmed the darker water. A ribbon of moonlight rippled across the glassy surface. Cassie felt as if she and Colton were the only man and woman on earth.

"You going to stay up there all night?" Colton asked.

Lost in the beauty of the night, she hadn't noticed he'd dismounted. Colton reached up, his hands slipping around her waist as he helped Cassie down from her mount. She touched ground, and his palms slid upward against her ribs. He tightened his grip then and drew her close.

"I've thought about this from the minute you walked down the stairs at your house," he whispered, running his hands through her hair and yanking loose the few remaining pins.

"We could've ditched the party."

"Oh, no." When her hair fell free, he framed her face with his hands. "Then I couldn't have shown you off."

"'Is that what you were doing?"

"Mmm. You were far and away the most gorgeous woman there."

She laughed, the sound ringing through the surrounding hills, and she shoved her thoughts of Vince Monroe aside. "And did you see that in a movie, too?"

"'No—that's my own."

"You're irrepressible." Loving him, she tilted her face up to his.

He sighed. "You know," he whispered, taking a pin from her hair and letting the long loose curl drop to her shoulder, "I thought I'd leave you alone for a week, maybe two. Give you time to realize just how miserable your life is without me, but I couldn't make it."

She struggled against a giggle and failed. "Twenty-five years of misery. It's a wonder I survived."

"A miracle," he said, taking another pin from her hair, then lowering his mouth to hers. His lips were chilled and tasted of Scotch. They fit across her mouth perfectly. With strong arms he pulled her so close she could scarcely breathe. He tugged at the zipper of her dress, and she felt the breath of wind touch her bare back as the silk parted,

She wound her arms around his neck, and he lifted her deftly from her feet. One shoe dropped on the bank, but she didn't notice. He carried her to the base of the very tree where so long ago they had made love.

Tenderly he laid her on the ground, her dress falling off one shoulder, her skin shimmering like pearls in the night. "I love you, Cassie," he whispered roughly. "I think I always have."

Her heart thrummed wildly, but she attempted to hang on to some tiny shred of her common sense. Placing a finger across his lips, she whispered, "Shh. You don't have to say anything."

"Wrong, Cass. I should've said what I've felt for a long time." He kissed the finger touching his lips and shuddered when she traced the outline of his mouth. "I didn't want to love you eight years ago. God knows I fought it. But I lost."

"No—"

"Yes." He tangled his hands in the wild strands of her windblown hair. "Why do you think I've been running away, Cass? Why haven't I married? Settled down? Had a family?"

She held her breath.

"Because of you," he admitted, his lips brushing over hers as her pulse quickened crazily. "Only you. Oh, I denied it," he conceded, "wouldn't even admit it to myself, but deep down I knew." With his tongue he tasted her lips, then forayed between her teeth, delving deep, tasting and exploring.

Cassie gave into the swelling in her chest, the ache burning hot and deep inside, the quiver of her skin as he brushed his hand across her breast.

"Marry me, Cass," he pleaded, nuzzling the hollow of her throat, moving his hands slowly across the red silk still draping her breast. "Say yes."

A thousand questions raced through her mind, a thousand questions without answers. "Shh," she whispered, searching beneath his shirt for the muscled wall of his chest. "Don't talk."

And he didn't, not until they were lying side by side, sated and sighing, arms and legs wound together as they watched a hawk circling in the moonlight. "I'm serious, you know," he said, levering himself up on one elbow and twirling one long strand of her hair around his finger. "I want you to marry me."

Cassie laughed. "And where would we live," she teased, "Beirut or Seoul?"

"Somewhere around here."

Shaking the pine needles from her hair, she eyed him thoughtfully. "And you'd be happy ranching?" She didn't believe him for a second.

"No. But I might be happy doing freelance work in the area."

"I hate to be the one to break the news to you, Colton," she teased, "but there hasn't been a major war around here in years."

"Maybe it's time I slowed down a little—"

"Ha!"

"—worked on stories stateside."

"You'd be bored," she said, wishing it weren't so. Unconsciously she traced the tiny purple scars on his shoulder.

"You wouldn't let me get bored," he insisted, throwing one leg across her and pinning her to the earth. "I know it won't be easy, because I won't be working an eight-to-five job, but I'll travel as little as I can."

"Why?"

"Believe it or not, I'm tired of covering my . . . butt."

"Are you?"

He seemed so sincere. His eyes were dark and serious. "I mean it, Cassie. Say you'll marry me."

His expression was a mixture of determination and love. For the first time since she'd seen him in the middle of her father's kitchen, she didn't doubt that he cared. "You're not kidding, are you?" she whispered, her voice filled with awe.

"No, Cassie, I'm not. I want you to be my wife."

"And everything else?" she whispered, thinking of the feud, her father, Black Magic's disappearance and their long, lost affair.

"Doesn't matter." He pushed his face so close to hers that she hardly dared breathe. "Marry me, Cassie."

Her heart took flight. He wanted her! He loved her! "Oh, Colton, yes! Yes! Yes! Yes!" Wrapping her arms around his neck, she sighed happily. Finally they'd crossed all the barriers between them and she was where she belonged, wrapped in the safety of Colton's arms.

Reaching into his pocket, he withdrew a ring—a diamond ring with a single winking stone. "Wear this," he said, his voice catching as he slid the ring over her finger. "It was my mother's."

Katherine's? "Oh, Colton." Her heart filled her throat, and tears pooled in her eyes when she thought of Colton's feisty mother and how she'd lost her life trying to save the horses. "You don't have to—"

"I've waited eight years for this," he said.

"Hardly—"

"Well, maybe I didn't know it, but I knew someday, if I did ever marry, I'd want my wife to wear this ring."

Cassie blinked rapidly. "Thank you," she whispered, her heart so full of love it threatened to burst.

"Don't thank me," he growled against her ear, "show me how much you love me."

"I will—oh, I will," she whispered, finding his lips and kissing him as if she'd never stop. She didn't think of the pain eight years before, nor the feud between the families, nor Black Magic. There was no room. Her heart, mind and body were filled with only Colton McLean.

Chapter Thirteen

C assie snuggled close to Colton, not caring that her dress was probably ruined, her hair a mess. Sighing contentedly, she closed her eyes as he drove from the McLean Ranch back to her father's house.

"Something's up," Colton said as he turned into the Aldridge lane. Ahead, though it was nearly three in the morning, the house lights were blazing. Across the broad expanse of yard, the broodmare barn, too, was illuminated. Yellow patches of light spilled through the windows.

"It's probably Sylvia," Cassie said as he braked the Jeep near the barn. She hurried from the Jeep and into the barn, where, as she expected, her father was settled on the top of an old barrel, staring over the slats of Sylvia's stall.

At her entrance, he glanced up, and his mouth tightened at the sight of Colton following her inside.

"Sylvia?" she asked.

Her father nodded.

Cassie grinned at the sight of a tiny black tail waggling as the filly nursed hungrily. Long-legged and spindly, the foal was coal-black against his mother's roan coat. Sylvia shifted, protecting her new one.

"She's a beauty," Cassie said, wondering at the lack of pride in her father's eyes.

"That she is."

"And so black."

"Same as Devil Dancer," he replied quickly, mentioning the foal's sire as he placed his hands on his knees and pushed himself to a standing position. He flicked a cold glance at Colton, then took in Cassie's soiled dress. "The party get a little out of hand?" he asked.

"A little," Cassie said, her eyes sparkling. Colton was standing behind her, with one arm slipped possessively around her waist. Her stomach had tightened into knots even though she'd never been happier in her life. "Dad . . ." she started, as her father slapped his hat against his thigh.

He glanced up, his skin losing some of its pallor, as if he expected what was to come. "What is it?"

"Colton and I are getting married."

Ivan's old shoulders slumped. His jaw slackened, and a heavy sigh fell from his lips. "I was afraid of that," he admitted, bracing one arm against the wall as if he'd been kicked hard in the gut.

The seconds ticked by, measured only by the drumming of her own heart and the soft sounds of the foal suckling nearby.

"I love him," she said simply. "I always have."

Ivan's throat worked. "And what's it got you, huh?" he demanded of Cassie before impaling Colton with his furious eyes. His face turned beet red, and one fist coiled angrily at his side. "Only heartache. And what did it get your mother when she fancied herself in love with a McLean? Nothing!" Big veins throbbed in his throat. "I always wanted what was best for you, Cassie. Always. I would have done anything to make you happy, but . . . ah, hell!" He kicked a water pail and sent it rattling down the concrete corridor, then reached for the door.

Colton stopped him with a hand on Ivan's arm. "Wait, Aldridge," he warned.

"For what?"

"To hear my side."

"I'm not interested!" Ivan roared, then glanced at Cassie and closed his eyes, obviously struggling with his temper. He shook off Colton's hand and glared at the younger man. "Okay—so talk."

"I'll take care of your daughter."

Ivan didn't say a word.

"I love her."

Cassie thought her heart might break right then and there.

"What do you know of love?"

"I know that I was a fool eight years ago. That I should have trusted her. That I made a mistake."

Ivan cast his eyes to a far stall. "So?"

"And I'll spend the rest of my life making it up to her if I have to."

Blinking rapidly, Ivan studied the floor. His voice had dulled from a roar to a whisper. "This is really what you want?" he asked Cassie.

"Yes!"

Ivan's Adam's apple moved up and down his throat. He struggled with words that wouldn't come. "I—uh—I won't stand in your way." Lifting his eyes to meet Colton's gaze, he added through tight lips, "You'll be welcome in my house anytime." Then, without another word, he yanked open the door and marched stiffly outside.

"This isn't going to be easy," Colton said, staring after the older man.

"Did you think it would be?"

"Sure—a piece of cake." He chuckled and drew her to him, taking her lips in his. He kissed her for an endless moment, then chuckled. "And if you think this was bad, wait until we talk to Denver."

"Oooh," Cassie groaned. "Let's not think about it." Happiness swelled deep in her heart. Resting her head against Colton's chest, she looked through the slats of Sylvia's stall just as the newborn turned his face to hers. For a minute she didn't say a word—just stared at the perfect little horse with the crooked white blaze. Her blood seemed to freeze in her veins as the curious colt lifted his head and tossed his ebony head. He was so like Black Magic.

Colton's eyes followed her gaze, and the blood drained from his face. His fingers curled tight.

Cassie's eyes pleaded with his. *Don't say it*, she seemed to whisper, though not a sound passed between them, *don't spoil this beautiful night.*

He didn't. His eyes narrowed on the little horse, but he didn't say a word. A cold stone settled in her stomach.

The stables seemed suddenly cold as if a wind from the north had silently blown through.

"I think I'd better go," Colton finally said, his voice suddenly distant, his eyes filled with an anger so hot it burned through her heart.

"You don't have to . . ."

He took a step toward her, then hesitated. "I think we both have a lot to think about." Turning, his broad shoulders stiff beneath his jacket, he left without another word. Cassie slumped against the wall, her fingers sliding down the rough wood. It couldn't be possible. Or could it?

Her feet felt like lead as she made her way to the open door and watched Colton get into his Jeep and drive away. Searching her heart, she tried to push her suspicions aside. Ivan wouldn't have stolen Black Magic; he *couldn't* have. The colt was sired by Devil Dancer and that was that.

But her throat was clogged with nagging doubts, and her

mind wouldn't quit spinning with misgivings. The coldness
that had started in her stomach chilled her heart as well.
Oh, please, she cried inwardly, *let me be wrong!*

She took several bracing breaths, knowing what she had to
do. Dread mounting with each step, she ran to her truck, found
her veterinary bag, then headed back to the barn. She didn't
like the idea of taking a vial of blood from a newborn colt,
but she had to know the truth. And she had to know it soon.

*And then what? What if you find out your father's been
lying to you?* Her legs threatened to give out on her, and she
had to force herself onward.

At the door of the barn she paused, glancing down at her left
hand. The diamond ring twinkled in the night, and she wondered if she'd made a gigantic mistake in not telling Colton.

"Too late now," she whispered pragmatically, and shoved
the door to the barn open again.

Colton didn't drive back to the ranch. He was too keyed up.
That foal—that new little Aldridge horse—had to have been
sired by Black Magic. Cassie had seen the resemblance, too.
Only a blind man wouldn't have recognized Black Magic's
genes in the little ebony colt.

"Damn it all to hell!" he ground out, instinctively driving
toward the hills. He couldn't ignore this—act like he didn't
know. Obviously Ivan Aldridge had stolen Black Magic a year
ago and bred his mare, Sylvia, to him. He must have stolen
him again this year, and this time the horse could've died.

The Jeep hurtled off the main highway and up the twisting road leading to Garner's Ridge and the old ghost town.
Once there, he climbed out of his rig and walked the desolate
main street. But he didn't see the decrepit buildings, sagging
porches or broken windows. No, each time he looked down
that street, he envisioned Cassie. Cassie pointing the barrel

of a gun at his chest, Cassie mussed and soiled as she pulled Red Wing's foal into the world, Cassie laughing, moonlight caressing her face as she rode the feisty little Lamont, Cassie as a girl, seductive and innocent, the lake lapping around her legs, and Cassie now, a woman, her throat clogged as she accepted his mother's ring, her eyes glittering with tears of happiness.

He kicked at a stone, sending it richocheting along the remains of a boardwalk, and wished he could just leave Montana and forget her. But the thought of chasing stories in war-torn countries held no allure for him. In fact, a life spent searching for the next front-page story seemed like exile. "Oh, Cassie, Cassie," he murmured, wondering how he'd ever become so maudlin, "what am I going to do with you? Just what the hell am I going to do with you?" He dropped his head into his hands.

By the time he finally left Garner's Ridge, the night was beginning to disappear as the eastern sky grew light. He turned into the lane of the McLean Ranch and caught a glimpse of cattle, white-faced Herefords, moving slowly through one field. This wasn't such a bad place, he realized with a jolt that rocked him to his very soul. He could find happiness here—and peace—as long as he could leave when he felt the urge. As long as Cassie was by his side.

He parked near the garage and had barely stepped out of his Jeep when Denver, nostrils flared, blue eyes angry, strode up to him. Still wearing suit pants and white shirt from the party, Denver didn't mince words. "Where the hell have you been?"

"Out."

"All hell's broken loose. Tempest died two hours ago."

Sickening bile filled Colton's stomach. He thought of the ornery stallion, and his throat constricted. "No—"

"It happened."

"Damn, how?"

"Pneumonia."

"But just yesterday he was better—much better." He couldn't believe it, wouldn't.

"That was yesterday. Last night he took a turn for the worse. By the time Curtis found him, he was too far gone."

"But the antibiotics—"

"Failed!" Denver's dark skin was white, the lines near his mouth deep grooves.

Colton's anger turned inward. He was the one who lost Black Magic, and he'd suspected all along who'd taken the beast. Ivan Aldridge. His soon-to-be father-in-law. "Sweet Lord," he whispered.

"That's not all."

Colton's head snapped up.

"By the time Curtis got hold of Craig Fulton, it was too late for Tempest."

"Fulton examined him?"

"That's right." Denver's eyes were dark with rage, though there was a tenderness akin to pity as he stared at his younger brother. "And he made a strange remark—one I think you should hear. He said he'd talked to another veterinarian at the Edwards's party, and that guy knew someone up here with a horse infected with strangles."

Every muscle in Colton's body went rigid. "Go on."

"Seems Vince Monroe had a horse come down with it right before Black Magic got the disease."

"Monroe?" God, was it possible? Was he wrong about Aldridge? "The funny thing is, Craig already told Cassie Aldridge about it."

Colton didn't move. "When?"

"Last night—at the party." The skin on Denver's face had drawn tight. "She say anything to you?"

"No."

"Strange, isn't it?"

Colton's lungs constricted. *Oh, Cassie—oh, love!* Why hadn't she told him?

As if reading Colton's thoughts, Denver sighed. Some of the anger left his face. "If it's any consolation, I think she's protecting someone—maybe Monroe, maybe her father. They're pretty tight these days. Let's go see what she has to say."

"And Monroe?"

"I've already called the sheriff's office. A deputy's on his way to the Monroe place right now. And there's a quarantine on his horses."

"I think I'd better handle this myself."

"I'm coming with you."

"Not this time!"

"But—"

"Denver!" Tessa's voice cried out through the early dawn. Colton turned to see her grab hold of a post supporting the porch while her other arm wrapped around her stomach, and she bent over, wincing.

"What—?" Denver spun on his heel, his face draining of color.

"The baby," she cried, forcing a brave smile, though her face was twisted in pain.

"But it's not time!" He was racing across the yard and up the steps in long strides. When he reached the porch, he surrounded her with his arms. "I knew we shouldn't have gone to that party," he grumbled. "Are you all right?"

She forced a brave smile, but another contraction hit her full force, and she clung to her husband, eyes squeezing shut, her mouth pressed into his chest to muffle her cry.

Colton saw fear on Denver's face and felt a pang of his own. Tessa's baby wasn't due for another six weeks. "I'll drive you to the hospital," he said, but Denver was already shepherding Tessa toward his car.

"I'll handle this! Come on, Tessa . . ." His jaw was rigid as he helped her into the car, then climbed behind the wheel and took off.

Colton stood in the middle of the yard for a second, then climbed back into his Jeep. Bone-tired, he let out the clutch. Why hadn't Cassie told him about the strangles at the Monroe ranch? Why had she wanted so desperately to deny that Sylvia's raven black colt was sired by Black Magic? To protect her father? Somehow Ivan was involved, and Cassie cared so little about Colton that she couldn't confide in him. His boot pressed hard against the throttle.

Cassie didn't sleep a wink, but watched as dawn turned the sky gray and she heard her father in the kitchen below. She listened as Erasmus barked to be let out and watched through the window as her father, his shoulders stooped, made his way to the broodmare barn.

With a heavy heart she climbed out of the bed, showered, stepped into faded jeans and brushed her hair into a sleek ponytail. "It's now or never," she told her reflection, and she steeled herself for what was to come.

In the kitchen she poured herself a cup of coffee and waited at the table. She heard her father's heavy step on the back porch, and her heart turned over.

Her cup of coffee, untouched, was cradled between her hands, as if to give her warmth as he walked in. From the stoop of his shoulders and the lines near his eyes, she guessed he'd slept no better than she.

"'Mornin', Cassie," he muttered, not bothering to remove his hat or boots. "There's something I think we should talk about."

The lump in her throat swelled. "Does it have to do with the new foal?"

"What d'ya mean?"

Her fingers shook as she opened her veterinary bag and

withdrew two purple vials of blood. "These," she replied, her voice the barest of whispers. "One of them is from the new colt, the other from Devil Dancer."

Her father sucked in his breath. "I see."

"Later, I thought I'd go to the McLean Ranch and take a sample from Black Magic. Even though I cannot prove who the foal's sire is, I can prove which horse isn't the father."

Dropping his head into one hand, Ivan whispered, "You already know."

So it was true. Her stomach quaked. "Oh, Dad, why?" she cried, tears filling her eyes. She heard the rumble of a truck in the drive, and she knew instinctively that Colton had returned. What could she say to him? How would she explain? Setting her cup on the table, she noticed Katherine's ring on her finger. Her lungs and eyes burned.

"I did it for you," Ivan said.

"Me?" she cried. "No . . ."

He studied his thumb. "It was wrong, I know, but the way I saw it, the McLeans had it coming. All they'd ever caused us—you—was heartache."

Colton stepped through the door, his jaw set, his eyes blazing.

Ivan didn't look up. "I wanted the best for you, don't you see? And I couldn't afford it. I'd borrowed everything I could to help you through school, to get you away from here and all those memories."

"Oh, Dad—"

"Vince came to me with a plan—and it wouldn't really hurt anyone. We'd just borrow the horse, use him to service our mares and then put him back. Improve our herd and give old John McLean fits. It worked, too."

A muscle jumped in Colton's jaw, but he didn't cross the room. He lifted one foot to the seat of a chair and leaned forward, his gaze set on Ivan.

"Then, this year, Vince says we should do it again. I wasn't too crazy about the idea—John was dead."

"But I was around," Colton surmised.

Sighing, Ivan nodded, his neck bowed miserably. "It was a mistake from the beginning. All it did was get you riled up and stomping over here." He cast the younger man a weary glance. "I wanted to keep you and Cassie apart, but the whole thing backfired."

"What about the disease?"

Ivan's old head snapped up. "That was an accident."

"Was it?"

"Vince brought in a mare he'd bought down south somewhere. She developed a fever right after she'd been bred to Black Magic. That's when I brought him back." He glanced at Cassie. "None of our mares had even gotten near him. Thank God."

"Damn it all to hell, Aldridge, do you hate me that much?" Colton demanded, kicking at the chair and sending it across the room.

"I did."

"And where did you hide the horses?"

"That was the beauty of Vince's plan," Ivan explained. "They never left your land, except for the ride. They were up on the ridge—up in a shack in the old silver mines."

"You old bastard!" Colton roared.

Cassie couldn't take her eyes off him. His expression changed from love to hate, to pity, to disbelief. When he turned his gaze her way, she recognized his anger . . . and his pain. "You could've told me," he accused. "Last night, Cass. At the party. You knew most of this."

"I wanted to talk to Dad first."

"That's the problem, isn't it?" Colton muttered. "You never have been able to face me with the truth. You put things off—delude yourself into thinking you'll confide in me, but you wait until the timing's right. Well, when would it have been right this time? Today? Tomorrow? Or after the wedding? Tell me, Cassie, were you planning to dupe me again—trap me into marriage?"

"No!" She shook her head vehemently. "No! No! No! You can't think—"

"I don't know what to think," he snarled, his fists curling, his eyes black with fury.

"Leave her be!" Ivan shouted. "She had nothing to do with this! I already called the sheriff's office. They're sending a man over."

"*What?*" Cassie shrieked, bolting from her chair. "What do you mean?" she demanded.

"It's over, Cassie," he said, touching her hair fondly.

"No! Dad, you can't be serious." Her eyes flew to Colton's. "Tell him! Tell him you're not going to file charges!"

"Tempest died, Cass," Colton pointed out.

"Leave it alone, Cassie," Ivan said, ramming his hat on his head and whistling to his old dog. "I can deal with anything comin' to me."

"No! I won't let you! Dad—you're it. The only family I've got. Don't leave me, too."

But the door slammed behind him, and he crossed the yard.

She whirled on Colton. "Don't do this."

He hesitated.

"Please, it won't happen again. Look at him, for God's sake." She pointed a shaking finger to the window and beyond, to where her father leaned down to scratch Erasmus's shaggy ears. "He won't hurt you—he can't. And . . . and as for the damage, I'll pay you for Tempest and Monroe's damned stud fees and any other expenses." She advanced on him, her own eyes burning bright, her fingers struggling with the ring surrounding her finger. "I'll even pay for the cut fence and the antibiotics, any amount of money you lost, but you can't, *can't* send my father to jail!" The ring slid off, and she slapped it back in his hand. "My father is my family. He sacrificed everything for me, and no matter what he's done, I'm standing by him."

"And against me."

"It doesn't have to be so black and white," she said, struggling to keep her voice from shaking. He was leaving her— again. Again he was refusing to listen to reason or any of her explanations. She knew Ivan had been wrong, realized his hatred went much too far, but he'd already suffered. She could see it in his old eyes, and to send him to prison for a crime he'd committed because of her . . . It would kill him.

"What about trust?" she asked, her voice shaking as she advanced on Colton.

"You couldn't trust me last night."

"I had to have my facts straight."

"Bah!"

"What about love?"

He blinked. "I always loved you."

"And now?"

His gaze held hers, and though he didn't say the words, she could feel the intensity, the love lurking deep in those stormy gray depths. She reached up and curled her fingers into the smooth folds of his leather jacket. "I didn't lie to you eight years ago, Colton, and I didn't lie last night. But I do need time and space to work things out in my own mind. I would never manipulate you into marrying me," she said, blinking back the hot tears. "In fact, if you don't want me, believe me, I don't want you." She pressed his mother's ring against his palm and closed his fingers over the gold band. "If your love isn't as strong as this stone, as never-ending as this circle of gold, as complete as the ring itself, then I don't want you!"

Colton's breath was a desperate rasp. His eyes locked with hers.

"I won't have a man who doesn't love me."

"Cass—" He tried to fold her into his arms, but she stepped backward.

"I mean it, Colton. All or nothing!"

"I do love you, Cassie," he said, his voice thick, his words a whisper. "And I can't imagine living without you."

She waited.

He swallowed, looking down at the ring in his big palm. "There's been enough hate already," he said quietly. "Enough pain. Enough loneliness."

Her knees went weak as he took her hand and placed the ring on her finger. "I love you, Cass," he said again, caressing her cheek. "No matter what happens, I want you to be my wife."

A sharp, painful cry escaped from her lips, and she flung her arms around him.

"Marry me."

"I will," she vowed, her arms circling his neck, her tears flowing against his chest until he tilted her face to his and kissed her with all the emotions roiling deep in his chest.

"This is forever," he pointed out.

"It better be!"

A month later Ivan Aldridge gave his daughter to Colton McLean. The charges against him had been dropped, and despite a nagging feeling that he was losing something dear, Ivan realized stoically that Colton loved Cassie. He'd treat her right.

As a bride, Cassie was radiant. Kneeling in a hundred-year-old church, her ivory-colored gown spilling over ancient boards, she vowed her love for Colton.

Ivan's old eyes misted.

"You may kiss the bride," the preacher declared, and standing, Colton took her into his arms, lifted her veil and slanted eager lips over hers. Cassie melted against him. Finally they were together, and nothing, nothing could tear them apart.

Organ music began to throb through the little church, and one small voice, that of Katy McLean, Denver's four-week-old daughter, rang through the chapel as wedding bells chimed loudly, pealing across the valley and sounding beneath the wide Montana sky.

Mr. and Mrs. Colton McLean walked together along the flower-strewn runner, and as the door opened, they started a life together as bright as the morning sun.

"You've done it this time," Colton said.

"Oh?"

"Now you'll never get away from me."

She giggled, holding her skirt up off the dusty porch. "Is that a promise or a threat?"

"Both," he murmured, taking her into his arms again. Colton felt her heart begin to pound as loudly as his own. Finally, he knew, he'd come home.